Sarah K. Marr started writing fiction at school, but got distracted. After studying law, anthropology and theoretical physics at the Universities of Oxford, Manchester and London, respectively, she finally returned to her first love and wrote *All the Perverse Angels*. She lives in London, where she spends too much time in art galleries and buys too many second-hand books.

ALL THE PERVERSE ANGELS

Sarah K. Marr

Unbound

This edition first published in 2018

Unbound
6th Floor Mutual House, 70 Conduit Street, London W1S 2GF

www.unbound.com

Text Design by Ellipsis

A CIP record for this book is available from the British Library

ISBN 978-1-78352-444-0 (trade hbk)
ISBN 978-1-78352-445-7 (ebook)
ISBN 978-1-78352-443-3 (limited edition)

Printed in Great Britain by Clays Ltd, St Ives Plc

1 3 5 7 9 8 6 4 2

for Beth
as true a friend as Watson

Dear Reader,

The book you are holding came about in a rather different way to most others. It was funded directly by readers through a new website: Unbound. Unbound is the creation of three writers. We started the company because we believed there had to be a better deal for both writers and readers. On the Unbound website, authors share the ideas for the books they want to write directly with readers. If enough of you support the book by pledging for it in advance, we produce a beautifully bound special subscribers' edition and distribute a regular edition and ebook wherever books are sold, in shops and online.

This new way of publishing is actually a very old idea (Samuel Johnson funded his dictionary this way). We're just using the internet to build each writer a network of patrons. At the back of this book, you'll find the names of all the people who made it happen.

Publishing in this way means readers are no longer just passive consumers of the books they buy, and authors are free to write the books they really want. They get a much fairer return too – half the profits their books generate, rather than a tiny percentage of the cover price.

If you're not yet a subscriber, we hope that you'll want to join our publishing revolution and have your name listed in one of our books in the future. To get you started, here is a £5 discount on your first pledge. Just visit unbound.com, make your pledge and type **angels5** in the promo code box when you check out.

Thank you for your support,

Dan, Justin and John
Founders, Unbound

CHAPTER ONE

Against the wall the blue lights came and went, came and went, and I remembered. If you really want to feel the drop, you have to close your eyes. And then the car journey, long, winding, through imagined landscapes, and all the while she spoke to me. The this-and-thats of my time away, and all of it hers and not mine because she had earned it and somehow I had not.

She made the pick-up by the glass doors where the set-down had happened three weeks ago. In that abrogation there had been a formal handover. In the collection there was no entry to the building, just a kerb-stop.

There were few material needs in that place. They even provided a toothbrush, wrapped in cheap plastic, with bristles that twisted off on the molars. So the small suitcase was thrown on the back seat and I threw myself in the front and leaned to kiss, but seeing no response faked down to reach my bag and take out water for the drive ahead. When we took a left and not a right I asked where we might be going and was told a break was needed, and so the car journey was long, and wound through imagined landscapes.

Our arrival was a breath, slow and deep. We were in the Cotswolds, she said, nestled as the Cotswolds nestle everything, in warm stone and antiques and second-hand bookshops with cats. The cottage was small, at the end of a path of herringbone bricks running between thickets of cross-hatched twigs, blackened by the fading winter light. On the gate the paint peeled around the ornately serifed "Rose Cottage". I mourned the flowerless tangles beside the path. Emily stepped through the threshold of the garden whilst I lingered with the cold, watching the

1

moon try to hide behind the smokeless chimney. She was unlocking the door with unfamiliar keys when I caught up.

"My clothes?"

"Inside," she said, and she may have been answering or telling me to enter, so I passed by her and in, with a switch clicking as she turned on the dim lights to search out the corners of the room.

"You're upstairs on the left," she said and jerked her head towards the thin, white-plank door with the black latch that I opened and, looking back, asked, "We're not together?"

She shook her head.

Stairs seemed new after single-floor accommodation with en-suite facilities and hot and cold running nurses, although running was never a good sign. Running followed from the buzzing start-gun and ended in inevitable victory for every competitor but one. But there were stairs and they rose ahead, and the space became darker until hesitancy began and the fragile light from below was blocked by her, but she was reaching, I could see, and then brightness returned. Two more steps and a landing with four doors: bathroom, large bedroom, small bedroom, and at the far end another thin, white-plank door with another black latch, and the whole effect made me think of Escher. The white planks would wait for me, so I entered the little room, my room, and found clothes in drawers, dresses in the wardrobe, and linens and towels on the bed.

I wished she had not done it.

"Anna," said a quiet voice and I turned, not expecting to see anyone. Emily was there. She held me. We held each other. We breathed another breath. I was sorry. She was sorry, if she should be sorry, yes, she should be sorry, so she was sorry, I was sure. She allowed me a smile, and repaid me with one of her own.

"I have to go back to work on Monday," she said, "but we have the weekend together, and I've cleared a lot of my clients. I should be able to stick to a nine-to-five. The village is nice. You'll be fine here. Are you hungry?"

I nodded and wiped my eyes and whispered my wish that she had not done it, but she just stiffened and told me I needed to eat. We ate pasta and drank apple juice. Our conversation was a shallow exchange

2

of words. The cottage was rented for the next three months, through to the new year. The village was small, but had too many cafés—she had not tried them but they looked pleasant enough—as well as a stationer's and two bookshops, both terribly overpriced, and one had cheap paperbacks out front, but she could pick books up from the house in London, no, she would go on her own. The room upstairs, past the second palisade of white planks, was an attic space full of the owner's possessions, and heaven only knew why it was not locked. There was no television, but we could get one, but why would we? So probably not, no, surely better without. There was plenty of food in the refrigerator. Pasta. Juice. Plates. Cutlery. Pills.

I started to feel sleepy. The world slowed down a little to give me a chance to reflect and recover. There were magazines stacked on a bookshelf and I flipped through one, looking at the pictures amongst a haze of grey alphabets. People were going to parties, babies were being born, weddings and horse races mingled. All from ten years ago and the faces of the people looked happy but their expressions could not tell me anything beyond the instant. There was no continuity, no flow, challenge, development. I needed art. The haze danced and I was asleep in my chair, not knowing until awakened gently, led upstairs, sat on the bed. The door closed. The light was on as I felt the cool of the pillow on my cheek, off for the morning's opening of eyes.

Saturday was Claude Monet: *San Giorgio Maggiore at Dusk*. He painted the view, despite his initial reticence, across the Venetian waters to the island, and the church which stands upon it. The church is an absence, lit from behind by the setting sun, a gap in the oranges and blues. No, not exactly that, because Monet was not using any black paint: the shadows are just the darkened colours of twilight. The church is a deadening, a stopped conversation, as if one had shouted into a cave and heard no echo.

Emily and I walked down the lane in the early morning, with mist rising all around, binding the walls of our own church, a few yards from the cottage. Emily talked of history, of Levellers and smallpox, but I was in Venice by then. It had rained during the night, before or after my light was turned off, but the timing did not matter because the rain left puddles and they reflected the reality of nature. The water was the levelling of all things, the lagoon from which rose buildings and trees and a yapping dog passing by on the end of a thin lead. I stopped. My reflection stopped. Emily stopped.

"Anna?"

I looked up. "Sorry, Ems," I said. "I was in Venice."

"You've never even been to Venice, Anna. We keep saying we'll go one day. We could make plans."

"But they gang aft agley, don't they?"

Emily took my hand. We walked to the nearest café and out of the freshly sputtering drizzle. Venice reappeared, warped through the drops on the window. A petite woman took our order on an off-white pad. I wondered if Monet's wife was short: Alice, of course, his second, as Camille had been dead for years when Claude was in Venice. Alice had another three years to go, although she had no idea.

"I thought we might drive to the countryside this afternoon, if the weather doesn't get worse," said Emily, between sips of hot chocolate. I took a mouthful of filter coffee through a layer of soapy froth. I swallowed.

"We should go to Italy for the coffee," I said. "And yes, the countryside would be nice. Did you bring my boots?"

Emily nodded and picked up a local paper from a rack beside the table.

"There's a book fair in the next village, if you'd rather do that," she said.

"Let's let the weather decide."

The weather toyed with us, lifting the mist with a seductive sun, then greying the world with cloud once more. Back at the cottage we warmed ourselves by the radiator, unimpressed by the dried flowers in the fireplace. As noon arrived the elements lost their playfulness and resigned themselves to sunshine. Monet painted Alice's daughter, Suzanne, in the sun, and there she stands, under an *ombrelle* and not a *parapluie*, though both are protections from extremes.

While Emily made sandwiches I found my boots and went outside to the back garden. There was little in it other than patches of unkempt grass and empty borders at the foot of old fencing. A roller stood in the corner, far too big for the place, waiting anxiously in the hope of a miraculous, lumpy lawn to give it some meaning. I banged my boots against it, filling the air with the sound of leather on metal and flecks of dried mud from a holiday in Yorkshire, making the pigeons take flight in the Piazza San Marco.

The back of the cottage was plain, red brickwork with a name which I knew existed but had forgotten: Dutch bond, English bond, James Bond. Michael Bond. He wrote the Paddington Bear books. The cottage was a séance for the ghosts of its previous incarnations: filled-in windows, long-lost doorways. In the roof, which sloped down towards me, a gable-fronted dormer window admired the surrounding fields. It was a later addition to the building, its sill holding only a peepshow of faded wood, unlike the striptease common to its flaking companions on lower floors. The room through the window was invisible. Darkest Peru.

"Anna!"

Emily was standing in the doorway to the kitchen, clutching a small rucksack to her chest.

"I've been calling you. Let's go."

We headed out to the car, leaving the lawn roller to its dreams.

"Countryside or books?" I asked, when we were on our way.

"Countryside whilst the sun lasts, then books if it's not too late."

I said I thought that sounded reasonable and listened to Emily as she talked about work: her team had been busy, new clients coming in, the chance of a partnership in a year or two, some staff changes. I wondered if he had left. I thought that was why she mentioned the staff changes, but maybe I was supposed to ask. Maybe I was just supposed to understand. Maybe we were in Venice and we were sinking, and the deadening of the church hid the sunset from us.

"We're here. Welcome to the late Neolithic."

My puzzlement was met with a grin which I thought it best to return with one of my own. Emily had parked the car to the side of the

5

lane, beside a thicket of trees and a stile in a two-rail, wooden fence. I followed her into the undergrowth and out again, into a soundless clearing where she could speak and I could only listen, where I could rage and scream and yet cause no vibration, as though shouting in a vacuum.

"These are the King's Men," said Emily, pointing at the circle of stones in the clearing. "There's a legend that they were changed to stone by a witch. There's another one around here called the King Stone. Same story."

The vacuum filled with a hiss of air.

"I'm going to explore," I said. I stood in the middle of the circle and turned clockwise, slowly, ticking off time, stone by stone. They were there when Monet's wife—Alice, Camille, either—died, when the sun set in Venice, when there was no Venice. They were there for my Venice. I thought of Paul Klee, projecting lines from his drawings, and the more they met higher dimensions, the better. The stones began to run at me, all except one. Against that one Emily leaned back and ate a sandwich. Intellect and soul operate in different dimensions, according to Klee. He said he painted in order not to cry. I walked away.

The path back through the trees continued on the other side of the lane, and I followed. There, alone, captured within iron railings, stood the King Stone. Later, on the journey home, Emily told me the whole story. A witch promised a king that if he could see the village of Long Compton after taking seven strides he would be king of all England. Whilst the king's men stood, craven, in a circle, he took seven strides and looked ahead, out over the countryside. Alas, his view was blocked by a forgotten hillock, and with no village to be seen the witch turned him and his men to stone. Never trust the promise of a witch.

I was the King Stone. I was the King Stone then, and I was the King Stone as a child. The circle was a place of sharing, protection and safety, not pure cowardice. The story was wrong. There, standing alone, was the sacrifice, the one given to the witch in hope of mercy for the others. I sat and rested against the railings, looking at the lane and trees. I felt my isolation and carried it back with me, towards the time of the stones, to a playground filled with other people's games. I had sat against railings before, years ago. They had defined the edge of safety. I let my eyelids fall to a raucous lullaby of crows.

Tabitha took my hand and pulled me towards the centre of the world. It would be fun, she said, and I was her friend. The centre of the world, and around me Tabitha and her friends, and they must be my friends, because we were all part of the same world. Round me they went, rhyming, cross-stepping quickly, ten paces then reversing and chanting, chanting. My eyes stayed on Tabitha, left then right, turn after turn, faster and faster. The held-hands of the circle, clutching, came closer to thighs, then unclasped and arms interlocked at crooked elbows, hands on hips, closer to me with the right then left, faster still, and the rhyming had the sow in the middle, and I was the middle, but the middle of the world, and Tabitha was my friend so surely I was not the sow. They wanted to be close because I was special. Arms around waists and no space between, and the stones running at me, embraces unravelled to fists. Crouching, and friends leaning over, friends of my enemy, and the sky blue, blocked, deadened. My name being called. Anna, Anna, Anna. Everything legs, socks, shoes and I wanted the railings back.

"Anna."

Anna, Anna, Anna.

"Anna. Wake up."

"I'm the King Stone," I muttered, opening my eyes.

"You're anything you want to be. Including hungry, I'll bet."

Emily pulled a sandwich from the rucksack and handed it to me.

"Bad dreams again?" she asked.

"Was I asleep for long?"

"About ten minutes. Perhaps we should go home."

I nibbled at the edges of the sandwich.

"No, it's early. I feel better now." With Tabitha gone. With my railings returned. "Let's go to the book sale."

"You're sure?"

"I'm sure. But sandwich first."

Klee ate sandwiches, I supposed.

7

It was late afternoon by the time we reached the hamlet to the west of our borrowed cottage. Outside the church hall, men in sensible knitwear were starting to load vans with cardboard fruit trays full of books. Emily kept the engine running and looked at me, but when I opened my door she turned the key and followed my lead. A despondent youth sat inside the porch, reading the *New Musical Express*. He resigned himself to taking our money. In exchange for our twenty-pence pieces we received the kind of coat-check tickets that I had seen used for country-fair tombolas.

"We're supposed to close in about an hour, but there's not many come out today, so... Still, there's a few left set up, so..." He nodded to his right, towards the inner door of the porch, and went back to his magazine.

"Thank you very much," Emily said, in a voice so bright and lilting that it could only be sarcastic. *N.M.E.*-man did not respond.

Inside, the hall was lined with folding tables, a few of which stood empty. One supported a battered tea urn, which must have seen VE Day celebrations, and a sponge cake filled with jam and ennui. The remaining tables held books. Emily gave me her "we could just leave" look, but I moved away to the first table, where shabby Penguin paperbacks jostled each other to attract my attention. I ignored their orange brashness and picked up a hardback from a stack towards the rear.

"*On the Butterflies and Moths of the Balkan Regions* by Edward F. Cousins. London. Nineteen hundred and three," I read aloud.

"Fascinating. Are you familiar with his work?"

"Aren't you?"

She grinned. "Well, I usually prefer my Lepidoptera from more northern territories, but... What can you tell me about the author?"

"Edward F. Cousins," I began, "was a distant relative of the Earl of Garthorp-Mundum and came to the title in later life, through the unfortunate deaths of many family members in Africa, in a terrible giraffe-based incident at a wedding."

Emily laughed.

"Oh," she said, "I knew about that, of course. It was the money from the inheritance which allowed him to pursue his hobbies."

"Which were?"

"Well, apart from being a voracious collector of even the most dangerous butterflies…"

"Yes?"

"Apart from that…" She paused. I think she must have realized that she was happy. "Apart from that, he used to record animal noises on wax cylinders and play them at parties. Oh, and he juggled goldfish on Sundays."

"He sounds like a dreadful man."

"Yes, I think I agree. Put down the book, Anna. We shan't have any part of his ill-gained legacy."

I put the book back in its pile and gave a little nod to the lady seated behind the table. She did not look up from her hardback, and seemed lost in historical romantic fiction, but, as we moved away, she said, almost inaudibly, "Goldfish? It was puppies."

We giggled our way around the rest of the hall. The offerings were the usual: cricketing stories, railway ephemera, collections of ghostly tales, a leather-and-gilt Burckhardt on the Renaissance, an India-paper Gombrich on art. As we left, Emily held my hand, cautiously at first, as though it might be too timid to be touched, but then with a practised familiarity. We stopped by the car and kissed. Emily had left the circle, joined me alone on the floor, across the lane, by the railings.

"Shall we talk about it?" I asked.

"Which it? It him? It me? It us?"

I shrugged. "Any. All. I know we tried before I… before, but maybe now?"

"You need to rest. It's getting late. I'll make dinner."

We drove home listening to the radio. A cold spell, said the weatherman. I thought of snowmen in the garden, years ago, before Tabitha and the railings, long before Emily. I had blonde hair that made my eyes shine pale blue. I would play and grow tired. At night my parents turned off the bedside lamp once I was sleeping. Sometimes I'd wake up in the dark, and call, and my mother would come and tell me to be brave. Or Dad would come and switch on the light and tell me I was already brave enough. I was always good enough when he was around, but he was not around, and Emily said that I needed to rest my blue eyes, so we were not talking in the car.

I fell asleep with the light on, again, that night. It was still on when I awoke the next day.

The note on the table said, "Gone to church. Food in cupboards and fridge. E." Whilst she ate of the body which was given for her I satisfied myself with cornflakes and milk. I took her to see *The Church in Auvers-sur-Oise* once, at the Musée d'Orsay. Vincent van Gogh arrived in the village, Auvers, just outside Paris, in late May, 1890. He had two more months. In those two months he painted a new canvas each day. Maybe he thought painting would chase away the inevitability of his death. Or he always knew how long he had, and counted down the blank canvases remaining to be filled.

It was sunny outside. The lagoon had gone and I headed to the little village polder, down the lane, towards the church. Singing, faint and subdued, came from within, drifting over the graveyard, a hairbreadth above the headstones. I stopped. The tune had an ordinariness which robbed it of identity, reduced it to a primal, religious incantation.

The lychgate was old, its dark wood textured by years of brushed-on preservative, its foundations dressed with lichen. It was wide enough to contain a bench, pressed up against one side of the woodwork and seemingly held in place by cobwebs and trapped leaves. I sat, listening. The hymn rose, fell, faded in and out.

Van Gogh's church is all curves in a miraculous balance. His church buckles and looms, but never seems precarious. In places it resolves into the straight lines of buttress and tower window, providing subtle anchors for the building. My church was everywhere perpendicular, or, at least, that's how I saw it. The fault might have been with my eyes, or Vincent's.

The hymn came to an end. I stood and walked on, to the heart of the village. All was golden, weathered sandstone. Later it would be busy, with tourists turning off the main road, chuntering down the sloping street, filling the parking spaces, peering from behind guidebooks, eating ice cream, scolding children. But in the glow of the morning light it was mine. It was an unwanted present, something thoughtful and considered, for which I ought to have been grateful, to have expressed my gratitude, but for which I held no real love.

At the bottom of the hill the road levelled before a humpbacked bridge carried it over a narrow stream. I wandered down and paused, looking into the waters below. The stream, which could be no more than a rill in summer, was swollen with recent rains, flowing swiftly, keeping the village safe. A winter leaf, brown and dejected, came down the stream towards me and on, under the bridge wall. I used to play Pooh-sticks as a child. The race was fun: the drop, the cross, the wait for the reappearance of the swimmers, the my-stick your-stick tension. But it was the eddies which really built the excitement: the *Starry Night* swirls that had the potential to catch and submerge. Sometimes you could see them, waiting, but sometimes they lurked beneath the bridge, like trolls, plotting to grasp anything which passed. I stepped across and waited for the leaf to show itself. Blue-green. Venice, receiving cargoes of lapis lazuli from Afghanistan. Blue-green. Venice, bringing ultramarine to Europe. Brown.

The worshippers were leaving as I walked back up the lane. By the door of the church a cassock and alb hid a small vicar, who shook hands with his parishioners as they departed. Emily was already at the lychgate.

"It was a nice service," she said. "You should try it sometime."

"I think I'm cursed to die outside the faith and unshriven."

"Well, anytime you want. What have you been doing?"

I told her as we walked the short distance back to the cottage. We sat in the front room with cups of tea, watching the religious stragglers go by at the end of the garden.

"That's Mabel Tamerlane," I said, pointing at an old woman in a faded blue coat. "She left the village when she was young to seek adventure."

Emily took a sip of tea. "Did she find it?"

"Oh, yes. Her life is full of tales of derring-do, illicit liaisons, and intrigue. There was a certain summer in Samarkand which would shock you. But she came back here, in the end, about twenty years ago, and now lives with memories and wonders if she should ever have left in the first place."

"And how do you know all this?"

"There are two names carved in the gate of the church. Mabel and Arthur. I'm inquisitive, as you know, and happened to run into the village historian whilst playing my solo game of Pooh-sticks. So, I asked him about Mabel. He's a strange fellow."

"I know."

"You do?"

"Everyone does. Some say he lost that leg in a bar fight, but the truth is that it got caught in the rigging of a whaling bark, in the treacherous waters around Nantucket. These days he drinks, to forget."

"You win," I said, and raised my cup in a toast to the victor.

Emily met my cup with hers in a porcelain clink.

We talked about plans for the day until we came to the conclusion that it was a day with no need for plans. She would potter around the cottage, maybe go for a walk, prepare some papers for the following day. I thought I might go to the bookshop, the one with the cheap books. First, though, I needed to rest. I slunk upstairs and lay on my bed, staring at the ceiling.

Van Gogh wrote about *The Bedroom at Arles*, about his painting, or the room itself, in the Yellow House. Perhaps they were the same thing, with the angles, and the walls falling in from above, and the two closed doors. His letter to his brother, Theo, described all the colours, the ones he applied with no shade or shadow: butter-yellows, lemon light-greens, scarlets, lilacs. Time has worked on the pigments. The lilacs have faded to blues, the floor has darkened. There is a patch of his ceiling, in a far corner, the same colour as the walls. My ceiling had cracks in the whitewash, running along the paths taken by the timbers above, or bisecting the space between them. Either way, the inflexible plaster had lost the battle. Still, it had done better than the Yellow House, damaged by bombs during the Second World War, demolished without reprieve.

I wanted to open more doors, to go into the hallway outside my room and see what lay beyond. Vincent had a guest room through one of his doors, ready for his friend, Paul Gauguin. The other led to stairs. In the cottage I had my own choices, and I wanted to turn left to the thin, plank door and open it and go up so that my stairs led only down. There were mysteries up there above me, mysteries that bent beams and cracked plaster, and walls which fell in, and I wanted to see them myself, to see them faded and darkened.

Sunday was Vincent, and pills, and sleep.

CHAPTER TWO

Friday, 14th October, 1887

Today I have missed Father greatly. What a curious admission: I had always thought that the first days of college would fill me with nothing but excitement, and that any homesickness from which I might suffer would linger in the shadows until the solitude of night. It is undeniable that the house is dispiritingly plain and indistinguishable from the other buildings in the vicinity—red brick and sandstone quoins are seemingly prescribed by good taste in North Oxford—but it is also too small for one to feel truly alone. Perhaps I miss Father because I know he would have enjoyed tonight's reception: he would have made the perfect chaperon.

At the start of the evening we girls crowded together in one corner of the room, finding safety in numbers. Yet, whilst we giggled like schoolgirls—a less than charitable observer would be correct in claiming that we are little more than such—Lady Diana Fitzpatrick entered the room, escorted by a certain reverend professor of divinity, whom I understand to be a friend of the family. Unwilling to have our juvenile natures exposed by this contrast, the rest of us began to circulate in a more appropriate fashion, much to the evident approval of Miss Callow and the other ladies for whom the running of the college has become such a calling.

How shall I describe Lady Diana? She is, in general, unassuming, which description runs somewhat contrary to her arrival this evening. On our first meeting, yesterday, at a small gathering of the students, both old and new—and even then numbering only sixteen in total— she introduced herself as "Miss Fitzpatrick, but my friends call me

Diana." I am only aware of her title because one of the other girls, whose name I now forget, delighted in sharing it with all who remained within earshot after Lady Diana's departure, as if her society knowledge were likely to increase her own social standing.

Lady Diana is undoubtedly beautiful. Her hair is blonde, but not of that garish hue which might suggest its achievement through the application of some form of oxide or acid; rather, it is the colour of pale honey, and the perfect match for her blue eyes. She appears young, but possesses that quality which I have seen in others of an aristocratic pedigree, that her youth does not disguise a mature beauty, but complements it perfectly. In truth, I find myself somehow lessened in her presence, as though the standards of those around me are adjusted to accommodate her comeliness and deportment, depreciating the value of any charms which I myself might presume to possess. I should have imagined that this would engender feelings of resentment or jealousy, yet I find myself approving of her, as though it is only appropriate that she exist just as she does. Although our social circles have little in common—conceivably only our attendance at college—I have hopes that I shall enjoy her company over the coming months.

Tonight's reception was described by Miss Callow as a chance to show her new girls to Oxford, to which she added—with a touch of venom I thought—"Or at least to those who are progressive enough to accept our presence." She was accompanied by her assistant, Mrs. Taylor, who, in the circumstances of such a small and new college, seems to be a general factotum in matters administrative. I find Mrs. Taylor to be a somewhat fussy woman: is that the price one pays in order to be valued in an academic environment, when one is not oneself defined by academic achievement or position? Certainly, she has shown nothing but a good-natured desire to be truly helpful to the girls since the day of our arrival, and one cannot find fault with that.

I, like so many of the girls, spent the start of the evening in our corner. This was as much the fault of those who failed to introduce themselves, and those who ought to have effected introductions, as it was the fault of our playing the *ingénue* role. Lady Diana's arrival created an atmosphere of more relaxed, though always formal, geniality, and introductions began in earnest. The men fell into two categories: those who were fellows of some college or other and thus untrammelled by duties of affection—though more through righteousness than statute, it seems—and those who were in the company of their wives. In the whole evening I met only one man who broke that rule, or so I thought. He was introduced to me by Miss Callow herself and, had I been less occupied with portraying the epitome of etiquette, and less distracted by the laughter of Lady Diana sounding from the far side of the room, I should have supposed immediately that this Matthew Taylor was the husband of our own Mrs. Taylor. I was, however, both occupied and distracted, and found myself, at least for an exciting and enticing first few minutes, talking to what I presumed to be the only "single" man at the affair.

Mr. Taylor is tall, four or five inches taller than am I, and I myself am often described as "willowy" by Mother. He was dressed smartly and entirely in keeping with the occasion, and yet somehow the cut of his cloth, or the looseness of his tie—which exposed just the slightest twinkle of collar stud—gave him what I can only describe as a poetic air. I should not want to give the impression that he is a louche individual: he had none of the extravagance which one is likely to associate with the Romantics. Yet there is, indeed, something romantic about the man. His eyelids droop—no, "droop" is too strong a word, and suggests a slow-wittedness in his character which is most certainly not the case—his eyelids hover above grey-green eyes, as though he is only recently awakened and taking in the start of the day, anew. I found myself quite disarmed and momentarily lost all concern for correctness. Indeed, so pleased was I to be conversing with one who confessed himself to be "an artist of little importance" that I poured forth a torrent of opinions on literature, leaving few pauses in which the poor man might say anything more. I spoke of Warber! It was perhaps a godsend that our Mrs. Taylor approached when she did. As she stepped closer with a low "Mr. Taylor?" it dawned upon me that this must be the man's wife, and the light-hearted "Aha! Hello!" with which he greeted her was all that was necessary to confirm my unremarkable, and much delayed, deduction.

There can be few people who have not experienced that intense burning sensation which accompanies a redness of the cheeks sufficient to guide the ancient ships at Alexandria. Now, as I grew suddenly voiceless before Mr. and Mrs. Taylor, I felt just such a fire. Mrs. Taylor, doubtless curious at the silence which befell our small group, bore a quizzical expression and I began to think, desperately, what one ought to say in such a conversational lull. I was saved by Mr. Taylor—thank heavens!—who turned to his wife and explained that we had been talking about my literary interests. My relief was short-lived: I became certain that Mr. Taylor intended to share with Mrs. Taylor all the details of those interests, a certainty exacerbated by the impropriety of those subjects on which I had expounded mere moments ago. Mrs. Taylor would hear of Warber, and of his book, and the thought of that was so unbearable that I even considered the pretence of a swoon to create a distraction. Ah! but I should have placed more faith in her husband, for he delivered a précis which gave me an air of erudition with no sense of impropriety whatsoever: I was the daughter of a publisher and, as such, in possession of a natural curiosity for the history of our country's literature. Mrs. Taylor had, then, nothing but a kind smile for me, and yet she did not follow with any kind words but asked my forgiveness as she needed to take her husband away from my company. Mr. Taylor thanked me for a most pleasant discussion, and turned to his wife without another word. I watched as she took his arm and walked with him—or led him, I believe—over to Miss Callow where clearly, since they left a few minutes later, they must have made their farewells.

"You will see them again through the window to your left," said a voice beside me, and I gave a little start. Lady Diana spoke with a cadence shaped from the same honey as her hair. I looked at her, feigning a lack of understanding of her comment. She cocked her head to one side, as if she were daring me to deny my interest in the Taylors, but placed her hand on my shoulder before I could utter a word in my own defence. She introduced herself, and I thought that she had forgotten my being at the college's small introductory soirée only yesterday. I was about to say something to that effect when we were joined by her chaperon, the reverend professor, who expressed slight distress that his evening's charge was causing him to follow her around the room.

"We must find time to talk soon," she said to me, with a tilt of the head, and then she moved off. I watched as she made her way over to a gentleman who stood by the very window she had indicated. The reverend professor, as ever, found himself governed by her decisions as to the path of her circulation, but she waited a respectable distance from this new gentleman, and it became evident that she knew the reverend would never allow himself to fail in his duties. So it was that he hurried past her and effected the necessary introduction, helpless to do otherwise. It was then that I came to understand that Lady Diana was perfectly aware of the formalities and that, in introducing herself to me directly, without the intercession of her chaperon, she had announced a perfect recollection of our previous meeting.

There was nothing singular about the don to whom Lady Diana was talking—I assumed him to be a don from his solitude and distracted nature, and the scuffs on his shoes—and it seemed odd that she should have proceeded so purposefully towards him. Then, from the smallest of glances back to me, I divined her purpose. There, in the small garden, framed and bisected by the woodwork of the window, appeared the Taylors. Husband and wife were no longer arm-in-arm, and appeared to be engaged in an argument which caused them, before they had even left the grounds, to cease their progression and face each other. Whatever the subject, first Mrs. Taylor and then Mr. Taylor, following her gaze, looked back at the college house. I was sure that they must have been able to see me, but could not avert my eyes for fear that my spying on them—for it was spying—would become an even more indisputable reality. Yet they did not linger on the building for more than a few seconds before Mrs. Taylor turned swiftly back to the path and made for the street. Mr. Taylor faltered, then thrust his hands into the pockets of his trousers, in a gesture which suggested equal parts resignation and resolve, and pursued his wife.

The sounds of the room returned—the clinking of glasses, indistinct mutterings, the gentle crackle of logs on the fire—and I looked around. The evening was coming to a close and guests were leaving. Most of the girls had a short distance to walk back to their lodgings, which are in the college house itself. Others have private arrangements within the city: their number includes Lady Diana, whose carriage was almost certainly waiting for her. After saying my goodbyes to Miss Callow I left as I had arrived, in the company of another student, a Miss Elizabeth Ashdown. She and I made each other's acquaintance on first arriving at the college, as our porters clashed on the narrow staircase of the house. We left our rooms simultaneously on hearing their assorted and creative oaths—eager to see what was causing such a terrible commotion—and shared an immediate bond. I think that she and I shall be fast friends.

My room is on the top floor of the college house, one of three garrets which I can only presume were originally intended for the lower type of servant. Elizabeth is in one of the others and the third is being used as a storage room, although I do not doubt that it will be converted to some form of bunk within the year, unless the college plans to move to larger premises. The furnishings are sparse: a bed of the creakiest iron, on which rests a thin mattress with which I fight in order to tame its more egregious lumps; an oak desk—with a slim volume of undistinguished poetry under one leg for balance—accompanied by an overly decorous chair; and the usual collection of wardrobe, chest of drawers, washstand, and washbowl and jug, these last being of the Chinese-blue variety with few enough chips to be serviceable but too many to be desirable. In the glow of the gaslight it looks thoroughly wretched. Oh! but the view through the little window! The spires stand white beneath the moonlight.

I am here—life exists, and identity. The powerful play goes on, and I shall contribute a verse.

Saturday, 15th October, 1887

Elizabeth and I breakfasted together. Breakfast is taken in a small room overlooking the garden to the rear of the house. It is a most tranquil spot. There was a single servant to assist with the meal. When one considers how many people are resident in our little college, it is curious that we employ only two maids-of-all-work. I had supposed that the intention was to reduce the weekly costs for the students. There is some element of that, as I pay 12s. each week for lodging, and the same again for board. However, Elizabeth has it on good authority that the lack of domestic servants is intended to bring the students together in their sharing of everyday tasks.

Elizabeth also informed me that the undergraduates of the University refer to us as "bonnets", and confirmed that our acceptance here is far from unquestioned. John Ruskin himself, that most esteemed of critics, only a few years past refused to allow "the bonnets" to attend his art lectures, arguing that such discourse was of no use to the female mind. According to Elizabeth, Mr. Ruskin claimed that we should "occupy the seats in mere disappointed puzzlement."

In truth, I find it somewhat difficult to comprehend my status as a student in this ancient university. Some lectures I may attend, some I may not, the decision seemingly at the whim of the lecturer, with Mr. Ruskin merely one particular case to demonstrate the rule. I face no residence requirements such as those imposed upon the men in their colleges. As for examinations, the University has seen fit to allow women to take only certain of them. The small body to which I so joyfully belong forms a secret cadre—by no means a complete regiment—in Oxford, sometimes accepted but oft-times spurned. We, its members, are subject to a level of caprice which, I like to imagine, will slowly be eroded by the actions of those who would see us in our rightful place, but who recognize the small steps which one must take to achieve that fine ambition.

After breakfast I discovered, waiting on the slightly battered oak table in the hall, a letter which—its bearing no stamp—I took to have been hand delivered. It is in the refined hand of Mr. Taylor.

Dear Miss Swift,

I do hope you will not perceive my writing to you so soon after a formal introduction to be an impertinence. I found our conversation yesterday evening to be thoroughly fascinating, and it was most unfortunate that other business required my early departure. Perhaps we might meet to continue our discussion? Although the weather is rarely fine at this time of year it has been sufficiently warm in the past week to allow for a suggestion of the Botanic Garden as a suitable meeting place. I find it to provide a sense of openness and vivacity, and I endeavour to take a turn there most afternoons.

I am most keen not to trouble you in any way, so let us say that I shall be in the Garden after lunch, between one and two o'clock, all this coming week, and should you be so kind as to accept my offer, I shall be waiting to meet you there on any day you may choose.

Yours very sincerely,
Matthew Taylor

I have spent much of today thinking about the letter. I do so want to talk with him again, not least as it is so rare that one finds a person, be it man or woman, with whom one can slip into easy reflection on matters close to one's heart. There is something which causes me to trust him, to an extent which seems both perfectly natural and inexplicable. By early afternoon I had decided that I should definitely not accept his offer: to do so would be highly improper. Now, however, it is late and the flickering light and shadows drive a certain sense of adventure—of possibilities—within me. It is that same adventurous spirit which drove me to come here, and which I share with Father, without whose support I should never have found myself in this room. I am persuaded that he would be proud of a daughter who expanded her horizons, and that I ought not to dismiss so quickly a meeting with Mr. Taylor but, instead, find some way to ensure that it might take place whilst retaining all possible propriety. Tomorrow I shall ask Elizabeth if she will act as chaperone. She is an older woman—I confess that I have thus far been remiss in asking her what brought her here, or how she came to find herself able to adopt the student life at her age—and she would seem to be a fine choice.

Sunday, 16th October, 1887
Elizabeth and I spoke together this morning, as we walked back from

chapel. She had much to say about Mr. Taylor and, aside from her acceptance of his handsomeness and agreeable demeanour, none of it was favourable. It is generally believed—I should say that Elizabeth believes it is generally believed, for such is the nature of rumour—that Mr. Taylor is an incorrigible philanderer and seducer of women. She attributed this information to "whispers" but from whose lips these whispers came she could not, or would not, say. She has heard tell from some that Mrs. Taylor is a perfect angel, enduring her marriage for the greater good of appearances and reputation. From others she has reports that the angelic Mrs. Taylor is the worst sort of Xanthippe, a scold from whom Mr. Taylor seeks shelter in the understanding arms of others. Elizabeth's tone, however, suggested that she tends towards a belief in Mrs. Taylor's possession of a flawless halo.

Thus it was with some surprise that I received Elizabeth's agreement to accompany me to the Botanic Garden, an agreement made with little of the reticence which her reporting of Mr. Taylor's nature had led me to expect. Were I to guess the reason for this contradiction, I should venture that it comes from an irrepressible curiosity, of the sort so often associated with those in whom rumours roost, and from whom rumours fly. There is a rare and valuable currency in those incidents which one can claim to have seen with one's own eyes, or to have heard with one's own ears.

So, it is decided: Elizabeth and I shall visit the Garden on Wednesday, shortly after lunch. Oh! I do have a sense of excitement, but it is tempered with a concern that Mr. Taylor and I shall not be permitted to talk as we might desire, for we shall be within earshot of one in whom a confidence is not to be left for safekeeping. Even so, in preparation, I spent the afternoon reading Warber in my room, with Keats ready by my side so that anyone who entered without pause would find me only lost amongst the nightingales.

CHAPTER THREE

On Monday I slept until mid-morning. The cottage was mine. Emily had gone to work without leaving a note to tell me that she had gone to work. I turned on the radio and set the volume to a level which kept me company. Outside, the rain fell to the lagoon, quenching history. I thought about calling Emily and asking what I should do, where I should go, but I decided that the day was a test for me, a chance to make my own decisions, and I would not miss the chance to shine.

The attic was dark behind the door. The clack of the latch stayed with me on the bottom stair, ready to climb beside me, into the shadows and dust.

"I shall click this light switch," I said to myself, "and it will have no effect. I shall toggle it, up and down, up and down, just like in films, and nothing will happen, but I'll press on, undaunted, feeling my way until I become accustomed to the light and then, slowly, the horror above will envelop me and my mouth will open to scream. Too late. Too late."

In reality, the switch blinked the staircase into stark existence beneath an exposed fluorescent tube. It filled the room with a subtle humming which swept down the stairs and into the landing, drowning out the faint sound of the radio from the kitchen, wrapping me in isolation. And behold, a ladder set up on the earth, and the top of it reached to heaven: and behold the angels of God ascending and descending on it. And I was Jacob, drawn from the Old Testament, surrounded by blue night sky and stars, and from above the gold of heaven cast down its light, bringing forth a staircase for the angels, cast from my dreams, sketched by William Blake two centuries ago. The dead ascend the staircase, children are carried aloft on gentle shoulders or led by the hand, and lovers reunite in an embrace. But nobody met me as I climbed towards the light, rounding the turn of the stairs, and instead of gilded warmth I found folded blankets, a broken record-player, mouldering books, packing cartons and tea crates. Piles of junk were crammed beneath the sloping roof, ready to tumble like the walls of Vincent's bedroom.

An ill-defined path ran down the centre of the room, broken with oak cross-beams which spanned from wall to wall, a little above floor level. I walked along, carefully, peering into boxes and under dust-sheets: tea sets from summers ago; photograph albums filled with faces, children carried aloft, lovers reunited; shellac 78s of classical and jazz music. Everything had a story to tell, but they were whispered, lost to me. The past seemed like a hologram: each object contributed to the whole; take one away and everything which remained lost a little focus, and so it would go, object by object. There, in the attic, the few remaining pieces sat in a past blurred beyond recognition, inviting me to draw the details for myself. Margot and Arnold could no longer use their tea service, as it had been a gift from Norman, who had turned out to be a frightful cad. Oh, how Judith and Patricia had enjoyed the stolen, carefree raptures of tennis that day, with the sun shining and Edith behind the lens of her Box Brownie. Robert was willing to make concessions in order to be with Miranda: he would play his jazz on Mondays, Wednesdays and Fridays, and she her classical on Tuesdays, Thursdays and Saturdays. On Sundays their spats would continue.

Where the dormer window broke the slope of the roof, the path branched to the side of the room. A bitter light dripped through the grimy pane, beyond the reach of fluorescence. On the floor to the left of the window a doll's house rested on top of a wooden tennis racket in a press. The plain, white face of the house was split down the middle and hinged at either gable-end. Tipped by the racket beneath, one side remained closed whilst the other lolled open, as though bombed-out during the war. Squatting down for a closer look I saw the shrapnel wounds continue inside. Shredded paper and mouse droppings covered the miniature furniture. I reached to open the remainder of the front elevation and everything happened at once: crying out, tumbling, a mouse, mice, all scurrying too fast for creatures so small, and my hands catching the floor to steady me, and the endless hum drowned out by heartbeats, my heartbeats, then alone again, and standing quickly to a smack on the head from the beam over the dormer and slowly, slowly, slowly, hand in hair, coming to stillness, rest, and breath after breath after breath. I laughed.

There was gold beside me, finally. In the dim light it refused to glow or shine or otherwise behave as it ought, yet still it called out. It shouted the presence of treasure from beneath a dust-sheet which had shifted as I fought to recover my balance.

"Yes," I murmured. "Wonderful things."

I took hold of the sheet, ready to face whatever might run away from me, or towards me. But once revealed, the only living things remained transfixed in the pigments of a painting. I knelt down, placing a hand on the top of the exposed frame to steady myself. The gloom did little to reveal the secrets of the discovery. The shadow details were lost completely, leaving the lighter areas to struggle into the attic as best they could. A woman gazed out at me, past a man, his face in profile. They did not belong there.

The dust could keep its stories. All but this one. This one was mine.

Simeon Solomon drank himself to death in 1905, or died in the trying. A short obituary in *The Illustrated London News* described him as lacking "that comfortable insensitiveness which leads along the happy middle way." There was no drink in the cottage, and even if there had been I would not have drunk it, alone. Pills, on the other hand, were allowed, prescribed, and mine to cherish or abhor depending on my mood which, in turn, depended on the number of pills I had already taken. Morning, lunch and evening pills were purple, and the night pill was yellow. But that was not why Solomon's painting was in my mind, with its woman draped in purple and its woman draped in yellow, embracing on a stone bench. Or maybe it was, partly. Inspired by poetry, Solomon painted Sappho and Erinna, two poetesses, together in a garden at

Mytilene, on Lesbos. Dead before we knew better, he thought they may have met, sharing islands and lifetimes. Not that he would have cared even if he had known the truth, because he was painting something allegorical, and not just in the doves and deer and flora with which he adorned the picture. Solomon's Sappho wears her pill-yellow gown, my nightgown, and leans in, one arm around Erinna's waist and the other on her shoulder. Sappho's eyes are closed and her lips rest on Erinna's cheek, but Erinna's thoughts are seemingly elsewhere: she looks out of the painting from beneath languid eyelids. It is as though she is lost to Sappho already, and her own hand, so lovingly resting on Sappho's, will be taken away, in a parting, because this cannot happen, or cannot continue to happen, and I hold Emily for the last time. Anna-yellow-pill Sappho holds, and her eyes are closed because she will not see the future as the purple pill sees it, as I saw it once.

People have written that the yellow-pill Sappho is androgynous, even masculine, but that is true of almost all the figures in Solomon's work. "The lineaments of woman and of man seem blended as the lines of sky and landscape melt in the burning mist of heat and light," wrote a poet of the time. Solomon's earlier sketch for the head of Sappho possesses a gentleness of line and softness of shading which emphasize the feminine. Seven years after spending time with the women of Mytilene he published a book, *A Vision of Love Revealed in Sleep*. Its frontispiece shows the narrator and his soul, two male figures that could be the twins of Sappho and Erinna. It could be Solomon himself, looking out of the garden, from under those languid eyelids, searching for a happy middle way.

The painting from the attic sat in front of the window, propped on the seat of a pine chair. The scene on the canvas was illuminated by moonlight shining through a mullioned window, slightly dulled with age. A couple rested on a canopied bed, in the shade of heavy, dark-crimson curtains, swagged and gathered. Several niches disrupted the lines of the surrounding stone walls, and in each niche stood a candle. One had been reduced to a wisp of smoke drifting upwards from a candlestick, whilst the others were close to death.

On the bed, the nearest figure lay propped against a collection of silk cushions in golds and greens. He wore a simple tunic of blue velvet, with a gold belt at the waist and pale tights ending in black, gold-buckled shoes. The profile of his face shared Sappho's androgyny. The second figure rested beside the first, towards the farthest side of the bed, her body partly obscured by the man who held her. His left arm was draped around her shoulders, and her head lay on his breast, red hair tumbling over his tunic. She wore a long, green dress which fitted closely above the waist, where it passed beneath a jewel-studded belt and loosened to flow down, over her feet. Her features were fine and well-proportioned. She was pale, except for a delicate blush on the cheeks. Thin brows arched gently above wide, brown eyes. She looked out, like Erinna, over her companion and beyond, to me, expectantly, as though she believed I had answers, even if she could not make her questions clear. I opened my mouth to apologize but the telephone rang and brought me home again. It was Emily. She asked how I was and I thought I should tell her about the attic, but then I caught sight of the woman on the bed and I needed to understand, if I could, so I said nothing of it and just yessed and noed and took my pills while Emily waited on the line, two purple, Erinna. Then goodbyes and I sat on the couch and felt the room exhale.

John William Waterhouse painted Hypnos and Thanatos—*Sleep and His Half-brother Death*—resting together, on a bed like the one which waited for me, propped on its chair. Sleep, eyes closed, clutches his red poppies for laudanum. Death, seemingly sightless, slumps beside him. But my two figures seemed too alive for Death, and too anxious for Sleep. Somewhere in the attic the whispered stories explained it all, but I could not hear and had to hope someone else had gained their confidence and broken the oral tradition.

The frame looked to be mid- to late-nineteenth century. It was too generic for earlier Victorian works, when each frame was individually designed to complement and extend the canvas it held. A flat inner frame overlapped the edges of the canvas, then gave way to a gently curving, concave surround moulded with intertwined flowers and leaves. The accumulation of dust and soot over the years had darkened the gilded relief, deepening shadows and softening highlights. At the top, the inner frame arched over the corners of the painting, pressing the walls in towards the bed and breaking any sense of depth which the painter had tried to achieve.

I scanned the surface looking for a signature, a date, anything that might give me a clue to the subject, but there was nothing. I turned the picture over. The back of the canvas showed between the wooden stretchers which kept it taut. On the top stretcher a fragment of paper read "ord": all that remained of the manufacturer's details. A green cloakroom ticket, number 734, was held in place by browning tape which curled at the edges and came away in my hands as I touched it. Simeon Solomon was arrested and charged with attempted sodomy. The man and woman on the bed wanted to tell me something, or to be told something, and either way I could not understand, and neither hear nor speak. Waterhouse's mother and younger brothers were taken by tuberculosis, Sleep and Death, his first Royal Academy exhibition. Solomon's soul showed him the way.

There was a fresh mug of tea on the table by the time Emily shook me by the shoulder. I thought her opening the front door would have awoken me, but no, not through purple pills. She sat down on the edge of the couch and ran her hand gently through my hair.

"Where did you find that?" she asked, nodding in the direction of the painting.

I propped myself up on one arm, taking the mug in my free hand and drinking slowly. The warm liquid made me realize I had not eaten all day.

"I'm hungry," I said.

"I brought Chinese. I'll get it."

Emily went into the kitchen and I sat up, still a little foggy, sipping my tea and looking at the painting. It was dark outside and the lighting in the room was too low to save the shadows from a return to their night. The woman peered out over a smudge of tunic, the wall behind her slipping away with the exhausted candles. The man stared ahead of himself. At what? There was no suggestion of light from an unseen window.

"So, tell me about the painting," said Emily, returning with a plate in each hand and cutlery sticking out of a trouser pocket. She gave me a fork and a helping of sweet-and-sour something with rice. I answered her between mouthfuls.

"Found it in the attic. And a doll's house with mice. But I left that. Don't know much about it. Late nineteenth century, I think. Not amazing. Not terrible. No signature."

I paused for another sip of tea and Emily took the chance to speak.

"I'm not sure you should have been up there. It's the owner's private stuff."

"Well," I said, "I won't go up there again. And I only brought this one thing down. And art is my thing after all. They wouldn't mind, probably."

Emily ate a few forkfuls of food before replying.

"Well, anyway… Did you say mice?"

"Just one. I thought more, but now I think one. It was living in the doll's house but I opened the front up and there it was. I'm sure it'll leave our house alone if we leave its house alone. What do you think of the painting?"

Emily stood up and stepped over to take a closer look.

"It's a bit dark," she said. "I wonder what the story is. There's always a story behind chocolate-box art."

"Chocolate box?"

"You know. The sort of picture you get on boxes of chocolate, for Mothering Sunday or grandparents' birthdays. Why is it two women, do you think?"

"It's a woman and a man."

"Are you sure? I know there's only one in a frock, but the one at the front reminds me of what's-her-name in that *Twelfth Night* painting."

She looked at me, knowing I could not allow her comparison to remain in such vague terms. And I knew she meant Lizzie Siddal. Poor, dead, Lizzie Siddal. She was Ophelia in a painting by John Everett Millais. Ophelia, floating, drowned, and Lizzie, addicted to Sleep's red poppies, lying in the cooling water of Millais's bathtub as he painted.

She was buried with a little book of her husband's poems: her husband, Dante Gabriel Rossetti, who disinterred her, who took his poems back from the coffin, stole them and returned her to the ground, alone. I walked over and stood by Emily.

"You mean Walter Deverell. *Twelfth Night* was his masterpiece, really. You're thinking of Lizzie Siddal as Viola."

"Letting concealment feed on her damask cheek," said Emily, and then, seeing my look of surprise, she added, "What? Shakespeare. You're not the only one with an education. Do you think this might be the same subject?"

"Maybe. There are certainly pictures of Viola and Olivia together. Deverell did an etching of them, with Siddal as Viola, again, disguised as Cesario. But I don't see why they'd be on a bed together, particularly. Even if that isn't a man."

I readied myself for an argument, but Emily just shrugged and said, "Now what? I suppose it wouldn't hurt if you did a little research."

"Maybe tomorrow. I'm getting tired."

Purple pills. Yellow pill. The two people on the bed, man and woman, two women. White pillow.

I rose a little before dawn, before even Emily was awake, Emily who had to drive to the station and catch the 7:40 train to London, and spend the day at the office. I did not have to work, but I was restless and threw on my clothes and tiptoed downstairs, picking up my keys from the hook by the front door before I left the cottage. I wandered down the lane to the churchyard and shared the dawn with Vincent.

Vincent had been dead for over thirty years when Stanley Spencer— Sir Stanley Spencer, but not yet—painted his own churchyard. He came over and joined us, Vincent and me, on the little bench by the graveyard wall, pushing his easel and brushes along in a pram. He pointed and whispered to us, but his eyes did not focus, and his descriptions were of Cookham, the village of his birth and the setting for his painting *The Resurrection, Cookham*. There was Christ in the church doorway, and there Hilda, his first wife, still resting in her ivied tomb, and Spencer himself, naked in front of us, his blushes spared by a small shrub. Stanley was amongst his friends, as alive then as when he painted them risen. Just as a little brook ran on, down past my church, so he pointed to the left of his church and spoke of his Stygian Thames, with the pleasure boats and tinkling piano, out beyond another Hilda, watching. The pointing hand darted down and to the right, to a third Hilda, smelling a flower, revelling in its existence. Dead couples rose from other tombs and plots. Wives brushed down their husbands, smartened them up, ready for their arrival in Paradise. I thought Stanley wanted to talk about his elder brother, Sydney, killed during the Great War, but Vincent heard the crows and he was back in Auvers with his wheatfields and dragging me with him and Stanley departed with his pram. Then Vincent left, as it was his time to leave, and I sat alone listening to the morning crow-caw of the trees as a trickle of sunlight lifted the mist. Sometimes, when I worked in the gallery, I had heard the pompous telling their children that to understand a picture one must climb into it, into the image and into the head of the artist. But that was the wrong way round. If you want to understand a picture you have to let the artist crawl inside you, guide you, accompany you and then, if you are lucky, leave you to your own trees and mists, to your own Resurrection.

I came back to the cottage to find Emily rushing around, grabbing bags and papers, a piece of toast hanging out of her mouth. She took a bite and pulled the remainder away with a hand which somehow balanced the weight of the bread against a cardboard folder stuffed with yellowing sheets of office paper.

"I thought you were still asleep," she said, conveying a delicate blend of concern and accusation. "Where have you been?" The note of concern had faded.

"Well, it was early. I didn't want to wake you. I went and sat in the churchyard. Fresh air."

Emily took more bites of toast, replying as she chewed.

"Well... I suppose... it can't do any harm. How is it... outside?"

"Cold, but peaceful. You'd better get going. You'll be late."

She looked around the room one final time, saw nothing she had yet to juggle, and made to leave. When she reached me she placed a kiss on my forehead and told me to call her if I needed anything. I nodded and opened the door for her. One of us said, "I love you." Then the house was mine again. I made tea and some toast of my own, and sat looking at the painting on the chair by the window, and out to the rose garden, disturbed only by an occasional car heading to work or to the station. For this is the suburb of the great city, belonging to his heavenly palace, in the heavenly Jerusalem. John Donne. Maybe he was thinking of Cookham when he wrote that. Stanley Spencer thought he was. It was time for a closer inspection.

The kitchen cupboards did not appear to have been changed since first fitted, sometime in the 1960s. White paint had stained grease-yellow from years of exposure to cooking fat. Diamond-shaped, frosted panes of glass added decoration to the doors, disguising shelves covered with curling, cracking paper. I found a couple of screwdrivers in the cupboard beside the door to the back garden. I was fairly sure that Emily would have wanted me to leave them in the cupboard, but she was not with me in Jerusalem and the painting needed me, or I needed the painting. Either way, I knew what I was doing. Back at the gallery I had the proper equipment, but a couple of screwdrivers would be enough to start the exploration.

Emily had cleared her papers from the dining table during her morning rush, and I moved my crumb-covered plate and empty mug onto one of the dining chairs. I brought a bedsheet down from the airing cupboard, folded it double and laid it over the table to protect the wood, and to protect the gilding of the frame as I placed it, face-down, in front of me. The canvas, supported by stretchers, was held in place by bent iron pins spaced at intervals around its four sides. Some of the pins had loosened over time, and I pulled them out by hand. Others could not be removed so easily but could be twisted to one side, out of the way. The remaining few I levered out gently with one of the screwdrivers, using my finger as a pivot point to avoid causing any damage. That was enough to release the canvas. I lifted it from the table, leaving behind the outer and inner frames and, around the edges, a set of small, thin spacers which had stopped wood and paint from coming into direct contact. Finally, the whole painting could be seen. I started scribbling notes on a pad from the kitchen, between cooking times and ingredients, don't-forgets and back-laters.

CHAPTER FOUR

Sunday, 23rd October, 1887

Dear Mr. Taylor,

I hope you will forgive me the delay in writing to you, which was caused, as I am sure you will understand, by the increasing demands of the academic term. Thank you again for the time which we shared at the Botanic Garden. Miss Ashdown has asked me to convey her warmest regards.

I cannot lend you my copy of Warber, as you requested—it is in a most fragile condition and I promised my father that it would always remain in my possession—but let me now tell you a little of Samuel Warber himself, and of his book. As you are no doubt aware, the life and works of this man are hardly an appropriate topic for the interests of Oxford students, whether they be man or woman, but I have no doubts that you will exercise the utmost discretion.

As is so often the case with authors of a certain antiquity, little is known of the man himself. He was born around the middle of the seventeenth century into what must have been a relatively well-to-do family, taking into consideration his education and access to literature. After the Restoration he attempted to fit the mould of libertine, and it was this endeavour which led to his publishing *The Strange History of Thomasin and Olivia* sometime before his hanging in 1676. Neither my father nor I are aware of any extant copies of this first publication, our own *History* being an example of a second edition, dated 1745. It is possible that the first edition was ordered destroyed, either because Warber's chosen subject was too prurient or—and I judge the likelihood of this to be the greater given the mores of the Restoration—because, in the telling, it was adjudged to be insulting to the monarchy.

Warber's story has many antecedents. Indeed, Warber himself writes in a weak imitation of sixteenth-century English: the book's title is given as *Ye Straunge Hystory of Thomysin & Oliuia*.

In 1534 an English text of *The Boke of Duke Huon of Burdeux* was published, translated from the Old French by Sir John Bourchier. Delightfully, the Early English Text Society has recently overseen the reprinting of Bourchier's work. It may be of interest to you that Bourchier's translation also brought with it the first mention of Oberon, king of the fairies, in English literature. Bourchier's main characters are called Olive and Ide—"Howe the emperoure gaue his doughter Olyue in maryage to the damoysel yde…"—but much of the story is unchanged by Warber. Such changes as he does make are surely designed to increase the licentious nature of the work.

Huon of Burdeux is itself translated from an early-thirteenth-century *chanson de geste*—a French epic romance—and its continuations, which include *Chanson d'Ide et Olive*. I have not seen the French work, but Father tells me that a printing of it is in preparation in Germany. The themes of *Chanson d'Ide et Olive* are themselves echoes of the story of Iphis and Ianthe, from Ovid's *Metamorphoses*, Book IX: "*Fama novi centum Cretæas forsitan urbes implesset monstri; si non miracula nuper Iphide mutata Crete propiora tulisset.*" A translation is unnecessary, of course, but I thought you might like to read the poetry of Dryden: "The fame of this,"—the transformation of Byblis into a fountain—"perhaps, through Crete had flown; but Crete had newer wonders of her own, in Iphis chang'd." My father tells me that some elements of Ovid's tale are also to be found in the earlier works of Nicander, as retold in Antoninus Liberalis's *Μεταμορφώσεων Συναγωγή*. Father read this in Xylander's sixteenth-century printing, although he hopes to view the original manuscript during his next trip to Heidelberg.

Do, please, forgive me if I have dwelt too long on the history of the piece. It is, no doubt, the story itself in which your interest lies, so let me now relate it here. Please indulge me, however, in allowing a few further observations regarding earlier works: I am, or aspire to be, an academic, after all. I trust you will recognize the extent to which the following has been Bowdlerized and understand the necessity of my removing much which is lewd and inappropriate.

King Florence was a fine king, in possession of a beautiful wife by the name of Clara. The two of them lay together as man and wife are intended to do, with the consequences which one might expect. On the day of the birth the King waited anxiously as the midwives did their duty in the chambers above his day room. After some little time had passed he heard the crying of a child, and his heart was filled with joy. The child, a daughter, was brought to him but as he held her in his arms he noticed the sullen faces of his courtiers and asked them how his wife fared.

"Your Majesty," replied a knight, "your Queen is departed to God."

The King handed the child back to the midwives and sat with his head in his hands, lost in grief. Throughout the coming days of mourning and burial, and on into the rest of his life, the King's only true solace was his daughter, whom he named Thomasin. She grew to be as beautiful as her mother, and the King adored her, often holding her in his arms and kissing her, eschewing the company of other women and giving no thought to the taking of a second wife.

So it happened that one day King Florence called together his lords and knights, and presented them with a great feast and marvellous entertainments. Afterwards the King bade them retire to the castle gardens and said:

"Sirs, you all know that I have a beautiful daughter, the Princess Thomasin, who has been courted by many kings and princes. I have never consented to a marriage, and I myself have never married because of the love I held for her mother. Now, however, I desire to be married, to take a wife in whom I might see again my poor departed Clara."

The lords and knights, hearing this, made much cheer and expressed great joy that their King had finally found a second chance of happiness. One amongst them, a knight called Sir Bartholomew, spoke out, asking the King to name his bride. The King replied:

"My lords and knights, I shall take my daughter as my wife, sharing with her the great love which I had for her mother."

Upon this, all present stood mute, until Sir Bartholomew spoke out again.

"My King," he said, "you know that I am your friend and faithful servant. Please hear me when I say that such a thing is forbidden by God. If you would so pollute your own blood then there is no end to the shame which will befall you. You would be unworthy to sit upon the throne."

"Sir Bartholomew," replied the King, "you are indeed my friend, and I have never had need to question your loyalty. It is for these reasons alone that I do not have your head removed from your shoulders for the words you have spoken. And let all men know that if they should repeat the claims you have made, they shall be put to death."

At this Sir Bartholomew ceased his protests, and all present averted their gaze from King Florence. Raising his hand the King summoned a page and told him to fetch the fair Thomasin. The Princess arrived forthwith and, seeing her loving father, joined him where he was sitting. The King embraced her and kissed her many times. The watching lords and knights observed her happiness and understood that she saw only the love of a father for his daughter. Then, however, the King stood and faced his daughter, placing his hands on her shoulders.

"My daughter," he said, "it has always saddened me greatly that you grew up without a mother. You are so like her in your beauty and your ways that sometimes I see her standing before me and love you even more. It is for these reasons that I intend to take you as my wife, and shall be your husband."

Horrified, Thomasin tried to stand, the colour fading from her rosy cheeks, but her father took firm hold of her hand and demanded that she follow his will. Again, the lords and knights appealed to King Florence to take pity on his daughter and to recognize the evil in his intentions. The King dismissed their protests and reminded them that if they failed to abide by his wishes he would see their heads removed. Then he ordered his daughter to retire to her chambers with her handmaids, that she might prepare for her wedding the very next day.

There was amongst the handmaids one who was old and wise and had served Thomasin since the death of Queen Clara. The Princess called her to her side, and bade all the other maidens leave. When the two of them were alone Thomasin begged the wise handmaid to help her escape to a far country, and the old lady, joining her charge in weeping, promised to do all she could. She left Thomasin in the chamber and went straight to Sir Bartholomew, telling him of her mistress's desire to depart in secret. Whispering, in a hidden corner of the castle, Sir Bartholomew told the handmaid of a plan to avoid the hideous marriage, and this the handmaid carried back to the Princess, saying:

"My Mistress, just as my brother, Peter of Aragon, rescued your own mother from the Saracens, so Sir Bartholomew will rescue you now from your father's intentions. The King has ordered you to bathe this evening, and you must go to the bath-house. When you return to your chamber, order the other ladies to bathe, too. I shall ensure that they spend a long while in bathing, and become tired and ready to sleep. Under your bed you will find hidden the clothes and belongings of a man. Don the clothes, place the sword on your hip and the spurs on your boots. Then, stealthily, head out of the chamber and to the stables, where you will find a horse readied for you."

Thus it was that Thomasin came to the stables as her handmaids slept. There she found Sir Bartholomew waiting with a horse, and bread and meat and two bottles of wine. He helped her into the saddle and she rode out, into the forest, until she was far from her country. Safe in those foreign lands, but eager to hide any weakness lest she be preyed upon, Thomasin became Thomas.

In the ancient versions of the story, those of Ovid and Antoninus, the child is brought up as a man from birth, as her father instructs her mother to kill the babe if it is born a girl. Warber, I suspect, saw more sensationalism in the later version, which he thus chose to adapt. His descriptions of King Florence's interactions with his daughter are far more elaborate than those in *Huon of Burdeux* or my relating of the story, and the gratitude of the Princess to her handmaid and Sir Bartholomew is similarly—how should one describe it?—extravagant.

On the significance of names, my father has suggested that Warber chose Thomasin and Thomas, rather than Ide, because of an occurrence in Virginia, earlier in the seventeenth century, which may have reached the ears of the gossips in London some years later. Perhaps Father is right, although I have my doubts: he himself has the history only through personal correspondence with a friend who resides in the state. A person by the name of Thomas Hall became the subject of much consternation amongst the townsfolk of Warrosquyoake, having been seen to dress in the garb of both men and women. Several inconclusive and no doubt highly intimate examinations of Thomas's body were made, and finally proceedings reached the General Court at Jamestown. There, Hall told how he had been christened Thomasine, and had been raised as a girl, before he cut off his hair, called himself Thomas and became a soldier. At the end of his service he returned home and became again Thomasine, until presented with a chance to sail for Virginia. It was then that Hall returned to his life as Thomas, for the most part.

On with our story. *Huon of Burdeux* spends several chapters on Thomasin's—that is, Ide's—heroic deeds at this point. Warber's volume is, however, too slim for such digressions, and he reduces this part of the narrative to a little over four pages. Thomasin runs out of money, sells her horse, and becomes the squire of a German soldier, bound for Rome. An attack by Spaniards leaves her as the only survivor and she flees, directly into the hands of brigands. Various scuffles ensue, which leave Thomasin riding away with five of the brigands dead and the severed hand of a sixth still clutching the bridle of her horse. Finally, she comes into the service of the Emperor of Rome, is knighted by him, and leads his army to a glorious victory against the Spanish.

Warber returns to his main narrative with the Emperor's lauding of Thomasin—whom, of course, he knows only as Thomas—for valiant deeds. Warber's handling of names and pronouns in this next section of the book is far from deft, and I fear that mine will be no better.

When the Emperor saw Thomas, garlanded in victory, he praised him effusively, and made him First Chamberlain and High Constable of all his lands and lords. The daughter of the Emperor, whose name was Olivia, fell in love with the brave and handsome Thomas. Her father, seeing his daughter's desire and himself loving Thomas as though a son, called him to his chamber and said to him:

"Thomas, my dear friend, I wish to repay the service you have done for me and cannot think of a greater reward than the hand of Olivia, my dearest daughter. When I am dead you may govern my empire as your own."

Thomasin was filled with dread that such a thing might happen, and that she might be discovered on her wedding night. She tried to persuade the Emperor that she was just a poor gentleman, unworthy of a daughter who should surely marry a fine prince. At this the Emperor became angry, unable to believe that anyone would refuse the honour of his daughter's hand in marriage. In the face of this ire Thomasin could do nothing but accept her fate and agree to the betrothal.

The wedding took place the very same day, with celebrations and feasting such as Rome had not seen since its first founding. After dinner it was time for the couple to retire to their chambers. Olivia went to bed, followed by Thomasin, and the servants departed, leaving them alone.

And now we come to the point at which Warber breaks away from all previous versions of the story. In Antoninus's telling, Galatea's child, Leucippus, becomes too beautiful to pass as a boy. Galatea prays to Leto, who takes pity on her and changes Leucippus into a man. In Ovid, it is Isis who hears the prayers of Iphis's mother, Telethusa, and turns Iphis into a man so that he may marry Ianthe. In *Huon of Burdeux* Ide manages to delay "ye thynge the whiche of right ought to be done bytwene man and woman" for fifteen days, through the fabrication of an illness, but finally he must reveal all to Olive. She is forgiving, but a page overhears the couple talking and conveys the news to the Emperor who, in turn, promises to burn Ide and his daughter at the stake if what he is told is true. Thankfully, an angel of Our Lord appears and declares that Ide is thenceforth a man and Olive shall bear his child: "The day past and the nyght came, and yde and Olyue went to bed togyther, and toke there sport."

Warber seems to have no time for such dalliances with divine intervention. It is quite possible that even he blanched at the idea of mixing his particular style of low writing with the godly.

The fair Olivia moved to take off her fine wedding dress of silk and lace but Thomas placed a hand on her shoulder and whispered, "Wait. Let us lie beside each other, and kiss and talk a while."

Thomas took his wife's hand and led her to the bed and bade her lie down beside him. This she did, resting her head on his chest and waiting for him to speak.

"My Love," said Thomas, "you know that I love you dearly, and that I think you the most beautiful woman in all of Christendom."

"My Love," replied Olivia, "I do know so, and I should hope that you know the place you have held in my heart for so long. Why now do you sound so unbearably burdened with distress, my Thomas?"

Thomas gave no reply. His fair wife, anxious lest her new husband be unwell, held him ever tighter and pressed her head against him until she heard the quick beating of his heart. After some little time, unable to hold her tongue any longer, she spoke again, hesitantly at first and then with ever-increasing courage.

"My Thomas, though I fear you may be ill, yet you seem well. Your body is strong and your heart beats loudly. Though I fear you may not love me, yet your words and your gentle touch tell me I am in your heart as you are in mine. Now I fear you may have some secret and that you are the one in whom true dread resides. I shall say only this to you, my husband, that had I been born Ianthe I should not have wished for Isis to change my Iphis."

On hearing this Thomas lifted the head of his beloved wife and kissed her gently. Then he asked her how she came to know his secret.

"My sweet Thomas," she replied, "I have always known. You are brave and strong, but these qualities are not reserved to men alone. You are wise and protective, but so too are our mothers. And you are beautiful, too beautiful for one such as I to miss your true nature. Now tell me, what shall I call you?"

Holding her tightly Olivia's Love kissed her, saying:

"My name is Thomasin, but I fear that if you call me by that name when we are alone you shall one day call me by that same name when others are present. You must call me Thomas, and must think of me as your husband, for if we are discovered your father shall have us both burned, of this I am sure."

"My darling husband," said Olivia, "you will always be my Thomas."

My dear Mr. Taylor, I now find myself quite unable to bring Warber's story to any true conclusion. As I have mentioned, Warber was most certainly in the business of publishing in order to further his ambitions, and to gain recognition amongst certain of the less-reputable members of King Charles's court. The continuance of his tale, which lasts a not inconsiderable number of pages, relates what one might term "the amorous interactions" between Thomasin and Olivia and, I reticently add, a maid who interrupts them later that night and is taken into their confidence and their "sport".

Suffice to say that, despite its lewdness, the Warber book is fascinating for its retelling of far older stories and its illumination of some aspects of Restoration sensibilities. Such, I am sure, was the thinking of my father when he came into his study on that autumn day and found me reading his copy of *The Strange History*, as I was relating to you at our last meeting, shortly before the rainstorm forced my sudden departure from the Botanic Garden. Surely there can be few who are as keen on the intellectual life as publishers—or, should I say, reputable publishers?—and this was certainly my father's reason for allowing me my interest in the book. Just as he feels that young ladies ought to be given the chance of a decent education, so does he comprehend that even the most delicate subjects—those deemed indecorous by polite society—have their place in an understanding of the world. "These qualities are not reserved to men alone."

I think even Father would be uncomfortable were he to know of my sharing this private part of my life with another. He does not know you as I feel I have come to know you, even in our short time together. There must be a moment in a liberated woman's life when she determines to take on the responsibility of judgment for herself.

I do hope we shall be able to meet again and continue our conversation. I shall discuss the possibility with Miss Ashdown.

Yours very sincerely,

Penelope Swift

Chapter Five

I tried to talk to Emily as soon as she opened the door, but she brushed past me and threw her briefcase onto a chair, giving me a look which strongly suggested that I keep quiet. She took off her gloves and put them in the pocket of her greatcoat, which she then removed and hung on the back of the door, beside me. Only then did she greet me with a perfunctory hug which seemed more protocol than affection.

"He came into the office today," she said. "I'm sorry."

"*Et in Arcadia*," I muttered, and went away from there to the woods and mixed with shepherds and lost my innocence or found an understanding, both, neither, and the shepherds were asking me about the inscription, asking me in Emily's voice:

"What do you mean?"

"There's death here, too, even here. We think we're safe, endless, but it, he, she always comes back, even in this place, even here."

"Anna?"

I looked at Emily's face, worried, questioning, and the room was back and her coat was hanging beside me with her gloves in the pocket.

"Sorry," I said. "It just reminds me of the Poussin painting. He's the tomb."

"Poussin's the tomb?" She took my hand and we sat together on the couch.

"No," I said. "So Nicolas Poussin paints this bucolic scene, right? Calls it *Les Bergers d'Arcadie*. Paints it twice, actually. The one in the Louvre is the most famous. All trees and mountains. Greenery and blue skies and fluffy clouds."

"I know this one. There's a tomb in the middle."

"Yes. Right in the middle. A tomb with an inscription."

"*Et in Arcadia ego.*"

"Right. 'I am here, even in Arcadia.' And shepherds have gathered around, pointing in amazement, trying to come to terms with the fact that death exists even there, in the middle of a pastoral Utopia. I mean, that's a simplistic interpretation but..."

I paused for a minute, but Emily's expression didn't change. I continued, talking more quickly, breathing more shallowly.

"But the tomb is huge, and old. How are we supposed to view the shepherds? They should have known. They couldn't be so blind as to believe they were endless. And the woman. Three men and a woman in the painting. The woman. She knows. She always knew. It's as if she brought them there to end their stupidity. Maybe gently, but it's still a lesson. And we should have learned, Ems. He is here. I should have learned. I should have known he was here."

Emily put her arms around my waist and pulled me to her. Our cheeks brushed against each other as I rested my chin on her shoulder.

"He's not here, Anna. He's never been here. He'll never be here. He just came to collect the last of his personal stuff from the office."

I felt—we both felt—the tears running down my face. Emily put a hand in my hair and stroked her fingers gently against my scalp.

"I only told you he came at all because I promised. Whenever I see him, I'll tell you. Here."

She leaned away from me and handed me a tissue from her pocket, small and white and scrunched up: a scared tissue.

"Thank you," I said. I watched her walk into the kitchen and take two mugs from the cupboard above the sink. She switched the kettle on and went to rummage for tea bags. White steam. Fluffy clouds. He was not in the cottage. She said that he was not there and she would not lie to me. Unless I was the woman, the one who knew, and she was a shepherd. Unless I was supposed to teach the lesson, to watch her point at the inscription on a tomb, point and trace her own shadow as it fell on the stone, trace his shadow as it fell over hers. And, as she did so, I would nod sagely and she would know that I was wise and a teacher. I blew my nose and she put the mugs on the table beside me.

"Tea," she said.

I picked up the nearest mug and took a sip.

"Tea," I said.

"I'm sorry. Tell me about your day."

I pointed to the dining table. The painting lay beside its empty frame.

"I noticed when I came in. You broke it?"

"No. I didn't break it. I slowly and carefully removed the canvas and stretchers from the frame. I know what I'm doing, Ems. I might be... I'm not... I know what I'm doing."

"Okay, yes. Okay. I'm sorry. I know you're good at your job. Did you find anything?"

"What do you want to know?"

"Anything. Everything. Who painted it?"

"I don't know. There's no signature. At least, none that I've found yet. No date, either. It's odd, but not unheard of, especially if the painter didn't intend to show it."

"Well, what can you tell me?"

I began to feel defensive, challenged to prove my worth. I stood up and walked over to the painting. Emily followed and listened as I pointed and talked.

"Well, it's in the Pre-Raphaelite tradition. Like *Ophelia*."

Emily cocked her head.

"We saw it at the Tate," I explained. "John Everett Millais painted it in 1852. It's quintessentially Pre-Raphaelite. The river banks are painted from nature. Or maybe from sketches from nature. The plants shown don't all flower at the same time of year. Full of romantic imagery. Looks a bit like stained glass. You know the one. Ophelia's floating in a stream, drowned. Her eyes are open. Lips are parted. Her dress is billowing around her in the water. You know. *Ophelia*."

"I always knew. Sometimes I just like hearing you talk," she said. "Go on."

"Right. Okay. Well, if you look here," I pointed at the top of the painting, "you'll see that these two corners are bare. The artist knew there were going to be spandrels. They're the arched bits at the top corners of the inner frame. They covered the canvas here, so he didn't bother to continue the painting beneath them. There are some patches of colour where he was testing his pigment and varnish mixes—"

"It's definitely a male painter?"

"No, I suppose not. Statistically though... There are a few pencil scribbles, too. *Ophelia* has the same thing: little daubs of paint where the spandrels hide the canvas. Splashes of colour, pencil sketches of birds, some sort of rat-like thing. They're all there, hiding in the corners above Ophelia, Lizzie Siddal, in Millais's bathtub beneath a willow growing aslant. Before her husband stole his poems from her."

Emily put her hand on my arm and I paused, regaining a tenuous sense of pace and focus.

"Anyway," I continued, "you can see that the ground, the layer on which the painting itself is made, is exceptionally white. Probably zinc white and lead white over the original commercial preparation of the canvas. It's part of what makes the colours look as vibrant, as glassy, as they do. The oil paint is made from pigment, little particles of colour suspended in a liquid medium. I think the medium might be copal and nut oil, or something like it. Maybe Roberson's Medium. That was popular at the time. See, around the edges the painting is slightly darker?"

Emily nodded. I could tell that I was testing the limits of her interest.

"That happens when copal mediums are kept away from light. Anyway, the refractive index of the medium, the amount it bends light, is close to that of the pigment it holds, so light passes through the paint without much scattering. A bit like when you drop a diamond in water. The diamond seems to disappear because it bends light almost exactly as much as the water around it does. So, the light goes through the paint—"

"The paint is the pigment and medium mixed together, right?"

"Right. The light goes through the paint and bounces back off the white layer beneath. It gives a kind of translucent appearance. Then you try to keep colours pure. One pigment in an area, not a mixture. You combine small areas of pure colour, so it doesn't start to look muddy. But from a distance you get a range of colours."

Emily took a mouthful of tea.

"Want me to go on?" I asked.

"I need to eat something. What about the artist?"

"Not much, but I have a plan to find out more. I'll tell you about that after dinner. All I can tell you now is that it was painted later in the 1800s. At least, I think so. Something about it makes me imagine someone painting based on other Pre-Raphaelites. Not imitating, exactly, but not innovating either. The artist is all right, but he's not astonishing."

"Oh?"

"Yeah. If you look closely you can see some of the sketching beneath the paint. Particularly where he used fugitive pigments."

Emily looked genuinely puzzled.

"Areas where the colour has faded. There are a lot of pencil lines, a really detailed sketch straight onto the white background layer, probably whilst it was still a little wet."

"Is that bad?"

"No, not bad as such. It was the way they worked. Sketching straight onto the painting, rather than creating preparatory drawings and transferring them when they were complete. But..."

"But?"

"But, look at a painting by someone as talented as Millais. The sketching underneath is sparse and fluid. He doesn't need much to allow him to paint, doesn't make many mistakes with what he does need. Here there's a lot of detail. The painter needs his hand held when he starts applying paint."

"So we're looking for a second-rate, late Pre-Raphaelite with a penchant for Shakespearean themes?"

"Well, 'second-rate' seems a little harsh. Just not first-rate. And I'm still not convinced by the Shakespearean theme. I do agree with you about the ambiguity of the gender of the front figure, but it's a calculated ambiguity. I think it's probably deliberate and part of the story. With all that sketching I'm sure the artist would have fixed it if it had been a mistake, even if he's second-rate. Could be a woman dressed as a man. Could be a man who looks feminine. Maybe something else. Maybe Shakespeare. Maybe not."

Emily said we should eat.

Nicolas Poussin, painter of shepherds, once wrote a letter in which he linked the nature of his paintings to the modes of Greek music. It may be that he had a complex system of composition, a system which created ratios of size and position between the elements on the canvas, enhancing the emotions within a painting. Then again, he was writing to a disgruntled client who thought the painting he had received was inferior to another of Poussin's. So, Nicolas may have been trying to get the guy off his back with whatever vague art-speak sounded like it might work.

Dinner was in Poussin's Dorian mode, held with an air both grave and severe. As he constructed painting through music, so we constructed meaning through the act of dining. Our representations lay in the scrape of knife on plate, the slurp of tea and orange juice, and the page-rustle of a newspaper. Finally, as I stood to clear the table, I said:

"I know how we can find out more about the painting, Ems."

Emily looked away from her newsprint and smiled a transparent smile.

"Oh? How?"

The removal of the frame had given me something, but not enough, not without returning to my gallery, discussing the piece with colleagues who specialized in the late-Victorian period, or with someone who did not know the period well, but knew people who did. Alison, who knew me, and cared when I needed her to care. Alison, who cared anyway. But the painting was shy and not ready for wider introductions. So I went back to the source, clicking open the small, black latch and being Jacob again, ascending, with the hum and the light above and the mice who would not scare me, I told myself, even as I was afraid that they would scare me.

Over by the window the light still stole through the dirt, but darker today, with clouds playing games in the sky, hiding Poussin's blue above them. The dust-sheet lay where I had left it, a small drift of snow and pale begonias warped by the crumpling of cotton. In my fear of mice—which I did not have, I reminded myself—I kicked it with my foot and stepped back. Nothing moved. I glanced at the doll's house. It lay sleeping, my handprints in the dust on its roof. The motes floated around me, filling my lungs with each breath.

Propped against the wall, visible without the painting for protection, an old bookcase held shoeboxes and papers, china animals, a stack of bathroom tiles, a tarnished silver mirror. A few brown-tinted paperbacks, tumbling from the bottom shelf and onto the floor, gave it some of the dignity of its purpose, but not enough to bring it back to life. It huddled, dead, buried under the detritus with poems to be reclaimed.

I picked up the nearest pile of papers and glanced through playbills and postcards, found the secrets of a washing machine from 1973 and a tape-deck from 1982, learned the notes to "Greensleeves". So went the rest of the loose sheafs, and each one made me less hopeful and more expectant, as if I were searching the places I thought least likely first, because stories should have a quest and the painting should demand that of me, that I struggle a little.

The first shoebox was full of jigsaw pieces, large and small, wood and cardboard, edge pieces that were straight, edge pieces that were curved, fractured pieces of stories, snatches of tunes, broken modes. A child's face, red-cheeked, missing an eye, had become trapped in a castle wall. Ducks rode a train into a tunnel of something purple, too blurry to make out, a little interlocking detail, robbed of context. Tabs and blanks and squares mixed with whimsies from a map of Britain, shaped like tourist attractions: Big Ben, Stonehenge, a jaundiced smudge which was probably the White Cliffs of Dover.

The second box was on the bottom shelf. One of the front corners had been replaced by a ragged-edged hole. I reached out and flicked the lid off, toppling a pile of paperbacks, trying to catch them, causing even more to tumble to the floor, and even as they fell something moved to my left and I wanted to leave, but I stayed because the story needed a heroine. Everything settled to dust and heartbeats. Nothing moved inside the box, nothing lived amongst the receipts, and fragments of paper, and mouse droppings. I could have looked through the contents in the attic, where they belonged, but the light was poor, I said, and the dust was bad for me, I said. I remembered that Jacob did not ascend the ladder himself, but slept and watched the angels, and I was no angel so I did not belong, I said. I left the dirt and books, the mice and their house-on-a-racket-press, and took the box down to safety.

The details were not for Emily.

"I found the receipt in the attic," I told her, pulling the folded, yellowing paper out of the pocket of my jeans. "We can use it to find out more."

She took the receipt from me and read it, or made the pretence of reading it, then placed it on the table and sipped her tea with an air of deliberation.

"Anna," she began, and the way in which she said my name caused me to stiffen, ready to defend myself before she uttered another word. "I don't see what we can do with this. I'm not going to ask the owners about their private belongings. We shouldn't even be in the attic. Right now you have their painting in pieces." She gestured to the other half of the table. "And now you want me to talk to them about some paperwork you found hidden up there?"

"Oh. Oh, no. We can't bother the owner. I'm sorry. I didn't mean to upset you." I sat back down and drank my juice, looking at her over the rim of the glass. "I thought we'd go to the auction house."

"The auction house?"

"Yes. We can find out who sold the painting. No need to bother the owners."

"Are you serious? Why would they even tell us? Even if they would tell us, why don't you just ring them? I'm not going all the way to—" She looked at the receipt. "Reading?" She paused and checked the address. "You want to go to Reading?"

"I do," I said, and wrapped both hands around my cool glass and looked down at the light bulb turned to sunlight by the orange liquid. "They might not tell us anything but I want to try. And I don't want to call because it'll be harder to persuade them if we call. And you said it wouldn't hurt, a little research wouldn't hurt."

"I did say that, but…"

"I want to go to Reading, please."

Emily examined the receipt yet again, but the address refused to change.

"And if we go, you'll be satisfied?"

She blurred in front of me, in salt water with the same refractive index as diamond. I nodded.

"Fine. We'll go at the weekend. At least call them and make sure they're going to be open."

"I did. They're open tomorrow. We can go tomorrow."

Emily rearranged her cup and spoon and the sugar bowl. Geometry, gentle modes of tension, Klee and Poussin. She looked straight at me.

"Anna, I have to work. I've missed enough already. I can't keep asking my colleagues to cover for me. We're a person short on the team. I can't ask them."

She ought to have been sorry. She had shown me the maggoty corpse in my own Arcadia, and if the truth was hard it was hard because it was her truth, and she had allowed me to ignore it, ignore even the possibility of it, until she showed me.

"I'm sorry," I said. "I understand. We'll go on Saturday."

Emily handed the receipt back to me.

"Thank you," she said. "I'm still not sure what good it will do."

I finished my juice.

I was Josephine Hopper for the rest of the week, sitting by a window, looking out and waiting for something. She sits at eleven in the morning, if the title of the painting—her husband Edward's painting, another work of confinement and loneliness—if the title tells the truth. *Eleven A.M.* She sits, Jo sits, but not Jo if we are not told. She sits staring out of her window at a missing view. There is only her body, almost naked, naked but for flat-soled shoes, naked on her chair, and outside only the stones of her building, and the windows of another, in shade, and the slightest hint of sunlight breaking through between them. It was grey outside my window, but at least I had a garden.

The painting, my painting, not mine, but yes mine, sat beside me. But Jo has only a table-lamp and an impossible chest of drawers, set between chair and wall, where no space exists to be filled, and the drawers are just fronts with handles, and their opening is defied by the chair which blocks their path. Everything enclosed. A curtain on the wall, a curtain which should be a door, a curtain which seems to hide... what? It must be another room, with another window, because the sun hits its back wall and how could the sun slip in without an invitation? Maybe it is a guest room, waiting for Gauguin, but far too late. And it is too flat, too flat to be a way out. No room. As flat as the garden outside the cottage. Rose bushes all empty sticks, and all and ever entwined, with their perspective stolen and no shadows for depth. Jo has shadows at least. They shade a wooden chair, partly visible and nobody on it.

My wooden chair had the painting on it. I had company, even if I did not know their names. Even if one stared away from me, the other looked out and wanted to hear something from me. And all I said was, "Soon." Aloud. Allowed to say that, as Emily was not there to hear.

Jo sits in Edward's *Automat*, too, one glove on, the other off—because one should not wear a glove to lift a coffee cup—waiting, or tired of waiting, or no longer waiting. Alone, with another empty chair. But there is depth in the window behind her, plate glass and the lights on the ceiling reflected into a darkness which is cheated of the mirror of her, of tables and chairs, because they might give comfort. Red lips, red apples behind her in a glass bowl, amongst oranges and bananas. Red roses outside my window, but not then, because they might have given comfort.

Emily brought the newspaper home each night and I read down the columns. On Thursday I wandered to the little bookshop, floating on the lagoon which had returned with the morning rain. Outside, the cheap paperbacks were sheltering beneath plastic sheeting. The pooling raindrops magnified Penguins and Puffins. I bought a battered copy of *The Hitchhiker's Guide to the Galaxy* with an acid-trip rainbow cover and the silhouette of a piper in the corner. The rain was falling again, bouncing off the streets, by the time I had walked back as far as the church. The cottage was within sight, but I was not ready for my own confinement, so I sought refuge under the roof of the lychgate and began to read the words I had read so many times before. There were no new plot twists, no new jokes, just old friends in familiar situations, and I welcomed them all. I began to feel the chill of the day but the cottage did not offer warmth and I took the path between the graves, into the church. I sat at the end of a pew, the end by a window, reading pages faintly dappled by the colours of the staining between the lead. Nobody came, nobody left. Wooden chairs with nobody on them and the only paintings were paintings of Christ and the stories of Christ, with no interest in me but for our mutual distrust. The light faded over the lost hours until I could no longer see the shapes of letters against darkening paper. I slipped the book beneath my coat and left, afraid that someone would come and switch on the lights.

Inside the cottage I could switch on my own lights. I hung up my coat and dropped the book onto the table just as Emily arrived. The sound of the front door made me jump.

"You're home early."

I tried to say it matter-of-factly but I could not remove an accusatory edge. Emily replied whilst facing the coat rack.

"I can leave again if you'd like."

"No. I'm glad to see you. I'm sorry. I bought a book."

Emily looked over and saw the book beside me.

"Surely you've read that before?"

She didn't wait for an answer so I could never say that she knew I had, and we had spoken about it, and it was one of my favourites but the radio series was better.

"Will you make a drink?" she asked. "I want to change and collapse

57

on the couch. Let's get Chinese or something."

We got Chinese.

On Friday I was Jo Hopper and on Saturday we left for Reading.

Chapter Six

Wednesday, 26th October, 1887

Mr. Taylor has responded quickly and effusively to my brief outline of Warber's story. Whilst expressing his sincere wish not to be the pedlar of an improper invitation, he inquires if I might like to call on him tomorrow at his studio, which is a short walk from college, and where he will be working all day. I, not being as much of a naïf as others have cast me, discussed his offer with Elizabeth. I have only known her for a fortnight but I am usually a fine judge of character. She is one of those rare individuals who manage to apply sound reasoning to affairs of the heart—is this, then, already an affair of the heart?—without the accompanying harshness of tone so often found in those called upon for advice. In truth, she was a little short with me when we spoke, but I attribute that to her being distracted by her studies. We are all aware that we "bonnets" must achieve with a greatness exceeding that to which we might aspire were we amongst the men of the University. Nevertheless, her advice, given generously, is that I ought to ask myself whether I should agree to such an assignation were it certain to become public knowledge. Beyond that, she would not—she "did not feel it was her place to"—advise me, but she has kindly offered to be my chaperone should I decide to accept Mr. Taylor's invitation. She ended our conversation by picking up a Latin dictionary and examining its contents with a studied exaggeration.

I have been thinking on the business for some time. The better part of my opinion is that I ought to decline the invitation.

*

I am slowly coming to understand that, with the presence of a chaperone, I shall be able to avoid the worst excesses of jealous and groundless gossip, should the encounter become public knowledge. Furthermore, I am certain in my belief that Elizabeth is from a most respectable family and could not be doubted if questioned. Besides, I conclude the debate with myself, Father and Mother have always been adamant that it is in the sharing of knowledge and experience—in both of which Mr. Taylor's holdings exceed my own—that we grow as individuals and find our ability to make a worthy contribution to society. *Experientia docet.*

Thus I am resolved and have decided to accept the invitation.

Thursday, 27th October, 1887

I believe that I may have done a most terrible thing, forced upon me by circumstances of fate which I do not dare ascribe to my own actions.

Mr. Taylor's studio appears a plain affair as one approaches along the curving path from the river. Its oppressive functionality, expressed by the red bricks of its walls, stands in contrast to the arc of water and open fields to be viewed from the large windows which adorn its northern side, providing light in the European tradition. To the right of the front door—a clumsy overstatement of wood, black studs and elaborate iron hinges—a small, brass plaque informs the visitor that the lower floor is given over to the teaching of languages, although I saw no sign of teachers or students. I rang the bell and heard footsteps, followed by the turning of a key. Mr. Taylor stood before me, looking not a little puzzled.

The reason for his puzzlement, that reason which I can only believe to be the work of the Fates, was this: I had come to our meeting alone. The circumstances were these. I had arranged to accompany Elizabeth to a morning lecture on the subject of the Peloponnesian War, and thereafter to walk with her, back up to college and thence the short distance to the river and the studio. Elizabeth, however, was not to be seen at breakfast, and on asking after her I was informed that she had taken ill with a cold and would be staying in her room. I really ought to have visited her there and then, but my schedule did not allow for the time, and so I called on her upon my returning to college after the lecture. I knocked on her door and, receiving no reply, opened it quietly, just as wide as was necessary for me to peer into the room. The drawn curtains and overpowering smell of camphor attested to the fact of Elizabeth's illness. The patient herself was facing away from me, with bed-covers pulled high over most of her head. The slow, laboured rise and fall of the sheets confirmed that she was sleeping. Not wishing to wake her, of course, I shut the door as quietly as I had opened it and returned to my own room.

I would be dishonest to claim that I do not know my motive for ignoring Elizabeth's absence and going against the rules of the college, which require a chaperone whenever one is outside its grounds, if "grounds" is not too grandiose a term for a moderately sized garden. The motive is simply stated: I chose to continue, alone, to Mr. Taylor because I wished to be in the company of Mr. Taylor. So it was that I found myself on the man's doorstep, without anybody's being aware of my location or intention, save for a sleeping student on the top floor of college.

If Mr. Taylor had any qualms about my attending his premises without a companion he most certainly did not express them: even his look of puzzlement, so evident on his opening of the door, faded to a gentle expression of recognition and delight, such as I had first seen at the Botanic Garden. He greeted me with, "Miss Swift! Thank you for coming. Please, step inside," and led the way through an unremarkable hall—which seems to serve as a general reception room—and up a staircase situated near the rear of the property. The stairs themselves are uncarpeted and have a musty odour, as though the damp weather seeps through the walls and rests there. Then, however, at the top of the stairs, Mr. Taylor opened a door and revealed the most marvellous room. His studio extends almost the entire length of the upper floor of the building, with two doors off at the eastern end—the end closest to the river—which lead to an office and a small but serviceable kitchen. I can vouch that the light in the room is exquisite even on an overcast, grey, autumn day: the northern aspect gives it a diffuse quality, creating gentle shadows which changed only in the smallest degree as Mr. Taylor and I sat and drank the tea which he had been kind enough to offer.

We talked of Warber. He asked if I had brought the book with me, as he had requested in his invitation, and I reached into my little satchel and produced it. Whilst he leafed through the pages I stood and, with his consent, explored the room in more detail. In one corner there stands a selection of stage properties and costumes such as one might expect to grace a Shakespearean performance: pikes, staffs and swords lean against rolls of paper which appear to be painted with the dark stones of some great, old building; tunics, trousers, bodices and dresses, in several colours and adorned with varying amounts of lace, hang on a small rack, above buckled shoes and plain black boots; a trunk, decorated as though to be carried on some tumultuous campaign, with muskets and fife and drums, is partly hidden by a pile of stockings. These more ancient accoutrements give way, farther along the wall facing the windows, to a miscellany of other items which promise settings from ordinary parlours to glimpses of magnificent halls, in periods from Georgian to modern. A rolled-up rug and two unprepossessing oak chairs rest on a *chaise-longue*, next to a cottage pianoforte which lacks ivory on several of its keys. The overall effect is one of slightly curated chaos and I fail to comprehend how one might make a single scene from the collection without the occurrence of evident, and doubtless embarrassing, anachronisms.

There are several canvases propped against the east wall, between the two doors. Here, too, there is an air of clutter, with large canvases leaning in front of smaller, and framed and unframed pictures mingling. At least on a cursory inspection, most of the canvases remain in their pristine white condition. Even some of those in frames are apparently untouched, and I can only assume that canvas and frame will be separated and reunited after the creation of an image. Of those canvases which already bear some trace of paint, I should judge that few are even half-way to completion. On each work in progress the unadorned areas of canvas shine a pure white, even in the dim light of an October afternoon, although that purity is interrupted by arcs and scribblings of pencil, slightly inset into the paint's surface. Some of the scenes show recognizable items from the piles against the walls. Only one has progressed as far as the beginnings of a figure, and on this the painted background surrounds a blank space, a phantom with crude, scratched features.

My exploration was interrupted by the sharp clap of my book's being closed by Mr. Taylor. He nodded towards the seat opposite him, which I had recently vacated. I sat down and we talked a little more. He wished to hear again the story of my discovery of the book and Father's willingness to accept, even indulge, my interest as just another secret between parent and daughter. Mr. Taylor—Matthew—asked about the other secrets and I told him of the time I fell into the puddle in the garden and covered my new dress in mud. Then he brought matters back to Warber. What did I find so interesting about the story? My initial reply was wrapped in the terminology of erudition, and filled with the branches which spread from the ancient roots of the story: the changes arising through the death of the old gods and the acceptance of the new, the political reflections hidden within each adaptation. Matthew stopped me after but a few minutes. He did so politely, with a furrowed brow of good-natured inquisitiveness still chief amongst his expressions. He asked me again—"What do you find so interesting?"— this time placing the stress on the "you" of his inquiry. My returning gaze must have spoken of nothing more than a lack of understanding, for he rephrased his question in such language as to justify my reporting it verbatim.

"Why," he asked, "does Miss Penelope Swift, a student of broad learning and delightful countenance"—I think he said "delightful" but it was certainly some such adjective—"Why does Miss Penelope Swift find a place in her heart for a book such as this, as scurrilous in its intentions as it is bawdy in its language?"

I tried to present an answer which would satisfy him, but stumbled over some incomplete yet overly intricate explanation. I recall that it included references to the great love stories of our past: Abélard and Héloïse, Troilus and Cressida. At my mention of Hero and Leander Matthew mumbled something into his cup about "Leighton's recent painting"—I presume that he was referring to Sir Frederic Leighton—which had engendered such favourable comments amongst the cognoscenti. I fell silent, my train of thought broken by this interruption, and he took the opportunity to ask me if I were not troubled by the unnatural aspect of the relationship between Thomasin and Olivia. I do not remember that I spoke in reply to this inquiry but, whether I spoke or whether my blushes were response enough, Mr. Taylor moved to sit beside me, with words designed to disavow any intention to cause me embarrassment. I turned to face him as he placed his cup on the nearby table. His gaze never left my own.

I have kissed a married man. I have been entertained by a married man, in the company of no other, and I have kissed him. I can tell nobody. I must tell nobody. Even writing in my diary brings with it the fear that it might one day be discovered, but I have to write it down. I can tell nobody but I must express myself. Otherwise I shall never come to an understanding of my actions, and I shall never learn from my mistakes.

Are they mistakes?

I must not see him again. I must not see him alone. I must not see him in the company of others.

I must not see him again.

I do not believe he would tell anyone of what happened for—surely?—to do so would be to ruin his own reputation and that of his wife.

He was standing by the kitchen window when I departed. I did not wish to look back, having left so precipitously, but I could not help myself. I thought that he was watching me, but his gaze seemed level, across the river and fields and on into the distance.

He stood by the kitchen window and all happiness had gone from his face.

I must not see him again.

Saturday, 29th October, 1887

Until last night I had hardly eaten since my departure from the studio on Thursday. On one or two occasions my lack of appetite provoked remarks from the other women, causing me to avow a concern that I might have contracted Miss Ashdown's sickness whilst visiting her in her room. I now see that this particular deceit was particularly ill-conceived. Yesterday afternoon the assistant to the Principal—Mrs. Taylor, no less—voiced her apprehension that I was unwell. She suggested, politely but firmly, that I take meals in my room and avoid the other students.

So it was that I found myself alone with Mrs. Taylor, with whose husband I had spent time just the previous day. The surprise I felt at my ability to form a coherent reply to her well-intentioned suggestions remains with me still. I had supposed that when I saw her next I should lose any semblance of composure, or—a possibility which truly frightened me—turn and flee without a word of explanation. Yesterday, however—perhaps because I was in the safety of my own room, perhaps because she stood between me and the door, rendering flight an unavailable course of action—I told her that I felt fine, and that whatever discomfort had robbed me of my appetite had passed. I told her this calmly and resolutely, and all the while I managed to avoid looking at her directly, busying myself with the rearrangement of books and the smoothing-down of the counterpane. To her comment that I seemed a little distracted I remarked that I was a victim of those stresses which are bound to affect the new student in her first few days of term: the absence of family and friends, unfamiliar lodgings, and a startling amount of lectures to attend, books to read, and essays to write. I was, I informed her, merely struck with a healthy mixture of excitement and trepidation. At this she walked forward and took my hands in hers, locking us together in an exchange which could not but require our eyes to meet. I am proud and ashamed, in equal measure, that I could maintain my light countenance as she told me not to worry and assured me that the staff, tutors and other students were all available to help me in any way possible. I thanked her—I think a little over-effusively—and she left, telling me, over her shoulder, that I ought to be sure to eat a hearty dinner now that I had overcome my temporary affliction. At the door she hesitated, as though about to turn and say something more, but if that were the case she obviously thought better of it, as she left directly. Then the door closed behind her and I was alone. I sat on the bed, believing I might cry, believing, indeed, that I ought to cry if I were any decent sort of person. Yet there were no tears, just a sense of disaffection with the world, or of its disaffection with me: it will continue to turn, and host the events which unfold, but will no longer pay attention to my behaviour, or seek to govern its outcome.

I came late to dinner, but the usual disapprobation of the college was muted, doubtless tempered by my "illness". Certainly, I heard no comment which might have been taken as a reprimand for my tardiness. Equally, my choosing to sit alone at a table by the garden window—a choice partly forced upon me by the absence of Elizabeth, who remains indisposed—was not greeted by invitations to join those who were already seated: it seems my quarantine is preferable to my company.

Lady Diana came into the dining room: she had chosen to dine with us! True, she did so on the first night of term, but since then her involvement with the rest of the girls has been limited to academic pursuits. I am quite sure that her need for the companionship of other students is ameliorated by an existing social circle—her family estate is not so distant from Oxford—and that the usual requirements of the college are supplanted by the desirability of her association. I watched her look around the room from the doorway and was somewhat taken aback as she recognized me and made her way directly to my lonely table. She sat across from me and greeted me with a friendly "Hello" to which I replied in the only manner I could imagine, with a formal, "Good evening, Lady Diana." She grinned as she removed her gloves, and reminded me that her friends called her "Diana" with, once again and somehow more strikingly so, the implication that I was her friend. For the first time since events at the studio I found myself relaxing, even if only a little.

What shall I say of Diana? She is enchanting company and we share several interests. We took the occasion of dinner to bemoan the fact that the University continues to oppose the introduction of a School of English Language and Literature. Our discussion touched on the great poets—after some debate we chose to delineate these as poets which we two appraise as great—and ventured into the fine arts, about which Diana is far more informed than am I. Yet, even in those areas which most evidently show the advantages of her class and education, she brings only the most gentle and enjoyable discourse, never slipping into the purely didactic. When she departed for her carriage I was left feeling nothing but a sense of close friendship with her, which surpasses by far that which might be expected from so short an acquaintanceship. I have a suspicion that she engenders such emotions in all with whom she engages, as a natural consequence of her breeding, but I wish to believe that the connection between us is born of a more mutual, equitable exchange: for every classical marble and canvas which she describes, I shall share lines from Byron or Keats; for the more modern, Whitman, and that the Whitman of America, not Rossetti's much-tamed edition.

Today, she and I are to spend the afternoon at the University Galleries. I find that I have written this entry whilst glancing out of the window every few moments, in expectation of the arrival of her carriage: this despite the fact that I cannot see the driveway from my window.

The carriage arrived a little before noon, and Diana and I, in the company of her tame professor of divinity, travelled the short distance to the Galleries. We alighted on Beaumont Street and entered the West Wing of the imposing building in which the Galleries are housed. The Reverend J.L. Parker, our chaperon, is a tall man whose hair exhibits a constantly shifting pattern of tufts and wisps, a product of his penchant for running bony fingers through the grey strands whenever he is talking or lost in thought. It is a cruel truth that his conversation is often bland in the extreme, but he has in his character one particularly agreeable feature: he is enthralled by art to such an extent that he pays little heed to those in his charge, at least in my experience. I have known men of learning who feel compelled to impart every last morsel of knowledge in their possession, whenever and wherever they may do so. The Rev. J.L.P. is not amongst their number. After our arrival at the Galleries—where I found the usual 2d. entrance fee had been waived through some connection of either the Rev. J.L.P. or Diana— after our arrival, the good reverend left us to explore alone and we were able to talk unencumbered by his presence, save for the occasional chance encounter.

Diana had with her an antiquated and dog's-eared copy of the *Handbook Guide* for the Galleries, and this year's copy of *Alden's Oxford Guide*. I had only my pocket note-book, a stubby little pencil, and a determination to learn from my surroundings and my companion.

We did not linger in the first gallery, filled with monuments by Chantrey beneath a frieze cast from the Elgin Marbles. It seemed cold and unwelcoming and I was glad when Diana took my hand and pulled me into the main sculpture hall. I found myself standing in front of a plaster cast of the Florentine Boar. Diana reached out and rubbed the nose of the beast. Then she looked to me, clearly expecting that I should do the same. I did so and asked her if she thought that our actions would carry the same weight as if we had been in Florence, in the Mercato Nuovo itself: that is to say, had we ensured that we should one day return to the Galleries? Diana said that she did not usually believe in such superstitions, but that she had stood in this very spot with her brother, some years past, and since they had rubbed the nose, and since she stood now beside me, she could swear to the truth of the legend. I wonder whether or not she really believed that her return was due to the polished nose of a plaster-cast boar. She asked me if I knew the story of the copy in front of us. She giggled as I took out my note-book and pencil, ready to write down what she had to say. I must have failed in my attempts to conceal the hurt I felt at her laughter because she suddenly adopted a most serious expression and told me that she thought my note-book was "darling" and hoped that I never stopped using it whenever I so desired. Coming from another, such a statement might have been received as a paradigm of sarcasm, but something about the way she spoke the words would not have allowed even the most sceptical of listeners to doubt her sincerity.

The story, which Diana had had from her brother as she stood before the plaster cast for the first time, is that a student was strolling in the woods which used to lie close to The Queen's College, when suddenly he was attacked by a wild boar. The poor young man remained calm in the face of what must have seemed his inevitable demise and, as the beast sprang upon him, he thrust his copy of Aristotle into its gaping maw. The beast fell before him, choked to death. So it is that Christmas is celebrated at The Queen's College by the serving of a boar's head and the singing of the "Boar's Head Carol" with its rousing, Latin chorus. Hence the presentation to the college of a boar cast in plaster, a cast which has since come to reside in the Galleries.

"*Caput apri defero, Reddens laudes Domino!*"

The booming, sing-song voice startled us. We both gave a frightened jump and turned to see the Rev. J.L.P., walking on without so much as a second glance in our direction, a picture of innocence. I looked at Diana who whispered, "A Queen's man," and then laughed so loudly that I felt sure someone would appear and scold her. Thankfully we remained unaccosted by the few other patrons of the Galleries, although an elderly gentleman directed a censorious stare towards us, and with it an intimation that he was wont to consider an afternoon's excursion incomplete without some opportunity to reproach the younger generation.

Facing an arrangement of casts of the Muses, under the watchful eye of Apollo, I performed a *tableau vivant*, standing first in front of Calliope, on the left, and moving clockwise from statue to statue, striking the pose of each. When I had reached Clio, the last of the nine, I returned to Diana and asked her which Muse she thought I might be. She replied, at once, that the *pose plastique* could not but indicate Terpsichore, but then, after a pause, she added, "Or perhaps Erato, if we are to draw comparisons with Lady Hamilton's 'attitudes'." It was an assessment to which one might react in any number of ways, depending on one's opinion of Lady H. I chose to cast my eyes heavenward and, with the slightest shake of the head, brought her back to Terpsichore. If that were the case, I told her, then she must be Euterpe, as even the Muse of Dance needs music. She disagreed. "Melpomene," she said.

I followed her as she moved swiftly through the remaining statues and ascended the great staircase. I quickened my pace to catch up with her, intent on finding the reason for her answer to my question: her identification with the Muse of Tragedy seemed so out of keeping with her demeanour. When I stopped her she told me that I ought to think nothing of her choice, that it had been nought but a silly reply to a light-hearted question. This she said as we stood in the ante-room of the picture galleries on the upper floor, where, hanging on the wall to our left, we saw Rubens's awful painting of a dead child with angels. We were agreed that there is something ghastly about the image: the gentleness of the cherubic angels, carrying the child to his paradise, do nothing to diminish the horror of the child himself. His lids are not quite shut, and yet there is no doubt that the eyes beneath see nothing. His skin is—what?—I cannot say. The colours are greys and yellows, their effect dull and muted. The whole gives nothing more than the sense of death, and neither Diana nor I could find any joy in the piece, only loss and melancholy. I shivered a little at the sight of it, and saw Diana do the same.

The University Galleries have a marvellous collection of cartoons by Michael Angelo and Raffaelle, done in preparation for some of their major works. They are kept in a fireproof room, according to the *Handbook Guide*. I cannot help but feel that the dreadful Rubens coloured my viewing, for the pieces which remain uppermost in my memory, and the ones on which I troubled myself to write in my little note-book, are all of a nature which goes against the brighter emotions of the day.

Handbook Guide, M. Angelo, No. 50, "Michael Angelo and his friend Ant. Della Torre dissecting a human figure, which lies extended on a table; the arms hang to the ground, and a lighted candle is fixed in the stomach of the body"—frightful, as one might suppose from description; candle jutting from ribcage; reminds one of lurid tales of bodysnatchers; Diana described the skinless figure as "*écorché*".

Handbook Guide, M. Angelo, No. 20, "Study from the Last Judgment—a demon gnawing the leg of a man; red chalk"—demon's face is leonine; sharp teeth visible sinking into flesh of man's calf.

Handbook Guide, M. Angelo, No. 51, "Five very fine studies in one mount, one of which is the Death's Head in the Last Judgment"—flesh still on skull; one eye socket empty; other retains eyeball although in deep shadow; gaping nose; Diana dismissed it as "repellent"; moved on to Raffaelle.

Handbook Guide, Raffaelle, No. 155, "Melpomene—a Study for one of the Figures in the Fresco of Mount Parnassus"—joined Diana looking at her; flowing lines and drapery; looks back over her shoulder; no vines or grapes in hair, or hard to see them, but carries mask of tragedy held to stomach; mask in folds of material looks like head of John the Baptist.

I left Diana looking at her Muse, and came before Raffaelle's sketch of *Jacob Wrestling with the Angel*. The opponents are central in the composition, holding each other by the arms as the angel raises his knee to Jacob's hip socket: "He touched the hollow of his thigh; and the hollow of Jacob's thigh was out of joint."

Handbook Guide, Raffaelle, No. 58, "Jacob Wrestling with the Angel"—looks like they are dancing, gazing into eyes; wings show this is an angel, less ambiguous than Genesis; we all have our struggles, but oft-times they bless us.

We were quiet during the carriage ride home. Our infrequent speech arose, for the most part, from the gentle inquisition of the

Rev. J.L.P., whose curiosity about our opinions of the Galleries was cordial, polite, genuine and entirely unwelcome. Lady Diana has a dinner engagement which requires her presence on the family estate, so I returned to my room alone. There, on our shared landing, I met Elizabeth, who looked much refreshed after her days of rest, and who greeted me with a heartfelt affection which lifted the weariness at the end of a long day. She and I dined together, for which she seemed grateful, although I suspect that my talk of today's outing cannot have been of the least interest to one who has not experienced the pleasure of Diana's company.

I retired early and have been at my desk since.

Sunday, 30th October, 1887

This morning, as we returned from the most tedious of sermons and the most dreary selection of hymns, Elizabeth and I spoke of Lady Diana. The subject was raised in the course of my rehearsing yet more of yesterday's diversions. Today, however, after a morning's service which was so awfully colourless, I found my memories circling around Diana's flights of introspection.

Elizabeth is by no means a well-connected woman, but she does possess a certain natural ability when it comes to knowing the lives of those with whom she is acquainted, even those at first or second remove. It would be uncharitable to say that she is a gossip but, rather, she is an open door, through which the facts may pass and find themselves stored away, if occasionally redistributed. So it was that she attributed Diana's melancholy turn to the loss of her brother in Burma, during the troubles of 1885: of the details she knew nothing more.

I wonder if I have found in Diana someone to whom I can talk about Mr. Taylor. I see now that the naturalness and ease with which Diana and I cemented our friendship are married with her own experience of tragedy. I should never compare the loss of a brother to my own situation. However, I do believe that there is a commonality in the isolation arising from, though not the nature of, these two events, which suggests that Diana and I might find some comfort from each other were we to discuss our respective sorrows.

Another letter has arrived, delivered by hand. Should I be asked, I shall say it came from Lady Diana. It is from Mr. Taylor. He is profuse in his apologies for his actions at the studio and assures me that such an occurrence will not happen again. All of this he does in language so opaque—"I do regret that my efforts as a considerate host were found wanting"—that any reader other than its addressee would see his contrition as relating to only the slightest of offences: the misremembering of a name, the serving of warm elderflower cordial on a summer's day, or cold tea on a winter's. He writes of the fondness which all artists feel for their muses, but only in the most abstract and dismissive of terms, "for did not Pygmalion experience a weakness for his own Galatea?" He wishes to meet me, and desires that I should sit for him in a scene from my "beloved Warber". Can I? Ought I?

Empta dolore experientia docet.

CHAPTER SEVEN

The auction house was part of a clot of low, brick buildings on the outskirts of Reading, no different from the other low, brick buildings which surrounded it in all their monotonous functionalism. We arrived late in the morning, when the day's trading was complete and the last of the buyers, bidders and watchers were leaving. A tall man stood by the door, smoking a hand-rolled cigarette from which he seemed to take no pleasure. I began to speak before Emily had a chance.

"Hello," I said. "We've come to inquire about a piece which you sold a couple of years ago. We thought we might be able to—"

The man interrupted.

"You don't want me." He reached an ochre-grey hand up to his lip and removed a piece of tobacco, flicked it to the floor and took another drag on his cigarette. "You want Mr Kemp." He pointed at the sign above the doorway which indicated that yes, Mr Kemp would be the person to see at "Kemp & Co. Auctioneers. House Clearances. Estate Sales. Valuations. Est. 1975".

"Thank you," I said.

Emily and I passed through the tobacco smoke and the doorway. Inside, the building did nothing to compensate for its lacklustre exterior. Fluorescent tubes hung from chains to illuminate white-painted walls and rows of folding tables. High, thin windows added the faintest hint of daylight. The table surfaces were varying shades of wood and Formica, visible after the morning's transactions, between the few items that remained unsold. Near the front door the tables gave way to ill-matched chairs and a raised platform which supported a battered lectern. Emily and I continued to the far end of the hall, where a large window looked into a small office. Beneath the window, stacks of old fruit boxes, some open, some closed, contained bric-a-brac which was presumably destined for the next auction.

I picked up a small statuette of the *Artemis of Versailles*. It felt cold against my skin: a Victorian bronze copy of a Roman marble copy of a Greek original. The lights hummed. Artemis stood, lean and strong, in a short tunic tied round at the waist. Beside her, a small buck rose up on its rear legs, as if trying to spring away. Her right hand reached over her shoulder to pull an arrow from the quiver on her back. Her bow was missing. Part of it was there, in her left hand, but the rest was long gone. There was a similar bronze on the *Titanic*, missing. The lights hummed like the attic. Artemis looked off to her right, towards whatever she intended to kill. She belonged in her cardboard box. Jigsaw pieces.

"It'll be in the auction next week, if you want it."

I gave the huntress back to her home and looked at the man who had just emerged from the office. He stood with his hands in his pockets. He was old, but he carried his age well, as though he were someone who should not be young.

"I can't sell it to you now, but if you can't make the auction I can bid on your behalf," he said.

"Thank you," said Emily, "but I don't think we'll bid on it."

Before she could continue I stepped forward and offered my hand to the man. He looked down at it then took it in his own and shook.

"Hello," I said. "I'm Anna, and this is Emily. We're really sorry to bother you. Are you Mr Kemp? The man at the front door said we should speak to Mr Kemp. We told him what we wanted and he said we should speak to Mr Kemp."

The man, whose subtle nodding confirmed that he was, indeed, Mr Kemp, said only, "Well?"

I tried to remain calm and confident. Emily was beside me, ready to take control again, to be the lawyer and speak to the witness, to question and explain. She was tall, serious, dressed in black, hair tied back, attractive, poised. But the court floor was mine.

"Well," I said, "we have a painting which you sold a couple of years ago. It's very important that we find out who gave it to you to sell."

"Even if I could lay my hands on the records, I can't give out the details, love," said Mr Kemp. He turned his head in the direction of the shelves behind his desk, laden with piles of box files and binders, stray papers and peppermint-striped printouts. "It's privacy. You understand."

The last statement was directed over my shoulder, to Emily. After all, how could anyone think that I could understand? Nevertheless, I pressed on.

"But it's really terribly important. There's no signature on the painting. I've looked. It's out of the frame, on the table, and I can see under the spandrels. But there's no signature. And then I was in the attic again. With the mice. I found the receipt."

I fumbled in my pocket and retrieved the crumpled shibboleth, but the gatekeeper of the office did not take it. He just repeated himself:

"I'm sorry, dear. It's privacy. You understand."

Again, it was Emily who understood. I could not understand. I tried to form a persuasive argument, maybe lie a little, but liar was not my part to play.

"I know it's Victorian," I said. "It might be Shakespeare. The picture, I mean. Olivia. I don't know. But you could check the files. Look for paintings. And we know when you sold it, so you could look by date. And who you sold it to. So there's that, too. But there's no signature, so I can't tell you any more." I was starting to cry. "But it's important. It will help. Knowing about it will help, because they're still together on the bed and we can know who they are."

Mr Kemp looked past me as I spoke. Emily put her hand on my shoulder and squeezed gently and I raised my hand to hers like Artemis to her quiver.

"Come on, Anna," said a soft voice which could not have been Emily because Emily would be angry and ready to fight. "We should go."

And then the same voice—which was Emily, who was not angry, who was not ready to fight—said, "I'm sorry, Mr Kemp. I told her we shouldn't trouble you with this. I'm sorry. Let's go, Anna."

I wheeled round, searching for Emily, not the Emily who spoke but my Emily, the old Emily, and she was standing there. It looked like she was standing there.

"We really should go," she said.

Mr Kemp had returned to his office, watching us over the desk through the big window of his paper aquarium. He picked up a mug and lifted it to his lips, lowered it and peered into it, looked disappointed, put it back. I wanted my Emily.

"I'm not going. We need these papers. He can help. He just won't." I was not yet sobbing, but my tears overwelled my lids and ran down to the corners of my mouth. "I need you to make him help me."

"He won't, Anna. He can't. Even if he wanted to, he can't. How would he explain it to the sellers when we turn up on their doorstep?" She paused and ran a hand through my hair, used her thumb to dry my cheeks. "Go and wait in the car."

"I need to ask him. If I don't ask him he won't help because he won't see how important it is."

"I'll talk to him. Give me a few minutes. It's better if I do it," said my Emily.

Outside, the tall man had finished his cigarette and was rolling another with a mastery which he showed no signs of appreciating. I dropped my bag by the side of the concrete doorstep and sat down on its edge, wrapping my arms around my legs and resting my chin on my knees. I was shaking a little. The gravel in front of me shaded from white to black, and I tried to focus on it, to find patterns, pictures, escapes. The tall man sat beside me and offered me the cigarette, holding it out between finger and thumb, without saying a word. I shook my head.

"No, thank you," I mumbled.

"Did you find Mr Kemp?" he asked.

"Yes. I talked to him and told him it was important but he won't help."

"Doesn't sound like Jim," said the tall man. He lit his cigarette and took a long drag on it, then exhaled the smoke through flared nostrils. I ran the tip of my shoe through the gravel, making a little labyrinth.

"Thing about Jim is, you catch him right and he's great. But you catch him wrong… Maybe you caught him wrong?"

"I was very polite. He doesn't understand how important it is."

"Well, how important is it?"

I turned and looked at him. His face was almost as grey as his hair, but tinged yellow around the eyes, with a hint of pink on the lips, and black stubble on his cheeks which faded to white on his chin and neck. Skin the colour of Marat, the French revolutionary, dead in his bath and Jacques-Louis David painting him as a hero with a gaping wound and Charlotte Corday, the Angel of Assassination, nowhere to be seen. Marat's eyes are closed, but the tall man's eyes were open and brown, and the turn of his mouth suggested sympathy, and he was there and Emily was not. I took a slow breath which smelled of tobacco smoke.

"We found a painting in the attic of the house we live in, and I want to know more about it," I explained.

"And you thought you'd show it to Jim and see what he thought? He does them valuations."

"No. I found the receipt in the attic. I went back and braved the mice. I found the receipt in a box. So I thought if we came here with it we could find who sold the painting."

"Oh, I don't think Jim'll tell you that, love. It's privacy, ain't it?"

My eyes followed a tiny minotaur as he patrolled his miniature labyrinth.

"You take care, love," said the tall man. He stood and left me alone with a gravel maze and no thread to show me the way home. I started to think about Alison, again. Alison could look at the painting. She had listened when everything had happened and she had come to see me in hospital, in the days before Emily came to collect me, because Emily had not come, not at first, and I had called Alison. So, she would help and not take it from me, but keep it all safe for me, give me a thread.

I heard footsteps and I thought that the tall man had returned, but it was Emily who walked past and headed towards the car. I decided that I could not leave without some more information because otherwise I would have to call Alison and I was wrong about her: she would pry and invade and take what was mine. Emily waved a strip of paper at me, without looking round or pausing in her journey across the gravel. I got up and followed her, scuffing over the labyrinth, burying my bull-headed guard in dust. By the time I reached the car Emily had buckled her seat belt and was sitting with her hands on the wheel and the engine running. She did not acknowledge me when I sat beside her and neither of us spoke until we were a few miles from the auction house. Finally my eagerness to know what she had done outweighed my fear of her temper.

"What—"

"Shut up," she snapped and fumbled in her trouser pocket, until she found the strip of paper. She handed it to me. It was torn from the pages of a spiral-bound notebook: the binding holes down the left-hand side gaped open, wounded. On it was written, in a scrawl I did not recognize, "Gerald Carter, Whitstable," and a telephone number.

"Is this…?"

"It's the number of the seller, yes," said Emily.

"Can we call it now?"

Emily reached over and plucked the paper out of my hand, passing it across to her right and putting it in a trouser pocket, away from me. I stared out of the window as the suburbs gave way to the ineffectual greenery of roadside landscaping.

"I'm sorry, Anna. It's just that… It's just… What you did in there wasn't fair."

"Fair?"

"Yes. It wasn't fair to that poor man, and it wasn't fair to me."

I lost my temper, and just as Emily directed her anger towards me so did I. Whatever Emily had done had worked, and I ought to have been able to do it because I was smart, as smart as she was, and it was not a legal disagreement, it did not need her specialist training, so why could I not stay calm? I had not even understood that I was not calm. I still did not understand but if she said I was not calm then I was not, and if she said what I did was not fair then it was not.

"I'm sorry. I thought I was doing well. I tried," I said.

"It's all right. I'm sorry I got angry. I just wish that sometimes you'd let me deal with things, trust me with them."

Trust.

I told her I was thirsty.

We turned off and parked by a soulless café where we sat and drank synthetic lemonade from polystyrene cups, and shared a plate of chips.

"How did you do it?" I asked.

Emily munched a chip, washed it down with lemonade, replaced her cup.

"I listened to what he was saying and used it to my advantage. Honestly, I used your outburst to my advantage, too."

"Outburst?"

She ignored me and continued:

"Kemp couldn't give us the details of the seller. Even if he'd wanted to, I could tell he wouldn't. He wouldn't compromise the privacy of his clients. You just had to look at him. He's been in the game too long to make exceptions to the rules. Anyway, I listened to what he'd said—"

"Which was?"

"I'm getting there, if you'll let me."

I studied the pattern on the plastic tablecloth.

"Sorry," Emily said. "I listened to his reasons for not giving us the details. I figured that if he couldn't give them to us perhaps he could use them himself, call the seller himself."

"And that's what he did?"

"Not at first. He pointed at all the paperwork, complained that he didn't need the hassle. So I used you."

"Me?"

"I explained that you weren't well, that I was looking after you, that the painting was important because it gave you something to do."

I bristled.

"Is that what you believe, Ems? That I need something to do? That I'm not well? Did you tell him why I'm not well?"

"Anna. Please. You know you're not well, weren't well before... Before. Anyway, it worked. He knew exactly where to find the paperwork. The place looks like a tip but it must have some sort of organization, even if it's just in his head. So, he pulled out whatever it was with the details and made a call."

"What did he say?"

Emily ate a chip and then another and another. Then drank lemonade. Then answered.

"I don't remember exactly. He just told the guy that we had found the picture and wanted to know more about it."

"And that was enough?"

"Yes. It surprised Kemp, too. And me. But he hung up the phone and yes, that was enough. He scribbled the name and number and told me he had work to be getting on with. And that was that."

"Thank you."

Chip, chip, chip. The last of her lemonade.

"No problem. Let's go home."

At the cottage we hung our coats and placed our shoes carefully beneath them. I asked Emily for the number so I could call Gerald but she said that it would wait until tomorrow, and then there was tea and purples, yellow on the side. Emily disappeared through the white-plank door and from above I heard the sounds of a running bath.

Jacques-Louis David was in his mid-forties when he painted *The Death of Marat*. There lies Marat, politician and journalist—a martyr for David and those like him—whom David came to praise, not to bury. Marat had a severe dermatosis, was covered in blisters and sores, except not in the painting because who would mention a skin condition in a eulogy? He spent all his time in his bathtub because of it, his unseen affliction, and that is where David places him, slumped over to his right with an arm hanging over the side of the tub and down to the floor. Echoes of Thomas Chatterton, the young poet, a suicide on a bed in an attic in Gray's Inn, London. Immortalized in oils by Henry Wallis. Chatterton, poisoned, his arm hanging over the side of the bed and down to the floor, his hand surrounded by torn manuscripts, and Marat holds a quill and the letter from Charlotte Corday which gained her entry to his rooms and gained him a single stab-wound below his collarbone. The bloody knife has been dropped on the floor by his assassin, who left, who went upstairs for her own bath. And the water had stopped running and was still. Charlotte did not run. She stayed and was tried and executed because, for her, it was the bather who had the guilt and his killer the martyrdom.

Paul Baudry painted the same scene, over seventy years later. The room is small and the man is smaller still in the foreshortened perspective of his ugliness with the blade in place and its handle jutting out, pointing to the resigned face of a waiting Charlotte. She stands scared but resolute in front of a map of France, of her France, with her hand still clenched around an imaginary knife which is no longer hers to hold. And all is still, but waiting, waiting, because Charlotte's future is the story. But all is still.

From upstairs there came the sound of water lapping the sides of the bath and I wondered if I should go and join Emily, but I had my map of France on the table there beside me, and Munch had joined us. Edvard Munch, who painted the death of his fifteen-year-old sister from tuberculosis, yellow-faced like the tall man. Munch, who waited until the twentieth century to paint a scene of Marat and Charlotte, where bath becomes bed and Charlotte stands as naked as Marat, and the blood on the sheets could be hers, and the ownership of betrayal is not in the painting but in the title, because we know the story even if the couple are shown as lovers. My France was on the table and I could have taken the paper from Emily's pocket and called the father of *la Patrie*, but Emily said it would wait until tomorrow.

It was late evening when Emily came downstairs and sent me away to sleep. I went alone as she settled down with a book. There was nobody in the bathtub whilst I brushed my teeth. I switched my own light off before closing my eyes.

Emily woke me the next day. She had already been to church. She woke me with a hand shaken by the vicar, and kissed me on the forehead with lips tinged with wine.

"Can we call now?" I asked.

"I have. It's all arranged. I made you a cup of coffee. Here."

I sat up, took the cup from her, blew on the coffee to cool it, stayed calm. Purple pills.

"I wanted to do that, Ems. You knew I wanted to do that," I said. No tears. Allowing tears would have allowed that she was right in making the call and my story would have been stolen.

"I know," she said. "But you were so tired and upset yesterday. I thought it would be best if I called and explained."

"Explained what?"

"About the painting. About how important it is to you, now."

"Now?"

"I mean, with everything that's happened. It's important. Don't get upset."

I did not get upset.

"What did he say?"

"It's all organized. I'll tell you when you come down."

She stood up and headed for the door.

"Ems," I began, but finished lamely with, "I'll be down for breakfast. Lunch. I'll be down in a few minutes."

Over bacon sandwiches she told me about Gerald. He had been delighted to receive the call, repeating several times that it was nice to know someone had an interest in the painting. When he last moved house he was forced to get rid of many of his possessions: there was no room for them in the new place. He thought he had some boxes of papers which might shed light on things. Would we like to meet in person? Emily said she had arranged for us to see him on Tuesday.

"You have work. Am I going alone?" I asked.

She shook her head.

"I'm going to take the day off. Well, technically, I'm going to work from home. There's no way you'll wait until next weekend."

"Thank you," I said and reached across to take her hand. She tolerated the touch of my palm on her wrist.

"But it's the last time, Anna. I really have missed too much work these past couple of months. The team needs me. They've been really good about it but there's a limit."

"So we're going to Whitstable?"

"We're going to Whitstable. It's a long drive, but we're not expected until early afternoon. I think we might drop into the flat on the way through London. I need some stuff from there."

84

"Can I pick up some books?"

Emily nodded with a mouthful of sandwich.

"Tomorrow I'll make a list of questions for Harold," I said.

"Gerald," she corrected.

"Gerald. What does he sound like?"

"Old, but sharp. I think he's lonely. We'll take him a cake or something. It's only polite."

Sunday afternoon was groceries and ingredients and the making of a Victoria sponge. Corday with a kitchen knife.

Chapter Eight

Monday, 31st October, 1887

I have read Matthew's letter a dozen or more times, and now comprehend its true nature. That which I had taken to be detachment is the writing of a man exercising caution lest his words be read by one other than its intended recipient. Matthew's abstraction is a deceit, but not one of which I am the target. No, I am clearly the Galatea to his Pygmalion, his desires made flesh. Why else would he ask me to sit for him? Such are these advances to me that his gaze can hardly be met by the same sight as greets my friends, or which I face in the mirror. I am become some Lamia, my daily appearance an untruth beheld by all but Matthew. It may be wrong of me to want to see him again, but surely it is crueller that I should deny him his muse, that those canvases skulking between kitchen and office should remain without purpose?

Tuesday, 1st November, 1887

After this afternoon's lecture—a tedious hour on the historical importance of Thucydides—I met with Diana. She offered me a seat in her carriage, which I was eager to accept. Elizabeth, with whom I had attended the lecture, did me a great kindness in allowing my departure whilst she herself walked back to college with others of her set. The lecture being a private occasion, solely attended by the women of our college, Diana was not in the company of her usual chaperon, and we were able to lean and loafe at our ease and talk a little during the carriage ride. We continued our conversation in my room, she having no pressing engagements until later this evening.

She is a free soul, even if prone to the air of sadness which one would certainly expect to arise from the recent death of a beloved brother. It would be too much to suggest that her behaviour is in any way scandalous, but it is certainly true that she casts a wide social net and faces no shortage of suitors, if her stories are to be believed. She conveys no individual details of these men, treating of them, rather, as one might expect a farmer to treat of his livestock: a collection of animals to be nurtured as a matter of duty, with only the lightest of fondness.

We spoke again of poetry—not, this time, of the greats, but of our own, more intimate passions, mine for Whitman and hers for Swinburne—and of literature. She quoted *Jane Eyre*: "It is in vain to say human beings ought to be satisfied with tranquillity: they must have action; and they will make it if they cannot find it." I told her of my love for that passage and how, when I was younger, but of an age to comprehend its import, my mother had read it to me. I pointed to the copy resting in a pile of volumes on the ledge of the window and then I, too, quoted from it: "Women feel just as men feel; they need exercise for their faculties, and a field for their efforts." Diana picked up the thread and we recited in unison: "It is thoughtless to condemn them, or laugh at them, if they seek to do more or learn more than custom has pronounced necessary for their sex." Then she laughed and listened as I spoke of my secret passion for *Treasure Island*, which led her to close one eye and exclaim a "Yo-ho-ho!"

Our spirits were so high, and the mutuality of our appreciation so evident, that I decided she ought to be shown the Warber, then and there. So close has grown our friendship, and so important is the book to me, that I could not but feel that to do otherwise would be to hide some part of myself from Diana, and thus, through selfish inaction, undermine all else that we share. I took it from the small leather valise which I keep underneath my bed. Diana was sitting by the desk, leafing through my tattered edition of Byron's poems. Finding "The Destruction of Sennacherib" she began to read aloud. I rested on the bed, with dear Warber on my lap, listening to Diana's voice as it galloped and panted through the lines of verse. On reaching the penultimate stanza she beckoned to me. I joined her and we delivered the final lines together until, on an otherwise quiet afternoon, the might of the Gentile, unsmote by the sword, had melted like snow in the gaze of the Lord.

My handing the Warber to her was met with a brief, inquisitive glance. I asked her to spend some minutes in reading the book and to tell me her impressions. Only then, I added, should I tell her its history and how it became known to me. She gently untied the old bootlaces which hold the covers in place and spent some twenty minutes with the book, making hardly a sound but for the occasional rustle at the turn of a page. I lay on the bed and diverted myself with the examination of some passages by Thucydides, in the light of our recent lecture.

When Diana had finished her reading—which must have been cursory but complete—she placed the book on the desk and smiled at me. She declared it to be "a funny little thing" and asked me to tell her how I came to own it. This I did, being good to my promise.

Mr. Taylor had been taken aback by the attitude shown by Father on finding me in his study, reading a book I had removed from a closed cupboard. In Diana, however, I could discern no such astonishment at the thought of my being discovered, afraid, only to have Father share his secret with me. On reflection, this reaction was to be expected of a lady who doubtless came out with great success and yet has been permitted, encouraged even, to attend Oxford: she must possess a most unorthodox father, a most persuasive mother, or both.

I used the Warber as an excuse to gain a better understanding of my friend's attitude towards those relationships which occur between two people, transcending their ability for rationality. I inquired what she thought of the book itself. Her reply concerned not the author's choice of subject but his use of language; that is, his adoption of a supposedly historical style. It could be, she suggested, that he was another Thomas Chatterton, a charlatan, faking early poetry in fear that works in his own style would never be circulated or held to be of any value. Her suggestion is persuasive, but not pressing. I again asked her for her opinion, being clear that I wished to hear her views on the narrative. She gave the story some deeper thought, and then said, "I quite like it. What do you think of it?"

It is curious that I found myself without an immediate answer when faced with the echo of my own question. I realize now that I, too, have invested my connection to the book with every nuance of technical appreciation—of language, of physical form, of historical placement—but have never troubled myself with deep reflection on the tale itself, even in these few days since Matthew asked a similar question of me. I know it by heart, of course, but that is not the same thing at all. It is as though I have become affianced to a gentleman on account of his dress and Cologne water, his turn of phrase and demeanour, and yet have never once devoted time to the essence of the man himself, the "who is he?" of it all. Facing a need to appraise that essence, I struggle to disentwine my feelings about the book from my feelings for Mr. Taylor, the two sets of emotions seemingly irreversibly tangled. I put down the Thucydides, which I still clutched in my hand, and stared at Diana, unable to speak a word. She must have sensed something of my distress as she gently assured me that we could talk on the subject at a later date, and that she would always be ready to hear my opinions but could most certainly wait. She stood, handing me the Warber, and excused herself on account of her needing to return home and rest a little before the evening. As she made for the door I followed and called her name with a breathless urgency which even I had not been prepared to encounter.

I divulged all. She sat beside me on the bed and listened as I told her of Mr. Taylor's invitation, our meeting at the Botanic Garden, my attendance at his studio. Finally, as I related the circumstances leading to his kissing me—or my kissing him, or some mutual kiss, I remain uncertain as to which—I could no longer retain the air of a mere factual explication and I began to cry. Diana placed her arm around me and comforted me with kind words, assuring me that women are destined to succumb to certain approaches, and that I should see myself as the victim of the piece, not the villain. She had heard stories of Mr. Taylor, she said, and described his wife as "long-suffering". Yet I am not convinced that she is correct in her insistence on my blamelessness.

The rest of my confession, undertaken after I had recomposed myself, pertained to Mr. Taylor's invitation to join him once more at his studio. It is an invitation to which I have not responded, as yet unsure of my response, which should unquestionably be to decline politely were I really blameless. Diana wished to know why I might not attend in the company of Miss Ashdown, as I had intended to do on my first visit. I explained that Elizabeth is well suited to the role of chaperone but that I fear she may be too free with the confidences of others. I did not say—but I shall admit here on these pages—that I do not wish to attend in her company precisely because she would be a most effective chaperone. Diana nodded and remarked that she might have a plan but could not be sure of its worth without first seeing the latest letter from Mr. Taylor. She read the letter through, twice, rubbing her neck with her free hand as I saw her do when she had fallen into thought at the Galleries. She asked me if I was sure I wanted to see him again, to which I responded honestly: I am not sure, but I am equally unsure of not wanting to see him again. In that case, she said, the only course of action is for me to meet him to clarify my thoughts. The letter, she reminded me, doubtless hides the possibility of future trysts in an offer to paint my image. I should, then, play Mr. Taylor at his own game, and agree to meet him to discuss the painting. She will be my chaperone and, should Mr. Taylor choose to proceed to paint a canvas, the two of us will pose together. She assured me—somehow in language which did not carry undertones of the separation of class between us—that the appearance in the painting of an Earl's daughter will serve to remove the stain of impropriety which might otherwise besmirch the undertaking.

So our plans were left when Diana departed. I have started to write a reply to Mr. Taylor and intend to rise early tomorrow, to complete it before breakfast and post it on the way to the first lecture of the day. I shall be in the company of Elizabeth, to whom I shall give the impression that I have written to an aged aunt of mine who lacks for company. I wonder whether this Machiavellian behaviour is born of recent necessity or constitutes an opportune manifestation of some innate talent.

Monday, 7th November, 1887

Lady Diana's carriage is due to drop her at college in a little under an hour. She has been occupied with social engagements and, I hope, some academic work since we last met. I have seen her only briefly, after one or two lectures, but I have read and re-read her letter of Thursday last, in which she expresses her excitement for today's "diversions". I draw from her words—from the assurance of her companionship—a heartening resolve.

I suspect Mr. Taylor disliked my insistence that Diana act as a chaperone: he was gracious but terribly formal in his acceptance of what he called "my terms". I fear there may be some tension in his first meeting with her. She must, after all, adjudge that her role includes the affording of certain protections to her charge. Under normal circumstances I might resent the impingement on my independence, but these are not normal circumstances.

I must get ready for her arrival.

I am back in my room. I can still hear Diana's carriage departing along the driveway. I am to dine with Elizabeth, who will want to hear news of my aged aunt, I'm sure.

> As though in Cupid's college she had spent
> Sweet days a lovely graduate, still unshent,
> And kept his rosy terms in idle languishment.

I shall see him again on Friday.

"The Assyrian came down like the wolf on the fold." That is what Lady Diana said to me yesterday, as we rode back from Mr. Taylor's studio and I told her of my desire to see him again, alone. I know what she meant, of course, but her tone also spoke of some element of her character. Her concern for my well-being seems married to an increasing, if still understated, hostility towards Matthew, his feelings for me, and mine for him.

Earlier in the day, when we left college, the world was softly paled by a frost which persisted in those nooks where the low sun cast long shadows. Diana seemed pleased to be engaged in "such an adventure", as she had it. She dismissed the carriage and we walked out together. I had supposed that effecting an introduction between Mr. Taylor and Lady Diana would be an awkward affair, but Diana took command of the situation with an ease born of her breeding and the confidence of one aware of her own charms. This she wears not, as one might imagine, with any sign of arrogance, but rather with the comfortable familiarity of a well-loved coat or pair of boots. She and Mr. Taylor were polite but somewhat studied: they appeared to be taking the measure of one another, as though preparing for some coming game of wits. As far as his attitude to me, Matthew seemed genuinely delighted to be in my company and I readily wove into his welcome those affections which he chose not express in the presence of others.

Upstairs, Matthew withdrew to the kitchen and left Diana and me to sit on the couch where—I am a little ashamed to admit, given what I hope was the seriousness of the situation—we whispered to each other. We fell quiet only when he returned with tea and a motley service of cups and saucers, making apologies for his chinaware. Lady Diana opened the conversation by saying that she was "led to believe he was a Pre-Raphaelite of sorts." Did he know Mr. Ruskin? If Mr. Taylor was affronted by this turn of phrase, or taken aback by the question, it could be discerned only in an almost imperceptible furrowing of the brow as he offered milk and sugar. Lady Diana was not to be deterred from her course and persisted in her line of inquiry, asking after his connections to the "highly respected artists" Mr. Jones—"Or is it

Mr. Burne-Jones now?"—and Mr. Morris, "both old Exeter College men." Again, though, Matthew remained calm and dismissive, saying that, whilst he is indeed in some form of correspondence with these gentlemen, he is concentrating his efforts on his own painting, and his social interactions have been quite deliberately curtailed. So they continued for the next few minutes, with Diana getting thinly hidden digs at Matthew and his artistic status. Did he feel that Mr. Whistler was successfully challenging the more traditional styles of painting? Was he influenced by the thrilling developments occurring in France? How had he been affected by the lowering of prices paid for art over recent years? Had he shown at the Royal Academy, or at the Grosvenor, "amongst the greenery-yallery"? Would he be showing at the New Gallery?

Mr. Taylor bore these questions with a diffident charm. As we drained our cups, I found that it was I who felt the need to end this inquisition. I did so by a swift but stern glance in the direction of Lady Diana, and by changing the subject to our posing for Matthew. What did he envisage for the piece? His eyes lingered upon me, and then his gaze moved across to Diana. He let out the slightest of sighs. His intention, as he informed us, had been to paint me as Warber's Olivia, looking out of a window, high in a tower, waiting for my love to return from some campaign. He allowed that it might not be prudent to title the piece as a scene from Warber, but that was, he felt, a decision for another day: the subject of the painting lent itself to many interpretations in keeping with other romances and idylls. Diana suggested that the confining walls of a stone tower might detract somewhat from the pastoral quality of an idyll, to which Matthew, ever-smiling, remarked that it was now a detail which would remain unresolved, as any composition clearly required the presence of both of the beautiful women before him. At that, even Lady Diana could not hide a subtle upturning of the corners of her mouth.

Matthew is a handsome man. I see, looking back, that I described him as "poetic" and "romantic". These observations are not without merit, but they do not get to the heart of the thing: Mr. Taylor, whether in features, carriage or character, is a handsome man. I saw something of it in the air with which Diana now regarded him as he spoke of his intentions for the painting. She gave a tilt to her head which I had seen previously only once, in her discussions with the younger men who attended that otherwise dreary college event at the beginning of term. Yet there was something in the stiffness of her posture—a degree of formality which I had not previously observed in her—that gave the impression of her warming to Mr. Taylor despite herself, rather than with the ease which I found in myself. Whatever the case, as he continued to speak she lessened her questioning and chiding, and listened with all the appearance of gentle fascination.

Mr. Taylor has yet to choose a suitable episode in which to stage our portrayal, but he does not want to abandon his idea of some scene taken from Warber. He cannot imagine my being anyone other than Olivia, as this is the image which has fixed itself in his mind, and with which his creative thoughts have been occupied these past weeks. All this he told us as his blue eyes locked with mine. Lady Diana let out a delicate cough and Matthew turned to face her, his expression unchanged. He asked her if she knew the story to which he was referring, to which Diana replied that yes, I had given her the book to read. She and I shared everything, she added, imbuing "everything" with a meaning which eluded Matthew, or which he chose to ignore. He continued by inquiring if Diana thought she would make a believable Thomas. Rather than rail at the idea of being portrayed in this masculine role, she exclaimed that it sounded "delightful fun".

Matthew gestured to a dresser close to the old piano, on which sat a brush and various clips and pins. He asked if I should be so kind as to fasten Diana's hair in some fashion which would, from front and side views, give it the appearance of being short. I endeavoured to do so whilst Matthew busied himself in gathering paper and sharpening pencils with which to sketch our portraits. The proceedings—our preparation and sitting—cannot have taken more than an hour. Matthew worked swiftly, his hand darting over the paper in arcs and curlicues as he captured first a likeness of Lady Diana in front and profile views, and then the same of my own face. Whilst he sketched Diana he asked me—when I attempted to stand and watch over his shoulder—to remain seated and quiet, and he required the same of Diana when I was the object of his gaze. The portraits he produced were accurate only in so far as their lack of detail enabled them to be a fair representation of our features. Sensing, I am sure, that we had been expecting a result which was—how shall I say?—a little more "polished", he explained that he prefers to adopt some elements of the approach taken by Sir John Millais and his followers, with few preparatory studies. These sketches, he averred, will serve as an *aide-mémoire* during his initial contemplation of the subject. Any more detailed outline is to be saved for the canvas itself, after a suitable layer of bright, white paint—called a "ground"—has been prepared upon it, prior to painting.

Diana makes a perfect Thomas in my opinion, and Mr. Taylor agrees with me. He said as much as he placed his sketches on an easel and stepped back to appreciate them. I am surprised that a change in the style of her hair can do so much to lend those delicate features an appearance which is both passably rugged and beautifully refined. There is within her some ability to tighten the jawline and lower the brow, which adds to the illusion of masculinity without removing an ambiguity which is much to be desired.

Matthew seemed distracted whilst we prepared ourselves for the return to college. He stood by the tall, north windows with his back to us. When we were ready to depart he followed us down the narrow stairs before passing us in the hall to hold open the front door. Here, as Diana stepped outside, he gently placed a hand on my arm and asked if he might speak to me in private. I turned to Lady Diana and lifted my head a fraction upwards and to the left, through which I conveyed to her my desire that she wait close by, but at enough remove to afford me a modicum of privacy. She, returning my gaze with what I took to be apprehension, departed to the boundary of the driveway and stared out, over the river. The sun was bathing the fields in ambered light. She might have been Ophelia, lost by the banks. Could beauty have better commerce than with honesty?

Standing by the door, whispering into my ear, Matthew asked if I should return on Friday, alone. He made no mention of an artistic requirement for my attendance, for which I am grateful as, otherwise, I think I should drown in a cup brimming over with the wine of duplicity. I am not proud to write that I almost agreed to the meeting with an acceptance of his terms, but a voice within me—a voice all the louder for the presence of Diana a few yards distant—gave me the strength to insist that I attend only in her company. Yet, I am not so strong as I should like to suppose: I am to arrange with Diana that I arrive a little earlier than she, or depart a little later. I fear that she will judge this arrangement imprudent in the extreme, but my true weakness is that I fear yet more the absence of another opportunity to be alone with Matthew.

"The Assyrian came down like the wolf on the fold."

CHAPTER NINE

I sat in the car as we drove through the morning fog, trying and failing to formulate questions for Gerald. An old, round biscuit tin, tucked down by my feet, held the finished sponge cake. On its lid J.M.W. Turner's *Fighting Temeraire* glowed in the last light of the day. It seemed an odd choice for a tin of biscuits, the final hours of a warship as it is pulled up the Thames by a tugboat, all funnel and smoke. The painting had been cropped to fit on the circular lid, robbing it of context: no more setting sun, no more waiting breaker's yard for the *Temeraire*, just a biscuit-tin-lid story. Once, there were two boats, a big boat and a little boat. The big boat had sails, and was proud of its history. "I was at Trafalgar in 1805," it would say. The little boat was much younger, and did not have any sails, just a tall smokestack that puffed out black clouds as it chuffed along over the waves. Sometimes, when the wind was low, and because they were best friends, the little boat would help the big boat, pulling it along over the calm waters of the Thames. Sometimes they would float and eat biscuits together. Then, one day, the little boat would not tell the big boat where they were going.

Emily had decided that it would be better for us if we stopped in London on our way to the coast, rather than on our return, to remove the risk of hitting the evening rush-hour. There had seemed little point in arguing. It was late morning when we arrived at our flat. I could have waited in the car but then she would have gone alone and left me there, and I did not want to be left alone with the Victoria sponge and the duplicitous tugboat.

Everything seemed familiar but unwelcoming, as though a stranger had moved into the place in my absence, silently, without changing a thing, and was lurking under a bed or in a wardrobe, resenting my presence. The flat, in size and location, was a testament to the earning power of a reasonably successful, reasonably senior solicitor. In decoration it was, with the exception of Emily's office, a visual pæan to the availability of cheap, junk-shop art and a manifestation of my dislike of modern reproductions. Where shelves of books did not intrude, prints and paintings hung from picture rails in columns of three or four.

"I'll be about ten minutes. Grab anything you need." Emily's voice came through the office doorway, followed by Emily. She continued, more quietly, "I think there's a suitcase on the bed. I was going to put some of your stuff in it but didn't need to in the end."

I had enough clothes at the cottage already: I was not there to be seen and, even if I were, the village was certainly not a hotbed of high-fashion sensibilities. Not that I myself possessed any high-fashion sensibilities beyond those bestowed by Emily's choices on my behalf. Books, though, were always a welcome and soothing addition to a room: a printed shipping forecast, hot chocolate with an evocative cover. I grabbed a few volumes on British Victorian paintings and painters, stacked them on the dining table and headed to the bedroom. The place was still a mess. I had expected Emily to have tidied a month ago, as soon as she had disposed of me at the hospital and driven back to London. I stepped over the larger portion of a smashed, pottery lamp-base and knelt before a short, wide bookcase of fiction, running methodically through the titles, left to right, top to bottom. I took out a slim volume in French, flipped through it and read aloud:

"'*Les infinies et fabuleuses montagnes où les chères petites adultères, toujours aimées, se pâment sans repos aux impérieuses caresses des anges pervers.*'"

"The fabulous mountains where the little adulterers, always loved, something without repose under the imperious caresses of the something?" Emily was still at the door. "Don't look so astonished, Anna. I'm not an idiot."

"I don't think you're an idiot. We just have different interests. I didn't think you knew Gourmont."

"I don't. School French, weekends in Paris and educated guesses. How did I do?"

"Not bad," I said. "There's a better translation, better than I can manage. Hang on. I'll find it."

I located the edition I wanted and ran a finger down the index until I hit the entry for Remy de Gourmont's short story, "*Danaette*".

"Here." I read from the translation. "The boundless, fabulous mountains where the precious little adulteresses, loved without end, drift upon their unrelenting swoons, beneath the imperious caresses of all the perverse angels."

"And? Why that passage?"

"Why choose it? I'm not sure. I've always liked it. Something about the sense of distance. Something about the juxtaposition of perversity and the angelic, about the inability to distinguish the two, somehow."

Something about adultery.

"Lovely," said Emily. "Well, throw it in the case if you want it. Let's get going. It's at least another couple of hours to Whitstable. We can eat on the way."

I placed the two books in the suitcase, then carried it, still open, into the other room and put it on the table. I took one last look around the room as I filled the case with the art books I had already chosen. Behind the couch, in the small space between its arching back and the wall, I saw a pillow, sheets and a duvet. The bedroom could accommodate two, and not always the same two, but not one, apparently. I headed downstairs, where Emily was waiting impatiently.

"It's another couple of hours, Anna. Let's go."

"You slept on the couch?" I asked.

"Let's go, Anna."

That was the only answer she felt I deserved.

Turner painted Whitstable, too. He was commissioned to create an original work to become one of the engravings in *Picturesque Views on the Southern Coast of England.* His subtle use of watercolours, the translucency of his sea, the small figures working along the muddied shoreline, the stumps of long-decayed groynes which lead the eye to a white horse trying, with help from its drivers, to pull a loaded cart along the final few yards to a solid track: all these combine to give a clear sense of the oyster beds in the foreground and the pretty seaside town in the distance, across the bay. Just to be on the safe side, however, Turner included a small, fallen sign in the lower-right corner which reads, "Whitstable Oyster Beds. Notice." In contrast, our road map was an unpoetic sheet of primary colours: pop art for cartographers.

Emily broached the subject of how we might handle Gerald once we arrived, opening with, "I don't know if you remember what happened at the auction house..." and building a predictable argument which centred around my allowing her to control the situation. I nodded in agreement. It seemed—as it so often seemed—the easiest response, and the one least likely to jeopardize my search for information. Besides, I knew I could behave as I pleased at Mr Carter's house: it would be too late for Emily to do anything then. She asked me where I had put the painting.

"I left it in my room," I replied, looking out at the fields, ploughed and walled by the rivulets of rain on the window.

"Why the hell did you do that?"

Two answers, public and private.

"Look at the weather, Ems. I was worried it would get damaged. It's still out of its frame. And it's not ours, remember?" And what if Gerald wants it back and can afford it? He might contact the new owner because he has our number because you gave it to him, you told me, so he can find out where we are and who owns the cottage. Then it will be gone, they will be gone, and I shall not be able to find out any more about them because their leaving will be a passing marked by death certificates and no more. I shall be Jo Hopper, alone with my window.

"Well, all right," said Emily. "I just hope you can describe it well enough."

"I can," I said, and directed my attention to the map. "We'll need to turn off to the left at some point. If we reach the blue we've gone too far."

Turner did not paint anything resembling Mr Carter's small, semi-detached bungalow. It faced a suburban road, looking across red pavers and concrete to other, equally unexceptional bungalows. Some of them had maritime-themed names: "The Sands", "Tide Cottage". "Oyster Shell House" had a low garden wall encrusted with oyster shells embedded in some chalky-looking cement mixture. The whole estate was already dated in excess of its age: a paradigm of seventies aspirational utilitarianism.

We had arrived at number 16—no name—to the twitching of a lace curtain. A man I took to be Mr Carter was standing by the open door before we had a chance to ring the bell. He seemed the perfect resident of his home: a short, elderly man, dressed smartly in an overarching theme of beige and brown. His hair was close-cropped on the sides of a balding head, and a wide but sparse moustache adorned his upper lip. He wore a cravat of emerald green and crimson, echoing the green-glazed pots which dressed the path beneath his front windows. He spoke without waiting for us to introduce ourselves:

"Hello, hello. I'm Gerald. You must be Emily and Anna. Now which is which? No. Let me guess."

He pointed at Emily.

"Anna. Am I right?"

Emily pursed her lips and shook her head, slowly, as though she were ashamed to have to prove him wrong, as though she were considering if she ought to lie and be Anna for the rest of the afternoon.

"Ah, well," Mr Carter continued, "never mind. Hello Emily! And you must be Anna. Hello."

He shook our hands and ushered us in. It was not until we reached the lounge that we finally had a chance to speak. I led the way, behaving as I pleased.

"Hello Mr Carter," I said. "We've come about the painting."

I spoke carefully and deliberately, not as I might if talking to an elderly relative, but as if I were drunk, and aware of being drunk, and finding it important not to seem drunk in company. Emily looked at me as if I were drunk.

"Yes, yes. The painting. Well, there's time for that. Tea?" said Mr Carter, gesturing towards a coffee table already decorated with china cups and saucers and a teapot under an orange, knitted tea-cosy.

I took the biscuit tin from Emily and handed it to him.

"We made you a cake," I said.

"Marvellous. Marvellous," said Mr Carter, appearing genuinely thrilled. "Take a seat. I'll go and get some plates. You're probably hungry."

We were hungry. Despite our plans, we had not stopped for food: neither of us could face sitting together, alone, making small-talk over another sullen, Formica table-top. Mr Carter disappeared into the hallway, leaving us side by side on the couch. The clink of china and cutlery drifted out from the kitchen. Emily whispered to me:

"I thought we agreed that I'd do the talking."

"I just said 'hello' and offered him the cake," I whispered back.

Mr Carter reappeared to ease the ensuing tension and to complete the still-life on the table with the cake, and a cake-slice, and side-plates, and cake-forks. Then, for a few minutes, everything was how-many-sugars, milk-or-lemon, napkins, small-slice-large-slice. When all was settled it was Emily who brought us back to her plan.

"We found a painting, Mr Carter. It used to belong to you," she said.

"Call me Gerald. Yes, you mentioned it on the telephone. I gave a lot of things to auction. I moved to this place and it was smaller, you see? I was in insurance. Retired. I couldn't keep everything."

"Well, the painting is very important," I said.

Gerald looked over at me.

"Oh?" he said.

Emily placed a hand on my knee.

"What Anna means," she said, "is that it's interesting. She works at a gallery and this sort of thing fascinates her."

"Ah," said Mr Carter. "Well, yes, I can imagine. May I see it?"

Emily looked at me.

"We didn't bring it, Mr Carter," I said. "Emily wanted to, but I was worried it would get damaged. The weather has been vile."

Emily took her hand from my knee. I pressed on.

"But it was the one with stone walls and the two people on the bed, with the curtains. A bit like the red in your cravat. One of them is resting her head on the chest of the other, looking out at you." And they want me to know who they are, and why they are there, and you might be the only one who can tell me that, and did you know Simeon Solomon was arrested for sodomy? Not that it matters, really, unless you think it does, of course.

"Do call me Gerald, please," said Mr Carter. "I know the one you mean. Nice thing, but nowhere to put it now."

He waved his hand around in a little circle whilst looking up at the ceiling, seeking to affirm the dimensions of his lounge.

"I can't tell you much, I'm afraid."

Emily took up the thread.

"Do you know how you got it? Could we trace it back that way?" she asked.

"Oh, heavens, no. It's a family piece. I inherited it when my father died. It was painted by my great-grandmother's brother. But no room."

Emily and I looked at each other. She must have been able to see that I was more relaxed and that I was not intoxicated and that I was no longer even trying not to appear intoxicated. She let me speak.

"Oh, I see. Can you tell us anything about him?" I asked.

"More tea?"

Mr Carter reached for the pot.

"No, no," I said, but Emily must have sensed that I was being rude, in some way which was unclear to me.

"Yes, that would be lovely," she said. "And some more cake, too, if that's all right. We're famished."

Mr Carter spoke softly but clearly as he poured tea and splashed milk, sliced and served cake. He seemed to be reciting something practised, as though he had engineered our meeting to give him a platform for a well-rehearsed oration.

"My great-grandmother's brother, Matthew Taylor, was a

Pre-Raphaelite *manqué*. He lived in Oxford for most of his life, with his wife, Constance. From what I understand she came to the marriage with money, so his failure didn't stop them from remaining reasonably well-off. He made some bad decisions, kept up with the wrong painters, missed the boat, as it were. Constance died before my father was born, but he kept going until I was two or three. My father said he seemed a decent chap, but then he didn't know him well. He'd given up painting by then."

He sat back with his cup balanced on a saucer in his left hand, stirring his tea with a little silver spoon, slowly and deliberately.

"What else would you like to know? I don't think there's anything more I can tell you."

"Do you know when it was painted?" I asked. "Or the subject? Or the people who sat for it?"

Emily thinned her lips into her best calm-down expression and took control from me.

"Really, any clues would be most appreciated," she said, with an elocution she normally reserved for clients and courtrooms.

Mr Carter took a sip from his tea and leaned forward, placing his cup and saucer back on the table, theatrically. He stood up.

"Follow me," he said.

Emily and I followed him, curious but wary, into a spare bedroom at the rear of the house. The room was spotlessly clean, and the bed meticulously made up for any visitor who might need to spend a night. The air of expectant readiness was broken, however, by a trapdoor which hung open from the ceiling, and by the ladder which ran down from the attic above. On the bed were three cardboard boxes of the type used for storing office files in bureaucratic archives. On each was scrawled "Papers" in thick, black marker pen. Mr Carter waved a hand towards them and beamed at us.

"I think you'll find these interesting, Anna," he said, and opened the first box.

I peered over his shoulder at the contents. It seemed to be a mixture of notebooks and papers, some printed, some covered with neat, copperplate writing.

"What is it?" I asked.

Mr Carter replaced the lid.

"They're from around the time that the painting was done. I had a bit of a rifle through, but I thought I'd leave the detective work to you."

I turned to Emily. She was checking the time on her watch.

"It's getting a little late, Anna. It's a long journey home. I don't think we have time to look at these now. Do you think we could borrow them, take them with us, Gerald?"

Mr Carter looked perturbed, and then crestfallen.

"Well," he said, "I'm not sure. They're from the family, you see. And…"

He looked at me, perhaps expecting that I would side with him and insist that we stay longer. It was true that I was keen to look through the boxes. They were full of treasure, surely. I had moved Turner's fallen sign—"Whitstable Oyster Beds. Notice."—and found beneath a chest full of gems, and gold and silver coins stamped with boats and the heads of kings and coats of arms. But if I looked at the hoard I would have to leave it behind and I wanted it with me, wanted to reunite it with the painting back at the cottage. I knew what Mr Carter needed to hear.

"The thing is, Gerald," I said, "if we borrow these I'll be terribly careful with them. I work with precious objects for a living. You can trust me. And of course we'd come back again, to return them and talk about our findings. You have our number. You can always call if you'd like them back sooner, or just want to know how I'm getting on."

I smiled as though everything were fine even though I was still in the deadened space of Monet's Venice, dark as the hole in the ceiling above me, in the spare room where Gauguin would never sleep, irrespective of Gerald's longing for company.

"Well," I said, not waiting for a reply, "we can load up the car after another slice of cake, right Ems? There's always time for another slice of cake." And purples and yellows.

"Of course," said Emily, poor Emily, for whom Turner's hoard was just more sand and oyster shells.

*

Mr Carter, holding his cup and saucer, occasionally lifting the cup to his mouth and sipping the lukewarm liquid within, watched from the front window of his tea-and-cake bungalow which Turner never painted. Emily had been right, it was getting late, but nevertheless I asked if we might drive to the sea, which was two minutes away, before we turned to the long westward journey. Everything was grey and empty. No little figures picked oysters. There was no struggling, white horse on the sands. The air smelled of seaweed and vinegar. A few seagulls circled overhead, or hopped around near the car, pecking at food wrappers blown to them by the wind.

"Can we go home now?" asked Emily.

I nodded and shut my eyes as she started the engine. When I opened them again the road signs were counting down the final miles to London.

"I'm sorry," I said.

"Don't be. It's good for you. It's going to be two, maybe three hours until we get back. You should sleep."

"I can keep you company, if you like. Read the map. We can talk."

"It's all right. I need to concentrate on driving anyway."

The world outside was all grass banking and small shrubs, ebbing and flowing in the sodium yellow of the lights, inconstant.

"Do you love me?" I asked.

Emily kept her eyes on the road.

"Of course. I wouldn't be here if I didn't. Not after everything. Why did you say that?"

"Because you didn't say it. After everything, you didn't."

"It's hard for me, too, Anna. I know it should be, and I shouldn't complain, and I don't, really, do I? But it is. I love you. Okay?"

"Can we listen to the radio?"

Emily turned the radio on and adjusted the volume. Whether or not it was her intention she set it to just the right level to fill an emptiness which might have demanded conversation. A sip of water. Two purples. The radio was not loud enough to keep me awake. The lights continued to wax and wane, little yellow moons rushing up the windscreen and eclipsing out of sight, and then they were just red-yellow fields, pulsing on my closed lids, until I travelled so far away that they, too, were swallowed by darkness.

The slam of Emily's door woke me. She was already halfway along the cottage path, head down to protect her face from the rain, shining a pocket-torch to guide her through the skeletal rose bushes which pressed in from either side. I undid my seat belt and waited for her to turn on the light above the front door. She headed back towards me with the torch as I got out of the passenger seat.

"It's horrid out. Come inside. We'll get the boxes in the morning," she said.

"No. I promised Gerald they'd be safe."

I opened the rear door and slipped the first of the boxes from the seat belt which held it in place.

"All right. Give it to me," said Emily. "You get the next one and follow."

I got the next one and followed. Emily passed me as she made another trip to the car.

"I'll get the last one and lock up. You put the kettle on."

As I got closer to the front door she turned and half-spoke to, half-shouted at me.

"Don't open the boxes. It can wait. Make tea. Toast if you want. The boxes wait."

That was the thing about treasure: it had waited so long to be found that it could wait a little longer, and it would be fine because it was safe inside the cottage, back where it belonged, with the painting. Outside, the rain could tumble, and the night could set in, and the roses could reach out, but the papers were safe. I put the kettle on and sat down. Emily did everything else when she returned with the final box. The painting lay on the table, and we drank and ate and warmed ourselves by the radiator. It seemed safe, the whitewashed room with the walls collapsing, and the yellow after purple, and time for bed, and I told her I loved her, too, or I think I told her, in the ebb and flow.

CHAPTER TEN

Wednesday, 9th November, 1887

Diana will meet me at the studio on Friday at two o'clock, which allows me an hour alone with Matthew before our sitting for the portrait. *Alea iacta est.* I have been giving thought to the ways in which I might get from college to the studio without a chaperone. In the end, Diana gave me the finest idea: I shall return to college with Elizabeth and make my excuses at the entrance to the driveway, claiming that Lady Diana is to meet me so shortly that it seems without merit to walk down to the main house and back to the gate. I no longer speak to Elizabeth of Matthew, and she, doubtless cognizant of the indelicacy of the matter, chooses not to raise it. There remains the possibility that she will wish to stay with me, but she is still recuperating from her recent illness, and the weather is so inclement that I cannot envisage her prolonging her exposure to the elements.

I am not at all sure how Diana judges my liaison with Mr. Taylor. At the studio, yesterday, she seemed to display a distrust of the man which bordered on loathing. Yet she softened when the process of making sketches had begun, and she was accommodating of my desire to speak to Matthew alone at the end of our time with him. Still, I had expected, when broaching the subject of Friday's rendezvous, to find her hostile to the idea of my spending time with him before she joins us. If I were to choose a single word to describe her reaction I should choose "resignation": there was a flatness in the tone of her reply which was a mere sigh away from outright disappointment. Why then did she agree to help me, and assist me in planning the necessary deceits? Does she share my enjoyment of Matthew's company? That thought does not create the feelings of jealousy which I might have supposed: she is, if my time with her has shown me anything, a good and true friend.

Thursday, 10th November, 1887

Mrs. Taylor accosted me in the entrance hall of the college house today. Her interest lay only with my academic progress, and her inquiries were couched in language of the most temperate and pleasant variety. She asked which lectures I was attending, and how I was settling into "the rhythm of Oxford." Had I enjoyed my day at the Galleries with Lady Diana? I must have displayed some sign of my surprise—that she had heard about our trip—as she hastened to add that she had learned of it from the Principal, to whom it had come from our friendly divinity professor, over some dinner or other. Nevertheless, I find it hard to believe that her question was asked without some subtle intimation that she was aware of my other activities. I cannot help but resent her, that she has the freedom to be with Matthew when she desires. I confess that I revel in the resentment, fearing that, in its absence, I should reflect so harshly on my own actions that I could not bear to face myself on waking each morning.

I am left with the uncomfortable feeling of being observed as I go about my business, almost as if some veiled threat had been made against me, and by one with both countenance and motive to issue it.

Friday, 11th November, 1887

I must rush and meet Elizabeth for breakfast and lectures. I do so wish that I might forego breakfast: a combination of excitement and nervousness has robbed me of my appetite. Then, however, I think that giving any outward signs of my condition would lead to indelicate questions from friends, no doubt witnessed by Mrs. Taylor. Am I stricken by some mania of suspicion? Surely, such an affliction would be understandable in one who found herself in my circumstances.

My visit to Matthew was a great success. I am tired and ready to retire for the night, although it is only a little after dinner. Elizabeth told me that I was "positively glowing" on my return, and that my outing with Lady Diana had clearly agreed with me. She suggested that we study together this evening, but I gently informed her that fresh air, whilst wonderful for the constitution, was anathema to later wakefulness, particularly when combined with the influence of a satisfactory evening meal.

Saturday, 12th November, 1887

How shall I describe yesterday without resorting to such superlatives as would render the account nought but hyperbole and the worst sort of melodrama? I shall try to follow the advice of Dickens's Mr. Gradgrind and stick to facts: after all, how clear the romance of Romeo and Juliet would remain were the pentameter abandoned and the story rendered in the most functional of phrasing. I have always supposed that my upbringing—the love of an intellectual father and the protection of an emancipated mother—would inoculate me, as the medical men say, against the excesses of emotion. Now I find myself dangerously close to a delirium of my own making.

Elizabeth saw nothing untoward in my plans to meet Lady Diana for lunch. When, returning after morning lectures, we reached the gates of the college driveway, I told her that I should wait there for Diana. She began by insisting that she wait with me. It was not, however, too difficult to dissuade her from this selfless action—as I had predicted—by reminding her of her recent illness and the importance of avoiding any chill to the lungs, and by reassuring her that Lady Diana is ever-punctual and was surely only minutes from arriving. I watched as she walked on, along the curve of the driveway, until out of sight. Two more of the girls with whom we had attended the lecture were a short distance down the road, and soon came to the gate. We exchanged greetings and I explained that my standing in solitude on a cold, autumn morning was necessitated by the imminent arrival of my friend. Once they, too, had continued to the college house I made my way up the road, and thence through parkland to the river and the studio.

Matthew was waiting there for me. When he opened the door, I could utter only a polite, "Good morning, Mr. Taylor. I do hope you are well." He let out a small laugh, and then apologized. My nervousness must have been clear from my words, and written on my face, which seemed incapable of demonstrating any form of enjoyment in my situation. I followed him inside and up the narrow staircase.

When the door to the studio opened I let out a little "Oh!" of glee at the results of Matthew's industry. There, in the middle of the room, where previously was only a great space and bare boards, a perfect stage-set now rests. No, "perfect" is not quite the correct description, as the resources of Mr. Taylor's studio are not those of the great theatres: here and there he has improvised features which will suffice for the composition of his painting without providing a precise model for every element of its completion.

Matthew made me comfortable and then disappeared into the kitchen. I took my note-book from my satchel—still with me from my earlier lectures—and scribbled short observations about the sight in front of me.

Item: a bed made from a varying selection of pallets balanced on a collection of bricks; aligned with the footboard towards the northwest; many sheets arranged on top to give the appearance of a mattress; more sheets and some cushions forming a large bolster at one end.

Item: attached to the rafters, ropes over which crimson draperies hang; these swagged to give the impression of curtains over the bed.

Item: rolls of paper on which are painted the likeness of a stone wall; one behind the head of the bed, the other to the southwest of it; a great fireplace and roaring fire drawn upon them.

Item: tall candle-holders of wrought iron, placed around the bed and between the bed and stone wall.

Item: two outfits on the bed, both mediæval in appearance.

Matthew reappeared and sat beside me, reading the open pages of my note-book, which I made no attempt to shield from him. He described his vision of the painting: Diana and I, as Thomasin and Olivia, will lie on the bed, she looking out towards the foot thereof, and I resting my head on her breast, looking straight ahead, out of the painting, as it were. We shall be recreating the scene in which Thomasin—here in the guise of Thomas—and Olivia are recently married and lie together for the first time. Thomas is to look worried, as he is filled with the knowledge that he has deceived his beloved and must surely lose her, and his life, when his secret becomes known. Olivia must seem simultaneously fearful and expectant: fearful, as she must surely dread the consequences of that which she already suspects to be the case, and expectant, as she has anticipated the arrival of this hour but must now wait until her husband is ready to impart his news to her. I asked Matthew if he thought it possible for Lady Diana and me to portray such mixed and delicate emotions. He avowed that he was confident of our success and that, should we find ourselves struggling, it was his duty as an artist to ensure that the picture was true to the narrative in all aspects.

I have sought to be coy when writing of events of an intimate nature, but on re-reading my entries for these days since my arrival in Oxford it has become clear to me that, taken in their totality, there is no ambiguity as to the nature of my relationship with Matthew. That being the case, no further harm can be done by my being more honest—that is, more candid—in these pages.

Matthew and I have been together, on a bed made from pallets and bricks, under a canopy of sheets hanging from ropes, hidden by a painted wall, in the cold heat of a paper fire which rippled in the currents of air within the draughty studio. We had scant time and Matthew wished aloud that we might have even a few extra minutes, for then, he said, he could be more gentle with me, and more caring, and show me the true depth and character of that love which he wished to express. Instead, we had only the interval until the arrival of Diana's carriage, for which we knew we must keep listening.

I had thought that this first time might hurt, for so I had been told by girls at school who, I am quite sure, knew no more than did I about these activities which occur outside the reach of the public gaze. Even now, with direct and personal experience, I myself cannot write with anything but soulless prose. There is no poetry in the way I describe my closeness with Matthew. I can only ascribe that absence to the difficulty I find in squaring our physical expression with the Romantic ideal with which my upbringing and temperament have imbued our love. Something of that ideal seems missing, as though we are listening to an orchestra from which the woodwind instruments have been removed, or gazing at the first, rough brush strokes of a painting that shows no promise.

If I showed my—my what? disappointment? yes, I suppose that is it—my disappointment, Matthew did not mention it to me. Indeed, on finishing, his concern was to ensure that all should appear a model of propriety to Diana, despite my undeniably solitary arrival at the studio. He hurried to dress, encouraging me to do the same, and then had me sit on the couch as he rearranged the bed-clothes and generally fussed about the place. I was about to comment on his reticence to be close to me when he stepped back and, with a nod of approval at his handiwork, sat, brushed a lock of hair from my face and pulled me to him into a deep, memorable kiss. When his lips drifted from mine we remained mere inches from each other, both, I think, waiting to see what the other might say. The rhythmic crunching of dirt beneath approaching hoofs crept between us and broke the spell. Matthew moved towards the door, and I stood beside the window, looking out over the fields.

I was still there when Matthew returned with Diana. She took my hand and told me that she was "as excited as one can be" to be sitting for the painting. I think that I was glad to see her. Matthew again explained the poses he wishes us to strike, for Diana's benefit, and suggested that she and I use the office to change into the outfits he had prepared. Diana thought it "perfect" but wondered if Mr. Taylor—who, she said, had a reputation to protect—ought not to be worried about the public's reaction to a painting based on such a bawdy tale. Matthew thanked her for her concern with a sharpness which, to my ears, seemed singularly devoid of gratitude. A minor scandal, he said, was just what one needed to attract the attention of the critics, in times such as these. Diana looked as though she were going to reply but settled instead on a gentle laugh and picked up the pile of costume clothing from the bed, where Matthew had replaced it before her arrival. I followed her into the office.

When we emerged I was the beautiful Olivia, the apple of her emperor-father's eye. My dress is velvet, of the same rich green as a holly leaf. It falls to the floor in gentle folds. Over chest and stomach a fine lacing criss-crosses the velvet with silver cord. A leather belt fastens loosely over my hips, high at the back but falling lower at the front to meet in a shallow "vee". It seemed a plain affair for such a high-ranking individual but Matthew told me that a silver, bejewelled belt will replace this thing of dull leather in the painting. My feet are bare, appropriately enough for a woman lying on her wedding bed on the night of her marriage.

Diana is—I struggle to find the word: "handsome" does not do justice to her beauty and, likewise, "beautiful" fails to speak of her handsomeness—but Diana is really a most striking figure in her outfit. She had become Thomasin, but it was only when I moved around and pinned up her hair that she was, finally, Thomas. From the front and sides it appears quite close-cropped, though not of such shortness as might detract from the comeliness of her face or the subtle ambiguity of her sex. Her tunic of sapphire velvet reaches down to the mid-point of her thighs, revealing long legs accentuated by sky-blue hose. She wears a gold, satin belt—to be rendered in leather, Matthew told us—and black shoes with gold buckles, which are perfect for a young husband who fears he may shortly have to flee for his life. My Thomas stood before me, with her hands on her hips. Then she stepped forward, took my hand and led me to bed.

I rested myself where I had lain so recently—where my thoughts had remained—leaning back on the bolster of sheets and cushions. Diana joined me on the side of the bed closest to Matthew, who was, at this time, occupied with his easel and brushes, his pigments and resins, and paid little attention to us. She lay beside me and raised her left arm so it passed above my head. I rolled onto my right side and shifted down the bed, moving my head forward until it rested on her breast. She lowered her arm so that it fell, crooked, across my back, with her left hand resting high on my hip. She took hold of my left hand with her right, settled into position and let out a quiet "ahem" to get Matthew's attention. He looked up from the business of sharpening pencils and gave a nod of approval.

Matthew made minor adjustments to sheets and curtains, lit candles, ruffled the folds of my dress and crossed, uncrossed and re-crossed Diana's legs. As he did so he talked to us of the process which he intends to follow. After he has sketched the scene directly onto the freshly applied ground he will paint the scenery, leaving space for the two of us on the bed. Next, he will complete our bodies and clothing. Finally, he will paint our faces into the small remaining areas of pure white. He may, he said, apply a second layer of fresh ground to these last spaces so they remain wet as he paints, following the technique of Millais: this will allow him to achieve an exquisitely translucent representation of skin.

Diana asked why we needed to be there at all before it was time to paint our likenesses. Would it not be possible for Mr. Taylor to use mannequins—she called them "lay figures"—until ready for us? The answer—which was then obvious to me, but of which I am now less certain—is that my posing is the pretext upon which all else follows. Matthew, perhaps not wishing to express aloud that which I thought so easily understood, retorted with some comment about the difficulties of attaining lay figures, and his opinion that using a fancy "scarecrow" to model a princess is not the way of a true artist.

We sat for two hours while Matthew sketched and hummed and hawed, and muttered to himself under his breath, occasionally satisfied with his work, more often critical of his latest arc or line. The canvas hides Matthew from his waist to just below his chin, and is about half as wide again as it is high. At times he crouched a little, clearly intent on some point of detail, reduced to a pair of legs beneath the expanse of white and wood. Occasionally he emerged from one side of it, bobbing like a buoy on water, closing one eye and then the other, moving his head first left then right before vanishing as quickly as he had appeared.

Finally, he stepped back and took in the whole of his creation. He seemed content, and was pleasingly jocund when he declared that it was time for real life to assert itself upon us. When we returned from the office—dressed in our drab, quotidian clothing—the canvas was facing the wall, and we had no opportunity to see the results of his labours.

Diana remarked that her carriage was not expected at college for another hour, but Matthew showed no desire that we remain with him any longer. He wished us a pleasant walk home and led us down to the front door. I ought to have understood that he needs his solitude to engage with the work of the day, to apply his critical faculties to their full extent, without interruption from the self-same models whom he is trying to sublimate into characters. Unfortunately, I let my emotions get the better of me, feeling that we were being dismissed sharply and without due gratitude for our efforts. I spoke to Diana, loudly, with words to the effect that we ought to be leaving as I was sure Mr. Taylor needed to tidy the studio and return home to his wife, who would no doubt be waiting for him. Matthew could not hide his scowl. I have not seen him angry before, but yesterday I most certainly did. Diana turned without a sound and descended to the drive, walking over to her familiar view across the river and fields. Yet Matthew did not give voice to discontentment. He told me that he would write with suggested dates for the next sittings, thanked me for my time, and asked me to convey his gratitude to Lady Diana.

I wrote yesterday of my visit's being a great success. Now I have had a chance to sleep on it, and write of it, and I find my own anger at his reaction to my mentioning Mrs. Taylor. Perhaps it was inappropriate for me to touch upon his marriage: he doubtless struggles to encompass his affection for me within the strictures of marital fidelity. I should be more understanding of his feelings. But what of my feelings? Can he not see that I, too, must struggle with the emotions which our intimacy brings to me? A word of reassurance from him, some gentle statement of his intentions, would make the greatest of differences. Yet I can see that it may be unrealistic for these expectations to be held by one who is leading a man to be unfaithful to his wife. Can I really ask of Matthew anything other than that which is freely given? I cannot determine the argument through which I might reconcile these two sides of my own role in the thing: the gentle lover and the scheming mistress. Do I deserve his love? Am I a victim, as much as—more than?—Mrs. Taylor? Does she deserve his love?

As we walked home Diana and I spoke of the studio but, each aware of some tacit agreement, we both ensured that the conversation centred on the artistic and narrative aspects of our time with Mr. Taylor. I told her of my wish to have hair as fair as hers. She assured me that she thinks my chestnut locks perfect for the role: they give me an air of "purposeful fragility". Then, as we came within sight of the college house, she said:

"The thing about lay figures, about using them, using full-sized dolls, instead of real people... The thing is, they are not hard to come by, and they are not inappropriate for princesses. They are, however, expensive."

CHAPTER ELEVEN

I awoke to an empty cottage and Venus. I had thought that I would rise early, keen to get to the boxes from Gerald, but yellow kept me down. I threw on a dressing gown that must have been Emily's, because it certainly was not mine, unless I had forgotten about it, and maybe I had, maybe it was from my mother.

The bathroom mirror was filled with well-known strangers. The student of Johannes Vermeer's *Music Lesson* looked off to the right, towards an instructor I could not see but could sense beside me, standing in black with a sash from shoulder to hip and his hand resting on a cane. And the student's face, framed by ringlets and bows, but only in the mirror, because she was painted from behind with dress and shoulders and no face but the one in the mirror: the mirror behind the virginal at which she sits, the mirror on the bathroom wall, the mirror on the wall in Jan van Eyck's *Arnolfini Portrait*. They arrived behind me then, the two figures in Van Eyck's reflected doorway, distorted by their mirror's convex surface, small and insignificant compared to the couple who are the main subject of the Arnolfini canvas, who were not showing their faces today. And maybe, just maybe, one of these small figures was Van Eyck himself, come to join me. I stared ahead, because they were not in the room itself, and nor was Ford Madox Brown—perhaps it was Ford Madox Brown—ready to receive a child I did not have to give but, then, he could not see me, I supposed. Brown only saw the woman in his own painting, *Take Your Son, Sir!*, the woman who held out her baby to him as she stood before the halo of a circular mirror: wife or kept woman, moment of joy or morality tale, or both. Who was I to judge? My Brown looked sadder than his reflection in the painting. My Brown was older, knew his son would die as an infant before the painting was finished, knew the painting would never be finished. All these joined me as I brushed my teeth, and all these left with the arrival of Venus, another reflection, another delicate resonance.

Diego Velázquez painted *The Rokeby Venus* in the mid-1600s. He was lucky to get away with it, given the Inquisition's displeasure at seeing naked women on Spanish walls. Venus faces away from the viewer, lounging on a day-bed, resting her head upon her crooked right arm, looking into a mirror held by her son, Cupid. I saw, in my mirror, the face of Venus just as I saw her face in the mirror of the painting, even though it ought not to be there at all, her face, because the angles are wrong, because light does not work that way. And she would know. Velázquez's goddess gave her name to the Venus Effect, the weird behaviour of mirrors in paintings, which reveal the reflection of their subjects to the viewer even as it is revealed to the subjects themselves. Somehow, impossibly, she admires her own image even as we admire it, as I admired it in my mirror, but mirrors do not do that: either she gets to look at herself or we do, but not both, not in the real world, at least.

My Venus, Velázquez's Venus, was slim but not thin, curvy but not Rubenesque, and maybe Velázquez used a live model and maybe he did not. In either case he painted her in a variation of the pose of the *Borghese Hermaphrodite*, an ancient marble which he saw in Rome, before it went to the Louvre but after it was placed on a marble mattress carved by Gian Lorenzo Bernini. If I shifted my head I could see that mattress, a perfect creation of feathers and warmth, but hard and cold to the touch, if I could have touched it.

I could touch the mirror, though, and did, moved the cabinet door on which it was fixed—opened, closed—and my reflection moved with it, cold, out of sight and back, with no Venus Effect and, besides, nobody to see it but me, and nobody sees the front of the Venus so nobody knows what lies between her legs. She was cut, once, with a meat chopper, by a Suffragette called Mary who came from Canada and was arrested nine times, force-fed, joined Oswald Mosley's black-shirted Fascists, left them, died. Venus was repaired and the cuts are almost invisible, like old scars on her skin, painful memories on her neck and back and hips.

I sat on the side of the bath and finished brushing my teeth, trying to clear my head and prepare myself to attack the contents of Gerald's boxes. I had seen a copy of the *Borghese Hermaphrodite* in Florence, in the Uffizi Gallery, and Turner—Turner who painted Whitstable and decorated a biscuit-tin lid—Turner sketched it, about a year after completing his watercolour of the Rivers Greta and Tees at their confluence. Ruskin used the watercolour in the Oxford Teaching Collection and must have guided his students to the background, between the trees, to the front aspect of Rokeby Park, once home to *The Rokeby Venus*. I stood and spat and rinsed and went downstairs to look for biscuits.

The boxes were stacked neatly by the side of the fireplace. I took the uppermost and placed it on the table beside the painting. It contained a mess of receipts, a tyre-pressure gauge, a mid-seventies Oxford telephone book, a collection of loose paperwork and policy documents which must have come from Mr Carter's time in insurance, and a plastic doll from the 1960s, judging by its torn, op art dress. I looked through the papers one final time, in case I had missed anything, but no, there was nothing there to help me. The second box turned out to be the one which Gerald had opened in Whitstable, but instead of examining the contents in detail I put it aside and opened the third. It matched the first: a mess of random papers weighed down by an old, digital alarm clock in a fake walnut case, missing two of its four buttons. Gerald must have opened one box and then assumed everything around it contained the same sort of materials. There was a certain pleasure in knowing that the detective work had been left to me.

I set the one interesting box on the table and began to sort its contents. In the hours after the Whitstable visit I had imagined that I would read the books as I removed them, read through their pages in a frenzy, look for the identity of my friends and the story they wanted to tell me. Instead, I found myself working methodically and calmly, bringing order, Klee's geometry, cool marble, gentle rivers. After about ten minutes I had arranged the Oyster Bed pilgrims into five congregations, neatly arranged on the table. The first was a set of three notebooks, each about six inches wide by eight inches tall, bound in marbled boards, with leather reinforcing the spine and corners. On the front of one of them a crumbling paper label hung by the last of its glue, identifying its owner and author as a Miss Penelope Swift. The other two covers each possessed a lighter area of similar size, where their labels had evidently rested, before the paste had finally withered with age. All three were diaries, their entries varying in length from several pages to little more than a date and a sentence fragment. Folded letters and ticket stubs peeked out from between a few of the pages.

The second gathering was also made up of notebooks, filled with the same, neat hand as the first, greater in number—there were eight of them—but with fewer pages. All but one of these were of a slightly larger page size than the diaries and contained notes in English, Latin and Greek. The odd one out was a smaller book containing both notes and sketches. Next came a small pile of envelopes, mostly empty, some with stamps, others delivered by hand, all addressed to Miss Swift. The fourth group contained a couple of old guidebooks, and the fifth was a jumble of personal effects including a silver mechanical pencil, more ticket stubs and an old pair of bootlaces.

When everything had been removed from the box, I found tucked into one corner a lock of reddish-brown hair, tied round with a light-green bow. I took it over to the painting and held it against the head of the nearest figure. It was far too dark. Held against the other figure it seemed to match, not perfectly, but I could believe it belonged to her, if I allowed for some artistic licence on the part of the painter. I lifted it to my nose and inhaled deeply. In its scent there was nothing left of the woman to whom it belonged, nothing to echo the sensations of her protector, who held her with those locks only a breath away. *Laisse-moi respirer longtemps, longtemps, l'odeur de tes cheveux.* And I wanted more but had only the smell of dust and mildew to shake memories into the air. I tucked it between the pages of one of the guidebooks for safekeeping.

There was some part of me that did not want to sit down and begin to read. I was afraid that the stories I could construct, built on a loose scaffold of connections, would always be better than the truth. Yet I opened the uppermost diary and checked the first entry.

Saturday, 1st January, 1887

A new diary for the start of a new year. Our guests left this afternoon and I believe that Mother and Father share my relief at the end of the annual descent of family and friends upon our home. I have given the rest of the day to reading the copy of *Strange Case of Dr Jekyll and Mr Hyde* which I received from Father.

The second diary started earlier, in mid-May of 1886, and the final one later, in the last days of August of 1887, when Vincent was in Paris, painting sunflowers and tangling balls of dyed yarn as he explored colour theory. Outside the cottage the sky was bright and the sun was teasing the night's frost into a facsimile of morning dew. Inside was a god-awful dull affair to me, a girl with mousy hair. No daddy to tell me to go, but I went, taking the earliest diary, wrapped in a plastic bag recently relieved of the bread and butter and eggs with which it arrived.

The village was clear. In the black tarmac the receding waters had left looking-glasses full of warm stone. Where fields showed through between buildings and walls, gates and fences, they lay fallow and still glazed with eddying mist. The village was Brigadoon, back for a day after another lost century, or seemed so until I reached the main road and a Ford Escort broke any spell cast over the place. A door sign told the world that the bookshop was shut, and would remain so until half-past twelve. There was no reason to suppose that the sign could be trusted on a mid-week day when the world was not around to rely on its accuracy. Next to the bookshop was a small café, with a blackboard outside promising the unseasonal availability of ices. Above a few rows of tiles—some white, some green, and white chips on the green ones—a large window made of small panes revealed tables and chairs. Several of the panes used bull's-eye glass, thick and distorted, twisting the tables into smears of light pine. The other glass was clear and even, showing the bull's-eyes for what they were, an affectation designed to give the place a false sense of age. I could see an elderly couple sitting as far from the door as possible, each nursing a cup of something steaming. They looked back at me without any sign of interest.

A bell tinkled as I entered and a short, round lady appeared from a door in the rear wall. She wore tweed as though it were a military uniform.

"Hello," she said. "Anywhere you like. I'll get a menu." She vanished back through the door and reappeared just as I sat down at a table by the window.

"I'll give you a minute to decide," she said and started her retreat to the safety of her kitchen redoubt.

"Oh, I'd just like a pot of tea, please."

The little round lady turned and took the menu off the table with a countenance which hinted at pleasant delight in having my custom but shouted ill-disguised contempt: all I wanted was a cup of tea, and even then I had not ordered until she had fetched the menu, and what was the point of that then? It started to drizzle again, little circles in the puddles, breaking the upturned houses and trees, sending clouds scampering outwards. I unwrapped my plastic parcel and placed the diary on the table. Tea arrived, served with shortbread biscuits and mild disdain.

Many of the early entries were short, one or two words, a single sentence: "Margaret has a new cat", "Weekend with the Bankses", and so on. July began with a longer entry:

Thursday, 1st July, 1886

Yesterday, Royal Holloway College was officially opened by Queen Victoria. It is a college for women only, and when I mentioned it to Father and Mother they approved. I told them that I felt it might be of benefit to continue my own education and they did not appear averse to the idea. Father, in particular, promised to give the matter some consideration over the next few months, although he expressed his wish that my academic performance continue to be such as to encourage him to look favourably upon my attending college.

There was little mention of art in the diary. Penelope's schooling was designed to impart the more ladylike pursuits required of a good wife. She spoke of literature and history quite often, but almost always in the context of her mother or father. Her mother did not seem to work but Penelope wrote of overhearing her discussing politics and the social upheavals of the day with her father: riots in Belfast, talk of a Women's Liberal Federation, a general election in July, not a year after the last. Her father, as far as I could tell, was something in publishing: on a few occasions Penelope described hearing her parents argue "about the new business" or "over the demands of the new bookshop." She and her father were close, judging by the regularity with which she mentioned him: sometimes no more than, "Spent an hour or two with Father," other times with more substance. One entry in particular caught my attention:

Saturday, 4th September, 1886

This morning I found myself alone in the house, but for Cook, who was busy in the kitchen preparing for this evening's dinner party. I decided to read but lacked anything of interest in my own room except for those favourites which are already much read. I went downstairs to Father's office, to search amongst the new books. I still do not know what possessed me, what caused me to behave so abominably, but I became caught up in my curiosity and opened several of the cupboards in the base of the large, glazed bookcase. It seems so ill-conceived now, as I write of it, but at the time I did not stop to consider my actions.

In the second cupboard I found an old book—MDCCXLV, London—which seems to be written, for the most part, in English from the fifteenth or sixteenth century. The short preface, however, describes its having been authored and published only some eighty years previously. That edition, it says, was banned and destroyed by order of the Crown. The story is entitled *Ye Straunge Hystory of Thomysin & Oliuia*. I had not even proceeded past the title page before Father entered at such a brisk pace that he was some distance into the room before he espied me at his desk. He stopped short and said, "Penelope?"

Sip of tea. Purple pill. I read on.

I braced myself for his anger. I had behaved in a way that caused me to feel guilty. How then could Father's reaction not hold a mirror to that guilt? Yet he showed no sign that he wished to punish me: sitting on the window seat, he patted his hand on the cushion beside him. When I rose he nodded towards the book on the desk. I picked it up and went over to join him. He took it from me, turning it in his hands, reading the spine, even though I am sure he already knew which volume I had selected. He asked me what I thought of it.

I told him that I had not had a chance to read any of the story itself, but that I found the title most intriguing. At this he handed the book to me, and told me to read it over the course of the next few days. I am not, however, to show it to Mother: she, according to Father, is not impressed by any fascination with literature which does not pertain to the modern woman. I have always thought it odd to keep secrets from either of one's parents, but, for a situation in which the distress or incredulity of that parent is an inevitable consequence of one's honesty, I am willing to accept such secrecy.

Then he kissed me gently on my forehead and sent me off to my room.

The rain had gathered pace, and its rapping on the window distracted me from my reading, even as Penelope took me into her confidence. I nibbled on a biscuit, staring out as Venice returned to the village and, with it, James Abbott McNeill Whistler. He was there, too, in Venice, before Monet, creating etchings for a commission. Diamond panes either side of a doorway, and a girl there, looking at her reflection. The woman behind—it looks like a woman, but so does Venus—holds her face to her hand and leans against the open door in encroaching shadow, beneath the chairs hanging above. And then the eye runs back, back over the steps, to lesser figures in a caner's workroom. Through my window the reflections shattered, running from figurative to abstract, just as Whistler's Venetian girl lost her twin to the finger-smudges of ink on the printing plate, a different smudge for each impression. The biscuit mixed with tea. Tweed returned.

"If there's nothing else, I'll just leave this here," she said.

Clearly, the option of there being anything else was entirely illusory. She put the bill on the table. It was slipped inside the tab of a black, leather holder. The paper aligned perfectly with the edges of the flap in which it rested. The pot was still warm, however, and not yet empty. I poured myself another cup and splashed in the last of the milk. The diary lay open but I held a new secret and was not ready to continue the story. My face blurred against the darkening skies as I focused out, out and down the gentle slope of the road to the bridge over the stream, where swirling stars hid beneath the dripping foliage of the bank.

Penelope Swift, daughter of a publisher, and an Oxford student, judging by the college address on the letters. Was she the woman in the green dress, looking at me from the picture? The lock of hair suggested that she was, but as evidence it was far from conclusive. Or was Emily right? Then the androgynous figure in the tunic was a woman, too, possibly Penelope, resting in profile, holding her lover to her breast. I wanted her to be the green dress, not the tunic. I wanted to share a look with her, to have her be imploring me, somehow, to give her answers. I wanted someone to rely on me, and there, in the green dress, was someone I could never let down, someone who could never let me down. Swirling leaves rushing under a bridge and then the waiting on the other side, waiting until she came home from work, waiting until she collected me from the hospital, waiting, and all a blur in the rain.

I was sitting in the lychgate again. I must have paid, I could not have left without paying, not with Tweed watching. My hair was wet. I shivered and moved to one end of the wooden bench, hugging the corner of the walls to keep out of the wind. The cottage was only a minute's walk away, but I had no desire for a waiting room, Emily's antechamber, with a fireplace that no longer held a fire. Above me the tiles syncopated a rhythm to accompany the music of the gutters and drains. Gentle creaks from overhead chairs, woven in the gloom behind diamond panes and there, outside, my reflection again, only I could not see it from where I sat so only supposed and then wondered if it saw me, on the steps above the canal, under the tiles of the gate, with the church looming.

There was a story in my plastic bag and in the neat piles back at the house. I could have read the whole thing in a couple of days, clear days, days without smudges. I could have skipped straight to the end. But maybe Keats had it right with his idea of Negative Capability: there should be no irritable reaching after fact and reason, and beauty should overcome all else. I shivered again as the dampness seeped through to my skin. Everything was tones of grey, everything but the pallid stone walls.

I was lying in a warm bath. I must have paid, I could not have left without paying, not with Tweed watching. Except I had been by the church, so yes, I paid, and then sat at the gate. Sitting at the gate, damp. Which is why I was cold and needed a bath. In my hands I held one of the old guidebooks from Gerald's boxes. I made a mental note to return it to the neat piles on the table before Emily returned. She would be angry if she knew I had risked damaging it with bathwater and bubbles. *Drawings and Studies by Raffaelle Sanzio in the University Galleries, Oxford.* I stopped at plate 77, *Jacob Wrestling with the Angel.* Under the engraving, in faint pencil handwriting which matched Penelope's diaries, was written, "We all have our struggles, but oft-times they bless us."

Once, when I was young, little more than an infant, I saw my father fight. It was the first time I saw him angry, and the last time I ever saw him. His opponent was not an angel. I held my empty ice cream cone in front of me, above the melting vanilla which ran and pooled on the concrete at my feet. Dad was telling the large man that he should apologize and buy me another, even if it had been an accident, and yes, I was small and not easily seen, but still… And then the man hit him and I thought it odd that it did not make any sound, but then nothing made any sound because Dad was falling, and his head was on the concrete, and if I fell like that I would cry but he was silent even when I knelt by him, when the man had gone and it was safe again. My mother rushed over and then some more people joined her, and when the ambulance arrived all their faces flashed blue in the lights. My aunt explained, late that night: she said it was a brain thing but it had a complicated name. I told her that my father would be able to explain it when he got back from the hospital.

Subarachnoid hæmorrhage. I looked it up myself, years later.

I was resting on the couch when Emily returned. She was preceded through the front door by a pizza box which she balanced on one arm, held above her briefcase. She approached the table but seeing it covered in papers she slid the box towards me and I took it in my hands.

"We can eat off the cardboard, on the couch. Then you can tell me the story." She nodded towards the papers and disappeared into the kitchen, reappearing with several squares of kitchen roll to serve as napkins.

"Okay. So, what have you found out?" she asked.

I replied between bites, suddenly aware that I had eaten nothing but biscuits all day.

"Not much. I'm not in any rush. They belong to a woman called Penelope Swift. There's a few diaries and some letters. And then various bits and bobs which all have to do with her being in Oxford. I just got to the bit where she actually goes there, in the diaries. The guidebooks are from there, and the letters are addressed to her college."

"When?"

"When was she there? Eighteen eighty-seven."

We ate our way through another slice each before Emily spoke again.

"Interesting. Early for a woman student. Anything about the painting?"

"Not yet, but I think maybe she's one of the people on the bed. I mean, she must have had some interest in art, in Oxford at least."

I reached over to the side-table and picked up the Raffaelle book to show to Emily.

"I don't know how you can do it," she said. "I'd read through everything to see what was going on. Then fill in the details afterwards."

"Well, you're a lawyer. I'm not. Maybe that's the difference."

"I suppose. Pill?"

Purple. Emily pulled out some papers and rested them on her lap. She trawled through them, decorating the pages with occasional, illegible scrawls in red pen. I tidied away the remnants of the meal then sat next to her, reading the Raffaelle's companion volume. On the first plate, beneath a trestle table holding a cadaver, Penelope had written "*écorché*—means skinless".

Yellow. Bed. We all have our struggles.

Chapter Twelve

Monday, 5th December, 1887

Diana brought me a gift today. To be precise, she brought three
gifts: two guide-books and a silver, mechanical pencil. It is a
pretty, fluted thing with "S.M" stamped upon it: the mark of
Sampson Mordan. Father has one of their pencils. I asked her to what
I owed this generosity and she replied that it is simply what friends do.
The guide-books include all the prints which we saw in the University
Galleries: one covers Michael Angelo and the other Raffaelle. They
are far nicer than Diana's *Handbook Guide*, each being filled with
marvellous engravings of the works. These, together with the pencil,
seemed far too grand a gift and at first I gently refused to accept them,
as it will be impossible to return the kindness. Diana, however, would
have none of it and placed them directly into my satchel. They are,
she explained, to be brought out and used as required and, she hopes,
often in her company so that she, too, may benefit from the purchase.
There was no reply to be made but a heartfelt expression of gratitude.

Friday, 9th December, 1887

This evening Matthew's wife joined me at the dinner table. It is not
unusual for her to dine with the students. Indeed, it is well known that
she has been tasked with the "pastoral care" of the college's charges, and
sees meal times as an opportunity to ensure that "her girls" are healthy
and content. Sometimes she departs with her chosen dinner partner,
presumably to talk privately about a particular trouble which weighs

heavy. On one occasion, and only one, I saw her bring a student to tears, but I remain charitable enough to suppose that this was engendered by some external misfortune which troubled the poor young woman.

Matthew and I met earlier today. We followed our routine: I arrived some time prior to Diana, allowing an hour or so of privacy before we heard her carriage approach. I almost wrote that these occurrences were unremarkable, but now I find it deeply troubling that I think them so. Certainly, all was the same as on previous occasions. My fear is that such a situation might ever become "normal" to me. It is as though the virtue of the thing—if it is virtuous at all—is to be found in its prohibition, or the romanticism of that prohibition. Perhaps I am desperately seeking to excuse my behaviour by creating a naive narrative of illicit love, realized against all odds.

Mrs. Taylor chose to refer to her husband in a most circuitous fashion, having first observed the niceties of inquiring as to my health and asking to hear my general thoughts on life as an Oxford student. Was I, she asked, finding time to indulge in any activities outside the confines of college? There was, without doubt, a test in this question, but its exact nature was hidden behind the inscrutable façade of Mrs. Taylor's unceasing smile. On the one hand, she might have known of my hours at Matthew's studio, and thus be seeking some confirmation from my response. On the other, if she knew nothing at all of my private life she may have been drawn to pry into my affairs by her own insecurities: after all, she was, in Diana's words, "long-suffering". If the former case, then a failure to mention my visits could do nothing but justify any suspicion that this was something untoward. If the latter, then I should be conveying information which ought to have been divulged by her husband and, again, there could be no escaping the same conclusion. As Father would say, I was on a very sticky wicket. I find myself thinking of this woman as my enemy; a woman who has done no harm to me, and whom I have inarguably wronged. She is, for want of a better epithet, a rival in love.

I smiled back at her then, over dinner, and recalled our recent meeting in the hall. As she was aware, I replied, Lady Diana and I had taken an opportunity to spend a few, pleasant hours at the University

Galleries. We are forming a close friendship and delighting in our shared interests. Mrs. Taylor took a sip of water, but said nothing. She looked at me with what I took to be an air of expectation. I could no longer bear the pressure of this wordless inquisition. I told her—with a care to avoid all sentimentality and embellishment—that I was enjoying sitting for her husband and then, without pausing for reply, asked her if he had made any comment on the painting which I might find instructional.

Then it was my turn to sip my water and wait. Mrs. Taylor placed her glass down with an unnecessary degree of studied precision. She dabbed her mouth with her napkin, closed her eyes and inhaled, and then opened them as the smile returned to her lips. It was, it occurred to me then, as though she were preparing for a piano recital. She played the piece with the greatest of skill: her husband did not often talk about his work; of course she knew I was sitting for him; it must be most enjoyable for me, and for Lady Diana; she must drop in one day and see how the painting is progressing. I remarked that her attendance would be delightful. Indeed it would, she agreed, and it would be nice to have the chance to advance our acquaintanceship. She glanced at the clock on the wall and made her excuses: she and her husband have an engagement.

I finished dinner alone, copying notes from the Galleries into the new guide-books, where they sit as marginalia. Now I am in my room, wondering if Mrs. Taylor does have an engagement this evening or is, as I sit at my desk, confronting her husband over the nature of his relationship with a student in her care. Diana and I are to visit the studio on Wednesday—Friday is the college Christmas dinner and we are all required to busy ourselves in preparations throughout the day—so I suppose it is then that I shall hear from Matthew if my actions today have caused him problems.

Wednesday, 14th December, 1887

Wednesday has been taken up with Millais, and Waterhouse, and

Sargent. I descended to breakfast to find a long letter from Matthew waiting for me in the hall.

My Dearest Penelope,

I am afraid that I shall not be able to meet you this week, as we had planned. Please do forgive my not writing to you sooner: I had hoped, until early this morning, that I should be able to attend the studio, but my circumstances and my disposition make it impossible to undertake further work on the painting at this time.

As you have no doubt surmised, my wife and I have had discussions about your sittings; discussions which have been at quite some length. I had, of course, informed her of my intention to have you and Lady Diana sit for me, and for two or three weeks she seemed untroubled. More recently, however, she has been prone to inquiring about each sitting on the evening after its occurrence. Was it successful? Were my models—a term which she somehow endows with an element of venom otherwise reserved for her descriptions of the more criminal elements of society—were my models sufficiently skilled to maintain a pose for any reasonable period? How was the set dressed? And so forth.

On the evening of last Friday she came home in a particularly vexed state and, finding me reading in my study, removed the book from my hands and demanded my full attention. It was, she told me, completely inappropriate that I should involve myself with two young students and that, were I not to cease this "madness" immediately, she would see to it that the appropriate action was taken by the college. I asked what might be the nature of this "appropriate action" and was given to understand that it would most likely involve your being sent down. I hope that you will easily imagine the vehemence with which I sought to deter her from this precipitous course.

Now, some four days later, the cooler aspect of her nature has gained dominion over the more heated. I should like to claim that this is due to my reassuring influence but, in truth, the greater part of her retreat is driven by an appreciation of Lady Diana's standing at Oxford, and in wider society. Any action taken against you, even if not precisely duplicated against Lady Diana, would no doubt still cause the casting of aspersions on Lady Diana's character. Clearly that is not something which my wife, or her employer, would wish to occur.

This being the case, you may wonder why I cannot meet you today and, indeed, why I bother to mention my wife at all. To answer the latter question: my reasons for telling you are twofold. First, your living situation renders it unthinkable that you and she will not continue to meet each other—say, over the course of some meal, as you did on Friday—and I should like to know that you have the information necessary to ensure an evenly matched and equanimous exchange of pleasantries. Second, and far more importantly in my estimation, I wish you to know that you are precious to me, and that I have it in my heart to protect you.

On the first question, I can only say that it is my disposition which causes me to cancel our appointment. You will recall that Lady Diana asked me about this year's Exhibition at the Royal Academy. Had I shown anything? It was an obvious dig at my abilities as a painter, for I am quite sure a woman of her background must have attended the Exhibition. Thus, she was asking either in the knowledge that I must confess my absence, or in the expectation that I had been there but hung so badly that she had not seen my work. I suppressed my anger at the time, and it has passed in the days since, but I find myself gradually losing faith in my abilities, and questioning the motivation for my continued pursuit of painting as a livelihood.

The Exhibition is a mire of double-standards and entitlement. What did Millais show this year? *Lilacs*. A young girl with blonde hair, wrapped at the waist by a wide, satin ribbon, who holds up the skirt of her white dress to form a shallow bowl in which rest the titular flowers. She looks up at what? The sky? The boughs of the tree behind her? God? She is beseeching, as though she expects some hand to descend and bring the plucked stems back to life. What is it all about, Penelope? It is—as is his *Nest*—a sentimental nonsense. The *Magazine of Art* agrees with me: "suggestive of the Christmas number style of art" and "steeped in the tritest kind of popular sentiment." But it is John Millais, and so the works are hung well and the public clamours for them. His other pieces are no better, even if slightly less mawkish. Two portraits—Hartington and Rosebery—are two dull subjects for two dull pictures: grey men in black coats. And *Mercy*? Another predictable tableau of French Catholics and Protestants, just as he painted thirty years ago. "Its not very lucid expression is unredeemed by any beauty of colour," says the *Magazine*. But this is Millais, Penelope. The man founded the Pre-Raphaelite Brotherhood. I swear one day he will be President of the Academy. Millais!

Waterhouse showed his *Mariamne*, which is the largest canvas he has produced to date. It is accomplished, certainly, but can you tell me the story of Mariamne? I suppose that you can: I envy you your education, even as it continues to flourish. I did not know the tale, or had long-since forgotten it. The catalogue, though, filled ten lines with the story. So why then do I wish to look at the painting? If I want stories I may read them in my Bible, or in all the other great books of this age. If I want to admire the skill of the painter then do I really care about the subject? I take from the Waterhouse his ability to paint a large canvas, and to capture a tale in oils. I want more, Penelope. I want a painting to make me feel something: not because of the technique it evidences, not because it calls up some woeful story, and not because it washes me in purest sentimentality. There must be something more. There must be something intrinsic to the art itself. If a painting shows me rain it is rain I wish to experience and not the image of rain. I want to hold the scene in my mind, close my eyes and feel each drop.

Ah! but then there is Sargent, back from Paris—where I hear demand for his portraiture has declined precipitously—and bringing the French style with him, to such acclaim. Do you know his *Carnation, Lily, Lily, Rose*? It is described as an "extremely original and daring essay in decoration." Penelope, it was a revelation to me. Two young girls, dressed in simple white dresses, face each other, but each seems utterly unaware of her companion, so intent are they on the task at hand; and what a task it is: so uncomplicated, yet so utterly perfect. Both girls are lighting paper lanterns, leaning over them so that their faces take on a subtle yellow-orange cast. They stand surrounded by lilies which gently reach above them, intertwined with more hanging lanterns, glowing softly. There is no mythology in the picture, no great historical tale, no self-important bombast. Everything blends in evocation: subject, composition, technique, all that Sargent has done. Stand in front of the painting and one is a child again, with a lit spill in one's hand, at dusk, beneath the lilies.

I did not even show, Penelope. Once again I had nothing to share with my peers, or the wider world. It is not that I have nothing to say, it is that I have not the language with which to say it. It seems I contend with quite the opposite problem to Millais.

So where does that leave us, and our Warber? I believe we ought to continue, Penelope, but let us not title it, else title it in such a manner as to leave interpretation to those who will look upon it. The painting—that is, the heart of the thing—should transcend the inspiration and exist as an object of intrinsic value. And it must be shown where it can best fulfil its *raison d'être*. The Academy is a dusty place. The Grosvenor is favoured by Burne-Jones and others, but I hear that it is full of internecine strife and may not last much longer. There will be somewhere new, I am sure. There is always somewhere new.

Do I convey my thoughts with any degree of cogency? I am tired. Can you see why I must delay our meeting until I am quite ready to return to the piece? I do hope so. I believe by the commencement of next term I shall have had the time I need. Is that awful of me, to ask that of you, that you wait? Please understand that my struggle is with my art alone.

With fondest regards, your friend,
Matthew

I was unable to get a message to Diana before she arrived at the studio. On finding the door locked she came to college and found me waiting. She said it was "a damned good job" that she had not sent the carriage away before trying the door, but her annoyance soon dissolved when she saw that I was upset. I allowed her to read the letter. She said that Matthew seemed genuinely distressed, but she could not, or would not, say whether she believed his explanation to be truthful, or a design to hide a deeper truth, one which undoubtedly involves his wife.

We sat in my room and talked for a while. Together, we drafted a reply to Matthew. I suggested that we write something short, but not brusque, but Diana was of the opinion that my cause would be better served if we were to craft a longer letter, engaging with Matthew's themes, lest I be perceived as dismissive of them in my brevity.

My Dear Mr. Taylor,

Thank you for taking the time to write and explain so thoroughly and completely the reasons for your being unable to attend our sitting yesterday. I hope you will not mind, but I took the liberty of showing the later pages of your letter to Lady Diana as I felt them to be of such a nature as to be personal but not entirely private. I remain aware that it is she, not I, who has the greater experience with the world of art. Just as you wished to demonstrate your desire to protect me, so I wish to show you that I am genuinely concerned for your happiness.

My father has of late been inspecting a forthcoming edition of the poet Keats's letters, and I have been permitted to read a little of the manuscript, from which I took down several extracts. I believe that two passages are of particular interest. In the spring of 1819, Keats wrote to his brother George and George's wife, asking, "Do you not see how necessary a World of Pains and troubles is to school an Intelligence and make it a Soul?" I believe that he was right to see our struggles as the tutors of our deeper understanding, elevating us above the mere beasts. So, my dear Matthew, I ask that you, too, might reflect upon your current worries and see within them an opportunity for improvement.

There is another letter worthy of mention. Two years earlier, Keats wrote to George and his other surviving brother, Thomas:

"It struck me what quality went to form a Man of Achievement... I mean Negative Capability, that is, when a man is capable of being in uncertainties, mysteries, doubts, without any irritable reaching after fact and reason."

I showed this quote to Lady Diana and we are both agreed that it may hold the key to your disenchantment, or some part of it. You rail against a painting which reproduces some episode from history or a well-loved tale, or "becomes the embodiment of myth" as Lady

Diana has it. It seems that you are troubled because these works are robbed of Negative Capability—robbed of their ability to entertain "uncertainties, mysteries, doubts"—because they are stamped with narrative by their titles and descriptions and left only as a photograph in oils.

It could be, too, that you see some paintings as too insipid to stir the imagination—Millais's recent efforts, for example—and that the possibility of the exercise of Negative Capability is removed not by some degree of pre-determination, but by a lack of visual stimulation. I should venture a third category to which you would assign failure, being those pictures which take to themselves a subject so familiar to all that, even without title or explanation, it cannot be open to interpretation and thus leaves its audience in want of opportunity.

Lady Diana told me the story of an uncle of hers—of whom you may have heard, but whose name I shall omit to spare his embarrassment—who writes novels of reasonable merit, which one might, if charitable, term "literary". Apparently he is in the habit of explaining these novels, in the course of drinks or dinner, to all who will listen, and in doing so is at great pains to ensure that they become ever-more attired in depth and meaning. Lady Diana says it has become quite the running joke in her family, and that "to act the Uncle D_____" has become a synonym for painting the lily; particularly so when the unadorned lily is not of an overly beauteous nature. This uncle, it seems to me, is guilty of committing the same acts against literature as you would accuse artists of committing against art: namely, an inability to produce work which derives its merits from within itself, speaking with its own voice, coloured by the experience and mores of its viewer.

I look forward to continuing our sittings in the new year.

With fondest regards, your friend,

Penelope

In truth, Diana was far less charitable in her assessment of Matthew than my letter suggests. If Matthew wanted to let the observers of his work construct their own narratives, she wondered aloud, then why did he not submit a blank canvas to the Academy, leaving them free to call upon limitless whimsy? I do like Diana—I like her a great deal—but she occasionally tends towards the insufferable.

She has invited me to spend the New Year with her on the family estate. I shall ask Father if I may, as soon as I arrive home.

Friday, 16th December, 1887

I have just withdrawn to my room after the college's Christmas dinner. It was a curiously cheerless affair. I suppose that all the girls, and Miss Callow's cohort, too, are keen to return to their families and distracted by thoughts of old friends and familiar faces. Diana did not attend, but she sent her apologies yesterday and was not expected. I felt lonely without her. I sat at a table with Elizabeth, with whom I remain on good terms, but who has taken advantage of opportunities to make new friends amongst the students, and whose company I no longer find as—how shall I put it?—"engaging" as once I did. Still, I made the best of my lot and talked with the other women, and laughed as required at the various *bon-mots* of the evening.

Mrs. Taylor was present, of course. She sat beside Miss Callow and, much to my relief, with her back to me. On the one occasion when she caught my eye—or I hers, I forget which—she gave a wan smile which amounted to a social politeness and nothing more. We did not speak, for which I am grateful. She left the dinner directly after Miss Callow's closing speech, whilst the rest of us remained behind for drinks and the singing of carols.

Saturday, 17th December, 1887

A day of packing, carriages and trains. Finally I am back home and in my own room. I find it less welcoming, and more suited to a child, than I remember.

CHAPTER THIRTEEN

On Thursday I stayed in the cottage, watching the rain hammer down and run to the waiting gutter as if it were late for an appointment. I spent my time with the diaries, reading a little then turning to some magazine or book for a while. Or I dozed by the window, waking to the sight of the painting on the table, where it remained, condemning Emily to meals eaten from plates balanced on her lap. If it troubled her she had been kind enough, or wary enough, not to say anything to me. I drank tea, ate toast and cake, eschewed anything of nutritional value. If someone had peered through the window they would have witnessed a scene from an advertisement for cat food: a woman curled up in jeans and an oversize sweater, thick socks on her feet and a mug held up to her lips, looking out of the window at nothing in particular. All that was missing was the cat.

I recalled a television commercial for instant coffee. In the darkness just before dawn an old, white Volkswagen Beetle pulls up to the top of a cliff, overlooking the sea. Cut to an interior shot of a young woman, her arms crossed over the curve of the steering wheel, her chin resting on them as she looks out into the lightening sky. She is clearly unhappy, even crying a little. She reaches over and fumbles in the glove box, looking for a heating element which is just the right size for the mug she keeps on the passenger seat. When she finds it she plugs it into the cigarette lighter and makes herself a cup of instant coffee. Then an exterior shot: the woman gets out of the car and stands. Her hands are cupped around the warming mug. She sips her drink. She allows the first glimmers of resolve and happiness to play across her face, washed with the gold of the rising sun. The soundtrack assures us that the coming day is going to be bathed in bright, bright, sunshine. I had always taken the whole thing at face value.

What if she had arrived earlier, with no dawn to greet her? Or suppose she had left the heating element at home? Or the coffee? Suppose Thomas Chatterton lay on the bed in his garret, tearing his writing paper into confetti, preparing for death, when a friend knocked on the door. They started talking about the past few weeks, how they stood at the finish line by Shoreditch Church gates and watched a costermonger run the first four-minute mile. His name was James Parrott and they had chatted to him when he had recovered his breath. And then life did not seem so bad to Chatterton, and he thought he should just go out for a walk. It was going to be a bright, bright day. One small shift and everything changes. A young woman drives off a cliff. A young poet finds his own voice and writes again.

What if Matthew Taylor had not been there, that first evening at college? Or had been preoccupied with his wife, or the possibility of a commission from Lady Diana? No sittings, no relationship, no painting. It seemed wrong that these events might not have happened: they had been validated by history, removing the potential for things to be otherwise even before they had occurred. Chatterton had to die, so his story would end with tragedy, so his death could be romanticized, so Wallis could paint him. Penelope had to kiss Taylor, had to give herself to him—or have him give himself to her—and then sit for him, weave Diana into their arrangement, even if she never saw the future before it happened, even if Diana always did.

Those first few weeks of sittings must have been awkward. Penelope arrived early, before Diana, on every occasion. She must have been breathless, tousled when her friend joined her, but the diaries never mentioned the two women having any conversation about Penny's physicality. Taylor showed nothing of her dishevelment in the painting.

I had my Penelope in the green dress, who looked out at me like Erinna in her garden, wanting answers. She was Olivia, and Diana was her Thomas, unless that was a trivial reading of the painting, too driven by the imposed narrative from which Taylor longed to escape. So, Penelope and Diana were on a bed, telling whatever story I wanted them to tell, or telling me something I was supposed to understand but could not, or asking me to write their history with them. Charlotte Corday was a heroine to some, a traitor to others, and that decision is forced by the paintings of her. There was no decision in Taylor's painting, no definitive tale. I wondered if reading the diaries would close off the possibilities of history even further, and if I had the right to do that.

Penelope had thought Diana insufferable for commenting that a blank canvas would provide limitless freedom, but it seemed a fair point in the light of twentieth-century art. I saw Yves Klein's *IKB 79* whilst at college. It is one of Klein's monochrome paintings, a single-colour canvas, titled for the blue of its paint: International Klein Blue, synthetic resin and ultramarine, lapis lazuli flowing with leaves under a bridge in Venice, Klein's vision of the infinite. I was with Alison, the same Alison who worked at the gallery with me, the Alison whom I would not trust with my painting. She took me to the Tate, and as I stood before the Klein, as I stood amongst visitors and speech and laughter and footsteps, she reached into her bag and handed me a cassette player, slipped the headphones over my ears. When I looked at her with questions she just nodded towards the painting and I let it fill my vision, pressed play, and everything was bathed in the hiss of a blank tape, unchanging, remorseless, the perfect shelter. Klein gave us his IKB, his blue, and Alison gave me the chance of a blue of my own, a blue which began still wrapped in its own construction, in pigment and canvas, wall and hanging, in the movement around me and the mechanics of amplification. Then I drowned and there was only colour and static, and the meaning of colour itself was lost in its constancy and the noise became silence. Sometimes I believed I had fallen asleep and was dreaming, and I blinked, hard and long, and the deliberate blackness brought back the blue and with it the sound and the there-and-then and I breathed again—gulps of air—and let myself float. Sometimes I told myself stories, sometimes memories, sometimes nothing at all. I think I cried. When the tape clicked to a halt I had been standing for half an hour and as the water seeped away, back into the surroundings, the image on the canvas was lost.

By the time Emily arrived home Penelope and I had shared Christmas dinner and I was lying asleep on the couch. She woke me with a gentle shake of my shoulder.

"Hey," she whispered. "Another hard day?"

"They're all hard days," I mumbled back, unwilling to open my eyes for an exchange which started with her beatification by work-ethic. She sat down in front of my hips and placed her hand on my head.

"I'm sorry," she said. "I've just had a hell of a time at the office."

I heard the rustle of a plastic bag, and the smell of vinegar and deep-fried food filled the room.

"Fish and chips. I thought we deserved a treat."

I opened my eyes. Emily kissed me on the cheek as I sat up. I think she expected me to turn and reciprocate but I just rubbed my eyes and assumed an air of confusion.

"What time is it?" I asked. "Shall I get plates?"

"It's half past eight, and yes. And bring some salt and tomato ketchup. I'm going to move the painting onto a chair."

"It has to stay flat, Ems."

"Then I'll put two of the chairs facing each other and lay it across them. Carefully."

I told her I would do it whilst she went to the kitchen. I was usually drawn in by Penelope, but as I lifted the canvas it was Diana who gained my attention. I knew Penelope from her diaries, knew more than just the facts of her name and age and address. But Diana remained somehow aloof, as though she had meticulously crafted both the person she was and the person she allowed the world to see. There, in the painting, she was disguised, dressed as a man, half her face hidden from view. In the Galleries she had chosen to be Melpomene, and by her hip the mask of Tragedy, the symbol of the Muse. And to me the mask seemed to gain a reality and Diana took her part in Allori's *Judith with the Head of Holofernes*. Diana as Judith, holding a severed head, set against her gold-yellow robes, cut off to save her besieged people from an Assyrian attack, cut off after she had seduced the general and filled him with wine. And the face at her thigh is that of Cristofano Allori himself, and Judith is his lover, and the ever-present maid her mother, perhaps, if biographers are to be believed. Of all the copies of the painting, Diana was the Judith of the Palatina Gallery in Florence, because of the eyes, the eyes of one who has seen horror, and whose lids speak of both resignation and defiance. But then, Judith is triumphant and Diana held only Tragedy by her hip, so perhaps there was only resignation in her eyes.

When Emily returned I still had the painting in my arms, lost in it. It fell to her to arrange the chairs. She brought pills with the ketchup.

Over dinner I told Emily that she had been right about the picture's being of two women, and told her about Penelope and Diana, and Taylor and Taylor's wife. She asked what happened at the end of the story and I told her again that I had not reached the end and that she was a lawyer. Our focus shifted to the food in front of us and the cottage sat quietly but for the ringing taps of knives on plates and the creak of chairs. Soon the plates were empty compositions of white, silver and red: Piet Mondrian rendering colour blocks in condiments. We began to talk again, with details of the day's activities and weather reports.

"Tomorrow I'm going to Barbroke," I said, gathering up the plates.
"Barbroke?"
I answered as I headed towards the kitchen.
"Diana's home. It's near here. There's a bus."
Emily followed me and leaned against the wall as I ran water into the bowl and added a squirt of washing-up liquid. We continued over scraping and suds.
"But why go there?" she asked.
"Well, Diana, Lady Diana, is a bit of a mystery to me. I don't know who she is, really."
"Do you need to know?"
"Yes. Yes, I think so. Penelope's about to spend the New Year with

her, at Barbroke, and I want to be there, too, to read what happens. Don't you think that's exciting?"

"I suppose. Wouldn't you rather wait until the weekend? I'll go with you. We can take the car. It's much easier."

I was prepared for Emily's suggestion. She was always sure that if mistakes were to be made then I was the one to make them. Her adopted role was she-who-picked-up-the-pieces, so she sought to pre-empt any opportunity for misfortune. She watched my hands moving in the cloudy water and I knew she was thinking about the sink at home and the tap running, the red spirals like raspberry-swirls in porcelain ice cream, pointillist poppy-heads at the margins. She never ran the film backwards, to before those frames, to causes, accusations, arguments. For her, the bathroom scene made us both victims of me, all previous sins forgotten. So I kept saying I was sorry and she kept telling me there was no need to apologize, all the while beseeching an apology.

"I thought about that, Ems," I replied. "It'll be really busy at the weekend, and you'll be bored. I'm going to be sitting reading from the diary for ages. It's just a short bus ride."

Emily dried a plate with a mauve-striped towel.

"Okay," she said.

"I'll leave after you in the morning. Be back before you're home. You won't even know I've been gone." Just like all the times I did not even know she had been gone.

"You'll have to tell me all about it when I get home, then."

She put down the plate and towel, and gave me a hug.

"I need to do some paperwork," she said. "Just disturb me if you want me."

I did not want her, not that evening. Purple, yellow.

Everything was white. The snow had started during the night, whilst Emily and I slept, or whilst I slept, at least. Emily often stayed up, working. Occasionally I woke to the sound of her talking on the telephone, too quietly to hear individual words, and she always told me it was America, and the time difference made it necessary, and I should be sleeping, and she said goodnight and kissed me on the forehead as though I were a child, and perhaps I was. And in the morning everything was white.

Emily was leaving as I came downstairs. She suggested I postpone my trip but I could hear the cars out on the High Street, and see little patches of stone cake showing through the icing on the garden wall. I shrugged and wandered off to make a cup of coffee, to the slamming of the front door and a fragile crunching as Emily made her way down the path.

The bus left from outside the Café of Our Little Round Lady and took about thirty minutes to get to Barbroke village, another Cotswold collection of postcard cottages with thatched roofs, a post office which sold souvenir tea towels, and an antique shop with the blinds down. "Reopening in January," read a note on the shop door, although it could have been years old: the shop could have closed during the war and never reopened. By the single road running through the village, just past a straggling pub, two gatehouses stood either side of a driveway which turned to the north. One of them had the appearance of a home whilst the other lacked roof and windows. In front of the derelict shell I found a green sign with gold lettering. Ahead, it told passers-by, lay Barbroke, family seat of the Fitzpatricks, which could be enjoyed for £4.50 on any day of the week during the spring and summer months, or Thursday to Saturday during autumn and winter. The text was accompanied by a sun-bleached sketch of a stately home, which did little to raise the spirits.

I took the diary from my satchel and opened it at a bookmark made from an old envelope: the day of Penelope's arrival. She did not have much to say. The train from London "had progressed at a snail's pace" and it was late at night by the time the carriage met her at the station and took her to the house, where Diana was waiting. Cook had a supper prepared for her, which she ate at the kitchen table with Diana, and then she went to bed, pausing only to write a few blunt sentences. The approach to the house was mine to discover.

As I passed close to the habitable gatehouse the front door opened and an old man stepped out, smoking a pipe. He took it from his mouth and pointed the stem along the driveway.

"Won't be open while another forty minutes or so."

"Well, I suppose the walk will take me a little while. I shan't hurry."

"You can stop at chapel. They open it early. Stop on way to the big house in mornings, and on way back."

"Thank you. I'll do that. It must be warmer in there than out here."

"Not much."

He retreated into the house.

"Nice to meet you. Thank you," I said, but I was talking to a closed door.

The curve of the approach quickly straightened and I found myself walking down a wide avenue towards a free-standing, stone triumphal arch, about half a mile away. On either side, visible through the bleached branches of trees, the landscape lay beneath a tenuous mist. The arch was oddly out of place in the quiet morning of Barbroke, asking me to look upon it and despair whilst the lone and level fields stretched far away. I had thought that it would frame the house, but the ground sloped upwards for another few hundred yards before dropping out of sight. It left behind a view of distant hills, pale in the sallow sun, dissolving into the avenue as though I had caught them in their march to the village behind me.

A red-brick wall marked the edge of a graveyard with a vernacular parish church at its centre. A weathered sign read, "Church of Saint Cecilia," and gave the times of services, which were held on the first and third Sundays of the month. If the doors were locked, it informed the would-be palmer, then the keys could be found with Mrs Tompkins, who ran the ticket office at Barbroke and could be contacted by telephone. The accompanying number had too few digits to have been updated within the past twenty years. A piece of paper, wrapped in plastic and fastened with drawing pins, made it abundantly clear that the building and cemetery were not the property of the estate. I passed through a rusting metal gate which filled the world with its shrieking, and walked down the short path between the graves.

The church was made of the same pale stone as the arch, but

weathering and hints of Norman architecture showed it to be much older. The man at the gatehouse had been right: the roof was still white with snow. I gave up hope of finding much warmth within.

Inside, the air hung still and expectant and swallowed up the sound of my footsteps on the worn paving slabs. Carved mediæval figures in loose-fitting robes marched around the base of the font which stood to my left. Its elaborate wooden cover was attached to the roof beams by a system of ropes and pulleys which ended in a complex, improvised knot tied around a metal peg in the door jamb. Next to the peg, set into the wall, a rusted metal box clasped a modern padlock beneath a small hole for donations. My twenty-pence piece made a hollow clank, its fall unbroken by other coins. A faded, black-and-white copy of Edward Burne-Jones's *Saint Cecilia* hid beneath the mottled glass of a cheap frame. In the half-light the background blurred to a smudge of ink, losing all the beauty of the stained-glass original. Only the lighter parts of Cecilia's gown and the small pipe-organ she was playing showed with any degree of clarity.

Magazines and leaflets rested on top of a bookcase of hymnals. They covered news from other churches in the area and charitable initiatives by the Church of England. A photocopied sheet, worth a suggested donation of ten pence, described the history of the church. Built in the early twelfth century, restored and extended at least once in every century since then, it was the only remnant of the original village of Barbroke. The homes which used to surround it were demolished during the construction of Barbroke House in the middle of the eighteenth century. The Fitzpatricks had rehoused the villagers, out of sight, away from the summit of the rise which lay to the south of their property. The church was still used by the locals and had been used by the Fitzpatricks, too: their box-pew could be seen at the front of the nave, overlooked by the pulpit to the left of the chancel.

The north side of the church had been extended to create an additional aisle, separated from the central space by an arcade. Between each pair of arches, in the spandrel at the top of the supporting pillar, hung a hatchment bearing the coat of arms of some past earl. The external wall of the aisle provided the backdrop for a series of chest tombs, each with a marble figure lying on top. The earliest and largest of these—the tomb of George, First Earl of Barbroke—occupied the middle position. On either side of George the tombs became increasingly recent. I walked to the western end. There was Albert, Diana's brother, killed in action in Burma in 1885.

A small sanctuary stood at the eastern end of the aisle: a raised footpace bearing an uncovered table. The table was dressed with the melted remains of two candles, in plain holders, and an unadorned brass cross. Behind it, acting as a reredos on the east wall, hung a large painting of Saint Cecilia holding a violin and looking heavenwards: a copy of a seventeenth-century original by Guido Reni. A pair of frayed red-velvet kneelers gathered dust in the corner. And there, beside them, the last of the Fitzpatrick chest tombs bore the date 1892, and a few lines attributed to Swinburne. I read them aloud to myself, quietly and without echo.

"Is it worth a tear, is it worth an hour,
    To think of things that are well outworn?
Of fruitless husk and fugitive flower,
    The dream foregone and the deed forborne?
Though joy be done with and grief be vain,
Time shall not sever us wholly in twain;
Earth is not spoilt for a single shower;
    But the rain has ruined the ungrown corn."

Diana lay in cold white, her head on a carved pillow with tassels at each corner which fell gently to the marble beneath. Her face, unlike those of her companions, was turned towards the nave. Delicate locks of hair curled from beneath her left cheek onto pillow and shoulder. Where the earlier sculptures presented attitudes of determination and resolve, Diana's eyes were closed and her mouth relaxed, peaceful. She had lost all her colour in death. Her right hand rested on her stomach, holding a book, closed but for the separation of pages on either side of the index finger which parted them, endlessly keeping her place, halfway, unfinished. Her left hand had fallen by her side, still clutched around the handle of an oval hand-mirror. Its glass pressed unseen against the folds of her gown, a hidden truth. Bas-relief flowers grew from the handle across the surface of its back. I had never doubted that Diana was dead, but I felt a sadness which arose from her having had so little life.

I sat on the floor, with my back against the end of a pew, pulled my knees up to my chest, wrapped my arms around them and hugged myself as I looked up at Diana. Algernon Charles Swinburne and James Whistler. Three "Symphonies in White", each one painted by Whistler, and the first just a woman in a white dress standing on a tiger-skin rug before a white curtain, but still rejected by the Academy in London and the Salon in Paris. The third accepted by the Academy, and the last of his paintings to use his lover as a model, and she another Jo H. but Hiffernan not Hopper. And the second, a woman in white standing by the hearth with one arm on the mantelpiece, and gazing into a mirror like Velázquez's Venus, so some say the reference was intentional. Swinburne, then, a poet who saw the second *Symphony* and wrote a poem, "Before the Mirror", which Whistler loved enough to paste onto the painting's frame. And in the church, in the cold, I could remember only a fragment that came to me with the white of the marble. "Soft snows that hard winds harden, Till each flake bite, Fill all the flowerless garden." Swinburne—Swinburne, friend and downfall of Simeon Solomon; who wrote of Solomon's blending the lineaments of woman and of man; whose poem "Anactoria" led Solomon to paint Sappho and Erinna in their garden; who turned against his friend, calling Solomon "a thing unmentionable", "abhorrent to the very beasts"—Swinburne must have been Diana's own choice, because who else would choose him, with his poems causing outrage, with his decadence, with his lesbianism and necrophilia and all? She chose him, and how could she be refused a dying wish? Swinburne wrote his "Hermaphroditus" on seeing the *Borghese Hermaphrodite* in the Louvre, and so the thread ran back to Velázquez, and Turner and Rokeby, and on, on to Swinburne's friend Burne-Jones, just plain Ned Jones when they met at Oxford, yet to create his "Cecilia of the Cheap-Framed Copy". Diana, surrounded by these lives, but having no real part in them, and at the centre of Taylor's painting through Penelope and with Penelope. Taylor and Penelope and Diana. Diana, the third symphony. And Emily and I, but then I should be the second, always the second, and he the unwanted third. I realized I was crying, quietly, secretly, hiding it from myself. Swinburne must have cried when his friend died: not Solomon—probably not Solomon—but Lizzie Siddal, poor Lizzie Siddal; for her he must have shed his tears.

I looked again at the ten-pence photocopied sheet to see if I had missed anything about the tomb, about Diana. There was nothing. These were the Fitzpatricks of Barbroke, and there was nothing more to be said, and I wondered if perhaps the pain of forced resettlement remained after all these years, a legacy of appropriation and class distinction. When I closed the door behind me the echo remained, trapped with Diana.

The sun had appeared whilst I was inside. I had noticed the change, fades of clouds coming and going, diffuse variations internalized by the fabric of the place, as though the church were replaying past illuminations as it pleased, to whatever effect it sought, for whatever audience it possessed. It seemed only natural. Outside, though, the brightness was stark and shocking and the day felt later than it ought.

I left the arch behind and walked slowly towards the house, just out of sight over the rise of the gentle slope ahead. Only once did I hear anything other than the crunch of my footsteps, the flap of wings, the susurration of frost falling from naked boughs. I turned, expecting to see a car approaching, but the avenue remained empty and I was puzzled until I noticed a van passing the entrance by the little house with the old man, heading along the road to the village.

From the summit of the rise the approach arced gently downwards and to the east, crossing an ornamental lake before turning again to the west to arrive at the front of the house. The grey-blue of the sky, the snow, and the stones of the building blended in the sunlight as though the whole scene were captured in a faded photograph. Only the clouds of my own breath brought movement and reality. I walked on, letting the cold convince me of my own presence. The trees left the sides of the avenue, giving way to sullen winter grasses and a brick building which looked to be part of an old stable block. A sandwich-board by the door was dressed in the same green and gold as the sign by the gatehouses. It entreated me, politely, to enter and buy a ticket, should I wish to go any farther into the picture ahead of me.

The ticket office was a sparse affair, a small room with a cheap bookcase against one wall and a table towards the rear. Behind the table sat a thinner version of the café's Woman in Tweed Uniform. She looked old enough to be the Mrs Tompkins of the church's sign, still waiting for a caller demanding the keys to the church, even after all these years. A Bakelite radio was playing something baroque. The sound of the door had caused the woman to look up from her paperback novel. It rested, open, on the table, with words pressed onto scratched wood and the cover upwards, adding a splash of pastel pinks and greens to the room. She spoke.

"Hello dear. Did you want a ticket for the house or just the gardens? It's four pounds and fifty pence for both. Two pounds for just the gardens."

"Hello," I said. "Is it possible to get a ticket for the house alone?"

Table Lady gave me a look which I ascribed to some blend of disappointment and pity, as if I had just told her that I had failed to get the exam results I needed for a place at university. She gestured towards a set of uninspiring leaflets on the bookcase.

"Oh, you wouldn't want to do that, dear. Barbroke is famous for its gardens. Always has been, since the eighteenth century. There's bits of Capability Brown all over it, if you take my meaning. And the autumn colours. But you're too late for those."

I handed over a five-pound note, receiving in return a printed ticket that looked like it came from a cloakroom and a handful of coins from a black tin kept under the woman's chair, for security, presumably.

"Take one of the white leaflets for the garden and a blue for the house, dear," Table Lady said as I turned to go.

I thought about asking her if her name was Tompkins, but she had the air of someone who was longing to perform, if only the opportunity arose. I decided I would be letting myself in for an hour of sciatica, and widowhood, and probably something to do with the requisitioning of the house during the war. So, instead, I thanked her, picked up the leaflets and returned to the white with the sound of Vivaldi's "Summer" fading behind me.

Table Lady was not wrong about the gardens, judging by the map in the leaflet. They were laid out as a relic of some forgotten eclogue. Pillars and urns brought Poussin to life through the death of those worthy of remembrance. Clothed in snow the territory was the map: shadows and stone translated to cross-hatches and lines, with only scale to differentiate between what I held in my hand and what lay before me. The little information which the leaflet provided left me with room to create my own stories. I had the names of landscape features and statues and buildings. I had the arrangement, the physicality, but I had no truth of them. The white world was my Klein Blue and I would find its reality in the silence, and its meaning in the sheltering voices of Penelope and Diana.

The approach passed through a break in a stone ha-ha which continued outwards to left and right and curved until lost to me. I walked between two more gatehouses, both in a state of mortal disrepair, and crossed over the lake on a weathered, three-arched, stone bridge. A series of carved urns punctuated its parapets. They looked out of place, an architectural afterthought, their incongruity amplified by their refusal to adopt the winter shading of the bridge. A few paces beyond the lake a path led off to the right, where a wooden arrow nailed to a tree suggested I would find "The Grotto" and "The Temple of Minerva". The temple was only a few yards from the main approach. A flight of three stone steps led up to four Ionic pillars which supported an unadorned pediment beneath a sloping roof. The row of pillars defined the front of a single room, with a bench against its back wall and niches on the two sidewalls. The niches, according to the leaflet, once held statues of Minerva, in a time when the plain, white walls were covered in murals depicting her victory over Ignorance.

I sat down on the bench and pulled a sandwich from my bag, eating it whilst taking in the view, first down the length of the lake and then up towards the house, partially obscured by trees. I could make out twin staircases. They reached upwards to a neo-classical frontage both elegant and awash with overstatement.

The snow had decided to fall again, gently but immodestly. Straying flakes danced through the pillars of the temple and fell on too-warm stone, vanishing as soon as they found the audacity to touch it, like the snows of Gourmont's "*Danaette*"—feathers from the wings of angels— crossing a window-frame threshold to caress their waiting adulteress. At Barbroke, that day, they returned to seek their advantage. I closed my bag and walked out, into the white, into Whistler and colourless blue, following Penelope and Diana's footprints up to the house at the end of the avenue.

CHAPTER FOURTEEN

Friday, 30th December, 1887

Today has dawned with a brightness that was not to be expected from yesterday's portentous clouds and flurries of snow. From my bedroom window I can see across that part of the estate which lies to the south of the house. There is a lake some distance away, which we must have crossed in the darkness, but which came as a surprise to me on opening my curtains this morning. There are small areas of woodland, and miniature facsimiles of temples in the Græco-Roman style. Two monuments remind me of the London Obelisk, and seeing it with Father, newly erected by the Thames: "A needle with no hole for thread," he said. Everything is blanched except for the lake.

This morning I expect to meet Lord and Lady Barbroke. Diana told me last night that her younger brother, Peter—the Viscount, now, I suppose—has been staying with friends and will not be with us until this afternoon. We made no plans for today, but I am hopeful that I shall see a little of this wonderful house and its grounds.

I want to write the events of this morning in some form of shorthand, that I might tell all as quickly as possible. However, I find myself sitting in pleasant surroundings, alone, and with no prospect of company for an hour or two. Thus, I have decided to make something of an exercise from the entry, and describe each thing in its fullest measure. If the only companionship I am to enjoy is my own then I shall make the best of it and keep a record fit to relate to Matthew when at last I can see him.

Breakfast was a grand affair, served in a room at the rear of the house. The walls are decorated with murals depicting scenes from Shakespeare. I ate toast and kedgeree beneath a bank where the wild thyme grows and Titania sleeps. Lady Barbroke told me that she commissioned the pieces to brighten the room, which had been ignored for some years and had grown, in her words, "devilishly melancholic."

Lord Barbroke has been called away to some business in the village and intends to stay there until his son arrives at the station, so they may return together. Thus it was that our party was reduced to three this morning. Diana seemed happy to allow her mother to hold the conversation. I did not mind this arrangement: the Countess was delightful company and as far from airs and graces—which she might so naturally assume—as Diana herself. She expressed the hope that I should not be too bored at the house over the next few days, and I assured her that I should not. I must, she told me, see the library, and the grounds—if the weather remained favourable—and the Bernini. Diana interjected that the Bernini was only a copy, to which her mother replied, "But of course it is, darling. Who would think otherwise?" So saying, Lady Barbroke subjected her daughter to the briefest of grave stares. Diana, in turn, looked at me with a slightly wide-eyed exasperation and muttered, under her breath but loudly enough for me to hear, "Great-great-grandfather." Then she addressed her mother: of course she planned to "show me the sights"; she was quite capable of entertaining a guest. Lady Barbroke's only reply was a weary nod of the head.

After breakfast the Countess retired to her private rooms to catch up on correspondence and Diana and I were left alone. She was distracted as we walked through to the main staircase and at the bottom step she turned and explained that she was feeling a little "all-overish" and would like to sleep a while. She asked if I should not mind spending time alone, and told me I should feel free to enjoy the house. If I needed anything then I had only to press the bell by any of the doors. I nodded my unavoidable acquiescence but then, as she ascended the gently curling staircase, I called out after her, asking that she show me the way to the library, at least. She beckoned me to follow.

On the landing at the top of the stairs a short, oak-panelled hall ends in a heavy door with brass fittings. Diana pointed and told me that it would not be locked, but the bookcases inside might be, and the keys were to be found underneath Socrates. She withdrew to her rooms with my "thank you" hardly out of my mouth. I opened the door and light flooded over me.

The library runs almost the entire length of the east wing of the house. On the south side the windows stretch from waist-height to within a foot of the high, ivory ceiling. Half-way up the remaining walls there extends a thin, oak balcony, supported at intervals by plain, stone corbels. The balcony is connected to the floor by a pair of cast-iron, spiral staircases, one at each end of the room. At the east a third spiral staircase—this one possessed of a wooden handrail— descends through the floor, disappearing into the gallery below. Apart from the south wall every inch is covered in bookcases, and every bookcase is filled with titles. Each case is identified at its top by skilfully executed numerals, in gold paint with a black outline, according to its location within the room. Below the balcony the cases are closed, some with glass fronts and others with an open-work of brass wires. Above the balcony the books appear more recent in date and less ornately bound, and here the shelves are open. For a while I circled the room, moving from case to case, reading the spines of the books: astronomy, medicine, a large section given over to the fine arts, literature, poetry.

Beneath one of the windows is a small oak desk, on which there sits an inlaid walnut box and, beside it, a marble bust with "ΣΩΚΡΑΤΗΣ" carved into its base. If one lifts the bust one finds the keys to the cases, just as Diana had said. Inside the box is a card catalogue, with each card bearing the number of a particular bookcase. On some cards the subject has been written beside this number, and occasionally struck through and rewritten in the course of some historical rearrangement. The rest of each card is taken up by a list of the books to be found on the shelves of its case: the books are not given in any particular order, but there are few enough of them in each case for this index to be somewhat useful. The book lists, too, are full of crossings-out and postils. Several entries announce a book "lost" or "lent but not returned".

I glanced through the cards and stopped at case 23, which was recorded as containing literature of the seventeenth century. In truth the list was a curious mixture of scientific and historical reports, descriptions of court proceedings, and the inevitable collection of Civil War pamphlets, both for and against the monarchy. I was about to replace the card and continue my tour with a perusal of the cases on the balcony when I noticed, written in faded brown ink, an entry reading, "Wrb, S., Ye Straunge &c." It seemed to me to be an impossibility, that this might be the very same book that now informs our painting.

Case 23 is at the east end of the room. I walked over to it with the card in one hand and the Socratic keys in the other. I peered through the glass, from book to book, to see if I could see the title which I sought, but I could not. Throughout the library many volumes have nothing written on their spines, and the thinner ones are collected together in green, cloth-covered boxes with cryptic, faded or illegible paper labels. The fourth key, of the seven which I held, unlocked the case and I began my search in earnest. I thought it unlikely that the book, were it the Warber, would be so thin as to merit inclusion in one of the boxes and so I began by methodically removing and examining those books which I could not identify by their spines alone. There are, it is true, some interesting works amongst them, but not one has been authored by Samuel Warber.

I found one of the cloth-covered boxes to be smaller than the others, and I decided that this would constitute the next object of my search. I was not disappointed for, on opening it, I was greeted by the sight of a leather-bound volume, roughly the same size as that belonging to Father. I opened the front cover without lifting it from the box, and saw there, on the title page, "Ye Straunge Hystory of Thomysin & Oliuia" and the name of the author, "Samuel Warber". This would be a worthy enough discovery for a day of gentle diversions, but then I saw the date of the book. It is there, at the bottom of the title page, in red ink, next to "London": 1670. This is a first edition of Warber, an original printing, quite possibly the only one in existence.

I sat down at a nearby desk, where the tall windows overlook the landscape. The sheep appeared as moving hummocks of snow in the distance. Slowly and with much care I lifted the book from its container but, before I had a chance to examine the prize itself, I exposed the items which it had previously hidden, secreted in a compartment beneath. A faded-green, silk bow holds a lock of hair—each strand is no longer than my thumb—its hue somewhere between brown and red, varying with the light which falls upon it. It rests on a pamphlet, which I removed, placing the delicate strands to one side. I copied down its title in my small note-book: "THE CONFESSION AND EXECUTION Of the Seven Prisoners suffering at TYBURN on Wednesday the 25th of October, 1676. VIZ. John Seabrooke, Arthur Minors, William Minors, Henry Graves, Richard Shaw, Katherine Picket, Samuel Warber."

I long to write more at this point, but a footman has just appeared and informed me that luncheon is shortly to be served in the mural room. He offered to escort me, but I assured him that I knew the way and should be there forthwith. Suffice to say that the pamphlet is the record of Warber's hanging. I shall return to it after the meal and make notes.

I was mistaken in thinking that I should spend more time in the library, for it is now quite late and I am writing before I sleep, having been otherwise occupied the whole of the remainder of the day, without any chance of return.

Diana and I lunched in the mural room. Lady Barbroke ate alone, sending her apologies: she was unavoidably detained with pressing affairs of the estate but looked forward to my company at dinner. I told Diana about my marvellous find in the library. She expressed an interest but seemed far less eager to share in my excitement than I had imagined she would be. She continued to clothe herself in an air of distracted preoccupation, but I felt it inappropriate to request an explanation or—to be more accurate—her countenance suggested that an explanation would not be forthcoming, however appropriate the request.

As lunch proceeded I was preparing myself for the news that she wished to abscond to her rooms, so I was most pleased when she asked if I should like to take a tour of the grounds with her. She glanced out of the window and told me that she had spare furs and boots, so I need not worry about the cold. Now, writing with an understanding of her reasons for wanting my company, I can see that the invitation was perfectly in keeping with her demeanour.

Suitably attired we walked south from the house, down towards the lake, on a curving path which took us past one of the monuments visible from the window of my bedroom: a tall, fluted column, with a carved ship at its top and a square pedestal for support. The lettering on the front of the pedestal—I assume it is the front as it falls beneath the prow of the ship—informs the reader that it is a celebration of the victory at Trafalgar, and a memorial to Nelson himself. To the rear, a second inscription gives the famous flag signal and, beneath that, the words, "They did their duty." Diana said that she had never cared for it, and thought it common-looking, but she said it with a smile, the first I had seen since my arrival. Then she clapped her hands together and walked off at a pace, down the gentle slope.

The northern bank of the lake stretched away on either side of us as we reached the end of the path. To our right lay a small island, linking two snow-dusted, wooden bridges to create a passage to the opposite bank. Farther to the west the ground quickly turned from open grass to woodland, and arching branches dipped down into the water at intervals. Eastwards, the landscape was all gentle drumlins of snow. There was a row-boat tied to a post a few yards away and, in the near-distance, a stone bridge, half-lost in mist, faded from existence before it reached the water. I must have crossed it by carriage on my arrival. At the waterside a thin layer of ice trapped roaming bubbles of air, and held dead reeds in place by their stems.

Diana made for the island. I followed, pulling my collar tight around my neck as the sun weakened above gathering clouds and the cold began to bite. On the island there stands a finely sculpted urn dedicated to Alexander Pope, with lines from his "Ode on Saint Cecilia's Day". They tell of Cecilia's having more power than Orpheus, as he only raised shades from hell whilst she lifts souls to heaven. Diana was already across the second bridge as I finished reading, and she called to me to hurry before the snow started to fall. It was too late: the first flakes appeared as I joined her by a pair of gatehouses and we looked away to the south, along a length of the main drive from the village. I wanted to ask her where she was taking me, but the fact that she had thus far chosen not to tell me gave me to think that there was little to be gained in the asking, and possibly much to lose, given the inconstancy of her temperament.

We passed through a ha-ha, which I had not seen from the house—that being the nature of a ha-ha, of course—and on, past a stable block, until we reached the wall of a churchyard. It is a pretty little thing, the church, and all the more so when clad in its winter finery. Inside, in the half-light, Diana walked across the nave to a line of arches. Each arch holds a pair of dark red, velvet curtains, separating the congregation from the family tombs of the Fitzpatricks. She parted the curtain on the far left and walked through, holding the curtain for me. Then, saying nothing, she walked away, back to the nave, leaving me alone. There before me, on the floor, was a marble sculpture of a young man in military uniform, lying on his back with his hands resting, one on the other, low on his stomach. Behind this figure, beneath a mullioned window, the four slab-walls of an unbuilt chest tomb leaned against the stonework of the church. I saw, propped against them, an inscribed plaque which memorialized Diana's brother. An area of the floor lay separated by the cleanness of its herring-bone brickwork and the brightness of its mortar. Diana has sat near this spot each Sunday since returning from Oxford, and at Christmas services, knowing what was hidden by curtain and brick, and what she must face in some horrid ceremony to come, when the tomb will be completed and the family will sanctify their loss once more. It was only with the greatest effort that I fought back my tears. I walked along the line of tombs, composing myself in readiness for Diana. Albert's tomb will be the penultimate one against the wall: there is one remaining space, beside the little altar at the other end of the row, doubtless reserved for the current Earl and his wife.

Diana was waiting for me in the porch of the church. I told her that I understood, and she nodded and took my hand. We walked, still hand in hand, back towards the house. This time we followed the route of last night's carriage ride, round to the right as we approached the lake and over the stone bridge. Diana was more talkative now, as though sharing her sadness had taken some of it from her. She asked me what I thought of Pope—I told her I had not formed much of an opinion— and then she drew out a leather-bound pocket-book, in which she has copied some stanzas from Swinburne's *Poems and Ballads*. These, she said, are verses I ought to come to know and appreciate: students at the Universities used to recite them from memory in moonlit college quadrangles. She told me it was withdrawn from circulation shortly after its first being published, and asked if that brought to mind any interest of mine. It did, of course, and I remembered making the connection in the autumn, when she and I spoke of our passion for poetry, and when I was too nervous to share my thoughts. One review, Diana said, described Swinburne as "the libidinous laureate of a pack of satyrs." How, she asked, could one not love the work of a man of whom such words were written? Then, for a few care-free seconds, her laughter cut through the surrounding tranquillity.

We crossed the bridge and broke from the main approach, turning to the east and following the path past some sort of miniature temple, until we stopped before a curious rock- and shell-encrusted, low building which sits above a small cascade. This, according to Diana, is supposed to represent the home of an anchorite, a sage to whom one could turn for wisdom. It is no such thing, it goes without saying. Nevertheless, even this elaborate folly adds a certain character to what is an already picturesque scene of trees and rill. Inside the "grotto" the little light which there is—particularly on overcast winter days like today—comes from an arched opening above the tumbling waters. It affords a perfect view down towards the lake. Diana explained that the gardens are laid out in two halves, split roughly along a line running from the front entrance of the house, across the water and between the gatehouses. The western gardens represent love and life, whilst the eastern, in which we then stood, are an allegory of learning and death. She should have liked to take me to the west, she told me, but the monuments there afford a lesser degree of shelter from the elements. I asked her if she might like to read some poetry to me as we admired the view. "Not here," she said. She took my hand again and we retraced our steps.

When we reached the temple Diana sat, at once, on a bench against the back wall, whilst I admired the murals. They portray a set of scenes in which a woman, dressed as a warrior, overcomes a much larger male opponent, amidst some tumult and a considerable entourage of admiring putti. It is all a little too florid for my liking and stands in sharp contrast to the grace of the two statues of Minerva—according to their pedestals—which rest in wall-niches on either side of the temple. In one niche she is portrayed aloof, in a military helmet and breastplate, a spear in her hand. In the other she is a more gentle figure, resting on the stump of a tree, holding a small owl before her.

Diana called my name and took out the pocket-book. This, she said, was the place for Swinburne, and the weather was perfect. The snow was falling heavily now, so one could only just perceive the geese on the banks of the lake, and the house, twice as far away, was as good as lost to us. We sat close together, for warmth and fellowship, and I listened as she read.

Suddenly I realize that I am no longer recording events for Mr. Taylor, but for myself. I have the Swinburne book with me now, as I write: not Diana's hand-copied poems but the published edition, bound in green cloth with gold lettering to the spine, entrusted to me by Diana when we returned to the house. In the temple she read "Dolores", slowly and with a measured lilt which muffled the world around and drew me to her words.

In the hall near my room there is a painting, titled on its gilt frame as *Landscape with the Fall of Icarus* by Pieter Bruegel the Elder. All one sees of Icarus are a few feathers drifting down from on high and a pair of legs protruding from a great splash upon the surface of the sea. He has fallen already: his waxen wings are melted, the drop is over. The other denizens of the painting pay him no heed: a sailor climbs the rigging of a galleon in the middle distance; the ploughman plods his weary way along the neat line of a neighbouring furrow; an angler casts his line and watches for a bite; the shepherd waits by his flock and gazes upwards in thought. Icarus is lost, lost to all he knew, lost to the blue which envelops him. And in the temple today, in the blue-white and the moment, I turned and laid my head on Diana's lap and rested my feet on the arm of the bench, and the snow fell and the words fell and I let my eyelids close. When she whispered, "Like lovers they melted and tingled," her breath was warm on my ear and I turned my head and met her lips and did not dare open my eyes to see her, not then; not then, when to add anything would be to take something away. Then her hand, removing my hat, and fingers running through my hair, and her voice stronger and more distant as she straightened her back and read on.

"Was it Alciphron once or Arisbe,
    Male ringlets or feminine gold,
That thy lips met with under the statue..."

I need write no more to remember the temple.

We walked back, across the clean, white grass in front of the house, with no care to find a path to guide us. Diana told me about *Buffalo Bill's Wild West*, which she had seen in May. Of the sharpshooters, she said she preferred Annie Oakley to Lillian Smith, finding the younger woman "dreadfully *déclassée* without ever having been *classée* in the first place." We had reached the door. Diana kissed me on the cheek— no more than a brush of the lips against my skin—and then we were inside. A new voice—new to me at least—greeted us, causing Diana to rush through the hall, dropping her hat and gloves behind her, with a cry of, "Peter!" I followed, more slowly, wondering what I ought to do with my winter wear until a maid appeared from nowhere and held out her arms to receive coat, scarf, and all.

The brother is, I suppose, handsome. Certainly, he is well mannered and an adequate, if reticent, conversationalist. He has something of the look of his father, with whom he returned this afternoon: well-formed features, in decent proportions, with the slightest heaviness to them, as though worn knowingly as part of the accoutrements of the aristocracy.

I dined with the entirety of the family for the first time since my arrival. Dinner was an enjoyable experience, but I was lost in the remembrances of the day past and glad to retire to my room a little earlier than usual, claiming a weariness born of yesterday's journey and the exertions of an expedition in the cold weather.

I keep closing my eyes and remembering the sensations of the afternoon: the chill of the snows, the warmth of her lips. Where I had supposed that apprehension would rush in, I find only excitement, as if I were arriving at some mysterious destination and saw ahead only the possibility of wonderful things.

Now there comes a tapping—she is gently rapping at my chamber door—and I must put down my pen.

Chapter Fifteen

I sat reading the diary in the warmth of the house, perched on a marble bench just inside a long gallery which ran east from the entrance hall. At the far end I could see a spiral staircase disappear into the room above. The blue leaflet confirmed that I was beneath the library.

I thought of the lock of hair, pressed between the leaves of a guidebook, back at the cottage. It did not belong to Penny. She had been growing ever closer to me, through her diaries and my presence at Barbroke, but she took a step away with the strands in their ribbon and hid herself, just a little. I wondered how the hair had ended up in Taylor's possession; how he had acquired any of Penelope's belongings, for that matter.

The house was virtually empty. As far as I could tell I was sharing it with one or two members of staff and nobody else. The marble bench seemed part of the building itself, out of bounds and only to be appreciated at a distance. Yet I was visible to the man who hovered in the entrance hall, keeping watch over the ground floor, and he said nothing to me, and gave no sign that I should stand. So I sat opposite a space once occupied by *The Blessed Ludovica Albertoni*. The statue had long-since been replaced by a photograph of the original: Ludovica, a sixteenth-century nun, lay in Rome, safe in the Church of San Francesco a Ripa. I looked up at the photograph from time to time as I read, recalling the work of the sculptor and wondering how good the Barbroke copy must have been to fool Diana's ancestor. In all probability it was not particularly accomplished: if great-great-grandfather wanted a Bernini then a Bernini it was.

The kiss in the temple was not the inevitable course of my imagined narrative, but its occurence made me realize that had it never happened I would have felt cheated, a victim of a peculiar *Weltschmerz*. The Bruegel, however, was an unexpected twist. I had stopped reading when Penny described it to me. The man in the hall knew nothing of the painting. He told me that most of the artwork had been removed during the war and little had been returned; told me that the long gallery held all there was to be seen; and no, the other walls were bare; and no, the private areas were empty or estate offices; and no, there was nobody else who might help. He seemed to resent my caring, as though it threw his own listlessness into the light, gave him his own reasons to hate reality, or caused him to be struck by his own, half-hidden disappointments. I had returned to my spot on the marble bench and he had returned to his coffee.

The Bruegel was interesting because it ought not to have been there. It was bought by the Musée des Beaux Arts in Brussels, in the early twentieth century, where it was later seen by W.H. Auden and woven into one of his poems. But I had never heard of the Fitzpatricks in its provenance, back before it was sold to the Musée by the Sackville Gallery. There is another version of the painting, one which is not by Bruegel, but then, even the Brussels copy may not be by Bruegel. In that other version Icarus's father, Dædalus, is still in the air, and Penny's shepherd is not lost in reverie: he is looking at Dædalus amongst the clouds above, watching him fly. So Barbroke had not held that copy, and Penny had seen something else. I made a note to look deeper but not then, when there was so much else to do. Auden's Bruegel has a small, pale patch of paint at the edge of the ploughman's field, and it is only when observed closely that it coalesces into the head of what must be a corpse, a body lost in the undergrowth and its meaning lost, too, or given the gift of multiplicity with the passage of time. No plough stops for a dead man. Penny did not mention it, so it was missing or she failed to notice it. Or she knew just what it was but had no place for more death that day.

Whatever the history of her Icarus, Penny had missed the reference that might have been closest to her heart: the words of Bruegel's inspiration, Ovid's *Metamorphoses*, the same as had given the world Iphis and Ianthe, the story told and retold before, finally, Warber had his Thomasin and Olivia. In Ovid the audience—the ploughman, the angler, the shepherd—see Icarus as a god, able to travel the sky. In the painting, though, they have not seen him, or do not care, or have turned away as he begins to fall, certain there is little to gain from seeing another human fail to match their deities. Or is it something more? A partridge sits on a branch by the angler, close to the ground as is its way, and relishes the sight of Icarus's failure, as well it might. Ovid wrote that the bird was once Talus, the apprentice of a jealous Dædalus, thrown from on high by Dædalus himself, saved, turned into a partridge, transformed by Minerva as he fell from her temple. I wished that Penny had seen all the connections. I wished I could tell her.

Ludovica lay still in her photograph, taking no notice of me. Her creator, Bernini, slashed the face of his lover to punish her for sleeping with his brother. He did not do it himself, but sent a servant. Bernini was too busy beating his brother half to death. Constanza Piccolomini, Bernini's lover, the wife of his assistant, but still using her maiden name: she paid a price for the affair, sent to an institution, scarred, whilst Bernini's contacts kept him out of trouble. And the bust he had carved of her, of his Constanza—when she was his—kept its beauty. *Dorian Gray* played in reverse. Diana told Penny the story as they sat, looking at the *Ludovica*, the one which Bernini might never have seen, the one destroyed during the Second World War, bombed where it rested, away from the troops at the house but not, it turned out, away from the war itself.

The photograph on the wall beside me had been enlarged from a negative which must have been tiny, or damaged, or both. The hard grain and wavering contrast hid the perfection of parted lips, heavy-lidded eyes, grasping hands; the flow and crease of the habit; the undulations of the mattress beneath, as hard and cold, as soft and warm as Bernini's mattress for the *Borghese Hermaphrodite*. Ludovica is… Ludovica is what? In ecstasy, certainly, lying supine, head thrown back onto her pillow, clothing crumpled. The fingers and thumb of her right hand are splayed, pressing gently through fabric into the yielding flesh of her breast. Her left hand rests on her stomach as though she is in pain, or holding herself down on the mattress. Penny and Diana sat there on New Year's Eve, the day after their time at the temple. Penny thought it "exquisite". She said that Ludovica, "beautiful Ludovica, looks to be in the throes of passion":

> Diana looked at me, and remarked that the saint certainly seemed fetching. Then she let a grin slowly form on her lips. She restrained herself from laughing, with some effort, until she saw in my own wide-eyed face that I had taken her meaning, and then she controlled herself no longer and laughed so loudly that I thought someone would take it as pain or weeping and come to her aid. It was infectious, however, and I could not help but join her, until we held each other and slowly regained our composure. Such a silly little pun to create such a stir, but its effectiveness said a great deal about the high spirits in which we find ourselves. And in truth, Ludovica does, indeed, appear to have been brought to a fetch by the touch of some unseen agency.

The couple spent the rest of their Saturday together, looking at the art and "assorted bibelots" in the lower-floor gallery, eating with the rest of the family, and, in the late afternoon, readying themselves for the dinner and party to be held that evening. Diana explained to Penny that it was to be a relatively small affair, not least due to the expense of June's celebrations for Queen Victoria's Golden Jubilee. There were around twenty people at dinner, whom Penny described as an "odd collection of relatives, minor nobility and army-types, and their wives, most of whom seemed to be elderly women determined to present themselves as far younger than they could reasonably be assumed to be." It was the usual white-tie affair, with two extra courses and the occasional toast for good measure. At the party afterwards a string quartet and a soprano provided the entertainment, which Penny and Diana found to be "dreadfully dull".

I had toured the downstairs rooms before settling in the gallery. The public areas included the room in which Penny had taken breakfast. Some of the walls had suffered from damp over the past hundred years, their murals erased and replaced with whitewash. There was no more resting place for Titania, just an emptiness where one might imagine her to be, amongst the thyme. It contrasted with the dining room, which had been decorated in the hope of recreating the nineteenth-century heyday of the house. A large, mahogany table was laden with porcelain place settings and crystal glasses, glinting in the light from two elegant, if gaudy, chandeliers. Other rooms were similarly decorated in late-Victorian garb, but their desire to be a facsimile was at odds with my purpose. When I drew my picture of Penny's time with Diana—from Penny's own words, and the painting, and the sculptures in the church—I retained the freedom to imagine the details as I wished. Equally, I could leave some ingredients out of focus, a blur of the period, without encroachment on the story I wished to tell: Klein wrapped in tape hiss, a Venice of shadows and subtle lights, a room leaning in on itself, supported by yellows and purples and my desire. So I had moved swiftly past the chairs and tables, the umbrella stands and sideboards, the red-roped areas with carefully typed explanatory texts perched on brass poles.

In the gallery there was breathing space. I exhaled and the room welcomed the intrusion. I had been there for quite some time, however, and I began to feel that I was attracting the attention of the man in the hall. Whenever I glanced at him he was lost in his newspaper, and never showed the slightest interest in anything but the sports pages. He was untroubled, still, that I had claimed the marble bench as my own. Yet I could no longer remain there, reading. There was a sense of social pressure that existed purely in the absence of any real society to cushion its effect on me. I could have lost myself if there had been crowds, families dragging unwilling children past me, elderly couples peering at labels and reading them aloud to each other, questions about tea rooms echoing around. I did not belong, and felt the need to portray some semblance of the casual visitor, or my own idea of a casual visitor. I stood up, placed the diary back into my bag and walked down the length of the gallery, away from the paper-reading man and towards the spiral staircase.

Upstairs, the shelves of the library were empty: those around the balcony completely so, those on the ground floor sparsely decorated with small porcelain statues and folded index cards. Each card gave a fragment of the history of the room: its architecture and decoration, the books it once housed, the story of their transfer to the British Library in the early forties. Penny's gold numbering remained, some numbers clearer than others beneath sediments of dust and soot. Case 23 was exactly where she described it, near the top of the staircase from the gallery. It held nothing at all, but in the case to its immediate left was a bust of Socrates, which I assumed must be the one which hid the keys all those years ago. The desk on which it used to stand was long gone, and with it the card catalogue. It was a library of all the stories never written.

The stairs to the balcony were roped off, as was the door at the west end of the room. The only exit was the staircase connecting library and gallery, except in the case of a fire, which a discreet sign suggested could be escaped by opening the forbidden west door. I thought that it must be awfully congested in the summer, when the house was busier, but looking around I started to gain the impression that it was never particularly busy. It seemed like a work in progress, a house which had lost its original purpose and not yet gained a new reason to exist. The idea of its being a public attraction had taken shape, somewhere, in some board meeting, but there was a long way to go before Barbroke House took its place amongst the pantheon of England's stately homes. I wished that it would forever remain on the sidelines, a destination for the few for whom it held a particular interest, but never host to streams of day-trippers. I felt a sense of ownership, as though I were a member of a secret society open only to those with some link to the history of the place. Diana had gifted membership to Penny, and Penny, even if she never knew it, was always going to bequeath the gift to me.

There were chairs set by the windows and, unlike the marble bench, clearly intended for the use of visitors. If there were any doubts in the mind of a cautious sightseer they were assuaged by a pink card on which was written, in a pretentious, uncial hand, "We invite our guests to sit and rest awhile by these windows. Please enjoy the view to the south, over the gardens and lake, to the gatehouses and approach." I took up the offer of a seat but faced into the room, towards the bare shelves. Behind me, angelic snowflakes were thwarted, and melted against the windowpanes, buckling the landscape. I opened the diary and read on.

Penny and Diana were in the library, on New Year's Eve. They came to get away from the party, as much to be with each other as to avoid unwanted company. Penny had been trapped in a corner of the long gallery, accosted by some friend of Diana's brother who wanted to know everything about Oxford. He had about him, even after several glasses of champagne, enough good breeding to ask Penny's opinion on every aspect of college life. He was not, however, well-bred enough to do anything with those opinions but cast them aside and provide his own in their place, based on experiences related to him by his elder brother, "a Balliol man". Penny suffered his advances for "probably only a matter of minutes, although it seemed like hours" before Diana appeared with two full glasses, and told the boy that he was wanted by Peter in the smoking-room. The boy left, asking Penny to wait for him. Diana had other ideas: she handed Penny a drink before grabbing her arm and dragging her playfully up the spiral stairs. I could see them in front of me as I read, talking and laughing together, temporarily free of the strictures awaiting them on their return to the party below.

I ran away from home when I was six or seven, wanting that same sense of freedom, but lacking the clarity of purpose to do anything but wander in unfamiliar lands. I remember how big everything seemed, designed for adults and not for me. My surroundings seemed to respire, breathing out and collapsing around me, before they inhaled and everything rushed away, left and right and up over my head, everything so distant that I longed for them to come back to me, to suffocate me again. The rush of them was like the fall from the top of the roller-coaster—after the climb, the click-click-click, Jacob on his stairs—down, down and Dad's hand in mine and my eyes shut tight as he had told me they should be. Icarus with Dædalus for company, only Dædalus died and Icarus ran away from home when he was six or seven, ran through the unlocked doors and away from the walls falling in from above. A nice lady stopped when she saw me crying, and asked where my parents were, and took me to the police station for telephone calls and a short drive home to a mother who had been facing a second loss. I have never been sure if one can be selfish when so young, and so alone, and so frightened.

In the library Penny tried to show Diana the book, her book, but Diana blocked the way, fought with her, joyously, and won with a kiss. Downstairs, the crowd was preparing to welcome in the new year. Not a sound came from the gallery below: everyone was back in the west wing, with warmth and food and drink. There were a few dulled cries for Diana, exhortations for her to return so as not to miss the stroke of midnight, but they were ignored. Diana told Penny that they should be together, alone, for the start of the year, told her that they should brave the snow, that nobody would see them if they sneaked out. Penny protested that it was cold and dark, but Diana asked her to show more faith and pulled her along, back through the gallery and into the hall. She ensured Penny's silence by putting a finger to her own lips and then slowly opened the lid of an oak trunk beside the door. Inside were two heavy coats, a box of matches and an oil lamp "which looked as though it belonged to a navvy." Outside, the snow had stopped falling. It was still possible to make out the ruts from the arrival of the guests' carriages. Music and laughter could be heard coming from the house, fading away as the two deserters followed the curve of the drive under the tall, black-painted gas-lamps which lined its outer edge. Beyond the grasp of the lamps the gardens fell quickly into darkness. Above them, the thin, bright arc of the moon played peek-a-boo amongst scudding clouds.

I shivered. At first I thought I was empathizing with Penny, but the library had grown cold, too. The sky outside was losing its light, not yet to darkness or even dusk, but enough for me to decide that it was time to head home. I would stop at the temple on the way back, and finish the few pages of the diary needed to bring me into the new year. There were other areas of the gardens to be explored, but they would wait for spring or summer, when I could come with Emily, when everything would be all right again, because time would have passed, and wounds would have healed, more purple, more yellow, just until the illness was gone, as it would be in summer. I could see the electric lights running from the house to the lake, and then out, across the ha-ha, all the way to the rise of the hill. I put the diary in my bag and walked from the dead library, down into the gallery and on, to the hall, nodding a goodbye to the man and his paper.

In the gardens the snow was falling more heavily: not faster but denser, each large flake trying to outdo the nonchalance of its neighbours, each more languorous in its descent. There was a bitterness which had not been present earlier, when the sun was higher and the clouds thinner, when the day was about arrivals, not departures.

Chapter Sixteen

Sunday, 1st January, 1888

We came to the start of the path which leads to the temple. Diana paused and lit the lamp. There was little chance of the dim flame being seen from the house at such a distance, particularly given the festivities in which its occupants were engaged. Nevertheless, she was careful to hold it before her and shield it with her body, so nothing fell behind but a slight brightening of the snow at the edge of her shadow. Then we were on the path itself and, more quickly than I had expected, upon our temple. The snow on the steps was crisp beneath our feet but after we passed between the columns we were walking on cold, clear flags. Diana placed the lamp on the bench and then sat beside it, and I beside her.

In front of us, all was dark and noiseless, but only almost so, for we heard the sound of the wind in the trees, and the occasional shiver of smaller branches as snow fell from bough to bough. The lake was black and even, except for fleeting dashes of silver when the clouds permitted an appearance of the moon. Wherever the geese had found shelter, they were keeping their secret. I turned to face Diana, thinking she would embrace me in some fashion, but she merely took off her glove and stroked my cheek, telling me that midnight was not yet arrived, turning my expectation to anticipation. I asked how we should know when it was upon us, but she told me not to worry and assured me that we had a little time yet. She took out her pocket-book, all filled with Swinburne, and began to read. I pulled my coat tight around me, moved closer to her, and rested my head on her shoulder.

She read "Love and Sleep". She read slowly and in a half-whisper which carried her words to me but no farther. As she approached the end of the sonnet I noticed a change in the bright patches which defined the house, otherwise concealed by snow-laden trees. Diana must have noticed it, too, for she increased her pace just a little and shifted so that we might face each other. As the final line dripped from her mouth the sky filled with a brilliant, white light. We watched a flare rise above the house, and heard the loud report of the pistol and the answering call of the awakened waterfowl. The snow shimmered on the branches by the temple, and the pillars before us cast their shadows in stark stripes over the murals and bench. Diana wished me a "Happy New Year" and kissed me as the flare sputtered and the black and white of our surroundings returned to darkness, but for the lamp's yellow glow. I asked her if she had known that the flare would mark the arrival of midnight. Yes, of course she had: her father acquired the pistol from a naval acquaintance some months back and had spoken often of his intentions, with what she described as "the excitement of a schoolboy."

I had started to shiver. Diana asked if we could stay for just a little while longer. Tomorrow, she said, the family would have their open house, and the place would be filled with a mixture of relatives and eligible young men. I was quite surprised to hear this: I had thought that the day's entertainments had replaced the more usual traditions. Diana explained that the night's celebration was also the idea of her father. The rest of the family had been unpersuaded of its merits, other than its being a welcome diversion at a difficult time of year. Thus reminded of our visit to the church on Friday morning, I placed my arm around her and, this time, gently guided her head onto my shoulder.

We sat, saying nothing, as the birds of the lake settled back to their sleep, and the guests slipped back inside the house, closing the large front door and confining the light to the hall and a few rooms of the west wing. The cold had reached Diana, too, and when we looked at each other we laughed at the blueness of our lips and the redness of our noses. She rose and took my hand in hers, pulling me gently from the bench to hold her for one last time before we returned. She whispered a line from "Anactoria" as we embraced:

"Like me shall be the shuddering calm of night."

Back in the warmth and noise of the house the Earl greeted us with a friendly "There you are!" and inquired if we had seen the flare. Diana remarked that we had indeed, from a vantage point in the gardens, and I, standing mute in the face of this sudden return to the prosaic world, nodded my agreement. This was cause for Diana's mother, who had been entertaining guests nearby, to come across and fuss over us. She hurried us to the fireplace to warm ourselves, worried that we might have caught a chill. Appropriately thawed, we were ushered into the billiard room to sit for Mr. Collins. Thankfully, carriages were at one o'clock and soon only the family and I remained. Lord Barbroke suggested a late breakfast at ten—to which all readily agreed—and we retired.

I awoke around six and returned to my own room whilst the rest of the house slept. I sit now, with the bed-quilt over my shoulders, writing and watching the snow fall. Outside the door I can hear footsteps as the servants begin to prepare for the day ahead.

Today began as Sundays begin, with breakfast and a short church service, to which we were taken in closed carriages due to the persistent intemperance of the weather. Diana sent down with her apologies: she was feeling unwell but would join us for luncheon on our return. I proposed that I go to her in her room to judge the severity of her illness, but my hosts insisted that she be left to sleep, and it was not my place to argue. It is my suspicion that Diana could not face another morning in the company of her brother's ghost and, moreover, that her parents were well aware of this reason for her remaining in bed. Not knowing that Diana had already taken me into her confidence, they were keen that I did not force her to broach such a distressing subject. The Earl and his wife and son—who must surely feel as Diana, must they not?—managed their emotions and, when at church, fulfilled all the duties of their position. Only once did I catch Peter stealing a glimpse over his shoulder at the dark curtains.

Diana was waiting for us when we returned, and we partook of an informal luncheon in the mural room. It was felt that since we were to spend the afternoon entertaining, with ample provision of food and drink, we ought to eat lightly. In all honesty I had then, and have now, no appetite: it has been stolen from me by the excitement of all that has occurred and by the short hours of sleep which last night afforded me. Diana announced that she felt much refreshed from her morning's rest and was looking forward to seeing old friends and making new ones during the remainder of the day. I found something disagreeable about the easy way with which she continued normal life in the face of what had passed between us, and yet I cannot list a single action of hers to which I took umbrage. As we sat she smiled at me, and my fears, whatever their nature, were lifted. All seemed well, at least here, in this place which belongs to us.

The afternoon was entirely as I had expected: a stream of well-intentioned callers and more introductions than I care to remember. Around three, however, I managed to ask Diana if she would come with me to the library, so I could show her the Warber. I told her that I should be on an early train tomorrow and it would be a pity were we not able to share such a discovery. She said she thought that one could make an exception to the usual *noblesse oblige* in such circumstances, and made our excuses with her parents.

We entered the library from the door at the top of the entrance-hall stairs and I led the way, across the room to case 23. It was about an hour before sunset and already the lower corners of the room were beginning to hide themselves. In the gardens the snowflakes flirted with each other, but the library was left to the two of us.

Diana listened patiently to my description of the book, the hair and the pamphlet as I took each of them out of the box, but I caught no sign of enthusiasm. I told her that she was hurting my feelings, that this was important to me and thus ought to be important to her. In reply she said, almost inaudibly, "It is important to you and to him." I realized I had not thought of Matthew for more than a passing moment—had I thought of him at all?—since she and I had taken our first turn around the grounds. Our sittings for the painting, which were once only footnotes to my times with the artist himself, have been transformed into mere excuses for enjoying the close warmth of my Thomasin. Mr. Taylor has waned in the waxing of Diana. Yet I have given no voice to this transformation. Diana left the library then, taking the spiral stairs, neither looking back at me nor giving me a chance to explain. I have not seen her since.

I replaced the book as quickly as possible, without any opportunity to take notes or study the pamphlet in greater detail. Downstairs, the Countess informed me that her daughter had started to feel unwell again, and was to spend the rest of the day in her rooms. I was not to worry, she said, for if the illness persisted they would call their doctor, who was a "wonderful man". Most likely, I was told, it was the effects of the cold weather, or the excesses of the season.

Dinner was accompanied by reminiscences of Oxford. The Earl was curious about the University itself, eager to know that the buildings still stand as they have always done, that Great Tom still sounds across the rooftops, that the "Hymnus Eucharisticus" is still sung from Magdalen Tower on May Morning. I politely reminded him that I have yet to spend a May Morning in the city—which seemed to cause him genuine embarrassment—but I expressed my conviction that the traditions continue unchanged. Lady Barbroke's interests lay with the nature of our academic work: the lectures which we attend, the organization of the college, the minutiæ of day-to-day life. Peter said hardly a word.

I knocked on Diana's door as I came up to my room, but she did not answer. I shall not see her tonight and I leave on the early train tomorrow, before breakfast, as I promised my parents that I should accompany them to the home of some great-aunt whose name escapes me. My head is full of contradictions and I do not know how best to resolve any of them, or if they may find any resolution at all. Some minutes ago I felt faint and opened my bedroom window. I stood and let the snow brush past me, or stop and rest on my clothing, cut through my skin in its melting, give me a physical sensation to take my mind from its spinning. I lost myself in the snow; lost Matthew, lost Diana, lost Warber, lost it all in the encroachment of winter. Now the window is closed again and everything is coming back. The only thing I can do, the only thing I shall do, is sleep.

Monday, 2nd January, 1888

I was awoken this morning by one of the maids, and left a short while thereafter, catching the first train back home. Diana was doubtless still sleeping and I did not feel that I ought to wake her. I placed the Swinburne against her door so she would find it when she emerged and know that I had departed. I think she wanted me to take it, to draw the thread beyond the confines of Barbroke, but I no longer trust my judgment of her wants and desires.

Mother and Father were glad to see me, of course, and wanted news of my "time amongst the aristocracy." I tried to affect an air of excitement but my heart was not in it. Those experiences which were of most interest to me cannot be conveyed to others, and particularly not to my parents, who were not taken in by my attempts at telling breathless stories of the great and good. In the end I excused myself as tired from my travels and in need of rest before the visiting of aunts could be undertaken. I lay on my bed with my eyes closed, waiting for Mother to open the door a fraction, peer round, and linger until she was sure I slept. Only after she had done so did I rise and move to my desk.

In the past hour I have written the opening lines of six separate letters to Diana, and one by one they have found their way into the waste-paper basket. It may prove difficult—it may yet prove impossible—to compose the substantive argument of the letter, but I do not know, as I have proceeded no further than the opening lines of greeting. No sooner has the ink begun to dry than I read what I have written and see that it is overwrought or insipid, extravagant or nondescript: anything but what is required. Indeed, I suppose I do not know what is required.

And then there is Mr. Taylor, my dear Matthew. Do I really care for him? Perhaps I am heartless to put such doubts to paper. Perhaps my heart is otherwise occupied. I wonder if he has abandoned me; but then, how could we have communicated? It is risk enough his writing to me at college, and at this time I most certainly do not possess an address to which he might send a letter without its being noticed by persons better left unaware of our correspondence.

Mother has just knocked and told me to be ready to leave in one hour from now.

Tuesday, 3rd January, 1888

Last night I retired the instant we returned, telling my parents that I was suffering from a headache. In truth, I had thought I should remain awake, restless, for much of the night, but I slept fitfully once I had extinguished the light. I dreamed I was back at Barbroke. I am unable to explain my own feelings or, indeed, to identify their character in any manner which might render them susceptible to comprehension. At times I believe Diana wishes nothing more than to be with me; at others I am quite sure she will never speak to me again. Yet I remain of the opinion that I have done nothing to wrong her. Ought I to have run from the temple, across the snow, away from the statues and murals and Diana, so that I might have been sure of retaining a friendship which I fear is in jeopardy? I wish I might talk to her, but I have failed to write with any acceptable degree of clearness, and it is still a fortnight until I shall have the opportunity to see her in person.

I have not spoken to Father about the Warber at Barbroke: such a revelation would work against two relationships which are both so awfully important to me. I should be reducing the worth of Father's copy and the breadth of his knowledge of the work—as he would see it—whilst simultaneously diminishing the value of something precious to me, as I still hold hopes of sharing it with Diana, that it might be possessed by the two of us and no other.

Tuesday, 10th January, 1888

This morning a parcel arrived from Barbroke. Mother was desperately keen to know the contents and began to protest when I insisted on opening it in the privacy of my own bedroom. It was Father who prevailed upon her to allow me some life of my own now that I have attained an age at which I may attend Oxford and form new social circles. It was interesting to discern, in the words I overheard as I took my leave of them, the strange reversal of the parental roles to which I have become accustomed. I was always Father's little girl as I grew up. It was Mother who most often and passionately expressed a desire that I exceed the limitations placed on me as a woman in modern society. Now it seems that it is Father who is ready to free me, and Mother who feels the loss of her daughter.

Inside the parcel I found the green box which had been hidden amongst the volumes in case 23 and, on opening it, the Warber, lock of hair and pamphlet, all in place. Resting on top of them was an envelope bearing my name.

Dearest Penny,

Knowing you as I do, I am quite sure that you are, at this minute, pondering how you might return this gift which you feel cannot be mine to offer, nor yours to accept. Please, put such thoughts out of your head. The box will never be missed and I am of the firm opinion that books belong with those to whom they offer the most pleasure. I have my Swinburne. You must have your Warber. Besides, my darling P., I know that you were eager to spend more time with the volume at Barbroke and found yourself unable to do so. Now you can take a closer look and see what you learn. At least I can be sure that your possession of the book itself, and the Tyburn pamphlet, will save you the trouble of writing copious notes. Will you share their secrets with me when we are together in Oxford?

Papa and Mama find you to be a delight. Peter keeps himself to himself, but he is not one to swallow his criticisms and his silence tells me that he, too, enjoyed the pleasure of your company. I, of course, have thought of little else since your departure and am deeply saddened that my shortness of temper spoiled our time together at Barbroke. I hope you can understand that I was not angry with you, but with the situation in which we find ourselves, a situation run through with difficulties.

Do you think what we share is improper? I have never been able to form a satisfactory division of life into proper and improper: both categories seem arbitrary in so many ways and change without any clear reason, so that what the Romans loved we abhor, and what we love they hated. Does that withstand argument, or am I trying in vain to excuse something within myself? I do hope I am not, for I truly do not feel that I have anything to excuse.

Please forgive my behaviour. I was a petulant child to become so emotional over the book. It reminded me so clearly that when we return to college we shall begin sitting again for Mr. Taylor, with all the complications which that entails. I want you to know that I now see how it may play to our advantage in giving us a chance to spend time together. Besides, I suppose we are not even sure that Mr. Taylor will wish to continue, after his last letter to you: the painting may remain ever unfinished as he pursues his dreams of abstraction.

Do you like him very much, Penny? I remember when we spoke on that night in college, the first time you saw him, and I watched you as your gaze followed him into the garden. He was with his wife then, of course. It must be hard for you, knowing that he is married, and not only married, but married to our own Constance Taylor. Please do not forget that I am your friend, someone with whom to share your concerns, someone to ease your distress.

It has been decided that the memorial service will be on Friday, 20th January, by which time all building works will have been completed. It will doubtless be an unspeakably sad occasion but it is best for all the family that Albert is finally laid to rest. Papa has always hidden his feelings from me, but I sense them—just the smallest amount—from time to time, when he seems preoccupied with thoughts which he cannot annunciate if queried on the matter. Mama has adopted all the social conventions of mourning, yet I have the unsettling notion that it is through the performance of what is expected that she avoids the need to face any real loss. Peter has always been quiet but, if pressed, I should say that he has been even more so since dear Albert's sleep. He chooses to remain within his own world not because it is a place he wishes to inhabit but because ours is a world he wishes to escape. If that all sounds a little melodramatic then I apologize, as I apologize for my own melancholia, which was so obvious during our time at the Galleries, I know. If I have an excuse it is that I am able to be open with you as with no other, and that hiding emotion from you is alike to betrayal, in my mind.

I shall not be coming up again until the following Monday, a couple of days after the start of full term. You must not think me lost to Barbroke. I should hate to imagine you at Oxford, worrying that I shall not return at all or, worse, that I have returned but failed to call on you.

Until then, I hope that Warber will keep you company.

Ever your affectionate,

Diana

After the signature she has quoted the final lines of "Love and Sleep", which I still hear in her voice from the temple.

And all her face was honey to my mouth,
    And all her body pasture to mine eyes;
        The long lithe arms and hotter hands than fire,
The quivering flanks, hair smelling of the south,
    The bright light feet, the splendid supple thighs
        And glittering eyelids of my soul's desire.

CHAPTER SEVENTEEN

D iana's letter was folded neatly between the pages of the diary. I read it on the bus as it meandered back to the cottage. There were only eight passengers but the melting snow on our coats was enough to steam all the windows to a milky translucence. A faded, grinning face was visible beside me, just two dots and a curve, so low on the window that it must have been drawn by a child, in other mists, sometime within the past few days. I rubbed my arm down and over it in an arc, then back again, clearing enough of the pane to see out to the world. There were no towns of any real size between Barbroke and our village, but the cars passing by, the telephone boxes and the bus stops were enough to rip away the layers of history. At Barbroke I had been part of Penny's world, and Diana's, and I had left something of them behind. I felt the distance between us increasing with each mile I travelled until, by the time I stepped off the bus, I felt unspeakably alone.

The village was quiet. It was too early for the evening traffic of returning commuters, too cold for tourists, too dark for me. Night seemed to arrive so quickly in winter that I could never shake the sense of its scheming behind my back, waiting for me to look away before it descended to oppress and confine. Sodium yellow, glancing off snowflakes, pooled on the ground beneath each streetlight as though huddled for warmth. The colour lost meaning in the absence of contrast, yellow to white and all else was shading. I watched my breath ascend and disperse, shifted my bag on my shoulder, sank my hands into my pockets and started for home. The snow was building again, coming down fast enough to defeat any lingering slush in the gutters.

I wanted shelter and warmth of a sort which I knew the cottage, and Emily, could not provide; and Penny and Diana would not yet have returned to the painting after their time at Barbroke.

Through the lychgate, away from the road, the graveyard faded quickly into an indecipherable *Totentanz* of greys and blacks, a smeared woodcut of the scene itself: fallen snow, falling snow, suspended snow, thick boughs which cut the scene in ink, branches juddering life into the cold; and beneath it all, always, the stones, worn but upright, patiently waiting. No pills today, not yet, left at home, forgotten in my hurry to leave and not missed in their absence. I sat beneath the roof of the gate and peered out, out to the waiting space, defining its individual elements without trouble, but unable to piece them together into a coherent whole. Caspar David Friedrich. Lines of monks, outside my grasp, always outside my grasp: walking towards them would ruin the print, stop the music, so I sat and watched, my own *Klosterfriedhof im Schnee*, a *Monastery Graveyard in Snow*. Friedrich painted it towards the end of the 1820s. In its middle distance stands the tumbled wall of a monastic church. Perpendicular windows—ruined, glassless—claw at the sky, high above an altar. The trees in Friedrich's foreground, winter-dead and stark, became the supports of the roof above my head, and the monks within the clearing, the monks processing to an empty doorway in a broken entrance, scattered before me to take their places throughout the cemetery. There was no colour, as there is no colour in the forest-break of Friedrich, stolen by the destruction of the painting during a bombing raid on Berlin. All that remains is an old, black-and-white photograph.

A coffin rests on the shoulders of the monks at the head of their column, already past one, two, three sets of steps and through the stone arch of the ruined entrance. Its time before the altar will be short, because in the foreground, by the dead trees, an open grave is prepared: a pair of spades for a headstone, stuck into the ground, eager to rain soil onto the coffin lid. The grave prepared and Diana waiting. I was cold, and drained by the company of cloisterers. The *Klosterfriedhof* belonged with things lost.

The cottage was warm, and the light switch brought colour rushing back. I kicked off my boots and hung my coat on its peg in the porch. Ten minutes later I was sitting on the couch with a cup of hot chocolate clutched in both hands, sipping it as I looked at Penny and Diana, back on their bed, in front of me. I was seeing Diana before she became the cold marble of Saint Cecilia's; but if Taylor followed Pre-Raphaelite practices, as he had claimed to do, then the faces were painted last, after the background and bodies were complete, so my Diana was painted after the kiss. Penny, too, must have finished the sittings looking out over the Diana of the temple at Barbroke, not the Diana of the University Galleries. I examined the expressions of the two women, wanting desperately to see something more of their story come through the varnish, but there was nothing new. Penny, as Olivia, still stared back at me with an air of expectancy. As Thomas, Diana's profile remained strong and protective, yet something in the turn of her mouth revealed a disquiet at her imminent unmasking. Or perhaps neither woman portrayed any such emotions. Perhaps I was reading into the painting what Penelope had told me in the diaries. Perhaps everything I saw was the product of Taylor's brushwork and imagination, just layers of pigment and copal, mixed and applied to a bright canvas. I sat back again and gave myself permission to imagine anything I desired. I imagined Penny glancing at Diana, trying to keep the corners of her mouth from turning upwards. But then, what if Penny just gazed at Taylor, seeing him, not Diana, as the one true constant in her life, even then, even after those days of unspoken promises? I pulled the diary from my bag.

There was no letter from Penny in reply to Diana's gift, at least not folded into the diary itself. I had glanced through the loose letters, too, and knew there was not one which fell early in the new year. It seemed unthinkable that there would be no note of thanks and, sure enough, on 12th January, Penelope mentioned a walk to the post office. She wrote at some length about her decision to keep the Warber, with the air of one who was justifying a decision after it has been taken, rather than weighing the pros and cons in order to reach it. I cannot say that I blamed her. I was sitting with the painting, surrounded by her diaries and letters, and I could entirely understand her desire to keep something she loved.

The handle-click and swing of the front door brought me back to the cottage. Emily entered amidst a swirl of freezing air. She stamped her feet and swore under her crystallizing breath. I hurried over to her, the diary still in one hand.

"They kissed!" I told her, then stood perfectly still, my face close to hers.

"What? Who kissed? Let me get in at least. It's taken forever to get home. The trains are just…" Emily trailed off and headed past me to the couch. "Make me a cup of tea?"

I made her a cup of tea.

"But it's only six. You're home early."

"I left at three. There was a general consensus that if we waited any longer we'd be spending the night in the office."

"You weren't tempted?" I did not ask it out loud, but the pause was enough.

"Anyway, I'm home," she continued. "Want to tell me about your day?"

I told her about my day. Except in reality I told her about Penny and Diana, with nothing of my own experience of Barbroke but the weather, the mechanics of transportation, and the implication that I had been standing in front of the objects which I described. I ended with Diana's letter. There was no place for the *Klosterfriedhof* in the story Emily wanted to hear.

"And there's no reply?" she asked.

"No, just a mention of a trip to the post office. She kept the book. She copied out a dedication scribbled on the final page."

"May I have a look?"

I hesitated.

"Or you could read it to me," she said.

"Of course. It doesn't say much. 'Hannah, mine owne Thomasin,' and Warber's initials, 'S.W.' Maybe Hannah was his girlfriend or wife."

"Or husband."

"Oh, you mean because of Thomasin. Do you think so? I suppose."

"I was being facetious. I'm sorry. Anna, do you think you're getting a bit too wrapped up in all this?"

"What else would I be doing?"

The conversation dragged on, and everything was my fault, my mistakes, my reactions, and blue and black and white and red. She was just tired, she said, and I am sure that she was, but I was angry, again, and wanted to turn it outwards into the room, into the cold. So I said his name. Once. No context, no adjectives, just a proper noun in our own deadened space. Then another name, Anactoria, and she frowned and asked what I meant and before I answered she told me not everything was about paintings, not everything was someone else's story. I said it was Swinburne, a poem, a pleading to a lost love, a pleading from one woman to another, a resentment, a search for consolation. The Venetian shadows returned. Then she was gone, over the frozen waters, into the cold and the snow. The lights of the car passed out of sight beyond the *Klosterfriedhof*, where the monks of the cortège, intent on their delivery, did not turn.

In the window Jo Hopper looked back at me. Even when she vanished in reflections of table and chairs, fireplace and couch, I remained motionless, deliberately seeing through myself so everything was painted in blurred patches of light and shade.

When he was thirteen Caspar David Friedrich watched his brother Johann fall through the ice on a frozen lake and drown. Knowing that, and knowing that he lost his mother at seven, and sisters, too, had changed how I looked at his paintings. Nothing could escape that history, his personal pathetic fallacy, or mine, ours, written over every landscape; his winters melancholic, his summers mocking. Most of his *Monk by the Sea*, about four-fifths of it, is sky. Moving down the canvas, dark green-blues lighten to a band of cloud with highlights hinting at an obscured sun. Then down into darkness again, to a sea in which Dylan Thomas would find Bibles. The bottom fifth is land, gently undulating in shades of sand and beachgrass. Nothing frames the image, nothing leads the eye as the trees lead to the *Klosterfriedhof*, the monks to the coffin, the gate to the church. A critic, Heinrich von Kleist, wrote that "when viewing it, it is as if one's eyelids have been cut away." Only the monk, the contemplative *Rückenfigur*—the figure with his back to us—steals the gaze. I stood before the painting, years ago, and thought I saw a vision of an existential sublime: a remorseless, endless beauty in the coming storm, defined in its breadth by the solitary man against whom it was set. But then, why is he there? Surely he is more than a slave to scale and composition, standing where he ought to be, on the golden section of the horizon, a tiny figure holding everything together even as he divides it into left and right, to please the lidless eye.

There are flecks of foam on his sea, bright as the brightest clouds. They are trapped between ground and sky, except where the sea disappears behind the body of the monk, who rises a little way above the edge of the land. Here the flecks transmute, become small birds, each just a few touches of white paint on the canvas, wheeling, flying upwards, some part of a soul, the closest of them low by the monk's feet, the farthest high in the clouds, lost in pale blue-greys. And, for me, the monk became more than just the immediacy of the figure he presented: he was my perspective, the one who stood by me as I entered the immensity of the painting, who started my journey, came with me and showed me that the others were wrong, that I could blink and return complete.

That was Emily, had been Emily: a companion by my side since our first meeting in a Soho bar. We stayed late, long after closing time, when the lights upstairs were off and downstairs was left to the two of us and our friends washing glasses and tidying tables. We would have found each other sooner but I had been in Glasgow for the second year of my doctoral studies and had returned to London only a week earlier. Emily had arrived in the capital just as I left, to start the first year of her master's in international law and human rights. Still, we were both regulars at the bar and our meeting was inevitable, even if its outcome was not. The rest of the story was pedestrian, if not to us, its protagonists, then to its audience, to our shared friends, to Alison. Emily received her master's after a further year and began to work with a large firm of London solicitors. I finished my doctorate and took a junior position at a gallery on Bond Street. We moved in together, had a cat for a while, until London traffic got the better of him. There were ups and downs but we managed, for a few years at least.

Then, one day, I blinked and there was no way to return. I was Caspar David Friedrich, thirteen years old and standing by a frozen lake. Brother Johann was gone and all I could do was watch the birds ascend.

I let my eyes focus. An artificial, Mondrian oblong became the open doorway to the kitchen. I fought myself in a gentle battle between hunger and exhaustion. Exhaustion won. Tea and purples, sloeblacks, yellows, sleep. Blue lights and wakefulness once more, for a few hours at least.

On Wednesday I awoke with a thought, a memory of something that had gained importance over the past days, something I had already found without realizing it. Jacob, the ladder, and the golden light from above, but silver, too, more star than night sky, among the ascending angels. I clicked the black latch and followed the choir, who sang with the hum of the light. If the mice were scratching then they stopped before I heard them, and I was alone with a forgotten past that had been appraised as worthless. The bookcase still rested against the wall, revelling in its exposure, offering me tiles and china, paperbacks and precious metals, dusty bric-a-brackery at prices too good to miss.

I heard a noise and turned, expecting the mice to have overcome their shyness, but the sound was carrying up the stairs from below, and I suddenly imagined that Emily was opening the door. Precious metals. I reached out and grabbed the silver mirror, pulling it to me in a cloud of dust. A roughly modelled swan, hollow between the wings, fell to the floor and broke into three pieces, never to hold toothpicks again. I hurried down the stairs, along the landing and down again, but there was no Emily. I peered out of the front window, but all that greeted me was a soil-shaded garden, damp and unwelcoming, set against the glass like a warder to keep me indoors. In the porch I found a menu for a local Italian restaurant, splayed on the tiles where it had fallen from the letterbox. I raised the mirror to my face and a green cloakroom ticket fluttered to the floor: 735. I started to rub at my blurred reflection with the cuff of my nightshirt, but found myself too hungry to wait for a genie. Penny looked out over Diana, watching me put the mirror on the table and head to the kitchen to forage.

The place was a mess and I needed to tidy, and I would tidy, just not then, not when I was remembering something, and not when I was famished. I vaguely considered going out to the Café of Madam Tweed but the weather was so foul, so blustery and wet, that I put together a slice of toast, a packet of crisps and a cup of tea, saying goodbye to the last of the bread and milk. I sat at the table and turned the mirror over. I had already known what I was going to find in the up-above. I had noticed it on that second ascent to the attic, when I retrieved the auction-house receipts, and I had seen it again, a few days ago, in the church at Barbroke. Flowers blossomed from the handle, pressed in silver, bruised with tarnish, a long way from the purity of white marble. I wondered how it, too, had ended its life in the remains of Matthew Taylor's effects.

A knock at the door made me jump. It was Alison. She stood in the porch, sniffing and blowing her nose. An etiolated thing at university, grown thin and wiry from late-night darkness and smoke-filled rooms, her features had softened, and she remained thankfully free from the air of fatalism and resignation that I saw developing in other friends. Her blonde hair was slightly darker, and there were the beginnings of lines at the corners of her mouth, but she still possessed the same smile, which privileged the left side of her face over the right. True, I had seen her recently, holding grapes and hopes for the future, but these changes struck me anew, as though we had parted at graduation and were freshly reunited at some overpriced fund-raising dinner.

Alison took on an air of seriousness with which she seemed ill at ease. I listened to her expressions of concern, which flowed with all the stiltedness of social niceties, however sincere their emotional origins. The real tension came when she tried to drive the conversation towards the general everyday, but away from my everyday. I assured her that I was coping and would be just fine.

When she noticed the painting she asked if it belonged to me and I told her that it did, and that I was researching its provenance. I did not ask her for her opinion, but I received it. It was one area in which she could engage me without the need for some desperate formulation of plausible pretence.

"So, late nineteenth then, I'm guessing. Pre-Raphaelite-y. Not bad, but not great. Romantic mediævalism, chivalry. Something Shakespearian. Or Malory? *Morte d'Arthur*. Grail legends. That sort of thing."

I nodded. "That sort of thing."

"Well? Where did you find it?"

"We bought it in an auction over near the coast. It's late nineteenth, as you say. I'm not sure who painted it. The faces seem to have been added late in the process. White ground visible in places at the edge of the canvas. Copal varnish. That's just a guess. The usual."

Alison let out an "mmm" of agreement as she walked around the painting.

"Subject?" she asked, but did not wait for a reply. "The foreground figure, the one looking out to the right, he's—"

"She," I interrupted, and regretted my correction.

"She? I suppose you could be right, yes. The curve of the tunic over the chest? She seems resigned to... What? Something's coming. And the other, how does she look to you? Beseeching? Reflective? Yes, reflective. She's not really looking out at the viewer. She's not really looking at anything. She's lost in her own thoughts. She's trapped by them."

"I really thought she needed my help."

"Your help?"

"Just someone's, I suppose. I think she is our invitation to become part of the story."

"What story, though? What did the auction catalogue say?"

"It must have said the same as the receipt. A late-nineteenth-century piece, artist unknown."

"Okay. What do you say?"

I was beginning to feel as though I were being cross-examined.

Soon she would shine a desk lamp into my eyes and I would give in and share everything with her and lose my Penny and Diana. Exhalation. Everything started to rush at me. I told myself that she did not know anything and that whatever I told her was her truth and she would be fine with it.

"Anna? What do you think is going on?"

"Well…" I took a breath and composed myself. Alison was wearing her unease again. "You're probably right that it's Shakespeare or something similar, but I'm not sure what. I think they've been there for a while, because of the burnt-out candle. They're waiting. They're waiting for an ending."

"An ending?"

"Yes. Whatever's going to happen, they believe it will be the end of something. The figure in the dress is resting on her love for the last time. That's what her eyes are saying. If you're right that they aren't looking out at us, it's not just because she's lost in thought, it's because she cannot see, would rather not see, anything of her future. And the nearer figure, the one in the tunic, is dispassionate, because she sees no other way to face whatever's coming. Or if she does, she doesn't want to show it to her lover."

Alison looked at the picture again.

"Yes," she said, "you could be right. Or wrong. It's hard to know without more information."

I had not lied about the receipt. There was no title given.

"I'm not sure we're supposed to know," I said. "We're each supposed to construct a story of our own. It's a single frame from a film."

"But a film has a script, a story it tells. It might be ambiguous, but there's a core narrative that drives each frame. Are you trying to talk about abstraction?"

I remembered having these types of debate at college, late into the night, fuelled by coffee and cheap alcohol. At some hour the audience would dwindle, plod home, leave the world to darkness and to me. There were never any resolutions. The system would have collapsed if we had ever reached a solid conclusion. People would have become worried about making a contribution, about sounding foolish. In the cottage, talking to Alison, that was exactly my worry: that, and her thinking me somehow incapable.

"It's more than abstraction," I said. "It's recognizing the possibilities within figurative art. Yes, it's limited, informed by, prescribed by the image, but it's still there."

Alison narrowed her eyes a little but said nothing. I could not tell whether she thought what I was saying was obvious or incomprehensible. I pressed on.

"Look. It's a cliché, a picture paints a thousand words. And it does. It does that easily. It would take at least a thousand words just to cover the detailed visual content of the painting. But there could be thousands upon thousands of words spent on its meaning and message, yes?"

Alison nodded. She pulled a dining chair from under the table and sat down.

"But it only takes a few words, a title, to close it all down. Those words force a specific meaning onto the picture, more than it shows. Suddenly the man in the mirror is the newborn child's father. The man on the bed is a dead poet. That's fine. But it steals a thousand other meanings. It's personal to the producer, and impersonal to the viewer. All I'm saying is, maybe the painter didn't want to do that, didn't want a figurative painting to become a narrative painting. Or did, but wanted it to show your narrative, or mine. Finding out more is precisely what you shouldn't do if you want to understand."

And even as I said it I knew that I was speaking for Taylor, not for myself, and that only Alison retained a genuine ability to impose herself onto the picture. If Penny were to remain mine she had to be a painting, not a photograph, and yet I was carving away my own chance of ambiguity, hacking at it, day by day, diary entry by diary entry, inexorably.

"Yeah. But that's nothing new," said Alison. "It's Gombrich's 'beholder's share', or the ultimate elliptical narrative. Everything removed but that single frame. We spent an age on this stuff, remember? I wrote a god-awful essay on it and you brought schnapps to my room, for consolation."

201

I did remember, but it was not like this, it was not personal, or important, or mine. I could feel myself getting upset. Alison continued.

"Besides, I know you. You'll discover every last detail and then it'll be an *Erased de Kooning Drawing* in oils."

"What do you mean?" I asked.

"You know. Robert Rauschenberg. Nineteen fifty-something."

I was starting to get annoyed.

"Assume I don't," I said.

"Rauschenberg has been painting his white canvases. The white ground of your Pre-Raphaelites, but without any more paint on top of it. Roughly."

"Roughly."

Alison paused, but I said nothing more and she hurried to fill the dead air between us.

"But he loves drawing, Rauschenberg, loves it and wants to capture it in the white-paintings series. So... Should I carry on?"

I nodded.

"So, he tries drawing on paper and rubbing it out, but all he ends up with is an erased Rauschenberg drawing. He knows that somehow that isn't right. What he needs to do is begin with art, art with a capital 'A', and who better than Willem de Kooning? Big artist, huge name. So he goes to see him—"

"He goes to see him with a bottle of Jack Daniel's and hopes he won't be at home, so that the art can be a piece de Kooning never even drew because he was away when Rauschenberg called."

"So you do know it?"

"I know it. I just don't see what you're getting at, Alison."

"Well, de Kooning agreed, right? Even if he was a little reticent, he agreed. He gave Rauschenberg a piece he considered important, and something that would be hard to erase. Charcoal, paint, pencil, crayon. It took Rauschenberg a month."

"And? What's your point?"

"There's no room left for your construction of narrative, Anna. The *Erased de Kooning* is a blank canvas, well, blank paper, but the narrative is defined by the process which brought it into being. It cannot escape its creation story. And that's what you'll do to this painting."

She pointed over to Penny and Diana. They rested quietly on their bed, untroubled by the discussion, however personal it may have become.

"You'll define it by the story of its creation," she said. "That's not a bad thing, nor good. I'm just warning you."

"Do you know what Rauschenberg said when he was asked how he saw the finished piece?" I asked.

"No."

"He said it was poetry."

Alison studied me. She was trying to read my emotions, I was sure, even as I tried to keep them unwritten. She shrugged.

"Yeah. Okay. Right," she said. "Why don't we just say it's Shakespeare for now?" She laughed.

I laughed, too. I could not help myself. It had been too long and I could not fail to take advantage of the opportunity. I sat on the couch and Alison joined me, sideways on the cushions with one foot tucked underneath her and the other resting on the floor. She took my hands in hers and explained that she was going to help with the move back to the London flat. I had always known there would be an end to the cottage. She asked me if I would like help packing. I told her I could manage.

Vincent left his bedroom, the one in Arles—lemons and lilacs—for an asylum in Saint-Rémy-de-Provence, in 1899. I left mine for London, on a Sunday, when Alison returned in her red car; left with purples and yellows, and with Penny and Diana on the rear seat. On Monday Alison and I visited a church, but we did not stay long, and left early, without farewells.

Chapter Eighteen

Monday, 23rd January, 1888

It is three days since I returned to college, and I do not think I have ever found Oxford to be so drab and dull. Elizabeth has been a friendly presence, of course, though she has become distinctly reserved in my company. I suspect that she has guessed the nature of my relationship with Mr. Taylor, but has neither the evidence to support her belief nor the backbone to raise the matter with me.

Mrs. Taylor remains inseparable from life at college. She and I are perfectly civil to each other, but nothing more. She would seek to expose me as some sort of fallen woman were it not that, in doing so, she would condemn herself by association, and Lady Diana, too.

It has hardly stopped raining for more than an hour since I arrived. Most of my time has been spent alone, in my room, reading in preparation for the start of this term's lectures. Occasionally I have been distracted by the new—that is, the older—Warber, not for its content but for its existence as an object and a gift. I left the second edition with Father, giving its fragility and need for protection as my reasons. He declined to accept my bootlaces, not feeling they were quite proper for the purpose of bookbinding.

I hold the lock of hair between thumb and forefinger, wondering to whom it belonged. Hannah? Or Warber himself? I must find something for Diana, to repay her the kindnesses of last term and the New Year. She should be arriving today, but since she is not lodging here in the college house I am not sure I shall see her until later in the week.

What of Matthew? Away from Barbroke, back within the familiar stones of Oxford, I am afraid that I may have jeopardized the relationship which he and I have allowed to form between us. I worry that Diana sees Matthew as Paris to her Romeo, but perhaps her last letter is more representative of a calmer demeanour than the jealous tantrum thrown at Barbroke. A mash is, after all, just a mash. She may be spooney on me, but she must see that we are of an age when these sentiments begin to gutter and die, and the realities of life take hold. I have the perspective of boarding-school, which she lacks, and therein lies the difference.

Matthew left a note for me. He seems to assume that I shall always be at college, able to receive his letters before his wife sees them and we are discovered. Unless, that is, he is indifferent to the possibility; but I cannot believe that to be the case as he takes the trouble to disguise his handwriting on the envelopes, however ineffectually. To date, however, we have been fortunate. He tells me that he has recovered from his pangs of self-doubt, and wishes to arrange further sittings. He was also kind enough to say that he has missed the pleasure of my company over the past weeks and is looking forward to our spending more time together this term. I replied yesterday afternoon to say that I should be delighted to sit for him again, but must wait until Lady Diana returns before making a commitment to precise dates and times.

My reply was the poorest of compositions. I struggled to express my feelings for him whilst simultaneously adopting an air of one who has been wronged. In one line I became too sentimental, and in the next too formal; in one thorough, in the next perfunctory. I am reminded of my attempts to write to Diana after my departure from Barbroke. I considered beginning anew, or even postponing the writing until today, but it was late and I doubted I should make a success of it under any circumstances. I hope to hear back from him later in the week.

Diana departed mere moments ago. To my great delight she called on me after dinner. She came into my room in a whirlwind of furs, which she proceeded to slough and throw onto the bed. She lay upon them, looked at me—I was still sitting at my desk, not having had opportunity to rise—and said, in a most affected voice, "Darling Penny! You must tell me all the news." Then she began to giggle and patted her hand on the coverlet. I sat beside her and she clasped my hands in hers and told me that she had missed me terribly and was so relieved to be back in Oxford with me. Other than a single "Diana" when she had first come through the door I had not said a word until this point, and when I did begin to speak I imagine I must have sounded like an idiot. My exact words were not much distant from, "I... You... When did you... I am so glad... Diana." She rolled over onto her side and curled herself around me so she could look up at my face. She had, she said, come straight to college directly her bags were off the carriage at her Oxford place. Everything at Barbroke had been a bore since I left, and she could not bear the thought of one more evening without "the incomparable delights of my companionship." I offered her tea. I think this must have offended her or, more precisely, its being a substitute for a more intimate response offended her. She sat up sharply and asked if I were not truly happy to see her. Thankfully I had had sufficient time to muster some degree of coherence, and I reassured her that indeed I, too, had been waiting impatiently for our reunion and was simply taken aback at her sudden arrival. This seemed to calm her. She leaned towards me and rested her head on my shoulder as she had done at the temple.

I had no real news to tell her. Nothing of interest has happened to me since I left Barbroke. I told her that she would not want to hear my stories of dinners with aunts and afternoons in the company of young cousins who live only to play at endless games of hide-and-seek. Diana repeated that her life had been much the same over the past weeks, and whilst I do not doubt the veracity of her account, her dinners and afternoons must have been on a far grander scale. She said nothing at all about the memorial service for her brother. If she wants to tell me of it then I am sure she will do so, just as she took me to the church when she was ready. We talked a little of the term ahead, of our hopes for our education, and of the events which we might attend, of which there were few for which we expressed real enthusiasm. We spoke of the University Galleries and our lectures, of Barbroke and that night in the Temple of Minerva.

Soon it was time for Diana to leave. She jumped up, every bit as quickly as she had fallen on the bed, and began to put on her furs. Then she paused and, reaching into her bag, which I had not even noticed in the blur of her arrival, she took out the green-covered copy of Swinburne which I had left resting on her bedroom door. I am to choose a poem—not today, she said, for it was already too late—which I shall read to her on some future evening when we are alone together. Then, as she was reaching to open the door, I remembered Matthew's letter. I did not say a word about it.

I hate the thought of upsetting Diana. She must be awfully delicate, these recent days. I am increasingly of the opinion that she has always been delicate, and that the air of confidence and social capability which she wears is as much a costume as her Thomasin garb.

Tuesday, 24th January, 1888

I wrote again to Matthew to let him know that a sitting at his studio would be possible on Friday. I have not yet decided what to say to Diana, but I was careful to leave the letter deliberately vague on the subject of her attendance.

Friday, 27th January, 1888

The weather cannot make up its mind what it wants to do. One minute it is pouring with freezing rain and the next it is perfectly fine and sunny. By rights it ought to be April. It was my misfortune to embark for the studio moments before one of the showers began, and arrive just as the sun appeared. Matthew put my clothes to dry near the fireplace and suggested that I wear a Japanese robe from his box of stage properties. It is silk, patterned with light-pink cherry blossoms on a background of dark fuchsia-red, and quite beautiful despite its being ragged in places.

We sat and talked, hesitantly, as though getting to know each other for the first time, which rested strangely with my state of undress. He told me that he had thought more on the representation of story in his painting. He remains uncertain as to the future course of his work, but has decided that this current piece—the painting of Diana and me—must be completed, and must be shown without a title or, if titled, must be titled in terms which identify the painting without being greatly prescriptive. He gave me an example to clarify my understanding, saying he would prefer to call a painting *Ship at Sea* rather than *H.M.S. Pinafore Encounters the Wrath of Poseidon*. Gradually we relaxed and events took their course.

I told Matthew that Lady Diana sent her apologies as she was unavoidably occupied with an engagement that had arisen only yesterday. He seemed untroubled by the news and asked if I wanted to sit for him, alone. If I did not feel as though I had deceived Diana previously—clearly a refusal to acknowledge an evident deception—it was brought home to me as I lay on the bed, propped on an additional pillow which served as Diana's breast.

As he painted, Matthew and I talked about Christmas. His time had been quiet and spent at home, in the company of family members and a few close friends. He had been up to London, but only to pass a weekend with an "old chum" by the name of Robert, who is now in publishing. I almost wondered aloud if he might know Father, but a bright, insistent voice in my head told me that to build any other ties between Matthew and my family, however tenuous, could bring nothing but trouble. I conveyed the dullness of life at home, and how I had missed him during the long evenings. Of Barbroke I spoke little, and restricted myself to details of the architecture, the library, the gardens, statuary and church. The same bright voice delivered a warning that talk of events, even an innocent luncheon or dinner, would be a betrayal.

Now, as I sit here, I do not see that there can be such a betrayal. Diana knows of my relationship with Matthew. Indeed, her fit of pique on the last day of my stay was caused by that knowledge. Do I resent her for making me resort to subterfuge today? I think yes, and that it is she who has betrayed me in her destruction of the gentle friendship which she and I enjoyed. Oh! but I remember the temple and the library and all the other marvels of Barbroke, and feel that we are closer than ever before and share something that is ours, and ours alone. Or is it only a mash? Diana gives the impression that it is more than that, but should I, too, not reflect that same impression if I knew no better?

No, Matthew heard only the most banal of stories about Barbroke, and he reacted to them all with a subdued interest. He made no inquiries after Diana. He did not even ask if she would be attending the next sitting, which we have scheduled for a week hence.

Once I had returned to my dry clothes I checked on the progress of the painting. Matthew has clearly been working on it in my absence, as a great deal of the background is now complete, leaving the two figures in partial detail, with small ovals of bright whiteness where their heads should be.

How shall I describe the painting? It is accomplished and, viewed as a whole, a fine likeness of the scene in the studio. As one would expect, Matthew has allowed his imagination to overtake the lacklustre truth of cloth backdrops and mothy linens. The result is a pleasing representation of mediæval stonework and draperies. I fear I may be damning with faint praise: in all honesty, the painting does not stir me to high emotion, and this even though I revel in the story it represents. What will another viewer take from it? For every Michael Angelo or Raffaelle there must be a thousand nameless artists whose work nevertheless bestows on our world some pleasing decoration. Before I left Oxford last year I saw in Matthew a man with a name that might stand with Turner and Millais. Now I see "Taylor" as though it were carved into the base of a decent copy of *Ludovica*, the creator of a reminder of greatness, but not greatness itself.

I made only a single mention of Mrs. Taylor, as I prepared to leave. I think I asked, "What of your wife?" I was almost persuaded that Matthew did not know of whom I was speaking, such was the mixture of tiredness and puzzlement with which his expression was endowed. It was as if he left the very idea of her at home when he departed for his studio. I could not articulate my question in any fashion more direct so I stood wordlessly and waited for some verbal response, half expecting it to be, "My wife? My dear, I am not married." It was not, of course. Matthew demanded to know what I meant by asking after her. I meant a great number of things. Did she suspect the nature of our meetings? What would she do if she discovered us? How could we continue our sittings if she objected? On and on the questions went, but not a one was spoken aloud. Yet Matthew's rising impatience was cause enough for me to find my voice: what did Mrs. Taylor know of our meetings? Again, I thought he did not comprehend the question, possibly not even the language in which it was posed, such was his portrayal of bewilderment. Then, just as I believed he was going to answer, he instead changed the subject and, announcing that he had a Christmas present for me, he hurried away, into the little kitchen. When he re-emerged he held a silver hand-mirror, tied round with a red, satin bow. It is beside me now. On the back, along the handle and around the edges, are flowers in low relief, which Matthew told me are lilacs, the flower of "the first emotions of love." I blushed furiously at his mention of love, and hugged him as I thanked him, to hide my glowing cheeks.

It is getting late and tomorrow I am to pass some hours at the Galleries. I felt obliged to return in the company of Elizabeth, to whom I have spoken so often of the afternoon spent there with Diana. I am expected to give her the Grand Tour, and only hope she will not mind my reading out of the guide-books for much of it. It will not be the same.

It is a beautiful mirror but I am beginning to doubt that I am worthy of its sentiment.

Saturday, 28th January, 1888

Home at last, after far too much time spent in the company of Miss Ashdown. We arrived at the Galleries a little after one—no waiving of the 2d. this time—and I steered the same course through the exhibits as I took on my previous visit. I found it impossible to relax: at every moment I expected Elizabeth to ask about Matthew or Diana. My conscience sat on my shoulder, whispering the truth to me, over and over, and leaving me convinced that my companion would hear, and question, and demand remorse. Yet I sit here having spoken not a word that might compromise the privacy of my relationships. Miss Ashdown contented herself with news of the beauty of Barbroke and brought to the conversation, in return, assorted fragments of gossip which were forgotten even before leaving the Galleries.

All of this would have remained unremarked upon in these pages were it not for the fact that the day of such uneventful boredom was a mere harbinger to her goodbye, delivered at the doors to our respective rooms. To my adieu she replied, "Do please be careful, Penelope. There are few as accepting as am I, even in a place as modern as the one in which we find ourselves." I stood open-mouthed—literally open-mouthed—as she closed her door behind her.

Damn her. Damn her and all like her. I have no heart for false friends.

Sunday, 29th January, 1888

I had decided that today would be the day on which I told Diana of Friday's sitting with Matthew. I had planned to be a terrible coward and tell her in a public place. However, the opportunity did not present itself.

We once again enjoyed—or were subjected to—the company of her tame don, the Reverend Professor Parker. I have not forgotten that it was he from whom news of our visit to the Galleries had started its voyage to the ear of Matthew's wife. He seemed less jovial than I remembered his being during our previous encounter. When he was across the churchyard, muttering to some other fellow in a dog-collar, Diana informed me that he had appeared at her Oxford residence on Friday evening and suggested that he accompany her to the Sunday service. She was invited to join him and his wife for luncheon at their home, which is quite close to college. She is sure that her mother organized the entire proposal, probably when the Rev. J.L.P. attended the memorial service at Barbroke. It was the first mention of the memorial since Diana's return, but I had no time to continue in that vein as the professor returned at a pace, as if suddenly gripped by a sense of negligence in his duties. Would he—Diana asked, without having consulted me—would he mind terribly if I joined the family for lunch, too? Since I was standing right there in front of the man there was little for the Rev. J.L.P. to do but acquiesce to Diana's request. He suggested to her that I might have other commitments but she assured him that I had not. She was quite right, but I still find it to have been somewhat presumptuous. The reverend called over to his wife and the four of us walked the short distance to their home.

Mrs. Parker is a short woman, but every bit as thin as her husband. The two of them make quite the pair: he stands at least a foot taller than his wife, and she must half-walk, half-run if she is to keep up with his strides, which even Diana and I struggle to match. Mrs. P. is softly spoken, and offers only a few short sentences between long pauses. Unfortunately, these pauses are rarely proceeded by any question or observation upon which one might easily comment. I was thankful for her husband's presence: without it our conversation would have been decidedly awkward.

The reverend became more light-hearted as we neared his home, as though shedding a character adopted when in church. He began to ask us about our time at Barbroke. Had I seen the library? Had there been a hunt? Even in my state of nervous suspicion, I could find nothing accusatory in his investigation. When it became clear that neither Diana nor I had any great tales to recount, he told us of his trip to Norfolk to stay with the family of an old school friend, by the name of Hector or Harry, I forget which. His stories were as flat as the Fens themselves, but I had to admire his gusto in relating them. I almost allowed myself to relax and enjoy being amongst company, but always the quiet, insistent voice, and Diana beside me in her ignorance of my deceit.

Luncheon was roast mutton and vegetables. We talked of our studies: what we hoped to achieve this term and our plans for the future, vague and insubstantial as they were. All seemed to be going swimmingly until the Rev. J.L.P. asked how our sittings with Mr. Taylor were progressing. Diana and I exchanged the same, surprised expression—all raised eyebrows and motionless cutlery—across the table. She, however, recovered far more gracefully and swiftly than did I. She replied in a voice utterly free from any hint that the question was unexpected. Mr. Taylor, she said, had been reconsidering his place within the art world and had advised us that our sittings would cease until he had "rediscovered a suitable way to please the Muse." If I were not feeling terrible enough at this point, the Rev. J.L.P.'s response ensured that my guilt was almost unbearable.

According to our host, he had had it from Miss Callow that Mr. Taylor's block had passed and he was keen to continue his work on our return to Oxford. Clearly, there are both up and down lines between Mrs. Taylor and our reverend. I stared at my plate as Diana informed all present that we—meaning she and I—were delighted to hear the news, and no doubt Mr. Taylor would contact us shortly to make arrangements. She looked over at me and all eyes followed hers until I thought I should be overcome with some dreadful hysteria and confess everything: Friday's sitting, my relationship with Matthew, the events at Barbroke. Then, just as I felt I must say something or appear dumbstruck, Mrs. P. suggested we rise and take an afternoon constitutional around the University Parks. The relief I felt at the table has since been supplanted by my fear that Mrs. P. had taken pity on me, which can only mean that she was aware of my distress, and quite possibly the reasons for it.

Away from the confines of the reverend's house our talk turned—thankfully—to the banalities of life. Our stroll extended from the Parks, to college. Diana and I took our leave of the Parkers and went straight to my room, where I did something which now seems foolish in the extreme: I gave Diana the mirror from Matthew. She saw it on my dresser, still with the bow around its handle, and asked me about it, and I could not think straight after all the events of the day. Oh! I ought to have told her the truth or, if not, some story about its being a Christmas present from my parents, or a relative, or an old friend from school. I ought to have told her anything but the words I found tumbling from my mouth: "Oh, that is... Well, it is... It is a gift for you." The instant I had uttered this nonsense I realized my mistake, but it was too late. Diana protested, saying it seemed an expensive gift. I, even in my turmoil, found the wherewithal to assure her that it was the least I could do after the kindnesses she had shown me over the past months. At that she threw her arms around me, kissed me on the lips, and told me I was more wonderful than she had ever dared to hope. A call came from downstairs to inform us that her carriage had arrived, and she, and the mirror, were gone.

Since that time I have done little. I ate dinner with Elizabeth. Perhaps I have judged her too harshly. We spoke only of irrelevancies, but her desire to be in my company seems genuine and I am left with the impression that hers is an open door should I need her help. She is older than am I, and there is an air of the maternal about her. I suspect it is this against which I have railed, rather than any contrariness in action or opinion.

Diana and I have a lecture together, tomorrow. She is to meet me here and travel with me, either on foot or by carriage, depending on the weather. I must tell her what has happened. I cannot bear the thought of disappointing her expectations so deeply. More than that, I fear I shall lose her because of these actions, which is to suppose that I have her now. At the beginning of the week I was reassuring myself that she recognized the nature of our friendship with the same clear-headedness as I ascribed to myself. Now I discover I am the one by whom the loss will be keenly felt, the one whose head is full of confusion and whispering voices.

CHAPTER NINETEEN

No more snow in London. No monks, no refuge. Hopper again: Jo, alone, with coffee and the darkness outside the window. Friedrich, watching everyone as they turned away. Friedrich, turning away himself, the anonymous *Rückenfigur* even he did not know. I saw the want of these people in the world outside and in the hand-mirror I had brought with me.

Taylor's painting remained faithful. It hung, alone, on the walls of the room in which I ate, worked and slept. I had removed all the other decorations—the mediocre acquisitions of just-so-many Sunday markets—no longer caring what Emily thought. And so it hung alone, and I shared my flat with Diana and Penny, for as long as nobody detected their change of address and came searching for them. It seemed only right that they were positioned where I could give them the companionship they deserved. I found them, after all, when they had been lost for so many years. Alison asked about them, on the occasions when she called to see me, which she did often. I told her that I was still researching, that it was too soon. She was glad I had something to keep me occupied. I wondered if she would change her mind, as Emily had done.

I continued to read the diary, of course. Penny told Diana about her sitting with Taylor, but she did not mention that he was the source of the mirror, realizing that nothing was to be gained by brutal honesty. They were in Penny's room: low lights, scattered papers underfoot and Chatterton on the bed, or something dying, at least. Diana asked Penny if anything more than painting took place in the studio on that first Friday of the new term. Penny told the truth and gained nothing by it.

Diana left without saying another word. But she must have returned to sit for the painting, because there she lay, just as she lay on her tomb. A painter possessed of greater talent could have worked from sketches and memory, but not Taylor.

I ambled through the pages which followed: a few days, a week, a few weeks. Almost every mention of Diana was a statement of her disappearance, an absence of letters, an empty seat at a lecture. Just once did she appear in person, a face in the window of a passing carriage. Penny could not even be sure it was Diana.

Penny's sittings continued, as did the affair with Taylor. Her reports of their hours together became abbreviated, more time-sheet than cherished memory, a grudging acceptance of the acts themselves and the nature of the actors. She had become the protagonist of her own story and unwittingly relinquished her authorship; except for the day she thought she saw Diana, passing along Broad Street amongst the stones of central Oxford. Then, at least as she told it, she regained herself for long enough to question, to put aside all justifications from circumstance and step out of her ingénue role. Perhaps that was why she declared herself uncertain as to the identity of the woman in the carriage: being sure it was Diana would have forced her to face the reality of her emotions. Having nowhere to run, she could not afford to experience something from which she desired to escape. So, she spent her time lying to Miss Ashdown and avoiding Mrs Taylor. She tried to make new friends but found that the time to make friends had already passed. She wrote to Diana, twice, but never received a reply and did not bother to keep copies of the letters she sent. She tried to decide if she ought to give back the Warber and the Swinburne, the silver pencil and guidebooks. In the end, after a week of contradictory entries, she concluded that they should remain with her unless there was an expressed desire for their return. She had lost her silver mirror to Diana, she reasoned.

I replayed their argument as I picked up the shards of broken lamp from the bedroom carpet. Penny's version of it was brief, anodyne and impersonal, as though she were setting out an inevitability as a lesson to others. It was her written interpretation of all those Victorian paintings conceived from a longing to pass on some moral message. The fallen woman loses all and condemns herself and her children to destitution, or she turns away from her corrupt life in an epiphany of divine clarity. In either case, the invitation to the viewer does not offer an empathy with the players, but only a reflection on their inherent nature, their failings and moral inadequacies, their ability—or inability—to save themselves. There but for the grace of God, they say, and only then if grace falls upon a vessel of unquestioning acceptance. Penny, eclipsing her role as Olivia, had become a character in a painting of her own, a portrait of her own fallibility. In that, there were echoes of what I wanted her to be: not some living person into whose life I intruded, but the idea of a person, an outline that I could sketch and adorn and make my own.

My thoughts wandered as I sat by the window, reading, looking for Diana, second-guessing Penny. I stopped whenever the words on the page started to blur and cast off their meaning: I would mark my progress, close the book and make a hot drink, or watch the to-and-fro of city dwellers on a London side-street. Once, I took down the painting and held it against the morning sun. The raking light added texture and depth to the surface of paint and varnish, showing me its alterations and corrections. I made brief notes. I read on with a drifting lassitude that might have suggested enjoyment.

It was Alison's idea that we go out for an afternoon. She tried to express her concern for me in words which papered over it, in proposals for activities which would do me good, rather than exhortations to avoid those which were hurting me. She wanted fresh air, I wanted warmth. She wanted to talk, I wanted peace. We compromised on an afternoon at the National Gallery.

Inside the Gallery, away from the cold of Trafalgar Square, Alison and I hardly spoke. We had made the trip before, many times, and there was little left to say. Then we found ourselves in front of one particular painting and I became lost in the horror of the thing.

I recognized the piece. I had been there too often not to have seen it, not to have appreciated its visceral presence, but it had never breached my academic armour as it did on that day. The little white card beside the frame read, "*Two Followers of Cadmus Devoured by a Dragon*, 1588", and beneath that, "Cornelis van Haarlem". There were a few lines of text explaining the scene, painted from another of Ovid's *Metamorphoses*. The followers of Cadmus go to fetch water from a well and are killed by a dragon which guards it. In the background of the painting stands Cadmus, driving his lance into the mouth of the dragon. It passes through the base of the skull, forcing the beast up onto its back legs as its front claws reach up, hopelessly, to slash at the weapon. But that is a vision of the future, time passing in the movement from front to back of the image in the frame. Come forward and one is amongst the followers' slaughter. I fell into the butchery and with it a tangible reality. Penny had her Michelangelo study in red chalk—the demon gnawing the leg of a man—but it was nothing compared to the painting before me. The lips of the dragon turn back on themselves to expose rows of white fangs. It holds itself in place with its front claws, tearing at the flesh of one of the two naked men on the ground. That man's upper body is hidden beneath the monster but his head is visible, torn off at the neck and dropped in the dirt, front and centre, eyes closed, mouth open, trachea gaping, a dark hole beneath rings of cartilage. And under that headless body the second man supports himself on his crooked right arm whilst he reaches up with his left, trying to pull the monster from him, trying to save himself, but failing, failing in the darkness which envelops him, failing because the dragon is biting his face off. The razored teeth pierce him and slice deep through the skin of his cheek. Rivulets of blood run down to his neck from each agonizing wound and the eyes of the dragon—the black, red-rimmed eyes of the dragon—stare out, beyond his prey, beyond the canvas, out at the next victim. I was the next victim. There was no way to move quickly enough, away from snaking tail, grasping claws, the long, red tongue that must be caressing the palate of the man before me. All I could do was cry, not quietly as at Saint Cecilia's but loudly, obviously, becoming the focal point of the gallery, bringing people to my side.

Alison put her arm around me and led me away. I had staunched the flow of tears and started to mumble a few words to her but she grasped my shoulder tightly and told me there was no need for apologies. We rested on a hard bench, facing Velázquez's *Rokeby Venus* as the goddess looked back at us from her impossible mirror. Old scars. Alison told me it was normal to feel as I did, normal after everything. She suggested we leave, but it seemed too early to me, and there was nowhere to go apart from home, which was not really home, just a place to store purples and yellows, blues and paintings. Home could wait. I sat up straight and gave the necessary smile, the one which would mean I could stay out a little longer.

"I'd like to see the Friedrich," I said.

"Which Friedrich?"

"There's only one. Come on."

We walked through the rooms of the gallery until we came to it: "*Winter Landscape*, 1811, Caspar David Friedrich".

"What do you see?" I asked Alison.

"How do you mean?"

"The painting. What do you see? What is it about? If you had to write a paper on it, what would you write?"

"Okay," she began. "So, it's a snowy landscape. The foreground's all white. A few tufts of grass poking through the snow." She pointed at several small patches of green. "There's a group of fir trees in the middle of the painting, five or six of them, and one or two more a little farther away. In front of the firs are grey rocks, boulders really. A man, maybe a boy, is sitting in the snow, with his back propped against one of the rocks. His hands are in front of his face, palms together. I'd say he's praying. He's facing a tall, thin cross, about half as high as the tallest tree, with a Christ figure on it which is maybe a third of its overall height. So, yes, he's praying. And he's disabled in some way because on a line from the bottom right of the canvas, across the snow to the man, two crutches have been left behind."

She waited for my approval, or some comment. I nodded.

"And?" I asked.

"And? Well, the obvious thing is the cathedral towards the

back of the scene, where the snow fades into a misty skyline. The cathedral rises from the mist like it's not real. Like a metaphor for heaven, maybe. It's behind a wall with an open archway. The wall is just as spectral. I suppose Saint Peter could be waiting there. Do you want more? The placement of objects on the plane, the ratios and sizes? The paint and varnish? I'm sure there's a technical bulletin somewhere."

Alison realized what she had said before I had decided if I wanted to respond or just walk away.

"I'm sorry," she said. "I think I'm hungry." She paused, then faced the painting again and continued, "It's about redemption through Christ. The man has found his Saviour, has made it through the snow to this point of closeness to God, and the gates of heaven are open to him. Don't you think?"

"I'm not as sure as I used to be," I said.

"No?"

"No. Looked at another way, the man has given up. He's stopped in the middle of nowhere, too tired to continue, too tired even to carry his crutches those last few yards. He's going to die there, alone in the snow. And knowing that he's going to die he prays to Christ in hope of heaven. So maybe you're right, and the cathedral is Friedrich's way of showing that his prayers have been answered. But part of me thinks that the mist and the fir trees hide the cathedral, block it from his view. It's really there, real warmth and sanctuary, but the poor traveller doesn't know it. He's like a man in the desert, giving up and dying of thirst when there's an oasis over the next dune. Maybe the cross shows he has someone to turn to, even then. The cynic in me sees it as the distraction which killed him."

Alison opened her mouth to speak, then closed it without a word. She shrugged.

"Still," she said, "at least he isn't getting his face bitten off by a dragon."

She waited until I reacted and then allowed herself to match my grin with one of her own, part relief, part gratitude.

"Yes. At least he's not getting his face bitten off," I said. "I'm sorry about all that fuss. I might have missed a pill or two somewhere. She's not reminding me."

"No," said Alison, taking my hand. "No, she's not reminding you."

"I don't want to sit and eat, Al, not right now. Can we walk a little? We could get you some chocolate or something, just for the time being. All right?"

"All right. Where do you want to go?"

"Nowhere in particular. I don't have a destination, really. Maybe Charing Cross Road, that direction?"

Alison agreed. We walked slowly along the northern side of Trafalgar Square, keeping our distance from the lions and Nelson, although they never even bothered to glance at us. The newsagent's on Charing Cross Road was thoroughly run-down and rendered utterly dismal by the gloom of the London winter. It sold chocolate and snacks, though, which satisfied Alison's immediate needs. I needed to walk, away from the dragon, away from landscapes and crucifixes, from a home that was not home, from friends that never were. It was a journey that existed merely to leave the point of departure.

We peered into the windows of the second-hand bookshops, at strange contrasts of cheap paperbacks and leather-bound casualties of a decayed aristocracy. Up towards Tottenham Court Road station, on the left, stood Foyles, the grandfather of all these booksellers. It moved there in the early years of the twentieth century. Diana never saw it. And then we were in Bloomsbury, where the Pre-Raphaelite Brotherhood was founded, about forty years before Penny went up to Oxford: Millais, Rossetti, William Holman Hunt, and more members to follow, coming together to express genuine ideas through the reflection of nature, to sympathize with the heartfelt, to eschew the conventional. We could have walked anywhere but we would still have been somewhere haunted by Penny and Diana. So much of London was involved in their lives, if not by location then by association, by the idea of the metropolis as the centre of Victorian society.

"You've hardly spoken," said Alison, as we headed back towards Oxford Street. "Do you want to talk about it? Would that help?"

"It? Which it? All the its?"

"Yes. All. Any. Emily. The cottage. The painting."

"Penny and Diana?"

"Penny and Diana. Art. Anything, Anna. Just a starting point. Something gentle."

She squeezed my hand and stopped walking. I had no option but to stop beside her. She moved round until she was facing me and took my other hand.

"You have to talk," she said. "I know it's hard, and I know it takes time, but you have to say something, if you can, if you're not too afraid. I shan't force you. But if you can."

Everything was blue again, draining the colours. I remembered when I was a child and my mother had explained how the sodium street-lamps gave out such a pure, yellow light that no other colours would appear, everything became shades of yellow. It was a terrifying thought to me, that something could steal the colours from the world and leave only one behind. But she explained it, it was science, and through the explanation it lost its ability to scare me. I wanted explanations. I wanted to listen, not talk. I wanted the woman—the woman who held my hand and told me everything would be all right—I wanted her to say the words to make it right, there and then. Nothing magical, nothing Eleusinian, swathed in ceremony and mystery. The electrons jumped from one place to another and when they did they gave out a bit of energy and that energy was light and the size of their jump made the light yellow. The blue was there because, because why? Because things happen? Because decisions were made? Because I did not hold an ice cream tightly enough, and because Emily went out in the snow? I was not ready to talk. How could I be ready to talk with all the yellows and purples missing?

"Not yet," I said.

We walked on, down through Soho, heading towards Piccadilly Circus. There were models working behind the red-lit curtains, according to signs by the doors, black marker running where the drizzle soaked the paper. We did not linger. The dwindling daylight and intensifying rain drove me forward with thoughts of a warm bus and a return to Penny and Diana, whom I could not escape, and from whom

I should not have tried to run. They were the easy part of life because they were immutable. All that they were, all they had done, was fixed, reduced to archæology. Or I was wrong. The rest, the complex blue, continued through me, so all answers were contingent, just stepping stones to something else, echoes of an irredeemably unsettled past. I could definitely have been wrong.

Alison was keeping pace, although I had no reason to think that my troubles were shared with her: darkness and rain were enough. But Soho had dragons that day, and I would not let them tear my head from my neck, or rip the flesh from my skull. I was strong and fast, and the fear was leaving me. I slipped my hand from Alison's and began to run, through the worsening rain, Alison calling after me, increasingly breathless. I slowed and turned, walking backwards along the pavement as the water dripped from the tip of my nose.

"It's all right, Al," I said. "If you keep up with me everything will be all right."

I ran on. The water in my eyes smeared the neon lights of Soho, the reds and yellows. I wanted lemon drops. I had lemon drops as a child. But no time for lemon drops when dragons were abroad.

We sat on the upper deck of the bus. Alison told me she was going to come home with me and cook dinner. I wiped my arm across the condensation and looked out at the world, just as I had done when returning from Barbroke. We were passing Marble Arch, where Samuel Warber was hanged by the neck until dead. The only remembrance was a circular, stone plaque set into the pavement of Edgware Road, with an "X" in its centre and "The Site of Tyburn Tree" carved around its circumference. The Tree was long gone: no sign of the three-legged gallows, each leg joined to the next by an overhead beam, a triangle which dispatched the condemned in a macabre, kicking chorus line.

"The great thing about buses," I said, "is that they don't stop at the firs. They'll take you all the way to the gates of the cathedral."

I rested my head on Alison's shoulder and slept.

CHAPTER TWENTY

Tuesday, 21st February, 1888

Matthew is tiring of me. He greets me with a familiarity that has ground to dust the excitement he must once have felt. Despite my having arrived early, this last sitting was precisely that: a sitting, involving nothing but my posing for him. It seems ridiculous that such a change should have come upon him so quickly. I have been led to understand that this is the way of the adulterer: passion born of the illicit, the new and forbidden, which fades as the affair—for it deserves to be named in accordance with its nature—passion which fades as the affair becomes quotidian. Yet I did not wish to believe it was true of him.

I miss Diana more with the passing of each day, and with a keenness which I thought I had reserved for Matthew alone. Apart from my one glimpse of her she has become a phantom, flitting through Oxford only at night, if at all. I have no idea how she might be continuing her academic work, which must suffer greatly from her lack of attendance at lectures and from the absence of fellow students with whom to converse. As regards companionship, no doubt she has an eager coterie here in Oxford and another in London, even outside the season. I have implored her to meet with me, to no avail. I have asked her to write, asked her forgiveness, apologized until the ashes ran over my penitent's head. I have received nothing in return. Now, as if losing her friendship were not enough, I fear for the continuance of my sittings, which are no longer clothed in the propriety conferred by her attendance. Voices are whispering and the whispers grow louder.

This morning I left another note for her on the table in the hall. It is no longer there so I can only suppose that she, or some servant of hers, has collected it. I sent to her a line of Swinburne, in hopes that the source will play to her romantic sensibilities, that the meaning will show my drifting from Matthew and the loss I feel in her distance, and that the dual evocation therein might outweigh thoughts currently dominated by my infidelity.

"I have lived long enough, having seen one thing, that love hath an end."

I must leave for afternoon lectures.

It is late, later than I ought to be awake and writing. I have a towel curled along the bottom of the door so that the light cannot escape to tell tales on me. She came, this evening, as dinner drew to a close. She came and found me in the dining room, as I sat by Elizabeth, sharing the meaningless events of the empty day. She came and she was angry. She held my note in one hand and placed the other on my shoulder and asked, in a measured, formal voice which I have never before heard from her, that I excuse myself so we might talk for a few minutes. She did not look at any other woman at the table. She did not wait for my reply before leaving—with the briefest of nods in the direction of Miss Callow—to wait in the hall. I made my excuses, telling my friends that I had heard Lady Diana had not taken well to the memorial service for her brother and that I should hasten to her side. I should say that not one of them believed me, but yet each one nodded as though she did.

In the hallway I greeted Diana warmly, with language adopted to convey my relief that she was well and confirm my happiness in seeing her. She remained steadfastly dumb, even as she held herself in a posture so stiff that I took it to indicate a barely suppressed desire to shout. She moved, wordlessly, to the staircase and I followed her as she ascended.

When we were in my room she began to lose the semblance of composure. She thrust the note into my hands and demanded to know what the devil I meant by it. Had I lost my mind? Was I trying to scare her into some form of submission? Ought she to have had the college send for a doctor? A constable? I watched the anger drain from her with each question. Her shoulders relaxed and her arms fell to her side, until she stood before me, her face downcast, tears on her cheeks, her chest rising and falling with shallow, gulping breaths. She pointed a shaking finger at the note, still crumpled in my grasp, and said, in the faintest of voices, "I thought I should find you dead."

How could I have been so foolish? "I have lived long enough." The line seemed so perfect for my needs, so pointed in its expression of my loss. Oh! but it was perfect because I knew the next line, wherein the real message lay: "Goddess and maiden and queen, be near me now and befriend." Diana did not have the book with her, and why would she remember every line, or have copied every single poem into her leather pocket-book? Ripped from the verse, alone and of itself, my note was nothing more than a final goodbye. I had been strewing flowers and uttering a benediction. I took her in my arms and ran my fingers through her hair. She grew limp and I should shortly have been unable to prevent her fall had we not moved slowly towards the bed. There we sat, side by side, each talking to the far wall of the room, or the floor.

Diana's ire had subsided with that first outburst. In truth I do not think she was ever really angry. What I had perceived as anger was fear and a longing for relief, each of these pressing upon her a range of emotions which found their expression in accusation and reprimand.

We spoke, at first, of our time at Barbroke, seeking to concentrate on a topic which belonged to us both, and from which we took comfort. Then Diana asked me about Matthew, and my reasons for deceiving her. She had never thought that she would immediately replace him in my affections, she said, only that we should talk on the subject and, together, find our way. I had not been unfaithful to her with Matthew, she said, any more than I had been unfaithful to Matthew with her. This I felt to be of little comfort, but I bit my tongue. My seeing him without her knowledge, and concealing that meeting, these were actions of a different complexion. In these, she said, I had behaved selfishly and without any thought for her. This much I already knew. I tried to explain. I told her that it had all happened quickly on my return to Oxford, and that I had acted impulsively, finding myself isolated and unaware of the true depth of her feelings. Is that the truth? I may be telling the stories I need to hear if I am not to believe myself the worst sort of friend.

As for the note, I apologized for that, too, and she accepted the honesty of my contrition. Indeed, I seemed to have brought her the relief which she sought. Had we turned to the essence of our friendship, had we taken the opportunity to express our feelings towards one another, I am not confident that she would have found it to offer any solace. I have not yet come to an understanding of my emotions. The love—is it love?—which I feel for Matthew has withered once more, just as his for me. It saddens me but it comes as no surprise. Diana is some other phenomenon entirely. I find myself thinking of the drawing by Michael Angelo: the demon gnawing at the calf of some poor man. Does the suffering unfortunate know what is happening, what creature attacks him? Or does he know only the pain, and wonder at its identity, and strive to comprehend and through comprehension find deliverance? Drawings of that type are always warnings to the living, are they not? No one has seen a demon, or felt its bite, and yet we look at the pictures and some dark memory rises: it is a memory of neither demons nor their bites, but of whatever we most fear. I fear those memories themselves. I fear them all the more for not knowing their source or their nature, for knowing only that they surely exist. Matthew did not bring them to the surface, as I might have supposed he would. Diana, however, throws out nets for them, dredges, casts lines baited with I-know-not-what. If it is not a physical act fastened hard upon the hook then it must be some emotion. If the reeling-in is not driven by the illicit made tangible then... What? It is something in the admission of love, the acceptance of the divine in one for whom such godliness should be proscribed. Or it is not. We did not require an answer and I should not have been able to provide one, even if we had.

Slowly, as we talked, we shifted, until we lay together on the bed. It was not that we were unaware of our movement, but I, at least, felt that speaking of it would break the ease of our transition from argument to gentle sharing. There was a fragility, acknowledged in that which we allowed to pass between us and in that which remained unspoken. I tore up the note and threw the little pieces above us. They fluttered down upon our faces like the feathers of poor, fallen Icarus; like the snowflakes of Barbroke. I watched Diana laugh and remembered how I adore to see her happy.

She left about two hours ago. I have been lying on the bed, alone, reflecting on the evening and what is to come in the next few days. On Friday I shall sit for Matthew, in the company of Diana. I have given her my word that nothing "intimate" will happen between Matthew and me. His recent paucity of interest should render it a promise which is not so terribly difficult to keep. I shall come to the studio a little later than usual and she will join me shortly afterwards. I shall have enough time to tell Matthew of her impending arrival without finding myself alone with him for a period sufficient for other purposes.

I am terribly tired. Diana is going to meet me in the morning so that we may attend our lectures together. I feel a certain calmness, but whilst it is a change which is to be welcomed I fear it may come before a storm. My academic progress has been woeful thus far this term. I shall see Diana tomorrow, but then I must sequester myself from society, and read, and annotate, and live the cloistered life of the scholar. Until Friday, at least.

Friday, 24th February, 1888

It has been a trying day. At least I faced Matthew and Miss Callow with Diana by my side. I am hopeful that these challenges—faced and overcome—are my Cape Horn, and now I may expect an easier passage.

I do not understand how Mr. Taylor can be so disregardful of my attentions and yet so furious at the interference he perceives in the presence of Diana. I met him before our sitting, as arranged, but arrived late. I told him that I had found it necessary to return to college in order to retrieve my gloves, having forgotten them and finding the morning bitterly cold after a few minutes walking towards the studio. It has been frightfully cold: the fields look like a scene from a Christmas card, covered in hoar frost and mist. Matthew seemed untroubled by my tardiness. Indeed, he seemed decidedly less than enthusiastic about our meeting at all, but I have become inured to that. Such was his generally-expressed apathy that I was a little taken aback at the vehemence with which he communicated his displeasure at the news of Diana's imminent arrival. Why had I not told him sooner? Could I not have written him a note? Was she returning for the remainder of the sittings? I did as I must and played the innocent. Surely, he needed Diana to finish the painting of Thomas, did he not? Had I given the impression that her absence was unending? He, of course, had no answers for my questions. We sat sipping tea, each constructing our own truths from the tension between us.

It came as a relief to us both, I believe, when the bell rang and Matthew departed to greet Diana. I could read no animosity in their countenances when they entered the room. True, Mr. Taylor was not smiling, but there was no sign of the scowl he had worn when he left. Diana was smiling, in that way of hers, just at the corners of her mouth. She hurried over and embraced me as I stood to greet her. Only two days ago we met for lectures, and lunch, and a gentle walk by the river, yet we held each other as though each of those days had lasted a month. Then, hand in hand, we hurried to get changed into our outfits, leaving Matthew to clear away the tea "set". When we revealed ourselves in character he was already behind his canvas, and we took our positions on the bed without further delay.

There is a feeling one gets when one has a secret and stands in the presence of those who are not aware of it. It is a sense of duplicity, and an undesired assurance that there must be signs of the deceit, visible to all around, as though one were handing out visiting cards bearing a hand-written note of the transgression. Such were my feelings as I settled my head on Diana's breast this morning. I cannot list a single aspect of our appearance from which even the most perspicacious observer might have gleaned the deeper measure of our friendship. Did Thomas hold Olivia a little tighter? Not so tightly that the strain showed. Was Thomas's brow softer than it had been? Not so soft that a person—even a person painting that face—would notice. Did I settle a little deeper into that yielding flesh? Did my gaze lose its focus and pass by Matthew entirely? If so, these subtle variations went unnoticed or unremarked. Yet they, and memories of Barbroke, were all that occupied my thoughts as I lay, inanimate, on the bed.

Occasionally Mr. Taylor asked one or the other of us to move her arm slightly, or adjust the tilt of her head, or some such refinement. He worked more slowly today than has been his habit on previous occasions, and spent more time to the side of his canvas, holding his brush at arm's length and squinting at the scene before him. Diana whispered in my ear that if he took much longer he would have to paint her as she slept, and I could not suppress a giggle which, to my horror, passed untroubled through the drapery of the bed and echoed around the room. All movement behind the canvas ceased. The steady rise and fall of Diana's chest halted abruptly: both she and I held our breaths, not inhaling again until Mr. Taylor returned to his daubings.

After three hours or so, Matthew told us that he had done all he felt able to do today. He thanked us for our time and began to clean his brushes without looking up again. I think I heard him muttering to himself, but I could not discern his meaning. Diana and I whispered to each other as we changed, not wishing to cause another disturbance. I watched as she undid the gold belt and removed her tunic, slipped off her shoes and hose, left Thomas behind and became Thomasin, and then, as she donned the clothes she had worn on her arrival, my Diana.

Matthew was in the kitchen when we emerged. He acknowledged us with a dismissive wave of his left hand. His right held a silver flask. As we descended the stairs we heard him washing dishes with an exaggerated clinking of glass and porcelain.

We had arranged for Diana's carriage to collect her from college, to allow ourselves the pleasure of a walk in each other's company. She asked if I thought we should be sitting again next week. I said I did not know. I shall write to Mr. Taylor tomorrow or Sunday to determine when—or if—he wishes to see us. Then Diana asked if I had chosen a poem from Swinburne for her. I had completely forgotten, overwhelmed as I have been with all that has happened during these past weeks. I did not judge this to be the best of replies and so told her that I find the entire book to be an *embarras de richesses* and am struggling to make a selection.

At about half the distance home to college Diana stopped walking and continued her inquisition. Had the intimacies between Mr. Taylor and me come to an end? This was an easy truth to tell: he and I have not discussed the physical aspect of our entanglement but I have kept my word. I shall continue to do my utmost to ensure that we do not find ourselves in situations which might afford him any such opportunities. It may have been an easy truth, but it was not one which met with Diana's complete approval. She expects me to be frank with Matthew, which can do nothing but worsen an already difficult and tense relationship. I took her hand and assured her that all will settle and we shall have what we desire, without the need for confrontation. I worry that she thinks me selfish. We walked on, however, engaging in gentle, natural conversation which suggested I had assuaged the worst of her fears.

Miss Callow was waiting for us on our return to college. We had hardly set foot in the hall when she appeared from the door of her office. She greeted us warmly, asking politely if we should mind—"once we had removed our coats and so forth"—joining her in the office for a few minutes, "to discuss some matters of college life." Such an invitation could be deserving of nothing less than foreboding, and Diana's tight lips and raised eyebrows did little to quell my fears.

The Principal's office—an office in which I have had, thus far, neither need nor opportunity to find myself—is an understated affair, much in keeping with the college. A dark mahogany desk is the only substantial item of furniture in the room, apart from the bookcases which line three of the four walls. The remaining wall frames two large windows overlooking the garden, with a potted aspidistra on a spindly stand between the two. Miss Callow was sitting behind the desk. She indicated that we should occupy the chairs across from her, which we did. I fervently hoped that she was about to address some administrative detail of our college membership, or seating plans for a dinner, or, indeed, anything but that which I knew was the reason for our presence in her office.

I have, yet again, been sheltered from the true egregiousness of my actions by Diana. Miss Callow dressed her observations in academic clothes. She said she had noticed a "deterioration" in our work which was causing her some distress. She inquired whether or not we were both entirely content, being up at Oxford. Or might we have problems at home with which she could be of some assistance? Diana and I dutifully apologized for our lack of academic success and shook our heads at the suggestion that we might be sad or troubled. Only then did Miss Callow submit that we were "spending a little too much time in activities unconnected with the life of the college." I was unsure of myself and unprepared to rally a defence. It was my Thomas who fought off the dragon. Diana began her reply by expressing the great love which her family has for art and literature, the deep affection which they hold for the University, and the delight they express that a daughter of theirs should be amongst the first women to enjoy the privileges of an Oxford education. She will have—according to her father—opportunities which will be the envy of much of the civilized world, not only academically, but in the experiencing of life itself, in witnessing the creation of beauty from the minds of the great. She may have been overly theatrical but, whatever the failings of her rhetoric, the point certainly hit Miss Callow. It cannot have hurt our defence that the Fitzpatricks are benefactors of the college, far in excess of any costs accruing from Diana's attendance.

Miss Callow responded with a terse "very well" and an admonition to improve our studies, for our own sakes and "for the sake of the college's reputation." We are, in short, to make her proud that we are her students.

This seemed to be the end of the meeting. Miss Callow rose and thanked us for our time. We expressed our gratitude for her interest in, and care over, us and made for the door. I did not dare look at Diana for fear that, in my relief, I should begin to giggle as I had at the studio. Then I heard my name being called and I turned to face Miss Callow once more.

"Miss Swift, I have asked Mrs. Taylor to help you with college life, to ensure you feel able to concentrate on your lectures and classes. She assures me that she will be most pleased to work with you in order to minimize any distractions over the coming weeks."

I repaid Miss Callow's infuriating, unwavering smile with one of my own, thanked her, again, for her support, and left to join Diana in the hall. She told me that her carriage would be arriving shortly and that she intended to meet it at the end of the driveway. I offered to accompany her, but she insisted that it was far too cold and that there was no point in our both catching a chill. She departed and I returned to my room, where I have been sitting at my desk, writing, ever since.

I keep expecting a knock at the door and a voice full of cloying kindliness to announce itself as belonging to Mrs. Taylor, just here for my own good, and what a good that will be, no doubt: what a good for Mrs. Taylor, that is, but not for me.

No knock comes. I shall read. I shall read Swinburne and I shall choose a blasted poem for Diana, and read it to her, if she does not run off again.

Saturday, 25th February, 1888

A note from Mrs. Taylor was awaiting me when I went downstairs this morning. She has decided that we should meet on Monday to agree upon the ways in which she might best help. If only her husband were as forthcoming with communications. I shall hide myself away with my books until then and see if I cannot gain an intellectual high ground which might make Monday's meeting somewhat bearable.

Monday, 27th February, 1888

The meeting was not at all bearable. I shall not waste ink on it. Suffice to say that Constance Taylor is as interfering an old busybody as I should ever have the misfortune to know. She wanted me to meet her again on Friday, and on every subsequent Friday: there was some allusion to the finer points of my Greek translations, on which I struggle to see the value of her opinions. Can it be a coincidence that she chose the day of the week on which I sit for her husband? I really ought to have used that as my excuse but I lacked the courage. Instead, I used Diana, saying that we met every Friday and I felt it was an important part of my college life, and of Lady Diana's, too. I think I was successful: at least, I have escaped the unwanted commitment for this week. Again, I am a participant in a charade—the real story hidden, unspoken— though now I am quite certain that both parties understand its nature exactly. It is only the niceties of society which shore up the walls and prevent them from tumbling down around me, and how long can they last? How long can we continue to live within the artifices of others? The clouds are scudding across the sky outside my window. The blue is coming and going, and I want it to steady.

Wednesday, 29th February, 1888

Diana is mine again.

CHAPTER TWENTY-ONE

I was still resisting the urge to run ever onwards with the diaries. I limited myself to a few entries each day, as though each small group were hidden behind the cardboard shutters of an Advent calendar. Besides, there was no need to read ahead to see that there was soon to be an end to the story. The last twenty or so pages of the current diary were blank, and I estimated that I had only a few weeks' worth of Penny's life before emptiness prevailed. I could not understand why she had given me so much—given me the painting and receipt, the diaries, the mirror and guidebooks, the building blocks of a biography—only to leave the whole edifice incomplete. But I read on, slowly.

There was nothing more than, "Diana is mine again," to explain Lady Diana's return to Penny. Perhaps she was too tired to write more, exhausted from the constant reporting of arguments, separations and rapprochements. Or perhaps she felt that a single sentence said all that needed to be said.

Penny was surprised when Taylor invited her to another sitting, asking that she bring Diana with her. I was not. It was in Taylor's best interests to finish the painting and, however hard he might have wished it were not the case, he did not have the talent to work from either memory or pure imagination.

Mediocrity of execution is no bar to the greatness of a painting. Mediocrity can be transcended by subject or composition, by a new perspective—literally or figuratively—or a new technique, by the story of the painting's creation or tales of its subsequent owners. Taylor's painting found transcendence in none of these. It was too late to the party, and too humdrum to make a splash when it arrived. Only for me, and for Penny and Diana, did it hold any great value. For Taylor it must have tantalized with the hope of success, with the recognition for which he yearned but which was never to come to him. Not that I could tell him, tell him not to waste his time, tell him that he was doomed to be lost to posterity, another name on a stone, writ in water. So, he went on, ignoring his better judgment and refusing to accept the dying of his pride.

Penny saw no such explanation for Taylor's perseverance. She leapt at Diana's suggestion that Taylor had some personal motive to finish the painting, deciding that he regretted his recent distance and was eager to rekindle their affair. She did not mention the specifics of her interpretation to Diana. Nor did she mention the inner conflict between her delight at Taylor's continuing interest and her horror at the choices it forced upon her.

The sittings continued. Taylor was withdrawn and abrupt. Penny started to arrive on time and with Diana, rather than early and alone. Taylor's wife interfered as much and as often as she could, but never dared to stop the sittings or even mention them, not whilst the Fitzpatricks' generosity might be jeopardized. Fridays remained the days on which Penny "had arranged to meet Diana." All other days, however, were shared with Mrs Taylor and, as a result, Penny's routine was increasingly centred on her academic activities. If anything, she welcomed the improvement in her standing within the college, but she wrote about her arguments with Diana, as Diana felt increasingly unable to see enough of her. The sittings became a focus for their relationship. The diary entries for Fridays often trailed off, saying only that she had spent time with Diana. Those details which she shared through her pen divulged only conversation and context, but always with a sense of well-exercised discretion, rather than an absence of intimacy.

There was another argument about the painting, but it was delivered in an envelope addressed to Emily. The letter was from the owners of the cottage, a Mr and Mrs Laycomb. They had been trying to contact her, but without luck. I had not been answering the telephone since I returned to London, except to Alison, to whom I had made a promise that I would take a call if she rang once, hung up and rang immediately again. Every other call was reduced to an echoing knell, a brief interruption to the stifling peacefulness of the flat. Emily would not have answered, anyway. Mondrian did not have a telephone in his house, for a while at least. I envied him.

The Laycombs were wondering if we had had cause to go into the attic for some reason. They were careful not to suggest any particular reason and their phrasing held an implicit condemnation of my ascension, for how could there be any justification for such a breach of trust? I knew that even if I told them I had been Jacob they would be unsatisfied with the explanation. They had noticed that some of their possessions had been displaced and, although they could not be certain, it seemed that one item might have been removed entirely. What it was, precisely, they would not like to say, but Mrs Laycomb did have a strong recollection of their having bought a painting at an auction some years ago, which was nowhere to be seen. They hoped we had enjoyed our stay, and so on. The letter was signed by Mrs Laycomb, but her husband, clearly finding his wife's tone unnecessarily conciliatory, had added a postscript: "We have checked the house and find the painting is most definitely missing. Please contact us to explain as I am sure we would all prefer to avoid any escalation. Henry Laycomb."

I put the letter with the others on the table, where it camouflaged itself into insignificance. The doorbell rang. I looked out into the darkening afternoon, down to the pavement below. Alison stepped back from the door and waved up at me, then poked her index finger against her opposite wrist and gestured down the street with her head. It was time to go out. I had an appointment. It had been a while. Alison gestured again, and mouthed, "Come on," at me with slow, exaggerated movements of her jaw.

When I was young there was a quality to waiting rooms which made me feel deserving of treatment. They were unlike anywhere else.

Libraries were just as quiet, and filled with the same shuffling and coughing, but their demands for silence seemed justified by the need for study. Waiting rooms were quiet because of a shared belief that waiting rooms ought to be quiet. There were no decorations on the wall, unless one counted posters about the dangers of smoking or the need for immunization. I always thought it strange that the women—it was always women—who worked behind the reception desk did not think their lives, and the lives of the patients, would be better for a little relief from stark, white walls and red-brown furnishings. It was as though some committee had decided, in the distant past, that a line was to be drawn between areas for the healthy and areas for the sick; a project best served by a puritanical aversion to comfort. Or maybe it was the smell: not quite antiseptic, with just the right blend of scents to let one know that there were people present, whom one did not know, with ailments one could not perceive, except in cases of hacking coughs, bandaged faces, scraped knees. It was all for the best. I could sit and wait without any worry that I might be a malingerer. Who would subject herself to that environment if not genuinely ill?

Lucy's waiting room was from a newer school, all soft furnishings and copies of Monet's paintings of the water lilies in his garden at Giverny. They represented a fraction of the hundreds of lily paintings which he produced. Several years earlier I had written a short piece on their creation as part of a pitch for a never-made television documentary. There are giant water lilies at Kew Gardens: a single leaf of *Victoria amazonica* can support the weight of a small child. I had seen photographs of children sitting on those lilies, and I thought about them as I sat waiting with Alison. But in that place, subjected to a manufactured tranquillity and washed over by almost-subliminal pan-pipe music, I found Monet's presence to be oppressive. I was drowning in shades of blue, and no number of blurry, green lilies were going to keep me afloat. I hated arriving early. Lucy always opened her door on the hour, and ended our sessions precisely fifty minutes later. There was no point in drowning for any longer than necessary. When I came on my own I always waited elsewhere, usually a café or bookshop, and had no need to sit with Monet holding my head under. But Alison did not want to be late, so I was sinking, sinking a little deeper with each ticking minute counted by the wall clock. Lucy appeared.

On that day, as in all my therapy sessions, Lucy did not start the discussion. For a while—six months, maybe a little less—I had been unable to bear the vacuum, and sought to fill it with anything which came into my head, monologue or soliloquy. However irrelevant my mutterings, Lucy would say hardly a word, nodding occasionally to show that she understood, a privilege I rarely shared. Sometimes I became frustrated with the sound of my own voice. I would fight, remaining wordless to see if Lucy broke first. She never did.

There was no need for another battle. I was in a talkative mood. I told Lucy about my being discovered by Emily, the trip to hospital, the time there, the nurses, the food. I told her about the cottage and the painting. I even told her about Penny and Diana, but grew too tired of hearing myself to include Taylor and the other cast of characters. And through it all she nodded, and the clock ticked on the wall, and water lilies drifted above us both. She asked me if I wanted to talk about Emily. When I shook my head she did something she had never done before: she told me that I needed to talk. The second hand swept round, caught up with the minute hand, the hour hand, the minute hand, the hour hand, and on and on and I floated, and cried, slowly, with control, and took the tissues she offered and did nothing with them.

At ten minutes to the hour I dried my face and lifted my gaze from the carpet. Lucy ought to have been leaning forward in her seat, hands together, preparing for goodbyes. Instead, she sat exactly as she had throughout the session, and so I was the one who said the next-times and rose, ready to swim away. Lucy said she wanted me to stay, that she had kept her afternoon clear, and I began to panic a little, and she saw and understood and pointed towards the chair and poured a glass of water from the jug on the little table by the window, and held it out to me, but it was just more water and I waved it away. I sat down, though, and said something about Alison, waiting for me outside. Lucy's "It's all right" let me know that they had spoken before I had even come through the door to the waiting room. So the clock ticked on and I changed the subject, to Oxford, to Barbroke, to Bernini, Bruegel, Friedrich, Monet, Venice, Emily.

Emily. The police had come to the cottage the morning after Barbroke, early. I was still in bed: yellows and sleep. She was gone. She had driven too fast and too carelessly and there was too much snow. She had gone out in the snow because of me. She had gone to find him. She had probably always gone to find him. He was at the funeral when I went with Alison and so we did not stay long, and left early, without farewells.

Lucy spoke gently and slowly, but she could not change anything, nor tell me anything new. I sniffed and listened, and nodded when I thought I should, and even, once or twice, when I agreed with her. There were the usual platitudes in her words, the reassurances of a future to be lived, but she made no real effort to console me. She gave me, as she had always given me, an unvoiced permission to experience my emotions, raw and unlimited, and I took it, for what it was worth. I had the facts, but I had always had them. There were few emotions, and that did not change, despite a concerted campaign of tea and sympathy. What did change was my increasing awareness of the gulf between how I was expected to feel and how I did feel. Alison and Lucy were of the opinion, as they both took pains to tell me, that I was either torn apart but unable to express it, or numb. I was not torn apart or, if I were, it was only to avoid the guilt I would otherwise feel. Nor was I numb, which I took to imply my going through everyday activities as though on a stage, reading lines and following directions: the play was the thing wherein they would catch my conscience.

I was Anna without Emily, but that was nothing new, and if its finality was novel it was not entirely unwelcome. I had Alison to help me. And Penny. Or she had me, or we had each other, but whatever the case she was there as much as Alison and she would notice if I fell from the sky, even if the shepherd did not and the ships drifted on in the bay. Lucy interrupted my chain of thought.

"Did you go back to say your goodbye?"

"No," I said. "I thought about going back to the church. There was no point. Everything was over. She wasn't there any more. I mean, she wasn't really ever there, was she?"

"Sometimes 'goodbye' is important, Anna. Especially if there was never a chance before…" She trailed off.

"I wonder if Penny said goodbye to Diana, before. Maybe afterwards. Maybe she went to Barbroke and took the mirror away with her. Met Taylor again, or never left him. So he ended up with it. Before it came to me. Do you think?"

"I don't know, Anna. Perhaps. Perhaps we'll never know. Even if we do, Anna, do you think knowing will help you?"

She kept repeating my name and I was growing tired of it, and growing tired of the tick of the clock.

"I think I should go, Lucy," I said. "I have things to do. Alison is waiting. She must be hungry. Thank you."

Lucy took out her appointment book, but I told her that I would call to make arrangements. Through the glass of the waiting room door I could see Alison. She was reading a magazine with a cover which suggested that last summer's fashions were going to involve orange and pink. She looked up as I entered and was already at reception, paying for the session, by the time I had walked over to her.

We stepped out into the chill of early evening.

"Did you talk?" she asked.

"About Emily?"

"About anything?"

"Yes. I talked about Emily. Take me home."

We rode in a taxi, without another word, until we reached the flat and Alison paid the driver and I let us in and made tea. I expected her to continue talking about Emily. Instead, she said:

"You have to give it back."

I wondered what she meant, and then I knew what she meant and began to wonder how she knew.

"Give what back?" I asked.

"Anna, you know. You have to give the painting back. It's not yours. I saw the letter."

"What the hell are you doing reading my post?"

I stood up. Alison put down her cup and gave me a look half pity, half exasperation. She reminded me of the ticket seller at Barbroke, horrified at the idea that I might not want to visit her precious gardens.

"It was on top of the pile, Anna. I didn't rifle through anything. I'm worried about you and I'm trying to keep an eye on you. I noticed and I couldn't just leave it. Sit down. Please."

I sat down.

"It is mine," I said. "They're lying. Ems and I found it in an auction over in Reading. It was cheap and she wanted to cheer me up. I don't know what they're going on about. I didn't take anything from the attic. Maybe Ems did, before she left."

"Emily wouldn't do that."

"There were lots of things Ems wouldn't do, but she did them. She might have gone in the attic before I even arrived."

Alison grabbed a digestive biscuit and munched on it whilst she stared out of the window. There was not much to see. The sky was a uniform yellow-grey, the closest London ever came to darkness, above ground at least. Most of the curtains were drawn in the row of Victorian houses across the road. When Penny was alive they must have been single houses for a rising middle class. Most had long-since been converted to flats: one at street level, another one or two above, and finally the basement, which always seemed to be called the 'garden flat' by estate agents, even when the garden was a tiny, concrete yard at the bottom of six-foot, concrete walls. I wondered how much longer I could stay, and where I would go next, and if it would be as colourless. I suddenly thought of Gerald, alone in his house in Whitstable. We had promised to return his boxes. They were not mine, either.

"At the cottage you said you bought it near the coast," said Alison.

"No. I said we bought it in Reading. We went to the coast because Gerald lives there."

"I don't know who that is. Who is he?"

"I told you. Gerald is related to Taylor, the painter, and we got his details from the auction house, well, Ems got the details and I waited in the car and talked to the man outside, and then we went to see Gerald because he wanted us to, because he lives alone, and he gave us the boxes with the diaries and the other bits and pieces."

"I didn't know that, Anna. You said the other stuff came with the painting. It's not yours, is it?"

"Come with me to see Gerald again. He might have some more clues. Then I'd know how it ends."

"If I come, will you give the painting back?"

"Just say yes, Alison."

"Yes," she said. "I'll come with you. Get me another biscuit."

That night I dreamed of dragons in the snow, amongst the boundless, fabulous mountains, but I awoke to fog and rain, a red-brick Venice, and Stanley Spencer in the churchyard by the park. Gerald answered the telephone on the first ring, and was, predictably, delighted to hear from me. He had been planning to call me soon, he said. He asked after Emily, and sounded a little disappointed when I told him that she was away, and that I intended to bring a friend along with me in her place, if that was all right. It was, of course. Alison had told me that she could shift her weekend schedules around, so I arranged for us to meet on Saturday afternoon. Gerald promised cake.

I sat on the couch, turning the mirror back and forth in my hands. Anna, lilacs, lilacs, Anna. Had the owners of the cottage missed it? They had only mentioned the loss of one item—the painting—and the mirror had been left on the bookcase, surely forgotten. Even if they checked, they no longer had the auction receipt and I doubted that they would trust their memories enough to accuse me of its theft. Then there were the diaries and guidebooks, and the detritus of Gerald's life, in boxes in the bedroom. He had not mentioned them, but it was reasonable for him to assume that I would return his belongings. I was not ready to do that, any more than I was ready to lose Penny and Diana.

I made my plans. Saturday was three days away and I could use that time to dig out my camera and tripod and take photographs of the painting. To do so properly, separating the frame and canvas once more, varying the types and angles of light sources, would take the best part of a day, I was sure. Then I would go to the local library and photocopy the diaries, and any other letters and scraps of paper which seemed worthwhile. I felt some relief in knowing that I could keep the information, but there was a bite in resigning myself to the loss of the artefacts themselves. I wanted the original *Klosterfriedhof* and not just a pre-war black-and-white photograph, not just a half-erased de Kooning drawing.

Before I could take on the role of archivist, however, I needed to finish my work with the original sources. I settled down to read the few remaining diary entries.

CHAPTER TWENTY-TWO

Friday, 23rd March, 1888

Woe is me! for I am undone; because I am a woman of unclean lips.

Tuesday, 27th March, 1888

I am home once more, and if my parents are aware of events in Oxford they are keeping their knowledge a well-concealed secret. Mother expressed her unhappiness at seeing me wan and thinner than she would like. Father fusses over me as he has always done, but talks now of books and business and my studies, in place of an affectionate interest in his daughter. I do that which is expected of me—eat my meals, attend church, listen to Mother read in the evening—but take every opportunity to withdraw to my own room, where I study or lie on the bed and think of her, and wonder if the next morning's post will bring a letter.

Last Friday began as previous Fridays had begun. Diana and I met at college and walked the short distance to Matthew's studio for the final sitting of term. I had with me the Swinburne, hopeful that I should get a chance to read to Diana, and she put it in her bag to protect it from the elements. We arrived just as the charwoman was leaving. She, recognizing us, let us into the building whilst noting how bitterly cold the weather was for the time of year, and declaring that she would hate to be the person responsible for our catching chills. Matthew was nowhere to be seen. He is a punctual man—that much may be said of him—so his absence struck us as unusual. Nevertheless, we agreed that he would have sent ahead in the event of a lengthy delay—a foolish notion—and that we might best spend our time in dressing for our roles.

I have always found it delightfully easy to make Diana laugh, and she, too, often gives me cause to giggle over the most mundane occurrences. So it was on Friday, as she became Thomas and I Olivia. We played our parts: I the loving wife and she the heroine who would be hero. She helped me on with my outfit, making much of my "passing fair" countenance and delicate limbs. I dressed her in her disguise, wondering aloud who would ever guess her secret and what woman would not swoon in her presence. We laughed and embraced. In the language of Warber, we passed the time in clyppynge and kyssynge, until Thomas took his new wife over to the bed. There we undid much of our work in dressing, and lost ourselves to each other, forgetting our surroundings. I realize, now, that I have always failed to find the words to describe these too-short times which Diana and I share. I shall be no more successful on this occasion. It is because the acts are not the essence of the experience, but only the private expression of that essence. That is to say, whatever I might write by way of description would appear to my eyes to be unbearably lascivious, lacking, as it most certainly would, the beauty of its inspiration. Diana and I may have laughed together at the rapture of Bernini's *Ludovica*, but we were afforded that luxury by the presence of the statue itself, which took away any weight which might otherwise have been given to our flippant, schoolgirl nonsense. On these pages there is no balance to be had, so I shall leave it at saying we lost ourselves to each other completely and, in our privacy, without shame. It was only in the ending of privacy that shame returned, and with it anger, hopelessness and cruelty.

It was Diana who first saw the figure in the doorway. She became stiff and unyielding, so that I was aware of some change upon her even before she reached down and shook me by the nape of my neck. I looked up at her and she gave the slightest movement of her head, her chin falling then rising, gesturing towards the door over my shoulder.

I do not recall who grabbed the sheets and pulled them over us— probably Diana, as I was still pushing the hair back from my face to see clearly—but within moments we were lying side by side, our immodesty covered, but covered far too late. There, at the entrance to the studios, where I thought I had discerned the figure of Matthew, stood Mrs. Taylor.

I am being called for dinner. There will be time enough to finish later this evening. I shall let Mother read to Father alone.

Dinner was a miserable affair, made all the more so by neither Mother nor Father discerning anything miserable about it: they are so inattentive to my condition. Mother asked if I should like to accompany her in some charitable work or other. Father thought I might like to join him when he next calls on his printers. I spoke when I needed the potatoes to be passed, or a little more salt. Then the meal was over and I asked to be excused, and Mother said she thought it would be nice if I spent a little time with them, and Father said he thought so too but asked if I felt at all unwell, and that seemed the easiest route for me to take. I affected a headache and took my leave of them. Now I am writing in bed and listening for the creak of the stairs, lest one of them appear at the door and I need to adopt the semblance of mild neuralgia.

Mrs. Taylor walked in silence, over to the table and chairs where we usually took tea. She sat down, unbuttoning her coat as she did so. Diana opened her mouth, presumably driven by an idea that an attack was imminent and might be prevented were she to express her own displeasure at our interruption. Whatever her reasoning, it clearly failed to state its case with any force, as no utterance came forth. For my part, I was transfixed by Mrs. Taylor's eyes. I could not read the emotions in her face, irrespective of any and all efforts to do so. It was as though all the thoughts which were churning within her had blended to give a constant stillness, as waves upon water mingle and destroy each other. I could hear my own heart beating, faster than it had ever beaten during exercise, louder than it beat when Diana and I were alone together. When Mrs. Taylor finally spoke it came almost as a relief. What followed was at times calm, at times heated, but always the dialogue of a final act.

She opened with a question. Had we seen her husband? Apparently he was "tight" when he returned home on Thursday evening, and the two had argued. We were not told the subject of the argument, but the sentence was spoken in such clipped tones, and followed by such an accusatory pursing of the lips, that I took the meaning, and I am quite sure that Diana did, too. Mrs. Taylor went on to describe her sleepless night, her arrival at the empty studio long before dawn, and her lonely walk around the less salubrious corners of the city in the early hours of the morning. Finding no sign of Matthew she had returned to the studio in the hope that he had found his way there whence he had spent the night. And so it was that she sat before us.

She ignored Diana and turned her full attention to me. Had I no shame? Did I fully comprehend the unnatural character of my activities? What would my parents say? How could I ever show my face in college again? These questions being rhetorical, she moved on to blackmail without waiting for answers. Indeed, both Diana and I were yet to speak.

Mrs. Taylor set out her terms. I am to have no further contact with her husband, in person or indirectly, through any form of communication. If I find myself in circumstances which offer the possibility of my meeting him I am to take whatever actions are necessary to excuse myself before he and I exchange a single word. The *quid pro quo*—if blackmailers can be said to offer such a thing—is her guarantee of secrecy.

Diana had pulled the sheets up and over her head. I cannot but feel anger at her cowardice in a situation which was as much her doing as it was mine. I could not witlessly succumb to Mrs. Taylor's demands, and fought back in the only way open to me. I informed her that were any mention of my personal entanglements to be heard beyond the walls of the studio I should be forced to act: I should make known the shameful behaviour of her husband in preying on one so young, innocent and impressionable. It was a weak threat, but I perceived that it might work if it played to Mrs. Taylor's own desire to avoid any hint of public scandal. Diana shifted downwards, deeper under the bed-covers.

Mrs. Taylor made no answer. Her head fell forward and her body heaved, slowly, in what I took to be an approaching crescendo of tears. Then, alas, I heard the sound she made: quiet at first, so that I thought she were keening under her breath, then louder and ever louder until the room was filled with her laughter. I asked her what had caused her such amusement, trying as best as I might to present a stoical exterior to the terror I felt. Her laughter continued, unabated. Diana's head appeared again, looking first at Mrs. Taylor and then to me, for some answer which was not mine to give. There was nothing to do but wait. I dared not press my question, as I knew each repetition would be filled with greater and still greater tones of shrill consternation. Finally, after what seemed an age, Mrs. Taylor regained her composure.

The reply came slowly and clearly, that each word might convey the strength of Mrs. Taylor's feelings and put an end to my unutterable stupidity. Did I really think she still had anything to lose? Surely I had heard the stories of her husband, even before he and I had undertaken our liaisons? One more rumour would make no difference. One more set of whispers amongst her friends, the staff at college, the students: what harm could that do except to me? I could claim to be the victim, or even declare that I had fought off unwanted advances, but they would say there was no smoke without fire, and there was I, a fine, sparking flint of a coquette.

It was my turn to lower my head, but I did so in order to cry, knowing I was beaten by this wretched woman. I have cried since—I cried this afternoon—but now I start to see Mrs. Taylor as the victim. I am the wrongdoer, and that is even harder to bear.

I told Mrs. Taylor I agreed to her terms. She rose and buttoned up her coat. I thought she would leave without another word, but at the doorway she turned and called Diana's name. Diana was already half-way to the office, eager to leave Thomas behind and, with him, Olivia. She had wrapped herself in one of the sheets and walked slowly, looking like the abhorred wife of some disgraced Cæsar. She stopped, quite motionless, on hearing her name, but continued to face the east wall, so that Mrs. Taylor addressed her back and bare shoulders.

"Lady Diana," she said, "I should have expected better of you." And then, with a callous grin for my benefit, she added, "I am disappointed that you have chosen to aim so low in your choice of—how shall I put it?—close friendships."

If I had expected Diana to leap to the defence of her "low friend" then I, too, should have been disappointed; but I held no such expectation. Diana's silence throughout the ordeal, and her cowardly disappearance from sight for the greater part of its duration, had already disabused me of any hope that she might rail against these final words of Mrs. Taylor. She once more took up her slow walk. When the closing of the front door reached my ears she was already within the office and no doubt well along in her hurried dressing. So it was that the stream of oaths and abuse which I directed towards her fell on a closed door and an unhearing wall. I had not the will to get up, and sat, seething, propped against the back of the bed in Diana's pose of these past weeks. When she reappeared she made straight for the door without a single glance in my direction. I thought to let her go and be done with the whole awful affair, but I called her name, and not as sharply as others might. She stopped, just as she had stopped for Mrs. Taylor, and lifted a hand to wipe dry her cheeks. She did not, however, acknowledge my exclamation but for the momentary interruption of her progress. She walked on, out of the studio.

I am tired. I am tired of remembering, and writing, and crying.

Wednesday, 28th March, 1888

It was the end-of-term dinner on Friday night. I lay on my bed, calculating precisely the best form of malady to feign in order to avoid attending. Then, as the time approached, I had the sudden, terrible thought that Mrs. Taylor had not kept her word, that she had told Miss

Callow—and anyone else who would care to listen—of my indiscretions with Lady Diana. I could not fail to attend, lest I condemn myself by a guilty absence. I dressed swiftly and joined Elizabeth at a table towards the rear of the room, far from the head table where Mrs. Taylor sat, talking to Miss Callow and the other tutors. In my imagination I saw her direct her gaze to our table during the course of some conversation, and then, pair by pair, the eyes of her fellow conspirators fell upon me, eager to pick out the leading lady of her tale. Lady Diana could provide no distraction: she did not join us that evening.

Despite my fears I discerned no evidence that Mrs. Taylor had breathed a word to anyone, either before dinner or after. During each goodbye from a fellow student I searched for any indication—any smirk or nervous tic, any reticence to spend time in my company— that might suggest an awareness of Friday's events, but found none. The tutors expressed their hopes that I should spend the vacation in productive studies, and not fritter it away with social events and frivolities. Not one of them, even Miss Callow, showed any deviation from similar addresses to the other students.

So, I have brought the story up to date. On Saturday morning I boarded a train back home and here I am.

I have neither seen nor heard from Diana since she walked away on Friday. I might write to her, but what could I say to convey the piteous amalgam of anger and desire which I feel towards her? I wish I had not been with her at Barbroke, for then I might not form such a clear picture of her, alone in that place, amongst the art and books, or walking in the gardens, or sitting in our temple overlooking the lake. I wish she would fade like some banished wraith, rather than haunt me as she does.

Friday, 30th March, 1888
A letter has arrived from Barbroke. Mother handed it to me, remarking on the quality of the paper and suggesting it had come from Lady Diana.

I tried my best to respond with just the right amount of enthusiasm: too little or too much and I should have faced a series of questions on the problems I was experiencing in my friendship. Mother is well-meaning but she can be tiresome, and I could not abide the thought of any delay in opening the envelope and reading its contents. I told her that I should take it to my room so that I might read it in peace, and compose a reply if one were needed in haste. Her face fell a little, as though in disappointment that she could not share in the news, but she said nothing as she handed the envelope to me.

Mother's disappointment was as nothing to my own on reading the letter. It was not from Diana. As soon as I saw that the handwriting was not hers I turned my attention to the bottom of the last sheet to see the signature, and in the hope that Diana might have added a postscript. The letter is from her mother, and there is no postscript.

Dear Miss Swift,

My daughter has been feeling a little unwell these past few days and has asked that I write to inform you of her decision not to return to Oxford this year. She and her father have discussed, at not inconsiderable length, her determination to end her formal studies and they are both of the firm opinion that her education would be better rounded by a foreign tour of some sort: preparations will take place over the course of the following month. I am sure that, as her friend, you will understand and support the choice which she has made.

On a personal note, I wonder if you might care to tell me of any incident which occurred in Oxford to bring about this change in her outlook. She had seemed so terribly excited to be going up last year, and, until these past few days, we had heard nothing from her but the most effusive praise for the place. I know that you and she were close. Might you please spare a few words to put a mother's mind at rest? I should hate for her to be running away from some youthful mishap, to be suffering the loss of her Oxford, solely because she feels unable to confide in her own, loving parents.

Sincerely yours,
Maud Barbroke

I have paper on my desk bearing the necessary addresses and date, but no more. I have no reason to suppose that the Countess knows anything other than that of which she has written. Her request for "any incident which occurred in Oxford" seems perfectly genuine. Yet there is no question of my divulging any detail whatsoever of recent events. Should I lie? If so, should I insist that nothing untoward took place, to the best of my knowledge, or make up some tale that will fulfil her need? I cannot do the latter with any sort of clear conscience, so it must be the former. But I cannot tell so flagrant an untruth in that manner, so that, too, must be wrong. I do not know what to do. I am writing these lines to occupy my mind and prevent it from racing in two directions at once: backwards to Oxford and Diana, and forwards to a future without her. The former is upsetting. The latter is almost unbearable.

Finally, after much deliberation, I have settled on a short, but polite, response. "Thank you so much for your letter. I shall miss Lady Diana very much. I am afraid that I am unable to shed any light on the reason for her decision. I can only surmise that her desire to travel outweighs other considerations."

CHAPTER TWENTY-THREE

The remaining diary entries were all short. They were mostly reports of dull days with parents, interspersed with occasional visits from old school friends. Miss Ashdown spent a weekend at Penny's house, despite Penny's damning of her after their afternoon at the Galleries. Nothing about her stay inspired Penny to regain the fastidiousness of her diary-keeping.

I had thought that Penny would follow Diana's example, but she returned to Oxford for the final term of her first year. She must surely have suffered through a vituperative internal dialogue in reaching her decision, but she did not take the time to write it down. The final entry was unremarkable: "Back at college. It will not be the same without her. Mrs. Taylor has already called on me in my room. I shall write more after dinner."

Blank page after blank page. Penny watched over me from her frame on the wall. It was as though I had entered into one of Friedrich's paintings and overtaken the figure dwarfed by the landscape: the monk by the sea, the lame boy staring at the crucifix, the pall-bearer at the head of the snow-bound procession. I had overtaken them all and turned to see their expressions, to see their reactions to the sublime, to beauty, to terror, to the knowledge that their sight was unshared and misunderstood. They stood behind me, doomed to loneliness, not for want of company but through the unavoidable magnitude of the world and the intractable uncertainty of their place within it. There was nothing in Penny's eyes. Whatever I thought was there I had put there myself, put there in my broken perspective. She was David's missing assassin and Baudry's heroine, Rokeby Venus and Borghese

Hermaphrodite. She was everything I wanted her to be and nothing of herself.

By Friday afternoon I had a new list of questions for Gerald and by evening I had thrown them away, remembering our first meeting: he would tell me all he chose to tell and no more. Asking questions would only fluster him as he served his tea and cake and revelled in having company. If the conversation kept to main roads then all would be well, but if it strayed onto lanes and tracks there would be no map to help.

I packed everything back into the boxes. Gerald would put them into storage and forget them, and when he died they would be passed to the next generation, assuming there was a next generation. And the cycle would continue—Penny's testament hidden away—or be broken forever thereafter, the boxes thrown into a skip with unwanted crockery and saucepans and shoes and clothes. All of Thursday morning, and most of the afternoon, I had been standing in front of the photocopier at the local library, duplicating every page of the diaries, guidebooks and notebook. I had taken a break for lunch and another for a trip to the bank, to get more coins to feed into the machine. If I closed my eyes I could still see the bright, blue-white light scanning across my retinas. The piles of copy-paper sat on the couch, carefully gathered and sorted into individual documents.

A little after noon on Saturday I heard the beep-beep of a car horn rising from the street and looked down to see Alison sticking her head out of her battered old Ford. She waved up at me and mouthed something. I cupped my hand to my ear so she would repeat it but it still made no sense. I lifted the sash window and stuck my head out into the cold air.

"What?" I mouthed.

"Roadtrip!" she shouted back at me. "Roadtrip! Roadtrip! Roadtrip!" Each exclamation was louder and more drawn out than the last. Across the road a couple of faces appeared at windows as Alison retreated back into the car, leaving me shaking my head and laughing. Five minutes later we were on our way to the coast, with Gerald's boxes on the back seat.

In suburban Whitstable "The Sands", "Tide Cottage" and "Oyster Shell House" were still standing, and Gerald's lace curtains still twitched at the slightest sound. He opened the door before Alison had finished parking the car.

"I'm afraid I didn't bring you a cake this time," I said.

"Oh, no, no. No matter, no matter at all. Think nothing of it. I have cake." He ushered us through the hall and into the lounge. He did indeed have cake, and biscuits, all laid out on the table, and from the kitchen the last, timorous whistle of a just-boiled kettle promised tea.

"It's lovely to see you again. Anna I know, of course. And you must be?" Gerald looked at Alison and then back to me, clearly seeking a formal introduction.

"This is Alison," I said. "She's an old friend of mine. She knows all about the painting and the diaries."

Gerald and Alison helloed their hellos and she and I sat down, next to each other, as Gerald disappeared into the kitchen. He returned with a tray on which rested a teapot, three cups, three saucers, three teaspoons, a sugar bowl with a pair of silver tongs half-buried amongst the cubes, a milk jug and a tea strainer. It must have been sitting ready for us, just needing the addition of water to the pot.

"We brought your boxes back," I said. "We'll get them from the car before we leave."

"Ah. Oh. Thank you. Yes. Did you find anything interesting?" Gerald asked.

I told him no more than I felt necessary to encourage his reciprocation, skipping details as I desired, reserving them for myself. I was close enough to see each stroke on the canvas, close enough to lose sight of the scene which they created, if I were not careful. Gerald, however, was forced to stand behind the red rope of the gallery, to peer at the image from across the polished floor. I had Penny and Diana, and Taylor, and Constance, and all the tangled mess of their relationships. He had only the names and the painting. I had the college and the Galleries and the studio and Barbroke. He had only Oxford. But most of all, I had Penny.

Gerald listened with what appeared to be unfeigned interest, stopping me between biscuits to ask about trivialities. I thought he was just trying to engage with the story. Gradually, however, I began to realize that he showed no curiosity about the story itself: his questions added an occasional brushstroke but did not open up the vista beneath his gaze. It was only when I came to the end of the much-abbreviated account, and Gerald had muttered, "Fascinating," that I thought to ask him a question:

"Have you read the diaries?"

"Hmmm?" he replied, then crunched on his fifth or sixth biscuit. Alison put down her cup and directed a frown towards me.

"The diaries, and the rest. Did you read them before you gave them to me?"

Gerald brushed a crumb from his lip.

"My dear girl," he said, "but of course. It's fascinating stuff, isn't it? New Year at Barbroke. That poor Mrs Taylor, Constance. I liked your telling of it. Much faster paced. Much more enjoyable."

I was not sure how to react. The stupid man had stolen from me and he sat there and talked about it as if his theft were nothing.

"Why didn't you tell me?" I asked. "And why give me all those other things? Why give me the receipts and other rubbish, if you'd already been through everything? Why do that?"

Gerald shifted in his seat. He looked first to me, then to Alison, where his gaze lingered, as though he hoped she would come to his rescue. In the end, evidently sensing that there was nowhere to hide, he spoke.

"She told me to."

"Alison?"

I asked without pausing to think, but before he replied I had caught up and knew exactly what he was about to say. I found Alison's hand on top of mine, gently squeezing my fingers together.

"No, no. The other girl. Emily."

Gerald started to speak more quickly and all I could do was listen to him, and my breathing, and the clink of his cup and saucer. Alison was moving closer and holding my hand tighter as though she wanted to get my attention, to take it from Gerald and make it hers, so she could control me somehow, as Emily had done.

"She called me to arrange our first meeting. She said you were interested in the painting and asked if I knew anything about it. Well, I said I knew all about it and I'd be happy to tell you both. It's always nice to meet new people. But she said that perhaps I could help her, you know, with your condition."

Alison reacted on my behalf.

"Her condition?" she said.

"Well, you know." Gerald was clearly flustered. He continued, talking to Alison. "No offence meant. Anyway, she asked if I had any papers that might relate to it, something to give to Anna so she could continue with her own investigations. Something to make it all a little more interesting for her."

"You collected up the papers and put them in a box to give to her?" asked Alison.

"Oh, they were already in the box, so that was easy enough. I added a few other items. Red herrings. To make the chase more challenging. I hope I haven't said the wrong thing. I'm sure Emily can explain it all far better."

I was not there any more. I was staring at a wall of creams and browns, greys and blacks, a wall whitewashed and forgotten. I was Velázquez's Venus, robbed of mirror, torn from Cupid, left to lie on grubby sheets. I was the Borghese Hermaphrodite, because who was to say otherwise when I faced away towards the wall, and hid my face from sight on a mattress that even Bernini could not redeem. I was Helga Testorf, Andrew Wyeth's model, painted by him, again and again, over more than a decade. I was Helga stripped of identity, no longer the Helga of the other paintings: the Helga with braids, the Helga with flowers in her hair, the Helga naked on a stool by an open window. I was the Helga of a single canvas, lying naked, face to the wall, hidden. I lay in the dim light with old plaster for company, a reclining nude, and felt nothing and shifted and saw the rusted metal hooks in the roof above me, above Helga, which looked so sinister and yet held only a line for drying, or perhaps a curtain. And then back to the wall, and the sounds of the room fading into the greys, and the squeezing of my hand getting harder, becoming the only feeling I had. I longed for Mary, Suffragette Mary, to come and slash at my neck and back and hips, to save me from the nothing. Someone was shaking my shoulder and I started to wake and move, as though I had been asleep and motionless, but I was not telling anyone where I had been, only that I was back, back to Alison saying, "Hey," and Gerald gone.

"Where's Gerald?" I asked.

"He's making a fresh pot of tea," said Alison. "I told him it was what you needed after a long day of travel."

"Did you tell him about... Did you tell him why she can't be here?"

"No. There was no need. He saw you were upset and stopped talking. I think he's more embarrassed than anything, to be honest. He probably thinks he's betrayed a confidence."

"Why would they conspire like that? Why would she have told him to keep secrets from me? After all the secrets she'd already kept. I thought she'd changed." The grey wall was coming back, but Alison's hand on my shoulder kept me facing her.

"I don't know if she changed. But I think she was trying to keep you healthy."

"Healthy is a fine thing," said Gerald, stepping out of the kitchen. "I brewed another pot. I'm sorry if I said anything to upset you. It wasn't my intention. Shall we get back to our girls?"

"Our girls?" I asked.

"Penny. Diana. I might be able to tell you more."

"Our girls?" I asked again.

Gerald started to speak to Alison, as though she were my keeper, as though in any minute he would ask her if I took sugar in my tea, or if I needed to use the bathroom.

"I only meant, well, you know. We both know the girls, through the diary. So, in that sense... You can see that, can't you?"

He asked the question with a sense of desperation. I took my hand away from Alison's and began to lean forward in my seat, but Alison took control of the situation before I had time to bring order to the script in my head.

"I think we'd best be going," she said. "We have quite a drive back. That's probably enough for today." She stood up. "Yes, I'd say enough."

I still had no structure to my words. Whenever they aligned I reached out to grab them and, in my anger, sent them flying, never pulling them near enough to speak. I stood up. The iron hooks in the ceiling were closer, more intimidating than ever. I lowered my head a little, followed Alison's feet to the door, listened to her goodbye to Gerald, heard her explain that everything was fine and I was just a little tired, and he understood, of course, but still apologized. Then I left them behind, by the door, and shivered by the car and could no longer hear what they said and did not look up at all. Alison joined me. She unlocked the car and started the engine, and I waited inside, listening to the laboured breathing of the heater, as she and Gerald unloaded the boxes. I did not listen to them. When the work was done Alison sat in the driver's seat, put her hand on my knee and asked how I was feeling.

"I want to go home. I don't like that man any more. I want to go home and forget all about him," I said.

We drove home. The daylight had hidden itself almost before we left Whitstable. Alison took the side-roads back to London. I think she wanted to give me time to find safety before we were amongst the memories of the flat. When we passed through woodlands the bare trees blocked the lights of villages so that each individual street-lamp and window blinked in and out of life and the woods sparkled. The dashboard glowed red and green. The warmth from the heater started at our toes and rose up inside the car. Red and green, and the will-o'-the-wisp yellows, and the hum of the engine mixed with the tick-tock of the indicators. Night-time swirls and a night sky above an asylum in Saint-Rémy-de-Provence. Alison did not wake me until she had parked the car outside the flat. I stayed awake only long enough for more yellow with hot chocolate.

On Sunday I woke up to find that Emily had already left for church. I pottered around the flat, turned on the radio to let it burble to itself as I crunched my way through a helping of bland breakfast cereal. I was halfway through rinsing the bowl before I remembered that Emily had not gone to church.

There was a parcel on the couch. I had noticed it earlier and then elided it as an unwanted intrusion into the morning routine. The routine was all that kept the memories away, but they had returned and there was nothing to lose in tearing off the shiny, red wrapping paper. There was a little gift tag: "Not sure if you'll still want this. Hope you do. I'll see you later. A." I sat at the table and set the gift down in front of me. It was an old book, *Oxford: History and Traditions*. The dust jacket showed the view across the quad of some college, towards the great, oak doors of a tall, crenellated gatehouse. It was a stylistic representation in black ink, printed with rough blocks of pale umber for the walls, green for grass, grey for shadow. The jacket was wrapped in a protective plastic cover: Alison had probably bought it from one of the shops on the Charing Cross Road.

The book offered a chance to know more about the place where Penny—my Penny—and Diana had met. It would fill in the details of the college, even the Galleries and the Parks. But maybe Keats had it right.

I had been to Oxford in the past, just for an afternoon, to meet Kathy, a school friend who had gone up the previous term. The world I had constructed for Penny and Diana gained its ink from the diaries, and its blocks of colour from that afternoon with Kathy. Early in the year, with the sun low in the sky, diluted by clouds, the colleges lost their glow. Greys ran into yellows and whites, walls became monumental as their stones merged with each other, bled of the contrast they needed for an identity. The Parks kept their green but hedged it round with black branches, cut it through with the stroke of a slumbering river. And then on, to North Oxford, its red brick always red whatever the weather: a Victorian stamp on the city, and even it could not resist the mellowing of the place in its ivies and gardens, those delicate refinements glossed on a brash upstart. I had not seen Taylor's old studio. Kathy and I had walked close to it, or whatever had replaced it, but there was nothing of it left to me. Nor would the book describe it, I was sure, if I were to open the covers and read.

I could have gone back, made a pilgrimage to the sites of the diary as I had at Barbroke, but what would I have gained? Barbroke was different. It had the luxury of existing in its own cabinet, a frozen curiosity. Oxford, for all its outward languor, layered its history, hid the old beneath new sediments: not the grand things, but the smaller ones, the people and places which strove for grandeur but were lost when they did not achieve it. Students and painters departed; studios shut their doors. Newer colleges grew and evolved, moved to better locations, built their own traditions and stories, left their past to books and photographs. Barbroke could not hide its timelessness in its solitude, and ticket office and gift shop. Oxford, though, could bury its history deep and conceal the truth of it beneath a patina of age and tradition.

I had already lost part of my story yesterday, when Gerald claimed his share of Penny and Diana. It was true he had seen them first, but we were not participating in some stupid teenage competition and his claim was not a reason to suppose he had rightful ownership. I looked at the painting on the wall. It was home, with me, where it belonged.

The mirror lay flat on the mantelpiece. Diana had grasped it, combed her hair, thought of Penny. I remembered a painting I had seen, somewhere, in one of the books which filled the shelves on either side of the chimney breast. It was a memory of a memory, because the connection had come to me before, in the church at Barbroke, and then flown as quickly as it had arrived. The morning brightened outside the window. The painting was in an old book, badly printed. Something large. A present from Emily, a reminder of her, given to me before all I had were reminders. I began to scan the books to the right of the fireplace. The upper shelves were small, full of paperbacks. The bottom shelf, at waist height, was actually the top of a cupboard below, and held larger hardbacks. On the far left was what I wanted: a set of German magazines bound into two volumes of some five hundred pages each, with *Jugend 1917 I* on the spine of one and *Jugend 1917 II* on the other. I retrieved them both and left them on the table whilst I disappeared into the kitchen.

With a cup of coffee to hand I began the process of leafing through the pages, waiting for an image to trigger some recollection. The first volume yielded nothing. A little over halfway through the second I found it: *Die Korallen-Kette—The Coral Chain*—by "Wilhelm Gallhof, München". A low-quality print of the painting covered the whole of the right-hand page and spilled over onto the left, leaving room for a single column of text which had, as far as my German allowed me to make out, no link to the image at all. At the bottom of the column was a piece entitled *"Zum Frühstück"*—"For Breakfast"—by Karl Ettlinger, which my poor translation suggested was a group of pithy observations on tolerance, pride and criticism. The last of these—*"Lerne das Konversationslexikon auswendig und Du weißt—garnichts."*—seemed to be a shadow of Keats: "Learn the lexicon of conversation by heart and you will know—nothing at all."

I turned the page but there was nothing there about *The Coral Chain*, either, just an article covering the death of Albert Weisgerber—a painter and an illustrator for *Jugend* itself—printed beneath a dark, charcoal drawing of German troops gathered at dusk for his funeral. Wilhelm was to join Albert in death before the end of the Great War. It was the only thing I knew about Gallhof, other than his name and the print of his painting in an old magazine. As for the woman who wore the coral chain, I knew nothing about her except that she posed nude for a painter called Wilhelm Gallhof.

The woman is thin, but not too thin, not skeletal. She lies on her back, diagonally across the canvas, her head in the upper left, her body lifted by pillows, and her feet pulled up, knees together and raised, so her calves rest against her thighs. Her head is tilted to her right, cheek resting on patterned fabric. Almost all of her, in fact, rests on different swathes of cloth. They echo the busy pattern on the curtain which hangs behind her, breaking up the monotony of colourless walls. Only her lower torso and feet rest on pure white, a bolt of floral lace running from one side of the bed to the other. She is looking into a hand-mirror, which she holds in her right hand so that only the rear of the mirror is visible. It, too, seems to bear some sort of pattern but it is only a smear of green-greys, purple-blacks and browns. It could be a woman dancing or just the reflection of the surrounding textiles, an abstract pattern or nothing but verdigris and polish. The coral chain, a necklace of red-pink spheres, wraps tightly around her neck once, twice and then takes a longer loop, resting on her collarbone, drawing a line across the top of her left breast and then rising up, away from her body, to her left hand where she holds it pinched between thumb and forefinger before it falls again and passes behind the arch of her neck. She is admiring it—the necklace—or herself, or both.

It became obvious to me why I had so quickly lost my association of Diana's mirror with the picture. The composition of the work, its colour palette and framing, did not allow my eye to linger on the woman's face, her necklace or her mirror. Instead my gaze fell downwards, over her breasts and down to her hips and the white lace, the light of the image. And there, just above her right foot, inviting me closer, four more loops of coral chain as an anklet, the focus of the entire picture. It was as if the woman, lost in her own reflection, had given me the chance to survey her, voyeuristically, illicitly. I was neither welcome nor unwelcome. I was unseen. I began to feel that I was doing something reprehensible in admiring the pages, that the woman had been tricked into posing and I was no better than Gallhof himself in my collusion. I closed the book and put it back on the shelf.

Penny and Diana watched from the wall. I had always believed that they wanted to be found, that they belonged with me, that they were mine. But perhaps they were Gerald's, or Taylor's, or belonged under a sheet in an attic, finally left alone with themselves. Penny looked out, across Diana and through the dulling varnish. I tried to read her face, her eyes, again, knowing all I knew, but she gave nothing away. Taylor just painted Olivia, concerned for her marriage, awaiting Thomas's revelation, unable to reassure her Thomasin that she knew who—what—was holding her. But no, she was my Penny and I was thinking too hard for want of anything better to do on a lonely Sunday.

I put *Oxford: History and Traditions* onto the bookshelf, unopened.

Chapter Twenty-Four

Barbroke, Thursday, 17th December, 1891

Dear Mr. Taylor,

I hope you are well. As you will no doubt recall, you received and accepted a generous offer for your painting *Waiting for Sunrise* shortly before it was due to be hung in exhibition. The purchaser of the painting, whom you may remember as a Mr. Cartwright, was sent on my behalf, having been instructed to approach you on my learning of the work's intended inclusion in a show open to the general public. Mr. Cartwright, recounting his negotiation with you, made me aware of the changes to the picture during the latter stages of its completion but I felt that, nevertheless, it ought to remain within the sphere of those involved in its creation.

The painting has, for these past two years, been stored in my private rooms here at Barbroke. Now, however, I find myself unable to remain in possession of it. I have given thought to its destruction, but that seems an act of barbarism to which I cannot be party. Miss Swift has surely no desire to be reminded of the circumstances accompanying its production nor, I suspect, does she find herself in accommodation which would afford her the privacy required for ownership. So, I have been pondering the best course of action.

Please understand that I, for my part, feel no shame in my role as Thomasin. Indeed, my parents have seen the picture and, whilst not enamoured of it, saw nothing in it which they deemed inappropriate. Their moral and intellectual attitudes are often modern, but then they are not burdened with an understanding of the story behind its painting, which might colour their opinions. Perhaps I should say "stories", since the subject of the painting itself is quite as controversial as the lives of the actors behind the masks. No, it is not my decision to pass the canvas to my parents, or any other relative.

You will certainly have guessed that the crate accompanying this letter contains *Waiting for Sunrise*. I imagine you have already opened it, impatient to see its contents. It is yours, Mr. Taylor. I give it to you for only two reasons. First, I believe you will have no desire to destroy it. Second, I believe you will now recognize that it is in your best interests to keep it from public view. Whatever efforts you may have made to calm the worst excesses of your wife's temper, I cannot see that the reappearance of the painting into your life would serve to ameliorate matters further. I suspect quite the opposite to be true. It is thus with some forethought that I have arranged for the crate, and this letter, to be delivered directly to your studio.

Yours sincerely,
Diana Fitzpatrick

~

Oxford

Dear Lady Diana,

Do, please, forgive the delay in my replying to your letter of 17th December: the Christmas season has found me unrelentingly plagued with relatives, friends and acquaintances, and hardly permitted a moment to myself. In truth, I have also been looking for the words with which to thank you for your kindness. Finding nothing appropriate coming to mind, yet aware of the terrible solecism of tardiness in putting pen to paper, I venture to respond, nevertheless.

Although I could not be sure of your man's involvement in the purchase of the painting, I admit to having had my suspicions. The price offered was generous: I make no false claims to greatness at this time, having, over these past four years, slowly arrived at an acceptance of the limitations of my abilities, at the cost of much happiness. I have of late lost all my mirth, as it were. I do not tell you this to encourage a little *Schadenfreude*, as the Germans have it. Rather, I hope that you will see some hint that the events in Oxford have left their mark upon me as they have upon you and Miss Swift, and that, as a consequence, I am far from the man you knew.

I want to assure you that the painting will be kept in my studio, carefully stored and free from the adverse effects of extreme temperatures, grime and dust. It is true that Mrs. Taylor would look unkindly upon the reappearance of the work, despite my best efforts to set matters to rights with her. That alone would be sufficient reason to keep it hidden. However, I should like you to know that even if Mrs. Taylor's wrath were not under consideration I should still abide by your wishes in the spirit of kindling a friendship which I too-soon snuffed out.

sent: 4th Jan 92

~

Henley-on-Thames, 8th June, 1892

Dear Mr. Taylor,

You were once kind enough to give me a small hand-mirror as a gift. I feel that, under the circumstances, I ought to return it to you. Here it is. I wrapped it carefully and do hope it reaches you without any damage. We have managed so terribly well, you and I, in avoiding the crossing of our paths these past few years. Now, however, dear Lady Diana is gone, and I wish to write those words which were never said— or some of them, at least—so that everything may be put behind us.

I read of Lady Diana's leaving in the London papers, shortly after her departure. I am sure that you imagine me to have been saddened by the news but I should like to ask you to understand how great is the pain I feel. After she returned to Barbroke my letters remained unanswered. Indeed, I stopped writing after my fourth letter vanished without acknowledgement. Now I shall never speak to her again.

I wonder still, as I have wondered over the past years, what your wife told you of that morning when she arrived unannounced at the studio. Am I the first to tell you that she was there at all? No, I cannot believe that. You must at least know that she spoke to Lady Diana and me. I think it in her nature to have threatened you just as she threatened us. Certainly, I never found myself evading your presence in Oxford and that would suggest that you played your part in keeping far away from me. I think I am safe in assuming that you know, at least, that Mrs. Taylor brought all things to an end.

Lady Diana wrote to me in her final days. I did not receive the letter until a reply was impossible. She must have planned it that way, giving the envelope to some servant to post when the time came. She asked me why I had not written, Mr. Taylor. I placed my letters on the table in the hall of college and yet they were never posted. For this I can only blame myself, and ascribe their interception to my own foolishness: I should have seen them into the postbox with my own eyes. Unless, of course, you think there is someone else I should blame.

Lady Diana's letter was short. She said she was sorry for everything that happened. Do you not think that kind of her? She asked if I could forgive her for abandoning me. She asked me if I could forgive her, Mr. Taylor. After being forced away by other parties, she still asked for my forgiveness. One day soon I shall return to Barbroke, to the church at the top of the rise. I shall stand in the stillness and remember her as she was in those days of Oxford, but I shall never be able to tell her that there is not, nor was there ever, anything to forgive.

She sent a few items of sentimental value with her letter. One was the hand-mirror which I now pass back to you, lest you think I keep it as some manner of souvenir. I never kept it. I gave it to her on the very night of the day you gave it to me. She did not know, of course, that you had ever laid a hand on it. Now she has returned it to me as a keepsake. No doubt she imagined it joining her other gifts: the note-book and silver pencil, the guides to the Galleries, the first edition of Warber. Oh! but of course it could not, even had I not given it back to you.

Was it you that took those precious items from my room during dinner, Mr. Taylor? Or your wife? And not just the note-book and other items but also my diaries and academic writings. Do you have them now, Mr. Taylor? I wonder. When I returned to my rooms to find them missing I thought I should hide away and never be seen again. I wailed, I am not ashamed to say. Yet I found that I had the strength to come down to breakfast the next day, and all the days thereafter. Keep them if you have them, Mr. Taylor. I no longer care.

Penelope Swift

~

Oxford, 11th June, 1892

Dear Miss Swift,

Thank you for your letter. I am saddened to learn that you had no place for my gift. I accept it back with a heavy heart but with understanding.

I should very much like to have you comprehend my part in events, since it does seem that I have been cast in the role of villain in this drama. I wonder if you might allow that we three were brought together by some external force; something one might call "fate" or "predestination". For my part, I can only say that I attended that first evening at the college with no intention whatsoever of making your acquaintance. As events unfolded I can honestly declare that I was never given occasion to feel that our relationship was built upon anything but shared emotions. On reflection that is not quite true, as I recollect a change in your demeanour, at least in its expression towards me, as your friendship with Lady Diana grew. Would it not be a curious thing if I had not reacted to that change which came over you?

I do not know anything of your diaries or the other items taken from your room. I was not even aware of their theft until your letter arrived.

Perhaps she is right.

~

Whitstable

Dear Anna,

I am sorry that I upset you when you visited last week. I was behaving as I thought best at all times. Anyway, I am sorry.

I had a few additional pieces of the puzzle to share, but you left before I was able to give them to you. So here they are. I would like you to keep them. I think they mean more to you than they do to me.

The four letters are the last ones in my possession which have anything to do with the story. The letter from Matthew to Diana is his draft of the correspondence but the scribbled "sent: 4th Jan 92" at the bottom certainly indicates that a good copy was posted. It seems that he never received a reply from anyone at Barbroke, which I consider only natural given the circumstances. The final letter, the one from Matthew to Penny, was never sent. The last sentence seems to be Matthew talking to himself before he put his pen away.

I don't know who took Penny's things. Maybe it was Matthew, to protect himself. Maybe it was Constance, keen to find out the truth or looking for ammunition to use against Penny, if necessary. Whoever stole them, they ended up in my family. I am sending them back to you. I know that you will take good care of them.

If I had the Warber I would give it to you, too, but that seems lost now, as is the pamphlet which Penny found with it in the library at Barbroke. The lock of hair is here for you, though, and also a short note on the pamphlet, written by Penny. The mirror was sold at the same time as the painting.

The photograph will explain Diana's letter.

What else do you think Diana gave to Penny? There is no clue in the letter, and the "items of sentimental value" certainly did not include the painting. Would you let me know, please, if you ever find out? There will always be tea and cake waiting for you in Whitstable.

God bless you,

Gerald

CHAPTER TWENTY-FIVE

The package I received with Gerald's letter contained all the items he listed, including a faded, torn photograph, only a few inches on each side. A woman sat stiffly on a chair, in front of a plain backdrop. Her body and legs faced slightly to the right whilst her head was turned towards the camera. Her hands were resting on her lap, one on top of the other. She looked dour, but I could recall few formal, Victorian portraits in which the sitters did not look dour. I held the image against the painting to confirm what I already knew, that this was Penny. I turned it over, to see if there was a date or location written on the reverse. There, in neat, pencil handwriting, I read, "Constance Taylor. March, 1886."

Rossetti—grave-robbing Rossetti—had done the same thing. Fanny Cornforth sat whilst he painted her for his *Lady Lilith*; sat and combed her hair, combed the locks that would twine around a young man's neck and never set him free, according to Goethe. They did not bind Rossetti. He freed himself less than five years after *Lilith*'s completion, returning to the canvas and replacing the face of Cornforth with that of Alexa Wilding. Rossetti may have thought Wilding's aspect more dangerous, or perhaps the buyer wanted the painting to match others already purchased from the artist. Not that it was important: I felt no better for knowing that precedents existed. There was no solace in academic analysis.

I could not escape the loss of my Penny. I had seen Diana as impassive in the face of Thomasin's fears, but with the photograph in my hand I saw in her only the forbearance needed to embrace an imposter. Constance had been watching me as she must have watched

Penny, and perhaps that was only right: she was hurt and Penny was the source of that injury, the knife twisting in the wound. So Penny was Emily, lost. But I was Penny, surely, after all this time. I must be Penny, or I could not help her, could not be helped by her.

There was a telephone number on the letter from the Laycombs. I called it. Mrs Laycomb answered. I explained that I had been somewhat over-enthusiastic in my curiosity, and she was gracious in accepting my apology, and my promise that the painting would be returned within the week. There had been, I told her, some confusion when we left the village: I had wrapped the painting in a blanket, intending to return it to the attic, but a friend had mistakenly put it in the car. Mrs Laycomb wanted to know my impression of it. I told her that it was pleasant enough, but nothing special. In return she declared that she thought it "a pretty thing" and was looking forward to hanging it in her London place.

Within an hour the painting was wrapped, addressed and deposited at the local post office. Diana's mirror was tucked inside the parcel, too: however much I might have wished it were mine, it was not, and I could not take pleasure from it—or take whatever it gave me—knowing that I had stolen it. I even included the photograph of Constance, who could never be my "pretty thing".

CHAPTER TWENTY-SIX

THE CONFESSION AND EXECUTION Of the Seven Prisoners suffering at TYBURN on Wednesday the 25th of October, 1676. VIZ. John Seabrooke, Arthur Minors, William Minors, Henry Graves, Richard Shaw, Katherine Picket, Samuel Warber. Giving a full and satisfactory Account of their Crimes, Behaviours, Discourses in Prison, and last Words (as neer as could be taken) at the place of Execution. Published for a Warning to all that read it, to avoid the like wicked Courses, which brought these poor people to this shameful End. With Allowance, 1676. London: Printed for D.M. 1676.

Did not people wilfully neglect all means of Grace, and abandon all considerations of their own Interest, and give themselves wholly up to the Perversities of Satan, one would never imagine, that after so many Monthly Examples as this City affords, of persons bringing themselves to shameful and untimely Ends, any should be so impiously bold as to follow the same Courses till they involve themselves in the like miserable Fate.

Samuel Warber barbarously murthered John Howard, to whom Warber owed a debt; whereupon his Intent turned to Hatred and Malice. In pursuance whereof, on the 20th of March last about 9 of the clock in the evening, he meets Howard in Shoe Lane and seizes upon him and holds him, and gives him a wound in the Neck. And having dispatch'd this Cruelty, left him dead, and went home. But it pleas'd God a Witness then declared who had murthered the man and duly proved the same at the Sessions; whereupon Warber was Condemned according to the Statute in that Case made and provided.

Before his Tryal, having an excellent hand at Limning, he had drawn most lively on the wall of his Chamber in Newgate, the Tyburn Tree. Since his Condemnation, he caused it to be underwrit with these lines.

> My precious Lord, from all Transgressions free,
> Who pleas'd, in tender pity unto me,
> To undergo the Ignominious Tree,
> I Suffer justly in my love for Thee.
> My Lord, I take the Drop with two clos'd Eyes,
> And from the Gibbet mount the glorious Skies.

When they were brought to the place of Execution (whither they were attended besides the people, with several Ministers) few of them spoke any thing considerable, unless to some particular Acquaintance; but by their Gestures seemed to pray secretly, and so were all Executed according to Sentence.

CHAPTER TWENTY-SEVEN

Thursday was an L.S. Lowry painting: *The Funeral*, more blues and greys, a dark church silhouetted against a scrubby white sky. Mourners gather around a grave, watched by a family outside the cemetery, watched from the thin, black railings. Two figures walk away along the footpath, an adult and a child. The child looks back, over her shoulder, at the scene amongst the headstones. A reviewer called Lowry's figures "struggling little creatures" but in *The Funeral* they cease their own struggles, just for a short while, and remember one whose struggle is over.

There were no gravestones in the garden of remembrance, just regiments of oblong plaques set on low, stone walls or along the edges of flower beds, visible but illegible from the car. The place was drained of colour, and the group of people leaving as we arrived were every bit as stiff and monochrome as Lowry would have painted them. Alison parked by the slouching, concrete chapel and asked if I wanted her to come with me.

"No," I said, "but thank you. I'll be fine. Are you all right to wait here?"

She reached behind her seat and produced a paperback copy of *Moby-Dick* with a battered, cardboard bookmark sticking out, about a third of the way from the end of the novel.

"I'll be fine. Go round the back of this building and head through the archway in the wall. You'll see another garden area where they keep the temporary crosses. I'll be right here."

I stepped out of the car and watched my breath rising, straight up on such a windless day. And maybe I would have been safe and warm inside but I was going for a walk.

The garden was small, but well tended. In spring and summer it must have blossomed into an uplifting space. It offered me only naked branches and soil: greys and blacks. Plywood crosses stood where grass turned to path and path turned to earth. The crosses were about eight inches tall and each one wore a typed label, wrapped in plastic and stuck to the wood with a silver staple. Sombre bouquets leaned against a few of them. Someone must have removed the older blooms because none of them seemed to have decayed, even during the current night-frosts. The flowers gave the place its only real colour, other than the insipid green of the lawn. I felt a twinge of guilt that I had not brought an offering, but Alison had told me that I need only visit for myself, that I was brave, that I was taking faltering, difficult steps to come to terms with loss, not to satisfy the expectations of anyone else. But then, maybe I needed to bring a gift. Some other day, I supposed. I sat on the grass.

The cross was just a clone of its companions, cleaner than some, dirtier than others. The label read, "Emily Pargiter," and then one too many dates, and a code which represented the intended location of her final memorial, I guessed. The ground was damp. I could feel the chill rising but then everything went away: every sensation, every birdsong, every car and child and mother and father on the streets beyond the walls, all the paintings and artists and stories. And nothing came to fill the emptiness. No emotions rushed in to fill the abhorred vacuum. I was abandoned by whatever words I should have said, ululations I should have cried, tears I should have wept. I was a struggling little creature, but I was never going to emerge from my struggles whilst I remained there, within the lifeless garden.

There was nowhere to go. If I wanted to leave I had to wish myself back, somehow, and I did not know how. I closed my eyes to the mildewed light, stayed out of place, stayed with her, stayed. Until the tapping began. Slowly at first, quietly, without rhythm. Then a faster tempo, and each of the taps losing its direction as it blended with others, until all around was a cacophony and only then did the falling drops begin to carry their wetness to me, and with it the rest of the world. I opened my eyes.

Alison met me between the archway and the chapel, and walked beside me, sheltering us both with her umbrella. Neither of us spoke. Back in the car the world retreated behind misted windows.

"I'd like to go to Barbroke," I said.

"Today? I mean, we can, but it'll get dark soon after we arrive. But we can."

"Please. I don't want to be trouble. I think it's the right thing to do. I need it. You said to do what I need."

Alison put her hand on my knee.

"Of course. But I have to buy a sandwich on the way."

She smiled at me and I smiled back, because smiling back did no harm. We left the crematorium, the gardens, the crosses and the plaques, and headed out to the west, towards Barbroke. Alison bought her sandwich and ate half of it as we drove, taking bites on the occasional straight stretches of country road where gear changes were unnecessary. We spoke, but without depth of meaning. I slept a little, not through tiredness but simply to shorten the journey. As we approached the village Alison began to bring me back to the then and there.

"Can I park at the house, or do we have to walk?" she asked.

"We're not going to the house, just the church."

"Can I park there? Do I need to find some change? I don't really want you to have to walk. You'll get soaked."

"You worry too much."

Alison shrugged.

"Someone's got to," she said. "So? Can I park?"

"There's no car park, but there's a long drive up to the house. The church is by the side of it. I'm sure you can park on the grass verge. You pay for entry farther on. We shouldn't need any money."

"Do you think the church will be open?"

I echoed her shrug.

"I think so. I hope so. They usually are. When I was here last time it was snowing. I hardly saw another soul. It was open then. It'll be open."

We turned into the avenue and stopped just before the stone arch. It was less impressive than I remembered, seen from the car windows, no longer framed by snow. Alison eased the car onto the grass by the brick wall of the churchyard. No railings, but the gravestones seemed as black, the church as oppressive, as anything in Lowry's Manchester.

"I'll wait," said Alison. She reached down and took the second half of the sandwich out of a crumpled paper bag by my feet. "I'm here if you need me."

Inside, the church was unchanged. It probably never changed. It was darker, though. I could see, once my eyes became accustomed to the murk, but I searched for light switches. I gave up after a couple of minutes and walked over to the north aisle. I sat on the floor, resting on the end of the pew opposite Diana's memorial, as I had done when I was staying at the cottage, on the day Emily had gone out into the snow.

Diana was my only real link. I had words from Penny, but everything visual, everything that gave me a tangible reality, had been taken, except for Diana. Diana was the constant, had always been the constant, even if her fixedness was obscured by Penny's instability. I was there to clutch at what was left, to ensure that at least a fraction of the jigsaw remained complete. I was there for so many reasons. I was there for no reason at all.

Silence had encroached upon me in the crematorium garden. It had slithered in from the surroundings, down from the trees and across the ground. It had taken me before I even noticed its approach. In the church I had willingly stepped into it, into the hush, crossed a threshold to be an outsider for a while: a choice, a statement of control. So it came as a surprise, as I sat in the charcoal-grey, when the lights above me sparked into life and a voice called out, "Hello?"

The man in the doorway stood by the switches which had hidden from me. He was in his seventies or eighties, shortened by time and a slight hunch to his back. His clothes were almost entirely black. Only a dark green sweater broke ranks, and that was concealed, for the most part, beneath a long, heavy coat.

"Hello," he repeated as I appeared from behind the pew. "I weren't sure there were anyone here, but there were a car outside."

"Hello," I said, unsure how to continue, feeling unprepared for conversations with strangers. Still, it seemed rude to leave it at that so I tried, "Are you the vicar?"

The man in black ran a hand through his thinning hair and walked towards me.

"No," he said. "I just take care of the place during the week. Open up. Lock the door at the end of the day. A sexton, really. Do I look like a vicar?"

"Well, you're very black. Your clothes, they're very black."

"True. There is a vicar, though. I can call him if you need that sort of thing."

"No, thank you," I said. "I was just looking around. And the tomb seemed beautiful. I just sort of sat down for a while. I can go if you need me to. I don't want to be any trouble. If you need—"

He interrupted me.

"No. No, you're fine. I can't tell you much about the tomb that you can't see just from looking. Diana Fitzpatrick. Eighteen hundred and ninety-two. She died young, same as her brother. That's his tomb." He pointed a slightly shaky finger towards Albert, at the far end of the aisle. "Shame, really."

"Shame," I agreed. "Do you mind if I sit down again?"

I sat down without waiting for his answer. He sat near me, on the next pew along, and introduced himself as Bill.

"I can't join you on the floor, love. Not at my age," said Bill. He pointed the same, shaky finger at Diana's tomb. "Swinburne. Interesting choice."

"Mmm," I said, and nodded slightly to show that I, too, thought it an interesting choice, but did not have any particular desire to discuss it at length.

"It's underlined in the book, so I've always thought that maybe it had something to do with her."

I had no idea to which book he was referring, but I did know there was the Swinburne, and it could be the same one, and it could have stayed at Barbroke all these years, another loose thread to be pulled. I tried to remain calm.

"Oh? Do they still have the book at Barbroke, do you think?"
I asked.

"At Barbroke? No. No, it's here."

"Here?"

"It's in the sacristy."

"Could I—"

"See it? Don't see why not."

Bill stood up and took a bunch of keys out of his pocket.

"Come on," he said and waited while I clambered to my feet.

The sacristy was cramped and musty. Bill explained that it had become a glorified storeroom. The vicar kept his vestments with him, partly because he used them at several other parishes and partly because anything left in old, country churches tended to succumb to the cold, damp and mice. A second doorway, in the far wall, must have led to the churchyard, but the quantity and age of the cleaning products stored against the door suggested that it had not been opened in years. Against that same wall, underneath a diamond-paned window, stood a low, oak cupboard with a stack of red-bound hymn books balanced on top of it. Bill fumbled with his key-ring until he found the correct rusty, iron key. He knelt down, unlocked the cupboard doors and felt around, inside the darkness of the shelves. Twice he let out an "Aha!" and his hand reappeared holding a book, but on both occasions he frowned in disappointment and placed the volume on the floor. I sat down on a dusty chair. Finally he turned to me with a here-we-are and in his hand I saw gold lettering on a green spine.

"It were a little before my time," said Bill, coughing as he raised himself from the ground and walked over to me, "but my understanding is that the daughter of the owner gave it to the vicar, sometime in the forties. Said her mother had wanted it to come back here. Well, it's been here ever since. I'll have a look if there's anything else."

He handed the book to me and went back to his search. At the top of the spine was the title, POEMS & BALLADS, and beneath, SWINBURNE. I turned the first few pages until I came to a dedication: "To my friend Edward Burne Jones these poems are affectionately and admiringly dedicated." It was not the printed type which made me stop. I must have let out a sigh because Bill gave me a thumbs-up. I read the faded copperplate.

"Darling Olivia, For our time together. You said you would choose a poem but I took them back to Barbroke with me. Choose one now, even a single stanza, even a single line. Love, Your Thomas."

Bill had returned to my side.

"Does it mean anything to you? Olivia? Thomas?" he asked.

"Perhaps," I said. "But I think you're right that Diana underlined the words. Where are they?"

I continued, page by page. Bill held up one hymn book after another, shaking each of them, before returning for a final sweep of the cupboard. After some forty pages I found the lines from the tomb, the second stanza of "The Triumph of Time", underlined, just as Bill had described. A few more page-turns brought another collection of lines, highlighted by a pencil stroke running down the left margin. In the white space at the bottom of the page was written, in Penny's familiar hand, "For D. I hope you like the choice." I read slowly, letting my finger run over each word.

I wish we were dead together to-day,
 Lost sight of, hidden away out of sight,
Clasped and clothed in the cloven clay,
 Out of the world's way, out of the light,
Out of the ages of worldly weather,
Forgotten of all men altogether.

The rest of the book was unmarked. When I reached the last page I turned back to Penny's choice and copied it down into a little red notebook which I had in my pocket. Bill was sitting beneath the window, waiting patiently. When I shut the poems away between their covers he stood and handed me a piece of card.

"I were looking for this. Thought it were glued in the back of the book but when I saw it weren't there I figured it must've fallen out," he said.

The card was pale green. In large, grandiose letters it proclaimed,

"Collins & Son. Photographers. Oxfordshire", and, added in pencil, "New Year 88." I turned it over and smiled at the two women, dressed in their evening gowns, still cold from their time in the Temple of Minerva.

Penny had returned as she had so recently departed. Standing beside her, Diana echoed the fluid beauty of marble, with none of the masculinity of Taylor's oils. Yet Penny's were the softer features: a delicate, oval face with dark eyes beneath gently curving brows, and the whole dominated by a wide smile that spoke of more than a reaction to a photographer's request. Beneath the couple, in the margin of the print, I recognized Diana's handwriting.

Bill busied himself with tidying the cupboard and I sat, gazing at the photograph. For me, Friedrich's black-and-white *Klosterfriedhof* had always been the ghost of a vanished original, but the image in my hand possessed an authenticity which brought its own solace. When I was ready I carefully placed it into the book, which I handed back to Bill. I was shaking a little.

"Look," he said, "this obviously means a lot to you. I can't give you the book, but I don't reckon anyone else will remember the photo. I bet the lady who left it didn't know it were in there, to be honest. Here."

He retrieved the picture from between the pages and offered it to me. I shook my head. In my moment with the two women, at Barbroke and in the sacristy, as the camera plate darkened and Bill restacked hymn books, I had come to understand that it was an end to our time together. I was ready to relinquish Penny to her Diana. And I discovered that I felt her departure less keenly than I had expected. There was, in her final passing, a rectitude which had played no part in more recent losses.

"No," I replied. "They belong here."

The door creaked open behind me. It was Alison, silent but showing her concern by the tilt of her head.

"Thank you, Bill," I said. "Goodbye."

He nodded slowly and, holding the Swinburne in one hand, started to rearrange the cleaning products in the doorway.

Alison and I walked back through the church. I hoped that Penny had been able to stand in the stillness and be with Diana one last time, and remember, and tell her that there was nothing to forgive. I spoke the words I had read in the margin of the photograph, my voice no louder than the whisper of my own breath.

"Like me shall be the shuddering calm of night."

It was dusk. The sky had cleared and the air had started to cool and crispen.

"She's gone," I said.

"I know," said Alison.

We drove away from Barbroke, just two more angels in the darkening blue.

ACKNOWLEDGEMENTS
& SECRET TREASURES

In making any attempt to list all the friends and family to whom I owe so much gratitude, I should be assured only of failure. It is my fervent hope that I have already thanked them personally and my express wish that they feel free to blight my email with justifiable vitriol, if I have not.

I am indebted to every member of the wonderful team at Unbound. I should particularly like to thank: John Mitchinson, for expressing such enthusiasm and support for the publishing of the novel; Philip Connor and Georgia Odd, for guiding the book on its initial, faltering steps into the world; Elizabeth Garner, for insightful editing married with a gift for drawing out the best of my abilities; and Anna Simpson and DeAndra Lupu, for managing the entire editing process with such sympathy to the text, and for putting up with my rarely-warranted stress.

Thank you, too, to my agent at Felicity Bryan Associates, Caroline Wood, for all her help, advice and patience. And to Felicity Bryan herself, for listening to my wild talk about *All the Perverse Angels* on a Tube journey from Angel to Baker Street, and for subsequently bringing me into the FBA fold.

Writing the novel involved a lot of research. Here are a few books in which you might be interested. Any errors in the novel are, of course, my own—although I shall probably blame them on Anna or Penny—and not the fault of the authors below.

The artworks in the book, with one notable exception, are all available online, where you will also find the guidebooks used by Penny and Diana: *Alden's Oxford Guide* (Alden), *Handbook Guide for the University Galleries* (Fisher), *Facsimiles of Original Studies by Michael Angelo* (Bell & Daldy), and *Drawings and Studies by Raffaelle Sanzio* (George Bell & Sons). Matthew's letter to Penny draws on *The*

Exhibition of the Royal Academy of Arts MDCCCLXXXVII (Wm. Clowes & Sons) and *The Magazine of Art* (Cassell), again both online. Not online, but without equal, is *Pre-Raphaelite Painting Techniques: 1848-56* by Joyce H. Townsend, Jacqueline Ridge and Stephen Hackney (Tate Publishing). I can also recommend Paula Gillett's *Worlds of Art: Painters in Victorian Society* (Rutgers University Press).

When it comes to poetry, you may not be able to get your hands on a Moxon edition of Swinburne's *Poems and Ballads*, as owned by Diana: only one thousand were published and all were rapidly withdrawn from sale when scandal descended. However, it is available in *Poems and Ballads & Atalanta in Calydon*, edited by Kenneth Haynes (Penguin Classics), or can be found online. If you would like to know more about the poet himself, try Rikky Rooksby's *A.C. Swinburne: A Poet's Life* (Scolar Press). Penny paraphrases Whitman in a couple of places—her spelling of "loafe" is not a mistake—and you can find his *Leaves of Grass* online. If you want to buy a copy, I'd recommend one of the cheap facsimiles of the 1855 edition, though others would doubtless disagree.

All of the books which precede Warber's *Straunge Hystory* can be found online in editions which existed in 1887, including Bourchier's *The Boke of Duke Huon of Burdeux* for the Early English Text Society. Schweigel's German translation of *Esclarmonde, Clarisse et Florent, Yde et Olive* (N.G. Elwert) includes the French text of *"Chanson d'Yde et Olive"*. Ovid's *Metamorphoses* is included in Walker's *Corpus Poetarum Latinorum* (George Bell & Sons), and there are many online translations. Also online is the *Metamorphoses* of Antoninus Liberalis in Xylander's *Transformationum Congeries*. If you'd like a translation of that—unavailable to Penny—then seek out a copy of Francis Celoria's *The Metamorphoses of Antoninus Liberalis* (Routledge).

If you would like to read more about the first women to study at the University of Oxford, Vera Brittain's *The Women at Oxford: A Fragment of History* (Macmillan) is online. So, too, are *The Accounts of the Ordinary of Newgate*, which provide contemporaneous, and often disturbing, records of the hangings at Tyburn.

Finally, *"Danaette"*—the story which Anna quotes, and from which the title of the book is taken—can be read in *French Decadent Tales*, translated by Stephen Romer (Oxford World's Classics). It is available in the original French in *Remy de Gourmont: Histoires magiques* (Petite Bibliothèque Ombres).

List of Supporters

Unbound is a new kind of publishing house. Our books are funded directly by readers. This was a very popular idea during the late eighteenth and early nineteenth centuries. Now we have revived it for the internet age. It allows authors to write the books they really want to write and readers to support the writing they would most like to see published.

The names listed below are readers who pledged their support and made this book happen. If you'd like to join them, visit www.unbound.com.

The author would like to express her personal gratitude to all the individuals listed, without whom the first edition of *All the Perverse Angels* could not have been published by Unbound.

Author's Circle

the McCallum family
Douglas & Margaret
John & Heather
Kelly & Rodrigo
David & Natalie

Sergio M.L. Tarrero

Robert Zeps

Patrons

Rodrigo Barroso
Pauline Batty
Jeff Boison
Evelyn Brown
Peter Brown
Sandra Cheetham
Laura Clemons
Aubrey de Grey

Ann Flower
Karen Hendrickx
Daniel Hook
Michael Kope
Simone Libman
Evelyn Marr
Luís Melo
   Dos Santos

Kim Ohh
Daniele Orner Ginor
Eduardo Pellegrino
Darren Reynolds
Garret Smyth
Doug Weiser

Supporters

Julia Adair
Bernard Alabaster
Charlie Amor
Kristian Andresen
Stephanie Aretz
Sandra Armor
Rachel Armstrong
Mike Auty
Susan Auty
Catherine B.
Karen Baines
Rives Dalley Barbour
Chris Barrett
Lisa Beal
Adrian Belcher
Oliver Bell
Emli Bendixen
Penny Benford
Barry Bentley

Kirstin MacKenzie
   Berge
S. Bear Bergman
Louise Blinkhorn
Matthew Booth
Mark Bowsher
Sara Jane Boyers
Keeley Bunting
Toria Buzza
Eleni Calligas
Adelaide Carpenter
Marie Caswell
Elaine Chambers
John Luke Chapman
Laura Clarke
Pamela Clayton
James Wm Clement
Ronete Cohen
Bill Colegrave

Stevyn Colgan
Malcolm Comley
Katie Commodore
Harald Cools
Anne Corwin
Alison Costigan
Jan Court
Pete Cumberland
Harriet Cunningham
Ryan Curry
Christopher Curtis-
   Nurisso
Laurent Curtis-Nurisso
Steven D'Souza
Nelly Dader
Tori Darcy
Jo Davies
David DeMember
Jameson Detweiler

Kevin Dewalt

Larissa Doswell

Emma Doyle

Haidée Drew

Aine Duffy

Vivienne Dunstan

Christine Ellis

Maria Entraigues
Abramson

Erasmus

Lisa Evans

Lisa Fabiny

Charlotte Featherstone

Naomi Frisby

James Frye

Sophie Fuller

Billy Furey

Colin Furey

Beth Gallego

Kate Gardiner

Laura-Jo Gartside

Ina German

Beata Górska

Amara Graps

Silvia Gravina

Darrell Gullion

Patricia Giangrande
Hamila

Dream Hampton

Nova Han

Happy Birthtime!

Baylea Hart

Barry Hasler

Janel Hayley

Maggi Healey

David Hebblethwaite

Linda Hepper

Elizabeth Hewitt

E. O. Higgins

Lucy C. Hirst

Richard Hodkinson

Paul Holbrook

John Holden

Roger Holzberg

Mark Hood

Richard Hope-Smith

Henry Horenstein

Paul Hynek

Cathy Imber

James Imber

Suzie Imber

Julie Impens

Maxim Jago

Alice Jolly

Daniel Jones

Branka Juran

Nik Kealy

Tyler Kellogg

Kari Kelly

Dan Kieran

Jill Kieran

Lindsay Kightley

Trudy Kightley

Patrick Kincaid

John Kluge

Ben Kohn

Abbey Kos

Maxime Kraus

Cassidy Krug

Kirsten Kruse

Catarina Lamm

Laurence Lawson

Mikey Lee

Jo Lee-Reynolds

Amy Lehman

Sarah Lessen

Jay Lewis

William ☯ Liao

Caroline Libman

Martin Libman

Myra Libman

Christen Lien

Gretchen Lindemann

Leon Little

Barbara Logan

Peter Mandeno

Allen Manser

Usman Mansoor

Tracey Marion

Diane McCallum

Stephen McGowan

Dario Meli

Hamutal Meridor

Arian Mirzarafie-Ahi

John Mitchinson

Guy Montrose

Amanda Morrell

Maggie Murphy

Carlo Navato

Philippe
van Nedervelde

Christine Joy Nichols

Bruno Noble

Oki O'Connor

Corey M. O'Hara

Myra Ottley
Andrew Pack
Blair Palmer
Lev Parikian
Julia Parker
Robyn Pearson
Kevin Perrott
Kate Pierce
Justin Pollard
Kacy Qua
Nicky Quint
Victoria Ramsay
S.A. Rennie
Cheryl Reynolds
Freda Reynolds
Jo Richardson
Julia Richdale-Ellis
Holly Rutan
Rosally Sapla
Zoë Schlanger

Nicole Scott
Jennifer Seale
Ruth Selman
Emily Prudence Shore
Niall Slater
Wendy Southern
Paul Spiegel
Janice Staines
Tabatha Stirling
Liz Stoelker
Christina Strickland
Helen Taylor
Maria Tejada
Louise Theodosiou
Mary Thomas
Mat Tobin
Prema Trettin
Zoë Tryon
Jennifer Tubbs
John Anthony Vaughan

Joao Vidigal
Natasha Vita-More
Matthew Waldman
Stan C. Waterman
Denise Watson
Noshua Watson
Aileen Webber
James Webber
Peter Webber
Joyce Webster
Kathryn West
Gaynor Whyles
Caryl Williams
Kate Williamson
Derek Wilson
David Woof
Andy Wright
Allan Wyatt
Benjamin Zealley